Romance Reveal Book Box

Katy Regnery

October 2018

a modern fairytale

Katy Regnery

The Vixen and the Vet

(Beauty & the Beast)

Never Let You Go

(Hansel & Gretel)

Ginger's Heart

(Little Red Riding Hood)

Dark Sexy Knight

(Camelot)

Don't Speak

(The Little Mermaid)

Shear Heaven

(Rapunzel)

Fragments of Ash

(Cinderella)

Swan Song

(The Ugly Duckling)

Fragments of Ash

a modern fairytale

Katy Regnery

FRAGMENTS OF ASH

Katharine Gilliam Regnery, publisher

This book is a work of fiction. Most names, characters, places, and incidents are products of the author's imagination. Any references to real people or places are used fictitiously.

Please visit my website at www.katyregnery.com
First Edition: October 2018
Katy Regnery
Fragments of Ash: a novel / by Katy Regnery—1st ed.
ISBN: 978-1-944810-37-5

CINDERS NOUN \ˈsin-dərs\
(PLURAL) ashes, fragments of ash

What's left when the raging fire burns out?
When the desperate, white-hot incalescence cools?
When the thick, black smoke turns to gray and then to white?
Cinders.
Fragments of ash.
Detritus of disaster.
Tiny pieces of "once was."
Delicate reminders of what is gone.
Blown away by a gentle breeze and lost forever.

—*K. P. Kelley*

CHAPTER ONE

Ashley

Thirty-four years old is too young to die.

At least, that's what everyone keeps telling me.

But then again . . .

She was *also* too young to get pregnant at fifteen.

Too young to become a single mom at sixteen.

Too young to be discovered at eighteen.

Too young to be an international supermodel at nineteen.

Too young to overdose at twenty-four.

Too young to be washed-up by twenty-seven.

Too young to marry my forty-six-year-old stepfather at twenty-nine.

Too young to die of another overdose at thirty-four.

She was *always* too young.

Consistent to the bitter end.

The thought circles around and around inside my head as I sit beside her grave with my stepfather's heavy arm around my shoulders and more than three hundred people—photographers, magazine editors, fashion designers, and other models—weeping prettily behind me.

In an instant, I am ashamed of myself. I should be thinking *kind* thoughts about her—about Tígin, my biological mother, whom most of the world believed was my older sister. Only three people know that I am actually her daughter: my biological grandparents, who sit stoically on my other side, and, somewhere in the crowd, my godfather, Gus, my mother's hair and makeup artist for the five years she took the world by storm.

My heart clenches as I think of Gus's eyes when he touched my arm earlier, offering brief condolences. Red and bloodshot. So much sadness.

I clutch the onyx rosary beads and look up at the priest, who clears his throat loudly.

"To many of you, Tígin, who was baptized Teagan Catrin-Mairwen Ellis, was nothing more than a public figure, a woman who flaunted her body for money and fame. A modern-day Mary Magdalene. But in the eyes of God, she was a child, flawed and beloved . . ."

Beloved.

The word makes me pause.

Was my mother beloved by God?

By *whom* was my mother beloved?

Not my conservative grandparents, who were deeply ashamed of her out-of-wedlock pregnancy, bastard daughter, and the endless pictures of her in bathing suits and lingerie that heralded the beginning of her career as a model. Their disapproval was her constant companion, and though she tried to shrug it off like it didn't matter, I heard enough phone conversations throughout my childhood featuring a drunken Tígin begging for their forgiveness. I know for certain that they never granted it, though they did deign to live comfortably off my mother's wealth, in the house she bought for them—first in Ohio, then in New York—with every luxury they could imagine at their fingertips.

Did *they* love her? I don't know. I only know that they didn't show it. And by withholding it, they forced her to seek it elsewhere.

Elsewhere.

I peek over my shoulder at the industry people who have turned out to mourn Tígin, pulling from my earliest memories her first few years as America's sweetheart.

In the beginning, when she was a natural blonde with a fresh-scrubbed face, bright blue eyes, and a winsome smile, they loved her. And my mother, starved for affection, basked in the world's approval. But for a sheltered, religious, eighteen-year-old single mother from Loveland, Ohio, it was too much attention and too much fame. It was too much money and too much unrequited approval for a love-starved kid. And like most kids finally out from under the yoke of oppressive parents, she started acting out.

As the years rolled on, she was increasingly erratic. She'd be hours late for a shoot, arriving with heavy-lidded, bloodshot eyes and ashen skin, her flat blonde hair still reeking of cigarettes smoked the night before. No amount of help from Gus could disguise the fact that Tig's girl-next-door smile and bright, shiny baby blues were fading under the strain of fast living. Embarrassed by her way-too-public drunken exploits and out of patience with her increasingly prima donna ways, the modeling world proved fickle in its love, abandoning her when she needed it most.

Invitations were revoked. Bookings dried up.

Contracts were not renewed. And the world that had once welcomed her as the next "it" girl looked away, or worse: stood aside, watching her spiral into a depression that she treated with *more* alcohol, *more* drugs, *more* destructive choices.

Leading to the most destructive choice of all . . .

Her husband.

My stepfather.

Mosier squeezes my shoulder almost painfully, his face thickset and blank beside mine. There are no tears in his eyes. No quivering of his lips. His wife is dead, her frail body in the coffin before us, but he is placid, almost bored. He married an out-of-control, washed-up, once-beautiful supermodel and brought her to heel. The last time I saw her, she was a shell of her former self: obedient, timid, and withdrawn.

The question circling my mind pauses at the forefront, still demanding an answer:

By *whom* was my mother beloved?

Maybe by Gus, whom she was forbidden to see after her marriage, owing to the fact that he was, according to Mosier, "a negro faggot" and a "bad fucking influence."

Yes, I think, as tears well up in my eyes, *maybe Gus loved her.*

I remember so many nights that he brought her safely home to our Hollywood bungalow. She'd be stoned and screaming, her makeup smeared from weeping as she broke glasses and vases and shouted terrible things at Gus and me. When her tantrums finally subsided and she was limp from exhaustion, he would carry her upstairs and bathe her naked body with gentleness and respect while I held a saucepan between her mouth and the bathwater so she could puke. I remember him tucking her into bed, humming some old-time lullaby as he ran his dark fingers through her light hair and she cried herself to sleep.

"Gus-Gus is here, li'l Tig . . ."

As the memories fill my head with a mixture of profound sadness and even more profound gratitude, I know for certain: *Gus-Gus loved her.*

As for me? Ashley Carys Ellis? Her "little sister"? Her secret child?

Did I love her?

I don't know.

I only know she is gone.

"To you, O Lord, we commend the soul of Teagan Catrin-Mairwen, your servant. In the sight of this world, she is now dead, but in your sight, may she live forever in grace. Forgive the many sins she committed through human weakness, and in your goodness, grant her everlasting peace. *In nomine Patris et Filii et Spiritus Sancti.* Amen."

She is gone, whispers my heart, which weeps the tears my eyes cannot.

"Amen."

***

"I'm so sorry for your loss, Ashley."

"Your sister was so beautiful! So full of life!"

"Poor Tígin. What a shame."

"You look so much like her! Have you thought about modeling?"

I move through the thick crowd of people at my mother's wake.

For the occasion, my stepfather has rented out a country club in Rye, New York, close to the cemetery, and the room is full of noxious white flowers and poster-sized pictures of my mother displayed around the room on shiny gold easels. I stop in front of one and stare. The photo predates her supermodel days, and it's always been one of my favorites.

She is eighteen and I am two. We are sitting side by side on a bench in front of my grandparents' stone church, wearing our Sunday best on Easter morning. Both blonde, with natural curls that frame our faces, our identical bright blue eyes look hopefully into the camera.

My gaze shifts to her, and it's no wonder she was discovered the same year this photo was taken, no wonder she became one of the most recognizable women in the world.

She is tall and willowy, her limbs long and tan against the cream sheath sundress she is wearing. Even with a quick glance, you can tell her body is naturally model-thin.

But it was her face that so captivated the public.

Her favorite photographer, Jacques Renard, once told *Time* magazine that he'd never worked with someone as classically beautiful. Tig's face was perfectly symmetrical: identical cornflower-blue eyes with long, dark lashes, high cheekbones, and a perfect, Grecian nose. Her lips were lush, but not obscene, he said, and her hair, which she kept blonde for the entirety of her career, was a stunning shade of platinum ash. The color was trademarked by Orion Beauty at one point and offered in salons everywhere as Tíg White.

A pretty mannequin, however, wouldn't have sold as many magazines as my mother did.

The thing about Tig was that there was an unexpected vulnerability in her gaze, the kind of longing wistfulness that every human being can relate to.

I recognize her expression now that I am the same age she was in the photo. She is hoping for something she believes is beyond her grasp. Dreaming of something, but scared it won't come true.

What was it? I wonder. *What were you hoping for?*

Success? Accolades? Fortune?

A year and five months later, my mother's face would grace the cover of *Vogue*'s illustrious September issue.

Is *that* what she had hoped for? Is *that* what she'd wanted?

Or maybe it was something deeper and more ephemeral, like belonging, or being accepted, or feeling loved, or knowing that she was safe?

I sigh softly. *Those are* your *dreams*, my mind whispers, *not hers.*

"She was *mad* gorgeous. Tragic perfection."

Gus stands behind me, staring at my mother's tentative smile with tears in his eyes.

"Gus!" I say softly.

He opens his arms to me. "How's my li'l Ash?"

I step into him, closing my eyes as I inhale the familiar scent of cloves from the cigarettes he smokes. *You smell like fall*, I think. *You smell like help. You smell like goodness.*

"Don't you cry on my silk threads, now, miss."

I lean back a little and look down at his shiny gray suit, perfectly fitted to his spare, wiry body. "I'm not crying."

"No," he says slowly, remnants of a sad smile fading into an expression of deep concern as he looks into my eyes, "you're not."

"I'm glad you're here," I say, quickly scanning the

room for a glimpse of Mosier, or his sons, Damon and Anders. I relax a little when I don't see them.

"I waited until they went outside for a smoke," says Gus, reaching forward to tilt my chin up so I'm forced to look at him. "But I'll be leaving soon. I've already been told once that I'm not welcome."

"You are!" I insist. "You *are* welcome! We were the only ones who really—"

"Hush, li'l Ash," he says, shaking his head as he places a finger over his lips. "Don't say it, or it might be true."

He releases me and reaches into his pocket, withdrawing a small silver case. He plucks a card from inside and presses the stiff cardstock into my hand.

"Our time's running down. If you need me, this is where I am."

I read the name and address of an art gallery printed in small type on the bottom of the card.

"She was clean," I blurt out, searching his eyes. "I saw her at Easter, and she was clean. She wasn't drinking. She wasn't taking anything."

Gus winces. "Baby doll, once an addict—"

"I'm telling you," I say. "She hadn't touched anything in years. *He* wouldn't allow it. She barely left the house, Gus. Where would she get enough heroin to overdose? I don't understand! I don't know how it happened!"

"She always found a way. It was *part* of her, baby. It's what she did when times got tough."

My mother was many things at the end, but as far as I knew, she was no longer a substance abuser. She hadn't taken so much as an Advil or sipped from a flute of champagne since she married Mosier. I'd watched carefully every time I was with her—no bloodshot eyes, no slurred speech, no shakes. Not to mention, Mosier and his goons had kept such a close eye on her, it would have been just about impossible to hide it from him.

"It doesn't make sense, Gus."

"I wish . . ." His jaw tightens as he takes a step away from me. "I wish we could talk more. Be careful, Ash," he says, taking another step back. "Keep yourself safe, you hear? And—"

"Gus, don't go yet! Please stay!" I whisper, watching as any trace of tenderness drains from his face. He straightens his back and neck, standing as tall as he can, his eyes dark and wary.

"My condolences, Miss Ellis," he says, his voice low and formal as his eyes flick to something—or someone—standing behind me.

"My father asked you to leave," Damon says to Gus as he puts a hand on my lower back.

To anyone watching, the gesture might seem conciliatory or protective—a stepbrother comforting his grieving little stepsister—but my body stiffens and my stomach churns from his unwanted touch, willing it away.

"I'm leaving," says Gus, looking back at me, his dark eyes sorry and concerned. "Take care now, you hear?"

"Please," I whimper, tears that I didn't feel at my mother's grave suddenly brightening my eyes and blurring Gus's retreating image.

But Gus, my fairy godfather, my only good memory from a fractured childhood, is already gone, and with an increase of heavy pressure on my back, I am guided away.

***

Hours later, in a private meeting room at the same country club, I am seated around a small conference room table with my grandparents, stepfather, and stepbrothers as an attorney reads my mother's will. Her estate belongs to my stepfather now, but she requested that all of her jewelry be passed on to me.

I am handed a list of appraised items, and I'm surprised that Tig was able to squirrel away a small fortune's worth of gems for me. I was certain she'd shot everything up her arms at one point or another.

Tígin's attorney, Mr. Blanchard, raises his eyebrows at my stepfather. "Is that okay with you, Mr. Răumann? That Miss Ellis keeps Mrs. Răumann's jewelry?"

His Eastern European accent is thick when he responds with a flick of his ringed hand and a shrug of his beefy shoulders. "What do I want with women's things?"

Vhat do I vant vith vomen's things? It makes him sound like a vampire.

Long ago, Tig mentioned something to me about Mosier being from Romania. She said that he was one of eight kids born to a poor couple at a time when the government offered financial incentives to mothers of five children or more. Apparently it was part of a program to increase the birth rate and population of the country, but it had turned a lot of women into baby machines, without the resources or desire to raise their offspring.

Mosier, like many others of his generation, had ended up in a state-run orphanage, and God only knows what had happened there to turn him into the man he is today.

"Fine." Mr. Blanchard looks at me and nods. "The jewelry is yours, Miss Ellis."

I feel the heat of my stepfather's gaze against my cheek, but I don't look at him. I nod at the lawyer, then look down at the table. Modesty and composure are of paramount importance at school, and after five years, I project both effortlessly, my face a veneer of peace and grace, no matter what's happening inside my head.

"Your late wife also asked that some of her remaining assets pay for the rest of Miss Ellis's schooling. I believe she attends . . ." He shifts some papers. "Ah, yes. The Blessed Virgin Academy? In New Paltz?"

My stepfather sighs. "She's eighteen. A woman. How much more school does she need?"

I stare at the table, clenching my jaw as these two men, totally unrelated to me, decide my fate.

"Miss Ellis," asks Mr. Blanchard, "how much school do you have left before graduation?"

I lift my head to look at the lawyer, who meets my steady gaze. It's early May. "One month, sir."

Mr. Blanchard nods, making a note before looking up at my stepfather. "And then there's college . . . grad schoo—"

"No college. No grad school. Not necessary. Ashley will work for me," says Mosier, his tone nonnegotiable. "I have plans for her."

Mr. Blanchard's expression is deeply uneasy as he softly reiterates, "I believe Mrs. Răumann wanted her sister to finish high school at the very least."

"Fucking . . .," Mosier mutters a string of expletives under his breath, then huffs with annoyance. "Fine. One month. What do I care? It changes nothing."

The lawyer looks slightly relieved and continues quickly. "Your late wife also asked that their parents be cared for."

I shift my eyes to my grandparents, who sit across the table from me. Despite the fact that I am their public daughter and biological granddaughter, we have never been close to one another. Whatever love they may or may not have had for my mother, they've had even less for me. They made no effort to hide the fact that I was Teagan's great shame, and they certainly didn't stop my too-young, emotionally unstable mother from taking me to live with her in Los Angeles when I was only five years old. Tig wanted to "try" being a mother. My grandparents were only too happy to get rid of me.

My stepfather purses his lips at the lawyer, the slight gesture full of annoyance. "What will be the arrangements?"

Mr. Blanchard turns to my grandparents. "Do you wish to remain in your home, here in New York State?"

"Umm . . ."

I look up, and my grandfather is staring at me, his lips tight and blue eyes beady. His gaze slides briefly to Mosier before turning to the lawyer. His Welsh accent is diluted from years in America, but I can still hear it. "No. We wish t' return home t' Anglesey now that our Teagan is gone."

The island of Anglesey, off the northern coast of Wales, is where my mother was born and where my grandparents lived before they immigrated to Ohio thirty years ago.

I can't help gasping softly, because if my grandparents return to Wales, I will have no blood family left here in the United States. My mother is gone, and I never knew my father. A slight panic makes my heart race. Not that we were ever close, but if they leave, I will have no one here but . . . but . . .

Mosier places his hand on my thigh under the table, and my breath catches because, despite five years of lecherous looks, he's never been *this* bold—never touched me *this* intimately. I try to jerk my leg away, but his fingers dig into my skin through the black fabric of my ankle-length dress. He is issuing a warning. I freeze, terrified to move a muscle.

"Fine," Mosier says. "I will pay for your passage to Wales, for your moving costs, a house of your choosing, and I will put a lump sum of cash in a bank account to ensure you are comfortable until you die." Mosier's fingers stroke me through the thin black crepe. His voice holds a sinister finality to it when he adds, "But you *won't* come back."

Mr. Blanchard speaks up quickly, his brows knotted in confusion. "Won't come back? But certainly they'll want to come and visit their other daughter from time to—"

"Agree," demands Mosier, ignoring the lawyer, staring at my grandparents.

My grandfather's cheeks flush, but he doesn't look at me, while my grandmother keeps her steely gaze trained on the table. I sense I'm missing something. *What am I missing?* I wonder, the question filling me with breathless panic. It feels like my grandparents and Mosier have previously worked out an arrangement for my grandparents to abandon me and Mosier to assume all responsibility for me.

"*Mam-gu*," I say, using the Welsh word for

"Grandma." "Please don't leave me."

When she looks up at me, her merciless blue eyes narrow to slits, cold as glacial ice, a frozen wall of deep and uncompromising loathing.

"Dyma'ch bai chi," she hisses.

I am familiar with this Welsh expression. It means, *It is your fault.*

My fault. Because I am a "child of shame."

By virtue of my very existence, I am to blame for my mother's fall from grace, her addictions, her death at thirty-four. I read my grandmother's eyes clearly and see the long list of my transgressions, beginning with my birth. What I don't see is love . . . or compassion . . . or sympathy. My grandparents are compliant in a plan to be rid of me, and it chills my heart through.

Swallowing back the bile in my throat, I drop her eyes. My stepfather's hand dips slightly toward the apex of my thighs. His fingers, terrifyingly close to my womanhood, slide back and forth for a too-long moment before he removes his hand. I exhale a held breath, grateful for this small mercy, and glance up in time to see him tent his fingers in front of his face, inhaling deeply through his nose and groaning softly as though smelling something delicious.

My skin crawls.

Mr. Blanchard clears his throat noisily.

"This is tedious," Mosier says, his tone annoyed and impatient. He drops his fingers to his lap. "Are we finished?"

"I suppose so," says Mr. Blanchard, his jaw tight and his eyebrows deeply furrowed. He straightens up the papers on the table into a neat pile and places them into a manila folder. He seems anxious to leave, and I feel ever more alone.

He places the file into a black leather briefcase, then looks directly into my eyes, his gaze strangely searing. It's too intimate a glance from someone I don't know very well. It makes me feel like his insight into my life and future are far greater than my own.

"I'm so *very* sorry for your loss, Miss Ellis," he whispers.

After a beat, he quickly looks from me to my stepfamily and my grandparents, nodding his head in sympathy to each of them, though I sense it is more for the sake of propriety than condolence.

His eyes return to mine for one last, lingering moment, and I cannot help the ominous chill that slithers down my spine when he repeats, "I am so very, *very* sorry."

CHAPTER TWO

Ashley

My grandparents bid me a curt and cold farewell in front of the country club before turning their backs on me and heading to their car. I watch them walk away, wondering if I will ever see them again. I don't think so, which feels unbelievable, even though I witnessed them agree to Mosier's terms. I have not lived with them since I was very young, and we were never close, but to be abandoned by my mother and grandparents on the same day makes me feel worthless and—*I recall the feel of Mosier's fingers on my thigh*—frightened.

A sleek black limousine arrives under the club's portico for Mosier, Damon, Anders, and me. As is standard with all my stepfather's employees, the chauffeur, Eddie, doesn't look me in the eyes or speak to me as he opens the back door of the car and waits for me to slide into the backseat. As soon as I am seated beside Mosier, across from Damon and Anders, the door shuts, and a moment later, we're in motion.

As we drive to Mosier's gated and heavily guarded $8 million house in Scarsdale, I hold my rosary tightly, close my eyes, lean my head against the window, and pretend to sleep.

What did Mosier mean when he said that I would "work" for him, and he had "plans" for me? We've never discussed my taking a job with him after high school. What is it he has in mind for me?

When Tígin and I first moved in with the Răumanns five years ago, it was summertime, and I was only thirteen, but Mosier forbade me to wear anything more revealing than a T-shirt and a floor-length skirt or loose-fitting pants, no matter how warm the weather. No shorts. No short skirts. No sundresses. And further, the T-shirt couldn't have a V or scoop neck. It had to cover me completely to the base of my neck. Having lived most of my childhood in LA, where I spent my entire summer running around in bathing suits, shorts, and tank tops, it was a difficult adjustment, but my mother insisted on my compliance, telling me that Mosier valued modesty and only wanted the best for me.

At one point, toward the end of that summer, Damon and Anders, who were sixteen at the time, were swimming in the pool on an especially hot day while my mother and stepfather attended an event in New York City. Even though Tig had warned me to stay in my room while she was gone, I got bored and lonely, and eventually found myself on the pool deck outside, looking for company.

"Anders," said Damon, who paused in the middle of a game of water volleyball, "look who it is: Aunt Ashley."

Anders flicked a glance at me. "You should go back inside."

"Why?" I asked.

But Anders ignored me, gesturing for the ball.

"Throw it back."

"No, no, no, bro," said Damon. "Our new aunt's *finally* come out of her room. We should be social. Welcoming." He looked me up and down in my shapeless, baggy pants and high-necked blouse. "Bet you're pretty cute under that outfit, huh? Tan all over from the California sun?"

Damon and Anders were identical twins, both dark-haired and dark-eyed, but Damon's eyes were flirtatious and playful, while Anders kept his gaze carefully averted from me.

"*Tată nu-i va place,*" said Anders to his brother, a warning in his voice.

"*El nu este aici. Taci!*" said Damon, waving his brother's words away and still staring at me. "Hot day. Why don't you come in? Join us!"

I grinned at him, shrugging my shoulders. "No bathing suit."

"*Dă-mi pace,*" said Damon, clapping his hand over his heart as he winked at me. "You got underwear on under those clothes?"

"Maybe," I said, winking back at him.

I'd unbuttoned my pants slowly, doing a little striptease for my stepbrothers before pulling my blouse over my head and throwing it on the pool deck. Clad in only white cotton panties and a matching bra, I'd executed a perfect dive into the deep end, joining Damon's team for water volleyball, despite Anders' disapproval.

An hour later, my mother and Mosier returned to find me on Damon's shoulders, serving the ball to

Anders.

"What the fuck is happening here?"

Vhat d' fuck ees happening here?

Damon gasped, scrambling to push me off his shoulders, so I fell backward into the pool. By the time I gurgled to the surface, my stepbrothers were pulling themselves out of the water, standing side by side on the pool deck.

"*Dracu' să vă ia!*" Mosier thundered. "There is only *one rule*! She will be *pure*!"

Standing by myself in the pool, my eyes widened with shock as his fist shot forth, breaking Damon's nose with a loud crunch before blackening Anders's eye with a quick jab that sent his head reeling.

"*Du-vă în pula mea*!" Mosier roared. "Get out of my sight!"

With eyes cast down, they ran into the house without a glance back at me.

Mosier turned from their retreating forms to look at me. Dark and furious, his eyes stared at me with unveiled disgust. His nostrils flared. His cheeks were almost purple with fury.

"Get out of the *fucking* pool," he growled. "Now!" He turned to my mother. "Get her decent!"

I lifted my body onto the side of the pool, and my mother rushed me inside to get dressed.

"Stop squeezing me so hard!" I cried, trying to pull my arm away.

"What the hell were you thinking?" she demanded in a tense whisper as she pulled me up the stairs. "How could you be so goddamned stupid, Ash?"

"I was just swimming," I said, still shocked at the

sight of my bloody stepbrothers.

"Practically naked!"

"But Tig," I said, "I swam all the time in LA."

"*Teagan*!" she hissed. "Not Tig!"

"Fine!" I yelled. "I swam all the time in LA, *Teagan*!"

She yanked me onto the landing and turned to face me, her eyes swimming with tears. "Mosier's house, Mosier's rules! How do you *not* understand that?" Pulling me against her with a desperate sob, she squeezed me tight, murmuring in my ear, "Grow up, Ash. Grow up fast."

Then she dragged me the rest of the way up the stairs to my room, where she chose my clothes: a long-sleeved white blouse with a ruffled neck and a long, flowy skirt. She told me I'd need to apologize to Mosier and promise to be better.

"Better? In what way?" I asked, feeling scared.

"Tell him that you'll be more modest," she said, nodding at me encouragingly, though her voice was laced with panic. "You'll . . . you'll be the little sister he never had. A *good* girl. Respectable."

"He's not my keeper!" I huffed, scratching at the itchy neckline of the fussy blouse.

"Yes," Tígin grated out, grabbing my upper arms harshly as she stared into my eyes, "that's *exactly* what he is now."

We walked down the stairs together in silence, hand in hand, then headed to Mosier's private office. My mother knocked, and we heard him shout, "Come!"

I looked up to see her jaw tense before she lifted her chin and pulled me into the room.

Mosier's study was the most intimidating room in the house. Sinister, too, with its smell of stale cigars and whiskey, its dark wood and leather furniture. A dagger with a sharp, shiny point was displayed on a credenza, and crossed swords intersected over a massive black marble fireplace. Underneath the sword was a plaque that read, *Christus remittit. Nos non oblivisci.*

Years later, I would learn the meaning of those Latin words: *Christ forgives. We don't forget.*

"Mosier," said my mother, her voice high-pitched and placating, "Ashley has something she wants to say."

His eyes, dark brown and disgusted, slid from my mother to me. Flicking them down my form, his face softened slightly at my modest appearance.

"So, *cenușă*," he said, staring at me from behind his massive desk, "you act like a whore and make me hurt my sons . . . and now you want to talk to me?"

Cenușă means "ashes" in his language, and it's what he's always called me. Never Ashley. Always *cenușă.*

My mother's voice is tentative. "She's just a kid, Mo—"

"Shut up," he spat without looking away from me. "Not another word from you." He lifted his chin a fraction of an inch, his eyes searing. "You come to me dressed like an angel now. But I seen you before . . ." His eyes lowered to my breasts, and he held them there. "Your tits on display. An *ispită.* Teasing. Sinful. Dirty. Naked in the pool with two grown men—"

"With your *sons*! And they weren't naked. Mosier, they were just swim—"

"You speak again," he said, lifting his eyes to my mother, "and you'll need a doctor. *Mă înțelegi?*"

She gasped softly and nodded, looking down at her feet as she squeezed my hand.

"So, little *cenușă*, little whore in training, what do

you have to say to me?"

My heart was racing and my entire body trembling. "I . . . I am so sorry. S-so sorry that I broke your rules."

"*My* rules?" he repeated softly, leaning forward and planting his elbows on his desk. He sniffed, then grimaced, as if what he'd smelled was distasteful.

"I d-didn't mean to upset you," I managed to say, gripping my mother's hand for dear life.

My stepfather stood up behind his desk, raising a shaking fist. "Upset *me*? You upset *God*, you cheap *târfă*!"

I didn't know what I was doing wrong, but I wasn't saying the right things. I was making him angrier. I glanced up at my mother to find the color in her face draining as she jerked me closer to her side, taking a step back and pulling me with her.

"Little whores who flaunt their bodies should be treated like the sluts they are!" he said, reaching for his belt buckle. "*You have to pay for your sins*!"

Coming around the desk, he advanced on us, his face dark red with fury as he jerked his belt from the loops of his trousers with a whipping sound.

My mother yanked me behind her back, shaking her head. "No! No! She's only thirteen! She's just a kid!" She was breathing so hard and so fast, I didn't know how she could speak. "Do it to me! Whatever you want to do to Ash, do it to me! *I'm* a bad example! *I* will pay! Please!"

He paused in front of my mother, his belt doubled into a loop, fisted in his hand. "You? You'll fucking pay?"

Her breathing was loud and shallow as I rested my cheek on her back, my arms clasped tightly around her waist.

"Mosy," she begged, "she is still pure. I promise you. She's pure. She is. She's pure as snow." Reaching for my hands, she loosened them so she could step toward my stepfather without me. "But *I'm* not pure. Not at all. I'm . . . bad. I'm . . . dirty." Her breath hitched as she stepped closer to him, one hand appearing behind her back to shoo me from the room. I backed up to the door, watching her, listening to her words and trying to process them, but I didn't understand what was happening. "Take it out on me. I deserve it."

"Yes," he said, his dead eyes scanning her body as he nodded slowly. "Yes, you deserve it."

"That's right. I deserve it," she whispered, her voice low and heavy but tinged with relief.

Then, over her shoulder, she made eye contact with me. And for the rest of my life, I would remember the dread in her blue eyes. They weren't vulnerable anymore, and they definitely weren't hopeful. They were barely hanging on. She didn't try to smile for me. In fact, her lips barely moved as she mouthed, "*Get out.*"

"Yes," said Mosier, adjusting the belt in his hands as he looked over my mother's shoulder at me. "Leave, *cenușă*. Christ will forgive you."

I didn't need to understand the inscription on the plaque over the fireplace to finish the rest of his thought: . . . *but* I *will never forget.*

I walked out of that study and closed the door behind me.

My mother's screams lasted for hours.

The next day I was sent for early enrollment at the

Blessed Virgin Academy.

***

My bedroom in Mosier's house has never really felt like my own space. It has just been a place to stay when I returned home from school for two months over the summer and for a few days at Thanksgiving, Christmas, and Easter.

School is where I feel most comfortable, surrounded by the nuns and laywomen who teach us and live among us, and Father Joseph, who has been my spiritual guide and confessor since I arrived at the Blessed Virgin Academy five years ago. He is the father I never had, and I long to see him now—to ask for his guidance and prayers for my future. At dinner, I will ask Mosier if I can return to school tomorrow.

I sit on the edge of the twin bed, which is covered with a pink and white toile comforter and has gauzy pink curtains tied back on either side of the headboard. It is a room fit for a princess, with white faux-fur carpeting, an overstuffed love seat in front of the white-tiled fireplace, and a shiny silver chandelier overhead. I loved it when I first arrived in Scarsdale but quickly grew to hate it. It feels like too much. Too fussy. Too ornate. Too expensive. How does one earn a room that costs as much as this one does?

I managed to hide Gus's card in my bra when Damon wasn't looking, and now I withdraw it, examining it carefully and committing the information to memory. I'm good at memorizing things. I always have been.

La Belle Époque Galerie ~ 5900 Shelburne Road ~ Shelburne, VT ~ 05482

Augustus Egér and Jock Souris, Owners

Jock. Hmm. I wonder who Jock is. *Someone special or*

just a business partner?

And Shelburne. *Where is Shelburne, Vermont?* I repeat the information over and over again inside my head, then flip over the card, grateful when it all comes seamlessly back to me. I rip the card into tiny shreds and throw the pieces into the white wicker trash can next to the powder-pink bedside table.

And not a moment too soon.

Knock, knock.

A crisp double knock. It's Mosier.

I haven't had time to process the way my stepfather touched me at the reading of my mother's will, but I feel jumpy and scared when I think about it. The way Mosier looks at me—the way he touched me today—it feels wrong. *All* wrong.

Knock, knock.

Louder now. More insistent.

Sitting on the side of my bed, I press my knees together under my skirt and call out, "Come in," with an unsteady voice.

The door opens and Mosier steps into the room.

My fifty-one-year-old stepfather, who believes he's my step*brother*, is tall, dark, and muscular. The sleeves of his shiny, dark gray suit jacket strain over his upper arms, though his pants are tailored perfectly. This is by design, of course, to show the world his muscles, to dare lesser men to take a swing at him and regret it later.

His hair, shaved to a half an inch and oiled, makes his head look like a glistening black bowling ball. It smells strongly of the product he uses, which is spicy and thick and has always turned my stomach.

I don't need to look at him to picture his face in my mind: he keeps a permanent five-o'clock shadow on his jaw, likely to cover the myriad pockmarks and scars that cover his skin. His eyes are dark brown, and his nose is crooked, likely from being broken multiple times and having never repaired well.

One time, when Tig and I were standing across the living room from Mosier and his sons, she drew my attention to his lips and lashes. His lips are full and pouty, and his jet-black lashes are so long, they look almost fey.

"It's like he had a shot at being handsome once upon a time," she'd noted in a bitter whisper, "before his black soul took over his face."

Since I've known Mosier, he's always left the door cracked an inch when we were alone in a room together. The fact that he doesn't today makes my heart race and my stomach flip over. I nervously stare down at my lap as he strides across the room in his dark suit to stand before me, a jarring island of dark masculinity in this fluffy pink sanctuary.

His black shoes stop beneath my gaze, and they are so shiny, I can see my hazy reflection in them.

"*Cenușă*, look at me."

I fold my hands so they'll stop shaking and look up at him.

"Mmm," he groans, tilting his head to the side and rubbing the black bristles on his jaw between his thumb and forefinger. "*So* beautiful." He drops his hand and tilts his head to the other side, cajolingly. "Don't you have a hello for me?"

"H-hello, *frate*."

"*Frate*. Brother. Hmm," he hums softly, narrowing his eyes at me. "Your sister is gone now. You can call me Mosier."

I gulp, unsure of what to say. Calling him *frate* was

his idea. It's what I've called him since the day we met. Why should we change it now?

"Say it," he commands. "Say my name. Say 'Hello, Mosier.'"

Why it feels wrong to say his name, I'm not sure, but he is staring down at me expectantly, so I whisper, "Hello, M-Mosier."

"Yes," he says, his plump lips lifting to a grin as he lowers himself to his knees on the floor before me. "*Cenuşă, cenuşă, cenuşă*," he moans softly, his mouth not far from my knees. "Beautiful *cenuşă*. My angel."

He hasn't touched me, but everything in me rejects his close proximity and the tenderness in his voice when he draws out my nickname and calls me angel. He smells strongly of thick, spicy hair oil mixed with cigars, and it makes my stomach bubble up uncomfortably. I don't like the way he is looking at me, and I don't like the way he touched me under the table during the reading of my mother's will. I didn't like the noises I heard coming from the bedroom he shared with my mother, or the screams I heard—more than once—coming from his study. I don't like it that my mother died of a drug overdose when I saw her two weeks ago for Easter and she seemed, well, not *okay*, maybe, but not *on anything* either.

There is almost nothing I like about the man on his knees before me. I wish he would stand up, turn around, and leave. Why is the door closed? Why is he here? What does he want from me?

My curiosity gets the better of me, and I look up at him, instantly sorry that I didn't keep my gaze down. Behind his dark brown eyes, I don't see kindness or compassion. I see insatiable want. I see ruthlessness. I see desire and demand.

I can hear the beating of my heart in my ears.

When he reaches out and places his hand on my left knee, I jerk it away.

"Oh, *cenușă*," he says, clamping his hand on my kneecap and digging his fingers through the thin crepe and into my tender flesh, "your modesty does you credit." He leans his dark head down and rests his cheek on my right knee, facing his hand. "But you will learn to *welcome* my touch." Rotating his head just slightly, the movement forces my knees apart, and he presses his lips to the fabric covering my lower thigh. "Or not."

"What . . ." I am breathless, trying to figure out what is going on here. "W-what do you mean?"

"Tell me, sweet *cenușă*, have you studied the Book of Deuteronomy? At school?" He lifts his head but not his hand, which he slides higher, kneading the flesh of my thigh through the black crepe of my skirt. "In Deuteronomy, there is something called a levirate marriage. You have heard of it?"

I am well versed in Scripture, but my mind is too jumbled to focus on the specific text he's referring to.

"I, um . . ."

"It is an ancient law that says that if a man dies, his widow shall marry his brother."

"I . . . I remember now," I gasp, desperate for him to remove his hand.

"But I am not sexist, *cenușă*. I believe it can work both ways."

I scramble to follow his meaning. "Both ways?"

"If I lose my wife, should I be alone?"

I suck in a deep breath, trying to focus on his words as his hand slides higher. It rests, hot and heavy, midway between my knee and the apex of my thighs.

"I don't . . . I don't know," I answer truthfully, feeling scared and confused.

"I don't think I should have to suffer loneliness. Do you?"

"You could . . . you could find someone new to marry," I whisper, his words starting to shape into an idea that I push against, that I am repulsed by. "When y-you're ready."

"Why wouldn't I be ready . . . now?" he asks, his voice low and mellow but underscored with an insistence that makes my stomach churn with dread.

"Tig. My s-sister. She was . . . she was your wife. You loved her. You'll n-need some . . . some time . . ."

"*Time*?" he demands, his fingers clenching my flesh so hard that I wince. He must notice my reaction, because his fingers become gentler, petting me as though trying to soothe me. "You are so innocent." His hand slides higher, rubbing my thigh insistently, his thumb closer and closer to a spot that the nuns and priests have forbidden us to think about, let alone touch—let alone let someone *else* touch. His eyes are mean when he looks up at me and asks, "Do you think I married your slut sister because I *loved* her? You cannot be that stupid."

I freeze, trapped in his intense stare.

"My little *cenușă*," he says slowly, leaning down to press his lips to my right knee before looking back up at me, "I married *her* . . . for *you*."

The room spins, and my stomach, which has been upset all day, heaves, bile and acid burning the base of my throat.

"F-for *me*?"

"I wanted you the first time I saw you. But you

were only thirteen . . ." His voice drifts off as his thumb circles and presses. "So fresh. So young. Beautiful. Pure. Do you know what I saw as you walked down Rodeo Drive next to your stupid, junkie sister? I saw someone I could mold into my own. Someone who would be everything I wanted in a woman. Pious. Modest. All mine."

This isn't happening. This can't be happening.

"But . . . y-you . . . you were married to m-my . . . my . . ."

"You're not listening," he says. "I married your whore sister *for you.* All for you, my little darling. A means to an end." His chuckle is low-pitched and pleased, and I clench my jaw to conceal a shudder. "The Bible says it's allowed. There is no need to feel shame. It won't be a sin for us to fuck . . ."

Fuck is a word I heard a great deal in my childhood when I lived with Tígin. But once she married Mosier, my mother stopped cursing, and such profanity has no place at school. Mosier and his boys curse regularly, of course, but the blunt crudeness of Mosier's suggestion still shocks me, prompting a surprised gasp.

". . . as soon as we're man and wife," he finishes.

As his thumb continues pressing against my inner thigh, his free hand drops from my knee to his crotch.

Man and . . .? He wants . . . No! No, this is impossible. My lungs freeze, and I stare at him, lips agape, eyes wide, burning with tears and horror.

"I have waited a long time to fuck you long and hard, my sweet *cenușă.* And when the beautiful bleeding is finished, I will fuck you until sunup. And then I will come to you again. Every night. All night long."

He mumbles something about my being his child bride as the hand in his lap rubs insistently against the growing bulge in his pants. I shudder because his words are terrifying and his touch is revolting, and despite how crudely specific he's being, I'm *still* trying to wrap my mind around exactly what he's saying.

My mother was buried this morning.

Is he actually proposing marriage to me on the night of her funeral?

I lift my head and meet his eyes. They are dark and dilated. Black-coffee brown surrounded by a thin ring of onyx. Drunk with desire.

Ruthless want.

"*Frate*, you can't—"

"*Mosier*!" he growls at me, the hand in his lap moving faster. "Get used to calling me Mosier!"

"You can't mean—"

"Yes! I can," he groans, his face bobbing slowly up and down. His other hand clasps my upper thigh and his thumb jabs into my womanhood. He slides it back and forth in rhythm with the hand he's rubbing himself with, and I am beset with a terror, a repulsion so strong, I can't help myself.

My stomach heaves and I vomit, without warning, all over his head, his hand, and my lap.

"Futu-ți pizda mă-tii!" he yells, jerking his hands away and falling backward into a sitting position, his face shocked and disgusted as my vomit seeps between the bristles of his hair and slides down the sides of his ugly face. *"Futu-ți dumnezeii mă-tii!"*

The taste of puke in my mouth makes me throw up again, and I buck forward over and over again until there is a small pond of regurgitated food all over my lap, dress, shoes, and Mosier's once-pristine, faux-fur princess carpeting. At this point, I am crying too, with vomit-laden saliva hanging in strings from my lips.

I backhand my mouth slowly and look at Mosier, who is now standing. My eyes slide up his form, stopping briefly at the massive, terrifying protrusion at the front of his pants before skipping to his eyes.

He lifts a finger and jabs it in my direction. "You will *welcome* my touch! You will *beg* for it!"

Never.

"Or you *won't*," he growls. "I don't care either way. I *own* you, *cenușă*. I *bought* you. Your body is *mine*! Your virginity is *mine*! Your pussy is *mine*! Your womb is *mine*, and I will pump it full of cum and fill it with son after son until you have built me a beautiful fucking empire, do you hear me?"

Oh, God.

He runs a hand through his hair, shaking out the puke from his ringed fingers with a sneer. "You and your junkie slut sister were a package deal. I bought *her* for *you*, you stupid cunt!"

This isn't happening. This can't be happening.

He leans forward and grabs my chin harshly, making me cry out with pain.

His voice is low and lethal when he speaks to me, so close to my face, I can feel the heat of his breath on my skin. His dark, furious eyes stare into mine. "And when one month of decent Catholic mourning has passed . . . the day after your goddamned graduation . . . you *will* become my wife, *cenușă*. Do you understand me? *Mă înțelegi?* And you will be the perfect, pious, obedient fucking wife that I have *waited* for, that I have *paid for*, that I fucking *deserve*."

"No," I mewl softly, tears streaming down my cheeks as I try to escape his grasp.

"Yes!" he cries, tightening his bruising grip on my

slippery skin. "To be quite clear, *sister*. You will be mine to *fuck* . . . any way I *want* . . . for the rest of my goddamn *life*. *That* is your future, *cenușă*. *That* is your destiny. *That* is the plan."

"Please," I sob, dropping my chin to my chest when he releases it.

"One month," he bellows, then turns and leaves the room, slamming the door behind him.

I fall back on the bed, drawing my knees up to my chest, and weep.

CHAPTER THREE

Ashley

One month.

One month.

One month.

Now his words at the will reading—*Ashley will work for me, I have plans for her*—make sense.

My job? His wife. His . . . baby maker.

Ana, one of the housemaids, comes up to take my soiled clothes and clean my carpet while I step into a steaming shower, resting my forehead against the tiled wall as I replay his words in my head: *I married your whore sister for you . . . Someone I could mold into my own . . . Pious. Modest. All mine . . . I own you,* cenușă *. . . Your womb is mine . . . You will be mine to fuck . . . any way I want . . . for the rest of my goddamn life.*

That is your future, cenușă.

That is your destiny.

I vomit bile into my mouth and spit it out, watching the bright yellow mucus slide slowly down the wall to the shower floor, where it is swept down the drain. If only I could escape so easily.

This was his plan all along. From the very beginning. To find a vulnerable woman with a young daughter or sister, and marry her . . . like some sort of perverted two-for-one deal. He planned this from the first day he saw us shopping together. Marrying my mother was a means to an end. And the end, apparently, is me.

A sob rips from my throat as my shoulders shake with the force of my weeping.

"Did *you* know?" I sob aloud, my pitiful voice drowned out by the rush of water. "My God, Tig . . . *did you know?*"

Did she sell us both—willfully—into this life?

Tígin wasn't a *good* mother, but she was all I had, and I believed, in her own way, that she cared about me. How could she do this to us? How could she sell us to someone as ruthless as Mosier Răumann?

Though I don't know very much about Mosier's business dealings, my interactions with him and observations of him and his life over the past five years have been enough to paint a picture of his character.

His house—a massive brick estate in Westchester County, New York—is surrounded by a high black metal fence, and a force of six men, in alternating shifts, always guards the perimeter of the property. They carry handguns and walkie-talkies, and none of them are allowed to look at me. If and when they ever did, Mosier was swift to blacken their eyes or break their noses, as he did his own sons' that day by the pool.

Anders and Damon were not allowed to be my brothers in any real way. We weren't allowed to swim together or watch TV alone. When I was home on breaks, a woman named Mrs. Grosavu followed me around the house. I was told that she was there to take care of me and see to my needs, but it always felt like she was watching me, making sure that I behaved a certain way, reminding me when I should be more modest, laugh more quietly, or cross my ankles. Over time, I saw her more as a jailer than a helper, and I was relieved, in fact, when I arrived home this past Easter and was told she'd taken a job somewhere else.

More than once, I watched Mosier dispatch his men after loud cell phone conversations in a foreign language, and though I wondered where they were going, I dared not ask. When I asked my mother, she replied that Mosier's business concerns were none of our affair.

At least twice, my mother and I were woken up and sent down to the wine cellar apartment in the dark of night. There, behind a fake door that appeared to be a wall of wine, we had every creature comfort, but an armed guard stood outside the apartment door, prohibiting us from leaving, until Mosier, Anders, or Damon arrived to take us back upstairs.

I know that Mosier is some sort of criminal, involved in the sorts of business dealings that could get a man, and his family, killed.

But I also know that he likes the high life, movie premieres and weekends in Vegas— always with a large security force, of course—and regardless of how dismissively he just spoke of her, my mother was a diamond on his arm because of her former status as a supermodel.

But I never suspected—not even for a moment—that *I* was a part of his plans. My God, did *she* know? *Tig . . . did you do this to me?*

I close my eyes, clasp my fingers together, and

pray: *Please, God, don't let her have known. Please don't let her have chosen someone like Mosier for me. Amen.*

When I open my eyes, I reach for the shampoo, pour some into my hands, and massage it into my light blonde hair, trying to stay calm.

Mosier called my school two days ago with the news of my mother's overdose and death, and the advisement that Eddie and Anders would be coming up to collect me for the funeral the following day.

At first I didn't believe the news. For as much as my mother had battled an intense substance abuse problem between the ages of twenty and twenty-nine, she had straightened herself out by the time she married Mosier. And I watched carefully over the next five years—every time wine was poured into her goblet at dinner, every time champagne was passed around at an event, she never took a sip, never even lifted a glass to her lips. I was home one month ago for Easter, and her eyes were sad and withdrawn, but clear. How could she have backslid so quickly and completely? And with Mosier's watchful eyes on her, how in the world did she manage to obtain heroin, let alone enough to overdose? And how—with a veritable army of security guards and house staff—did no one find her until she was dead?

I have so many questions, but I am frightened to ask Mosier or his sons what happened. I don't think I would get a straight answer, for one thing, but after our conversation in my bedroom, there is a more pressing and immediate concern on my mind:

I am meant to be the child bride of a monster thirty-three years older than me, for the sole purpose of breeding him sons.

I lean back and rinse my hair, placing my hands

over my heart.

Sex. Something I know almost nothing about. Something my mother knew a great deal about.

I remember her bringing men over quite frequently when we lived in LA. I was meant to call them all Uncle. Uncle John. Uncle Frank. Uncle Ken. She'd walk in with them, point to me watching TV, and say, "That's my kid sister. Ash, this is Uncle Wes. Say hi."

I'd say hi without looking away from the TV while she'd lead them into her bedroom. I'd turn up the volume of whatever show I was watching so I couldn't hear her moans and screams, his grunts and groans. When they were done, my "uncles" didn't stay long. They'd slip out quickly when the deed was done. The front door closing was my cue to bolt it, turn off the TV, and slip down the hallway to my bedroom.

By the time was eight, I had figured out, more or less, what my mother was doing. I had my first kiss—with the son of one of my mother's old supermodel friends—when I was ten, and I let a boy from school touch my breasts through my shirt in the janitor's closet when I was eleven. Looking back, I was probably on track to lose my virginity by thirteen, but that just happened to be the year that everything changed.

My mother met Mosier the month after I turned thirteen.

Within three weeks of meeting Mosier Răumann via a high-end Hollywood matchmaker, my mother married him and moved us to his home outside New York City. She told me that he was her sugar daddy and we'd never have to worry about anything else for the rest of our lives. She told me that New York would be just as fun as LA and we were going on an adventure. She told me I'd have a new father and brothers, and a chandelier in my room, and wasn't I just the luckiest kid who ever lived?

Once we got there, I didn't feel very lucky. My favorite clothes were taken away and replaced with a Mosier-approved wardrobe. I was no longer allowed to leave the house unaccompanied. I was not to speak unless spoken to. I was enrolled in a religious boarding school, away from my mother, after just a few weeks there.

We arrived at his house in June, and all summer, Tig's bright blue eyes lost a little more luster every day. Once, when I asked her if we could go back to LA, Tig told me, without much confidence, that it would get easier, and besides, she added, Mosier would take care of us . . . no matter what.

It's recalling that "no matter what" now that sends a chill down my spine and makes me think that Tígin *did* know of his plans for us—and, ultimately, for me.

Turning around, I rinse the conditioner from my hair and quickly soap and rinse the rest of my body.

Mosier promised I could return to school until graduation.

Which means I have exactly one month to figure out what to do.

***

At dinner, Mosier sits at the head of the table, I am seated at his right, and his twin sons sit across from me to his left. The last time I visited, my mother sat between me and Mosier, but I have taken her place now, and it feels all wrong to me. I wish, just for tonight, we could have left her seat vacant in remembrance, but Mosier has already outlined his plans for our future, and remembering my mother doesn't fit with the fantasy he's created.

Mosier invites Anders to say the blessing, and Anders offers it in Latin, which is standard at Răumann family dinners. Even my mother knew how to give at least one blessing in proper Latin.

"Amen," mutters Mosier, picking up his spoon with a sigh. "Now we eat."

Mealtimes have been mostly quiet affairs, with Anders and Damon forbidden to glance up just for the sake of looking at me or my mother. They were only permitted to look at us if one of us was speaking, and even then, their expressions were carefully schooled to be impartial. To be honest, I was always grateful when we managed to get through dinner without conversation, which means my stomach is a mess of butterflies because *I* have something to say tonight.

"Mosier," I begin softly, keeping my eyes down, waiting for his permission to continue.

His spoon clinks against the side of his soup bowl with annoyance. He is still upset with me for vomiting on him. "What?"

I gulp, looking up at him. "I haven't been to confession in two days, and my classes resume on Monday. I wonder if I may return to school tomorrow?"

He stares at me, his eyes slipping down to my chest and resting there. My breasts are covered by a navy blue silk blouse, but the heat of his eyes makes me feel naked.

"No," he grunts.

My whole body tenses. *Is he reneging on his agreement to let me finish school? Oh, God, am I trapped here? Does my sentence begin* now*?*

"I have to be in Newark tomorrow," he says. "I

can't take you until Wednesday."

I relax, my shoulders lowering and my swimming head clearing a little.

"Oh," I murmur, looking back down at my soup.

"I can take her," offers Damon.

My neck snaps up because the Răumann twins and I rarely spend any time one-on-one, and it's a daring suggestion.

"You? Ha! And I'll send a fox to take care of my sheep." He shifts his gaze to Anders. "You'll take her."

Anders has always been the quieter son, the smarter son, the son that Mosier trusts more.

"I was supposed to join you in Newark," says Anders softly, his handsome face tightening in protest.

"So what?" demands Mosier. "Now you'll go with her."

Anders clenches his jaw as he nods. "Yes, *Tată*."

"*Yes, Father*," mimics Mosier, picking up his soup spoon. "She is *pious*. Pure. Devout. She wants to confess her sins with a priest, for God's sake! You could learn something from her devotion, you fucking mongrels." He slurps a mouthful of soup. "Now we eat. All of you, shut the fuck up."

I lift my spoon and chance a quick glance at Anders, surprised to find he's doing the same: glaring back at me with narrowed eyes. We stare at each other for a long second, for as long as we dare, before turning our attention back to the soup.

***

The next morning, I look out my window to see Mosier and Damon slide into the backseat of a town car and Eddie slam the doors shut. I breathe a huge sigh of relief, knowing that I won't see Mosier again for a month. Though I haven't the slightest idea of how to escape his clutches, I am determined to figure out an alternate future for myself once I return to school.

I am packed and ready to go at eight o'clock when Ana arrives at my room. She tells me that Anders is on a phone call for Mosier and wants to leave at nine. With half an hour of quiet time, my mind turns, once again, to Tig.

When Tig was twenty-one, after two years of splitting her time between Manhattan, Milan, and Paris, she settled down in LA, where she was cast as a prima donna supermodel in a sitcom about a fashion magazine. That was when her addiction began in earnest. During her years of modeling abroad, she'd gotten a taste for champagne, martinis, and cosmopolitans, but it hadn't become a problem . . . yet. She'd been jet-setting; she was very popular and in constant demand. Being so busy had kept her from the viselike grip of addiction. But once she settled down in LA, where she rented a bungalow and hit the club circuit every night, her behavior deteriorated quickly.

After three years on *Lure Me*, she overdosed one night.

I found her in the bathroom, out cold on the tile floor in a pool of drying vomit. I called Gus, who called 911 and my grandparents. My grandparents stayed at a hotel near the hospital until Tig was discharged and admitted to a rehab center in Ojai. Then they returned home to Ohio. Gus stayed at the bungalow with me. I was eight.

Those sixty days when I lived with Gus? They were, arguably, the happiest days of my life. He often had early calls for makeup and hair, but he'd take me with him, slipping out to drive me to school at eight. He was waiting for me every day at three o'clock on the dot, his blue chrome VW bug shining in the California sun. He was a loving and patient substitute parent, feeding me dinner at the same time every night and reading me a story before bed. For those two months, he didn't go out at night and leave me alone, and I knew a safety and security that I'd lacked since moving to LA.

When Tig came home, I knew I should have been happy, but I felt a deep, almost profound, sense of loss. A pure, unalloyed sadness. Saying farewell to Gus was gut-wrenching. Though I still saw him often, it wasn't the same. I missed having him around *all* the time.

My mother was fired from *Lure Me* following her overdose, but it didn't matter. Her name had been in all the magazines and newspapers, and all publicity is good publicity. Modeling jobs started coming in again. People celebrated her recovery, and Tig basked in her revival. For a little while, at least. But the problem with rehab is that it didn't change my mother's surroundings. Old habits die hard no matter how much you want to change. Three years later, Tig was using again: out drinking at clubs every night, snorting cocaine, and occasionally shooting up in her ankles to avoid track marks on her hands and arms.

And then one day, just after I had turned thirteen, we went shopping together on Rodeo Drive.

Shopping with my mother wasn't an unusual activity. She loved dressing us up, then posing for pictures when we were spotted by paparazzi. She was wearing sunglasses, of course, to hide her bloodshot eyes.

Her credit card was denied that day. I remember it clearly because it had never happened before. She pitched a fit at Fendi, throwing a three-thousand-dollar powder-pink leather clutch at the saleswoman when she cut up Tig's denied credit card. We were escorted from the store by security, and I vividly recall Tig hissing, "Fendi is shit. This whole street is nothing but overpriced shit!"

That must have been the day Mosier saw us walking together.

Was it before or after the scene at Fendi? I wonder, standing up from my bed and crossing my bedroom to the door. I unlock it, opening it as quietly as possible, and peek out at the hallway. My mother and Mosier didn't share a bedroom, and before I leave, I want to take a look in her suite of rooms. I don't even know what I'm hoping to find. I only know that I can't shake the feeling that I'm being lied to about her death, and I want to know the truth.

I step into the hallway.

Not long after that day on Rodeo Drive, my mother got a call from Chanel Harris-Briggs, the top Hollywood matchmaker, who had her own reality TV show called *Soul Mates*. She said that she had a new client, a very wealthy businessman from Manhattan, who was insisting on a dinner date with Tig.

My mother laughed at the phone call at first, but when her credit card bill came the next day, she called Chanel back and said she'd take the date. In a gesture that totally got Tig's attention, Mosier sent his jet to LAX to fly her to New York for an overnight date. When she got home the following day, she said we were moving to the East Coast.

I'd never met Mosier. She'd only met him once.

"He's a sugar daddy, Ash. He'll take care of us," she said, wiggling her fingers so that the five-karat diamond solitaire ring would make rainbows all over our bungalow.

The main condition of Mosier's marriage proposal?

No more drinking. No more drugs.

Tig ignored this condition for the two weeks leading up to our move, partying her ass off all over Beverly Hills on Mosier's dime as a moving company carefully packed all our belongings and had them shipped to New York. When we arrived, my mother and I were separated at the airport without explanation. I found out later that she was taken directly to a detox facility, while I was driven to a hotel in Manhattan, where I remained with my grandparents in adjoining rooms for ten lonely days.

On the eleventh day, we were collected by Eddie and driven to an Orthodox church in Brooklyn.

My mother didn't smile when she saw me. In fact, she didn't even make eye contact with me. But I'd never seen someone so changed, so quickly. Her cheeks were hollow, and without Gus to do her makeup, she looked sick instead of chic. Her hair, which had always been blow-dried stick straight, was heavily curled and piled on her head like a Disney princess at the prom. Though a simple white slip dress would have been her choice, her wedding gown had a massive, poofy ball-gown skirt, and was covered with hundreds of beads that shone like diamonds in the June sun. She went through the motions of the day in a quiet, dutiful manner that was foreign to me. She smiled for pictures, but otherwise kept her eyes down and her thoughts to herself.

But her hands didn't shake like she needed a fix.

I never saw them shake again.

Moving quickly, I scurry down the hall and turn the knob to enter her room, sliding inside and closing the door behind me as quietly as possible. My mother's perfume has permeated every surface of this suite, and I stand just inside the door, leaning against the paneling. I let my eyes close, and I breathe in the scent, half expecting to hear her voice.

Kid? Is that you?

Sudden tears burn behind my eyelids.

Yes. It's me.

Did you know? Did you choose this for us? For me?

How did you die, Tig? How and why?

I make my way through the dimly lit foyer, my feet making no sound on the plush carpet as I near her bright bedroom, where morning sunlight streams in through the floor-to-ceiling windows. But as the room comes into full view, I stop short. A man sits at the foot of her bed, his head cradled in his hands. Staring more closely at the back of his head, I realize it's Anders, and the subtle movement of his shoulders tells me that he's crying.

Then I notice something pink sticking out from under Tig's mattress. I squint, realizing that it's the tip of a hot pink feather. I'm curious about it, but I'm not supposed to be alone in a bedroom with Anders. It's probably best if I slip out and—

"Get out," he mutters without lifting his head.

I have never been particularly close to Anders, but the agony in his voice makes my breath catch.

"Get *the fuck* out," he says softly, still hunched over. "You can clean in here later."

He thinks I'm the maid.

My eyes skitter to the pink feather, and I step forward, reaching for it.

"GET THE FUCK OUT!"

I pull hard, and a journal, with a hot pink feathered

pen securely attached, slips from between the mattress and box spring. I grab it before it can smack on the floor, then bolt from the room before he turns around to see me. Cradling the book against my chest, I slam the foyer door shut, then race down the hall to my room.

Trembling, I bury the book at the bottom of my suitcase, hoping to find some answers later . . . as a hundred new questions fill my head.

CHAPTER FOUR

Ashley

The drive to New Paltz takes about an hour, and we are driven in a town car by Mosier's secondary chauffeur and part-time gardener, Cezar.

Anders sits to my left, staring at his cell phone, and the leather bolster between us remains down for the entire ride. We don't speak, though I can't shake my curiosity about Anders' unexpected presence in my mother's room this morning. Why was he there? And why was he crying?

I think back on their relationship, but can't pinpoint anything that would indicate that they'd been especially close. I wasn't around very much over the past five years, but I did spend a few days with Tig at Thanksgiving, Christmas, and Easter every year, and returned again for two months over the summer.

Had Anders become close to her? Perhaps loved her as a mother figure?

I don't know very much about Mosier's first wife, but her portrait still hangs in his study, with a candle burning beneath it at all times. In the painting, a woman sits in a formal, wingback chair beside a pool, wearing a white dress and veil. She holds a red rose and pink pearl rosary, which Mosier gave to me on my sixteenth birthday. She's looking to the left, so it's hard to make out her face, but a blonde curl escapes from beneath the veil, and her profile beneath the heavy white lace is very pretty. I don't know how she died, but I imagine she meant a great deal to Mosier if he still has her portrait displayed.

Her sons have barely ever mentioned her, though I heard her name once.

Rozalia.

Rose.

"Anders?"

"Hmm?" he grunts, not looking up from his phone.

"How old were you when your mother passed away?"

He glances at me, his face expressionless. "Four."

I nod, looking at the folded hands in my lap. "You must have missed her."

"We moved here soon after," he answers, flicking a look at the rearview mirror and meeting Cezar's eyes briefly.

It's the longest conversation we've had in years, but I press on, aware that we'll be arriving at school in the next ten to fifteen minutes, and the next time I have an opportunity to speak to Anders might be as his—*gulp*—stepmother.

"When did my mother start using again?" I whisper, looking over at him.

His jaw tightens as it did at dinner last night, and his eyes, shiny and profoundly miserable, meet mine, blinking twice in quick succession. "She wasn't . . . I mean . . . I don't know."

"She'd been clean for years."

He doesn't answer me, just closes his eyes and swipes his hand back and forth over his lips and chin.

"I don't understand," I continue. "I just want—"

"It doesn't matter," he says. "She's gone. Let her be gone."

My shoulders slump, and I glance out the window as we turn off the highway.

"*Please,*" I whisper, my eyes burning again as they did this morning when I smelled her perfume. I think of her diary hidden in my bag, and hope that if Anders won't talk to me, at least her journal can shed some light on her last days.

We stop at a traffic light, and Anders mumbles something.

"What?" I ask, turning to face him.

"She loved you," he murmurs, his eyes glistening as he blinks at me again.

No. No, I don't think she did.

"Did she tell you that?"

"She didn't have to," he answers.

She didn't love me, my heart protests. She couldn't have. She sold us to Mosier. She sold me to a monster in exchange for a powder-pink Fendi clutch.

"I don't think—"

"She *did,*" he growls. "Now shut up."

Turning back to the window for the remainder of the ride, a single tear slips down my cheek, and I realize it's the first I've cried for her since the moment I learned my mother was dead.

***

I am relieved to watch Anders and Cezar drive away, leaving me at the front door of the conventlike building that serves as both dormitory and dining room. Across a small, well-kept quad, there is a two-story, stone academic building with a dozen classrooms for the fifty-two girls who attend middle and secondary school here. Between the boarding and academic buildings is the Chapel of the Blessed Virgin, the focal point of the small campus. And in the middle of the quad, there is a statue of Jesus on the cross at the head of a square pool with a fountain in the middle that bubbles soothingly.

I am home.

There are seven girls in my grade, all of whom are like sisters to me. We board, with the juniors and sophomores, on the top floor, each of us in a very small, simple room that has a bed, dresser, desk and chair, sink, and small mirror. There is a common lounge area, with comfortable couches, reading lights, and puzzles and board games, where we are encouraged to spend time in study, play, or prayer.

There are no televisions. No phones except the one in Mother Superior's office on the ground floor by the kitchen. No full-length mirrors. Nothing that would encourage worldliness or vanity. Blessed Virgin offers a simple, quiet upbringing for young ladies whose families desire a careful, ultratraditional, Catholic school experience.

My peers are at class, but at 11:45 the bells will ring for midday prayer in the chapel, and they'll return to the dining room at noon for dinner, followed by afternoon classes, music, and fitness. Evening prayer runs from 4:45 to 5:15, and supper is served at 5:30 every evening.

I climb the stairs to the third floor, noting that I have about an hour before midday prayer and dinner to unpack my bag and freshen up. I place my freshly laundered clothes back in my dresser and change into my school uniform: a crisp white cotton blouse, belted navy blue skirt, navy ballet flats, and navy cardigan sweater monogrammed with the school crest in crimson. I brush my hair and French braid it into a long, blonde tail that almost touches the waistband of my skirt, then secure it with a simple navy blue rubber band.

With more than forty minutes to spare, I pull my mother's journal from the almost-empty bag. While part of me is desperate to know what's inside, there is another part of me that is scared of what I will find. I sit down at my desk, staring at the cover.

It's a picture of Marilyn Monroe kneeling on a pink bed with a pink pen between her teeth. A round puff of feathers on the back of the pen rubs against her cheek, and her smile is wide, as though kneeling on a bed with a fluffy pen in her mouth is the most fun she's ever had. I place my hand over the cover of the journal and close my eyes, offering up a quick prayer:

Dear Lord, whatever is in this diary, I pray it gives me answers, even at the cost of peace. I need to know what happened to Tig, Lord. I feel like I can't move forward until I know more about how my mother lived and how she died. Please help. In nomine Patris et Filii et Spiritus Sancti. *Amen.*

Taking a deep breath, I open my eyes and begin.

Day #1 of THE NEW YOU!

Dear Diary,

Jesus, that's cheesy. Can I be that cheesy? I guess I can. Who's going to read this sad shit except for me? No one. That's who.

Besides, look at that fucking header: THE NEW YOU!

(I just threw up in my mouth.)

Dr. Covey gave me this journal on my last day of rehab. She said it might help me stay strong if I wrote down my thoughts. Yeah, right. That was over two years ago, and this thing has been sitting in my drawer, collecting dust since then.

All that crap they taught me at rehab about One Day At A Time and You Can Do This is bullshit. That's the first thing I want to say. None of it helps. None of it makes me stop. I know I should stop. I even know it's going to kill me. Know what? I don't care. How pathetic is that? I don't give a shit if I die except . . . Fuck. Except for the kid.

My fucking parents would put her in a home so they wouldn't have to look at her, and then what? Just turned thirteen with little tits and a sweet ass. She's cute, just like I was. She'd be raped ten ways from Sunday before she was fourteen. Gus would try to take to her, but he's barely better off than me, moving from one sadistic son of a bitch to another before his ass barely has a chance to stop bleeding. I'll OD and Gus will die from fucking AIDS and they can bury us side by side for all eternity. Ha. Fuck. It'd be funny if it weren't so fucking sad.

Besides, the kid. The thousand-weight anchor tied to my neck. I haven't been free since the day I had her.

I see her eyes when I bring someone home. I try not to look, but I see. She hates me and thinks I'm a slut. Well, I am a slut. And she can hate me all she wants. I'm all she's fucking got.

We were doing okay for a while there. I got clean. The kid was going to private school. I don't know when things started to slip. I only know they're fucking slipping now and I should stop using but I can't. I fucking can't, okay?

I missed this morning's job call and they hired Jane Fake Tits Simpkins to do the shoot instead. A little late and I'm out. Well, fuck them. If they want Fake Jane, they can have her. I'll find a different gig. Miranda says I'm a pain in the ass and poison and no one wants to shoot me, but fuck, I'm also Tígin. Youngest bitch to own the catwalk since Twiggy. So she can just unwad her granny panties and call me when she's ready. Fucking Vogue or Elle or someone will call. And until then, I'll use this journal and do my own fucking rehab for a while.

I'll go One Day At A FUCKING Time and say to myself, TIG, You Can FUCKING Do This, and I'll make the kid macaroni and cheese for dinner and let her watch Survivor with me later because she likes that.

I'll get myself back on track.

It'll all be okay.

Tig

Xxxxxxx

Day #2 of THE NEW YOU!

Dear FUCKING Diary,

FUCK MIRANDA.

FUCK FUCK FUCK FUCK FUCK HER.

FUCK HER SAD PATHETIC LIFE AS A FUCKING AGENT BECAUSE SHE COULDN'T CUT IT IN FRONT OF THE FUCKING LENS, which is exactly what I fucking told her.

A catalog? A fucking catalog? Are you shitting me? It's been four weeks without a job, so I call you to see what's up, and you offer me a fucking catalog shoot?

Do I LOOK like a fucking catalog model to you, you nearsighted fucking cow?

"What do you say, Tig? It's the best I can do."

Know what I said?

I said, "SHOVE YOUR FUCKING CATALOG JOB UP YOUR FUCKING ASS."

So she said we're done.

Just like that. After 8 fucking years. WE'RE DONE.

Well, FUCK YOU, MIRANDA, and good luck getting 8 years out of Fake Jane.

I was done with Wilhelmina anyway. I'll find someone else

to rep me, for fuck's sake.

I called Gus and he said to send Miranda flowers and say I'm sorry and take the catalog job. And then, while I'm talking to him, the fucking landlord calls AGAIN for April rent, but fuck him too. He can cool his fucking jets. I'll come back. I ***always*** *come back.*

Fuck the landlord.

Fuck Gus.

Fuck Miranda.

Fuck this journal.

And fuck the kid looking at me with big eyes, hoping I'll stay home tonight. No fucking way. I'm going out.

Tig

Xxxxxxx

CHAPTER FIVE

Ashley

I close the journal with a smack, then stand up from my chair, staring at it like a coiled snake.

I remember those days right after my thirteenth birthday, right before my mother met Mosier. It was just a handful of weeks, but Tig was off the rails, drinking and smoking every night, barely alive when I left for school, barely awake when I came home, only to start the cycle all over again at nine or ten that evening.

It was a messy, desperate, chaotic time. While she was spiraling, I was just trying to get through seventh grade without a mom, without a dad, without anyone.

She loved you.

I remember Anders' words from this morning and lift my chin in defiance of them. *Loved* me? She doesn't even use my name in her journal. If anything, I was an inconvenience to her suicide plans. Love? I don't see it. I don't see a hint of it. Only some grudging responsibility toward my not getting raped.

Wow, I think, shaking from the crassness of her

thoughts about me. *What a mother!*

She can hate me all she wants.

"Good," I sob, turning away from my desk and Marilyn's gaudy smile, "because I *do* hate you!"

My classmates hug me as I take my assigned seat at midday prayer, and later Sister Agnes sits beside me at dinner. Mother Superior says a special prayer for Tig's soul, and my spirit and my heartbeat slowly return to normal as I allow the sweet peace of school to envelop me.

But what I really long for is time alone with Father Joseph.

Father Joseph is one of two priests who work at the Blessed Virgin Academy and the only one who works there full-time, living in a small rectory adjacent to the chapel. He is in his sixties, with white hair and wrinkles, but after Gus, I love him most in the world. Though our relationship is mostly confined to the confessional, we occasionally have long talks about life and faith. I once clocked our longest talk at almost two hours. The way he listens to me, stopping me now and then to clarify a point or offer feedback, tells me that I am heard. And I place a premium on being heard, since so few people in my life have cared to listen.

He doesn't hug me or kiss me or smile at me any more or less than the other girls at my school. He doesn't favor me or go out of his way to make me feel special. But he *gets* me, and he is more of a parent to me than Tig ever was.

He loves me like Jesus loves all of us—in an otherworldly, fatherly way that has no beginning and no end, given freely not because we deserve it or have earned it, but because something in his heart is called to love us no matter what. Sometimes I wonder if Father

Joseph's unconditional love is what stands between my life and a life like Tig's. Because of him, I believe that God loves us. Because of him, I want to be good.

And I desperately hope he can help me.

Confession is offered six times a week, but Father Joseph is in the confessional only on Wednesday and Saturday mornings, so I have to wait a day until I can speak to him.

I am up by five o'clock to shower and dress.

I have avoided Tig's journal over the past two days, though it feels like Marilyn's face taunts me with her sexy grin whenever I glance over at my desk. I tried turning it over, but the back of the journal has her rump in the air, and Lord forbid one of the nuns sees that! Part of me wants to put the diary in the back of my desk and forget about it, but a larger part of me is gathering the courage to go back and read.

I need to understand her. Tig. Teagan. My fake sister. My secret mother. I want to know how she died.

At six o'clock I walk across the quiet campus and enter the Chapel of the Blessed Virgin, relieved to see that the green light over Father Joseph's side of the confessional box is lit, which means he's available. Because not many teenage girls relish the idea of getting up at dawn to chitchat with a priest, I know that we're not likely to be interrupted.

I open the heavy wooden door to the right of his and step inside the small, dark, quiet space. I kneel down on the velvet-covered hassock and cross myself. When I open my eyes to Father Joseph's dimly lit profile behind the metal screen that separates us, my tired soul lifts.

Surely here I will find my way.

"Bless me, Father, for I have sinned."

"How long has it been since your last confession, my child?"

"One week," I whisper, the words strange in my ears.

How in the world could my life have changed so materially in one short week?

"Continue."

"My sister passed from this world," I say, "and I don't know how to feel. My mind wandered at her funeral. And . . . and my feelings have been very mixed, very confused, since she died." I pause, as I often do during confession, to let Father Joseph speak.

He clears his throat. "It is normal to feel confused after the passing of a loved one. There are things we wish we'd said, questions we wish we'd asked. Did you have a chance to say good-bye to her?"

"No," I whisper. "Her death was sudden and unexpected."

He takes a long, deep breath, then releases it. "All the more reason to feel unsettled, my child."

My eyes burn with tears, but I blink them back, which reminds me of Anders in the car. "My mother's stepson seems very upset about her passing."

"All members of a family, no matter how close or how far away, will grieve differently."

"But she wasn't his actual mother."

"Do you begrudge him his feelings?"

"No," I say quickly, leaning forward to prop my elbows on the shelf between us. "I just didn't realize he cared about her."

Father Joseph is silent for a moment before

responding. "Be careful not to make assumptions, my child. Your sister's passing could have stirred up memories of his own."

I think of Rose's portrait and nod. "Of course."

"Spend time in prayer. Seek the voice of God in your quiet moments. He will comfort you. He is the only one who can give you the peace you long for."

"Thank you, Father."

We are silent as I absorb his words, a sliver of that promised peace descending on me from his voice alone. I close my eyes and breathe deeply, letting the air expand my lungs and nourish my blood. It is so good to be back at school . . .

. . . except my time here is finite. And my future looms heavy and horrible on the horizon after graduation.

"Father," I start, but my mind fills with images of Mosier kneeling before me, his hands trespassing on forbidden, sacred parts of my body. A renewed sense of horror sends a chill through me. I clench my eyes shut as I shudder. "F-Father, my . . . m-my . . . he . . . he . . ."

"My child?"

I open my eyes and blurt it out. "My stepfather has plans to marry me."

"Your . . . *stepfather*?"

"Y-yes. My m-mother's husband. He . . . he says that I m-must marry him. He cited the Book of Deut—"

"Miss Ellis," he says sharply.

"Father?"

"Who is this *stepfather*? I read your sister's obituary not three days ago. As I understand it, your *parents* are both alive and still married to one another."

Oh. Oh, my God. Oh.

"My step*brother*!" I cry, realizing like a bolt of lightning my mistake. I have never told anyone at Blessed Virgin that Tig is my biological mother. Not even Father Joseph, whom I love. "I misspoke, Father! I meant my . . . my step*brother*!"

There is movement in the box beside me, and Father Joseph stands up. A moment later, the door opens and slams shut. Inside the confessional, I am frozen. I don't know what to do.

"Miss Ellis, come out of the confessional."

On shaking legs, I stand up. By telling the truth, I have exposed my lies. In church. To Father Joseph. Turning the doorknob slowly, I step outside, into the small chapel, keeping my eyes down.

"Look at me, miss."

Clenching my jaw, I raise my eyes and look at him, my nerves fraying by the second.

"We appear to have some confusion. You referred to the man married to your late sister as your *stepfather* with some conviction."

"No." I gulp. "F-Father Jo—"

"Yes. 'My mother's husband.' That's what you said. You were very clear a moment ago." His light blue eyes bore into mine. "Your *sister's* widower is your stepbrother. Your *mother's* widower would be your stepfather. We cannot move forward in our conversation without transparency. So please tell me the truth: which is it?"

I stare at him with wide eyes, my jaw slack, my mouth dry. I can't lie to him. I can't.

Father Joseph takes a deep breath and sighs, nodding his head, his eyes shifting from suspicion to sympathy before my eyes.

"Miss Ellis," he says, gesturing to a pew. "Sit down."

On legs of jelly, I make my way to the pew and lower my body. For most of my life I have been forbidden to speak of Tig as my mother. My grandmother's name is on my birth certificate. Gus knows the truth only because Tig told him one night a long, long time ago when she was higher than a kite. But no one else on earth knows.

Except now . . . someone does. And as he takes a seat in the pew in front of mine and turns around, propping his elbow on the back of the pew between us, I can see understanding in his brown eyes.

"We are formal in the confessional," he says gently, "but I know it's you when we speak on Wednesday mornings, Miss Ellis. You are the only student who comes to confession on Wednesdays, and, *I* confess, I greatly look forward to our conversations, to watching you grow and mature into a fine young woman." He pauses, pursing his lips for a moment before continuing. "But you are also one lamb in a larger flock. My *beloved* flock. I know all of my students, and I pray for all of you regularly." His eyes search mine. "I know, for instance, that your older sister recently passed from this life, Miss Ellis. I know that she, and her husband, were financially responsible for your tuition. Your parents, as I understand it, are Welsh, and chose to be little involved in the lives of their daughters."

He knows the script of my life cold.

He cocks his head to the side. "Look me in the eyes and tell me that the information I have stated—

that was written on your admission forms—is true."

I can't. I look away.

He sighs heavily. "Miss Ellis, you are a Catholic. I am a Catholic. Though times are changing, in some families, a child born out of wedlock is still considered a point of deep shame for those of our faith. In the confessional, you referred to your sister as your mother and mentioned a stepfather. I need to reiterate that, before we can continue, there *must* be transparency between us, or I will be unable to guide and counsel you. Was the woman you have identified for all of your life as your *sister*, actually your *mother*?"

The tears crowding my eyes slip onto my cheeks, scalding a path to my jawline.

"Yes," I murmur, staring down at my lap, still unable to look Father Joseph in the eyes.

"I see."

"I'm sorry I lied to you. I broke the Ninth Commandment."

"Yes, you did," he replies gently, "but you obeyed the Fourth by honoring your mother and her wishes to appear as your sister in the eyes of the world."

I look up now because I am so grateful for his kindness, for the way he understands, for the way he takes my years of deception and forgives it in an instant.

"Thank you, Father," I whisper.

"Are you an only child?"

"Yes, Father."

"And your sister—I'm sorry—I mean, your *mother* was married several years before her passing, yes? To a man named Mosier Răumann. Your *stepfather*."

"Yes, Father."

"Now we can proceed. Please repeat what you told

me in the confessional, Miss Ellis."

Using the backs of my hands to wipe away my tears, I look up, meeting his eyes. "He . . . well, it appears that my stepfather has had a plan in mind for q-quite some time. He wants me to . . . I mean, he *insists* that I marry him after graduation."

"Insists?" asks Father Joseph. "But marriage is a union of mutual consent."

"He is very . . . forceful."

Please help me, I silently pray. *Please, Father, please help me.*

Father Joseph winces, his eyes deeply troubled when he looks at me. "Aside from the fact that you do not appear to welcome his suit, he is considerably older than you."

"Yes, Father. Over thirty years older."

Father Joseph recoils, leaning away from me as I impart this information, though his eyes remain fixed on mine. Finally he raises his chin. "Miss Ellis, in the eyes of the church, a relationship between a stepfather and his stepdaughter is considered consanguinity. Incest. It is utterly forbidden."

"He believes I am his sister-in-law."

"Yes, of course." Father Joseph nods. "And that is why you must tell him your true identity. Make it clear that you cannot marry him. It would, after all, be a mortal sin. Once he understands that you are actually his stepdaughter, he will withdraw his offer."

I don't care either way. I own you, cenușă. *I bought you. Your body is mine! Your virginity is mine! Your pussy is mine! Your womb is mine, and I will pump it full of—*

A crazy, high-pitched sound escapes my lips. It's an ugly laugh, and it echoes through the sacred space, eerie and all wrong.

"Miss Ellis?"

"Y-you don't know him," I say, my voice wavering. I take a deep breath, trying to steady my nerves, to no avail. "Father, believe me when I tell you: he will *force* me to be his wife. No matter what."

"He would place your very soul in peril?"

In a heartbeat, I think. *He doesn't care about me or my heart or my soul. He feels that he owns me. He made that very clear.* Feeling hopeless, I let my head fall forward and cover my face with my hands, fear and shame washing over me like cold rain.

A long silence lies heavy between us before Father Joseph speaks again. "Miss Ellis, perhaps your grandparents could speak to him? They could explain that your mother was very young when you were born and they stepped in as parent figures for you?"

My grandparents are already back in Wales, but I recall their faces across the conference table at my mother's funeral, and I am more certain than ever that they knew of Mosier's plans for me, but were persuaded to look the other way in exchange for a comfortable life. Or maybe they just hated me so much for existing that they didn't care what happened to me. Or maybe they were glad that I'd be forced into marrying Mosier, thus damning my soul to hell. That's possible too.

"They have left the country," I say softly, "and won't be returning."

"Why not?" he asks, his eyes narrowing.

"My stepfather will only provide for them financially if they remain in Wales. I wasn't sure at the time, but now I believe he deliberately got rid of them so that they couldn't interfere with his plans to marry me."

Father Joseph sighs deeply. "Your father? Is he in the picture at all?"

"I never knew him," I say. "My mother never told me who he was."

"I am sorry," says Father Joseph, his eyes sad, but ever kind. "Without family to intervene on your behalf, Miss Ellis, I will take it upon myself to contact your stepfather and explain—"

"No! Please no!" My eyes must be wild as I lurch forward in the pew. "He would come and get me. He would take me. I would be trapped with him. Please don't say anything to anyone, Father. Please don't call him!" I sob as I recall the terrifying crudeness of his plans, the dark ruthlessness in his eyes. "He was very clear about his . . . *desires*. He wants me to have many children for him and—"

He holds up a single palm to stop me. "I don't require any further detail."

"Don't call him," I say, my voice breaking in a sob.

"Calm yourself, my child." He pats my hand gently two times. "You must see that he deserves to know the truth."

"Please," I beg him. "The moment he hears from you, he'll come up here and take me. He's powerful, Father. Determined. He'll come and get me, and then I'll be under his control. Indefinitely. Forever."

"You're distraught," observes Father Joseph, looking at me closely. "I think you might benefit from a few days away, Miss Ellis. Your mother was only buried on Monday. You need a bit of time somewhere quiet to make peace with her loss."

I consider this for a moment. Being sent away from Father Joseph and my school sounds scary on one hand, but on the other, the further I can get from Mosier, the better.

"While you are away, I will call your stepfather and explain everything to him." He shifts in his seat. "Your grandparents are abroad, but do you have somewhere else to go? Just for a few days while this situation is sorted out?"

"No. There's no one. I'm all alo—" *La Belle Époque Galerie ~ 5900 Shelburne Road ~ Shelburne, VT ~ 05482.* Of course. Gus. "Yes. There *is* someone. My mother's best friend. My godfather."

"Your godfather." Father Joseph's face relaxes. "Would he take you in for a few days? If you could spend a few days with him, it would give me an opportunity to speak to your stepfather on your behalf and iron this out."

An instant plan materializes in my mind: if I could get to Gus, maybe, just maybe, I would be safe from Mosier. I could hide there with Gus for a while. Forever.

Gus. His name is a benediction in the fury of my mind. I remember the happy months I spent with him while Tig was in rehab, the welcome sight of his face at the funeral on Monday, and a warm feeling washes over me, my heart thundering with sudden hope.

"Would you like to use the phone in the rectory to make arrangements?"

"I don't need to," I say, wiping away the leftover tears on my cheeks. "I know I'm welcome." *At any hour, anytime.*

"Very well. I'll write out a pass for you. You can leave on Friday evening when you've finished your classes for the day. I will drive you to the train or bus station myself."

"And you'll contact Mosier?"

"Yes. Let me be very clear, Miss Ellis: I feel strongly that he *deserves* to know the truth. Seen in a certain light, he is as much a victim as you are, lied to by his spouse for the entirety of their union. I ask you, also, to search your own heart. Relationships between stepparents and stepchildren are often challenging, but perhaps he is not as bad as you fear. Perhaps his offer to marry you was just his misguided way of making sure you were cared for after your mother's passing. But if he has Christ in his heart, he will understand that a marriage between you is impossible."

Mosier's face, furious and determined, appears in my head, and I shiver, reaching for Father Joseph's hand. "He's into . . . bad things, Father. I'm afraid for you."

"What sorts of bad things?"

I don't know how to answer—where to begin. When I flounder, he continues speaking, and the moment is lost.

"Come, now, Miss Ellis. I am a priest. God will protect me." He pats my hand before releasing it. "But I am certain I won't require protection. Your stepfather is a businessman, right?"

I nod slowly, wondering if Father Joseph can possibly understand the kind of sordid "business" in which Mosier deals.

"Then I'm sure he's a reasonable man. I have complete faith that once he learns the truth, he will withdraw his offer. And then you can return to school *and* be reconciled with him."

The way Father Joseph says all this, with such quiet conviction, makes me wonder if it's actually possible.

It's not really that I want a relationship with Mosier and his sons after my graduation from school—in fact, now that a plan to connect with Gus has formed in my mind, I know exactly where I want to go when I finish school—but I would like to part with my stepfamily on good terms. We did have my mother in common, after all.

"I have no money to get to Gus."

"Sister Agnes can prepare a picnic supper for your travels, and I will give you bus or train fare," says Father Joseph, "so that you can get to where you need to go."

I nod. "My godfather lives in Shelburne, Vermont, Father. Do you know where that is?"

"I don't. But we can look for it on a map and figure out how to get you there." For the first time since we started speaking, he smiles at me. "Mind you don't get too comfortable in Vermont, now, Miss Ellis. I expect you'll be back here with us by next week."

Seen in a certain light, he is as much a victim as you are . . . Your stepfather is a businessman . . . a reasonable man . . . Perhaps his offer to marry you was just his misguided way of making sure you were cared for after your mother's passing.

I mull over Father Joseph's words, testing them out to see if they resonate with me. They don't feel right, but then I have always been uncomfortable around Mosier because our life changed so drastically when we moved in with him. Perhaps Father Joseph has a point, and I am just too close to the situation to see it clearly.

Have I been unfair to Mosier? He is crass and crude, of course, and the security around his house has always made my mind spin stories of evildoing, but he also paid for my education and was financially responsible for my mother and me while they were married.

Confused by my charitable thoughts, I frown, very certain of one thing: "I think he'll be very angry."

"He has a right to anger," says Father Joseph. "He was deceived by his wife for many years, and the revelations I share with him may be painful for him to process on several levels. But I have faith that once he has all the facts, he will realize that caring for you in the future cannot include marriage. Trust me, my child. Trust in God."

Trust in God, I think, taking my first deep, clean breath in days and feeling all my bunched and aching muscles finally relax.

I brave a small smile for my savior and protector. "So I can just go stay with Gus for a while? Just like that?"

"You've completed all of the requirements for graduation, Miss Ellis. Besides, you're eighteen. An adult. You're free to go where you please. But, yes. I will write out a pass for you to take your leave of us for a week or so. The time away will do you good. I'm certain of it." Father Joseph smiles back at me. "Meanwhile, I'll sort things out with your stepfather, and you can return to school when you're ready. How does that sound?"

With a sigh of intense relief, I nod, and my smile widens.

It's a plan. A real plan. A good plan, with the best man in the world at the helm. I am so hopeful for its success, my shoulders slump, and tears of gratitude begin to fall. "Thank you. Thank you so much. I was so frightened, Father. So scared."

"There is no need," says Father Joseph, rising as

the bell rings for breakfast. "What we have here, more than anything, is a misunderstanding, my child. I am positive that once we clear it up, all will be well."

***

On Friday evening, while my classmates are summoned to supper by a herald of bells, Father Joseph drives me to the Poughkeepsie Amtrak station, and my eyes fill with tears as I wave good-bye to him from my window seat on the train.

As far as my friends and the sisters know, I am spending a few days off campus with a family friend, something that happens regularly among Blessed Virgin students. But my heart isn't light like theirs would be. Since Wednesday morning, I have been deep in thought and prayer, and what I'm doing on this train can be summed up in one word: *escape.*

I am escaping.

Lying in my bed for the past two nights, staring up at the ceiling, I have replayed Mosier's words in my head on an endless loop: *I married her . . . for you. I own you,* cenușă. *I bought you.*

The past five years have been a waiting game for Mosier, which makes me wonder if it's a coincidence that one month after my eighteenth birthday, my mother mysteriously dies. The timing is unsettling, to say the least.

As the train pulls away from the station, I wave to Father Joseph one final time, watching as he turns away from the platform and walks back to the parking lot. When I can't see him anymore, I face front, wondering about his meeting with Mosier.

He promised not to call Mosier or set up the meeting until I had left town, more out of consideration for my feelings, I believe, than because he believes my stepfather capable of nefarious action. Even today, on the way to the train station, Father Joseph reaffirmed his belief that once Mosier understood the circumstances of my birth, he would withdraw his offer of marriage.

I wish I had Father Joseph's faith in Mosier, but I don't.

I have far more faith in Mosier's hair-trigger temper and ruthless will to get what he wants. I think the revelation of my parentage will throw my stepfather into a fury, but I do not believe it will deter him from his plan to have me.

It's a little after five o'clock, and this train will reach the station in Westport, New York, a little after nine, which leaves me several hours for reading. I take a deep breath. It's time to face my demons again.

Leaning down, I tug my bag out from under the seat in front of me, unzip it, and find Tig's journal.

Day #8 of THE NEW YOU!

Dear Diary,

Big day.

BIG FUCKING DAY TODAY.

I took the kid shopping on Rodeo for shits and giggles and because FUCK MY LIFE I needed a break from feeling like shit. So I put on this ridiculous Zimmermann romper from last season that practically showed off my cooch and I told the kid she could borrow whatever she wanted from THE closet. Of course she chooses my 24" Alexander Wang jeans because she's a skinny little cunt and she knows I can't fit into them.

Cue mother-daughter magical bullshit, strutting our stuff on the Drive, when this dickhead in a limo pulls over and rolls down his window.

Kid is licking an ice cream and staring at headphones in the B&O window, so I step over to the car and lower my Gucci aviators. WELL?

Fucking asks me, HOW MUCH? like I'm a pro.

What a douche.

HOW MUCH? I ask him back, HMM. FIVE MILLION FUCKING DOLLARS AND A MANSION IN THE COUNTRY.

DONE, says the fucker, looking at the kid, then back at

me. I'LL BE IN TOUCH.

Smiles at me, rolls up the fucking window, and drives away.

Okaaaaaaaay. Weirdo.

I turn around and see this little rich bitch walking toward the kid. Zero style, fat as fuck, but she's got a light pink Fendi *bag on her shoulder and fuck if my kid doesn't deserve a* Fendi *bag too.*

I grab her arm and we go to Fendi, *but* FUCK ME *my cards don't work and they get out the goddamn scissors to cut them up. I pitch a fucking fit because* WHY YOU GOTTA BE A BITCH, MARY? *They obviously know who I am because they ask security to escort "Ms. Tig" from the store.*

The kid gets all nervous, pulling my arm and saying she doesn't want the bag anyway. So I throw that shit right at the cash register lady and tell her what I think of her. The kid drags me out the door, gets us a cab, and gives the driver our address before the cops can come.

I DON'T NEED A FENDI BAG, *she says, like I'm a useless piece of shit, and it takes everything inside me not to smack that self-righteous tone out of her voice.*

I call Gus to see where we're going tonight, but he doesn't answer. Fucker's probably getting it hard from some homicidal thick-dick with daddy issues. He needs to be more fucking careful.

When we get home, the light on the answering machine is blinking.

Fuck my life, please let it be work.

And it IS.

Well, sort of.

It's a different kind of job altogether.

Get this . . .

The Hollywood Matchmaker, Chanel Harris-Briggs—side note: WHAT THE FUCK KIND OF NAME IS THAT?*—wants to set me up on a date with the guy from the limo. His name is Mosher and he's loaded.* IF I AGREE, *he'll* *send his* FUCKING JET *for me on Saturday, so we can have dinner in* NEW FUCKING YORK.

IF I FUCKING AGREE? ARE YOU FUCKING KIDDING ME?

SURE, *I say.* I'D BE DELIGHTED TO DINE WITH MISTER MOSHER.

ROWMAN, *she says.* MOSHER ROWMAN.

GREAT, *I say.* SATURDAY IT IS.

So she tells me about how a limo will pick me up at four o'clock, we'll be dining in Manhattan at nine, and I'll be home in LA *the next morning on the red-eye.*

MR. ROWMAN IS HAPPY TO SEND OVER A NANNY FOR THE CHILD, *says Chanel* FUCKING *Hairy-Tits.*

But the kid would rather have Gus be her babysitter because she likes his gay ass way better than she's ever liked me, so I say NO THANKS, IT'S COVERED.

I hang up the phone and I have to admit that maybe Mam was right.

GOOD THINGS HAPPEN TO PEOPLE WHO DON'T DESERVE THEM.

I just might have found myself a fucking sugar daddy, just in the nick of fucking time.

Tig

Xxxxxxx

Day #11 of THE NEW YOU!

Dear Diary,

FUCK.

FUCK FUCK FUCK.

What am I going to do? What the fuck am I going to do?

I'm at the Hillendale Treatment Center in Irvington, New York. I got here today. How? FUCK! Buckle up. Here's how.

Remember the guy from Rodeo Drive? The old guy who I went to New York to meet? That was two weeks ago and a fuckload has happened since then.

He asked me to marry him that night. On our first date.

I figure he's fucking around, so I said, OKAY.

I mean, everything had gone according to schedule. His jet had picked me up at LAX. A helicopter flew me from Newark to Manhattan. I walked into the swankiest restaurant in town only to find out he'd rented out the wine cellar.

Caviar? Yes, please. Champagne? Don't mind if I do. Filet mignon? My favorite.

And get this—he doesn't lay a hand on me the whole time. Pulls out my chair. Buys me dinner. Doesn't say much, and no, he's not exactly a looker, but fuck, it's like being on vacation.

He's drinking his wine at one point, but he pauses and looks at me over the rim of his glass.

I WANT TO MARRY YOU, TEAGAN, he says.

I'LL GIVE YOU FIVE MILLION TO BE MY WIFE.

Thinking he's kidding, I shrug and say, OKAY.

REALLY? he asks. YOU'LL MARRY ME?

That was when I realized he was serious. Like, totally, 100% serious.

Huh. Okay.

I did some quick thinking . . .

I have no work coming in. I'm broke. I've already sold most of my cool bags and shoes on eBay. Thank God I keep my jewelry in the bank, or that'd be gone too.

I'm basically at the end of my rope, and like the good guy in an old Western, this rich motherfucker pops up out of the fucking blue and says that he'll give me five million if I marry him. The kid and I can move into his mansion in New York. He'll take care of us.

That's what I wanted, right? Five mil and a mansion?

Right.

TWO WEEKS, he says, still staring at me in this intense fucking manner. YOU COME BACK TO NEW YORK IN TWO WEEKS AND MARRY ME.

I smile at him and ask him for ten thousand to hold me over until the wedding, half wondering if he'll tell me to go fuck myself. But, nope. He snaps his fingers and some dude leaves the room where we're eating and comes back with the cash.

Fuck.

Then it was REAL real.

Anyway . . . I go back to LA, party for two weeks like my hair's on fire, and spend the ten grand. He sends people to pack up our shit and yesterday he flies us out here. Except, when we got to the airport, Mam and Tad are waiting for the kid and Mosier is waiting for me.

TAKE ASHLEY TO THE HOTEL, he says to my

parents.

Then he takes my arm, escorts me to a limo outside, and we're off.

OKAY, I think. We haven't even fucked yet. Now that I'm here for good, he wants some time alone.

WHERE ARE WE GOING? I ask him.

YOU'RE GOING TO DETOX, he says, staring down at his phone as he sits across from me in the car.

Detox? Did I fucking hear him right?

WAIT. WHAT? I DIDN'T AGREE TO ANY—

I'M NOT HAVING A CURVA JUNKIE FOR A WIFE.

CURVA? DOES THAT MEAN FAT?

IT MEANS SLUT, he says, looking up from his phone.

I've only met him in person once, but we've talked on the phone a few times, and he's never used this tone with me. All we ever talk about is how much he can't wait for me and the kid to move in and be a big happy family. A chill goes down my spine, but I'm pissed too, and I concentrate on my anger, letting it build up quick.

WHO THE FUCK DO YOU THINK YOU ARE? I scream, lunging across the seat at him.

But this fucker, for all his considerable girth, is fast. He reaches out and grabs my neck, squeezing it just enough to make me dizzy.

SIT BACK, he says softly, leaning me back against the seat. AND DON'T EVER FUCKING DO THAT AGAIN.

I blink at him because my eyes are burning. I can't get a deep breath.

YOU'RE GETTING CLEAN, he adds, kneeling on the floor between the seats as he stares up at me. His eyes are cold. His voice is quiet. His fingers hurt.

Finally the pads of his fingers release and I take a deep

breath.

What the fuck just happened?

I reach up and massage my neck. His fingers are going to leave marks.

MY WIFE DOESN'T ACT LIKE A SCORPIE CURVA. He sits back in his seat, unbuckles his belt, and unzips his pants, taking out his semi-erect dick. NOW SUCK ME OFF.

I stare at his cock for a second before skipping my eyes to his. WHAT?

IT'S AN HOUR TO THE PLACE. He glances down at his penis, which is getting thicker by the second. SUCK IT.

FUCK YOU, I whisper.

This guy is fucking crazy. I'm getting out of this. I'm not marrying him. Fuck this.

YOU HAVE A LOT TO LEARN, he says.

He reaches for the back of my neck and yanks my head into his lap, my cheek landing against his meat. I struggle, but he keeps his iron grip on the back of my neck.

IF YOU BITE ME, he says softly, I'LL KILL YOU. I'LL SLIT YOUR WRISTS AND MAKE IT LOOK LIKE SUICIDE. NOW SUCK IT.

I felt like I was going to pass out again, but I licked my lips, reaching for his cock and guiding it into my mouth.

I'm surprised I didn't snap the fucking hinge of my jaw.

I had his dick in my mouth for at least forty fucking minutes before he growled and clenched, cumming in hot jerks down my throat that made me gag.

His hand loosened on the back of my neck and I leaned up, backhanding my lips and wiping away the tears on my face as he stared at me.

I don't know what I expected. A compliment? Thanks? Something?

But he just stared at me, finally reaching down to zip up his pants and refasten his belt as the limo pulled into the driveway of the treatment facility.

Mosier kissed my cheek in front of the attending physician and said he'd be back in a week. A FUCKING WEEK.

MY KID? *I asked him, realizing I'd barely thought of her since the airport.*

AT A HOTEL WITH YOUR PARENTS UNTIL THE WEDDING, *he said. Then he tilted his head to the side, gently caressing my cheek with one stubby finger.* SHE WILL BE BEAUTIFUL, I THINK . . . LIKE YOU.

Everyone always said shit like that to me. She's my spitting image. It's true.

It occurs to me that he's told me I'm beautiful in a roundabout way, and this is the nicest thing he's said to me since I fucking arrived, and it makes me feel something. What? I don't know. A little less scared, maybe. And that's the first time I realize it: I'm <u>scared</u> of him.

BE A GOOD GIRL, *he says, his eyes going cold again as he drops his finger from my face.* BE A GOOD GIRL, TEAGAN.

They didn't take this diary away from me. In fact, Dr. Kazmaier said journaling was a "step in the right direction" and told the orderlies to let me keep it.

I'm in my room here and it's plush, but there are fucking bars on the window and the door is locked from the outside. It feels more like a jail than any other treatment facility I've been in.

I have no phone in my room and they took my cell away and after two weeks of hard partying I'm starting to feel like shit. Shaking and hot and cold and like I have to throw up. Fuck. Withdrawal. It's fucking starting already.

Maybe this won't be so bad? Maybe detox will be good for

me? Maybe an older man like Mosier will be good too?

I don't fucking know.

I only know it feels way too late to turn back now.

Tig

CHAPTER SIX

Ashley

"Miss . . . miss, wake up. I think this is your stop?"

I open my eyes with a soft groan, wondering who's shaking my shoulder. Leaning my head away from the window, I turn to the older woman sitting beside me.

"Hmm?"

"We're stopped in Westport. Isn't this your stop?"

I whip my head to look out the window at the train platform.

"Yes!" I drop my knees from the seat in front of me, and Tig's journal falls to the floor with a smack. I lean down, scrambling to grab it, and shove it into my backpack.

"You better hurry, honey. We'll be leaving in a second."

"Thank you," I say, hefting the pack onto my back and standing up.

The older woman sidesteps into the aisle, and I follow her, turning to grab my small suitcase from the overhead shelf.

"Good luck, honey," she says with a sympathetic

smile.

"Thanks," I say, knowing how much I need every bit of luck I can get.

I rush down the aisle to the door, blocked by a conductor who's approaching from the other direction. He grins at me. "Losing you here, princess?"

I look over his shoulder at the door. "Yes."

He clicks his tongue. "Shame. You were nice to look at."

I have heard versions of this sentiment, from the syrupy sweet to the retch-inducing crass, since I was a little girl, so I let it roll off my back.

"Thanks. Can I . . .?"

His eyes get mean for a second, like I did something wrong, like I didn't hold up my end of a bargain I never agreed to. "Sure." He leans halfway out of the aisle, but still blocks it enough that I will have to slide my body against his to reach the door.

I clench my jaw, sucking in my breath so I will touch him as little as possible.

"Bitch," he mutters softly as my face slides by his.

Inside, I feel the ugly word like a punch and blink in surprise, but otherwise I don't register any emotion. I stare at the floor as I walk the few steps to the sliding door and step out onto the platform just as the warning bell rings. I keep my back to the train as it whooshes by, finally leaving me in quiet darkness.

Father Joseph researched my route for me, and I know that the ferry terminal in Essex is a twenty-minute ride north. The last ferry to Charlotte, Vermont, leaves at 9:30 p.m., so I don't have much time. I find a pay phone and dial the memorized number for a cab company. They tell me they'll have someone there to pick me up in two minutes, so I sit down on a bench and wait. Reaching inside my backpack, I find the Mets baseball cap smuggled into my backpack by Father Joseph, twist my hair into a bun, and stuff it into the hat as I smush it on my head.

The parking lot is dark and empty, and I gulp nervously, hoping I'm safe here for a few minutes.

Safe.

Safe.

The word, the most coveted I know, brings sharp and painful tears to my eyes. *Will I ever know what it feels like to be safe?* For most of my tumultuous life, safety has been a distant and unattainable dream.

When I lived with my grandparents, I felt their scorn.

When I lived with Tig, I felt her indifference.

When I lived with Mosier, I felt his malevolence.

When I lived with Father Joseph, I felt his impermanence.

And now . . .

My grandparents are gone.

My mother is dead.

My stepfather is a monster.

My confessor is far away.

Here, in the dark, a transient figure in a town I don't know, I am utterly alone, and for a desperate and terrible second, I am positive I will *never* know safety. Scorn, indifference, malevolence, and impermanence? Yes. Sure. Safety? No. Never.

My hand clutches the handle of my suitcase until my knuckles turn white in the light of the buzzing overhead lamp.

Trust in God.

Father Joseph's warm and welcome voice washes over me, calming my racing heart just as headlights approach. A taxi stops in front of me, and I scramble from the bench into the backseat, lugging my suitcase in with me.

"Ferry terminal, right?"

"Yes, please," I say.

"Come in on the nine o'clock train?" he asks, pulling away from the curb.

"Yes, sir."

"Sir, huh? Hmm. Manners. That's new."

I push the button under the window, and it lowers, the evening breeze cool on my face.

"So," he says, "you're headed to Vermont, huh?"

"Yes, sir."

"You seem kinda young. To be traveling alone, I mean."

I don't answer because there isn't anything to say. I am young. I am alone.

"Not chatty, eh? Well, do you mind music?"
"No, sir."

"Heh. 'No, sir.' Okeydokey."

He leans forward, and pop music fills the car.

At school electronics are frowned upon. There is no cellular signal on campus, and Wi-Fi is available to students only from seven until eight in the evening, so if you want to text someone or look at your Instagram page, you have about an hour after supper.

If you need to call someone, there's a communal telephone in Mother Superior's office, or you can ask to make a call in the rectory. There's no TV in the common room either—only puzzles, books, and games—and no audio system.

So I haven't heard much pop music, except during the rare time I spend at Mosier's house. And even then, only my mother ever listened to Top 40 music, and my stepfather and -brothers hated commercial American music in favor of Europop with words that I didn't understand.

I'll be there, sings the voice on the radio, and I take a deep, bracing breath of the wind blowing on my face. *I'll be there for you.*

I have no idea who the singer is, and maybe her words should amplify my loneliness, but they don't.

Trust in God.

The words make me feel strong for some reason. Maybe because, as much as Father Joseph was only on loan to me, he still facilitated this escape. And as much as Gus doesn't know I'm on my way to him, he will welcome me with open arms.

I could let my past get me down. I could do that, but sitting here in the back of this taxi, driving through the night to a ferry terminal that will take me across black waters to an unknown town in another state, I make an important decision:

I don't know what lies ahead for me, but I promise myself I will come out whole on the other side. And when I do, I will find the safety I crave, even if I have to create it myself.

***

We pull into the small ferry stop at Charlotte thirty minutes later, and after the boat is docked, I walk from the lower level onto the dock with three other foot passengers. There is no terminal here, as the ferry is mostly used by commuters, but there is a small ticket booth, and I'm relieved to see that there's someone inside. I knock on the window, and an older woman looks up at me.

"Help ya?"

"Yes, please," I say. "May I use your phone?"

"Don't have a public phone here."

It's about six miles from here to the address on Gus's business card, and Father Joseph, who looked up the ferry stop on the internet, warned me not to try walking it since the roads between the ferry and Gus's house are heavily wooded on both sides.

I lift my chin. "Do you have a cell phone, ma'am?"

She looked up again. "Yeah. Why?"

"May I pay you something to use it, please?"

"Ya don't have a phone?"

I shake my head.

She rolls her eyes with a huffing sound. "I'm coming out. I'll let you make a quick call."

I watch through the window as she closes and locks the window, puts her denim purse on her shoulder, turns off the lights in the little building, and exits via a side door. She steps over to me, looking up at my face thoughtfully for a moment before squinting.

"Do I know ya?" she asks.

Because of the startling likeness between me and my mother, I have also heard this question many times in my life. People see her face in mine, but it's just different enough to throw them off. Sometimes I have used this to my advantage, but not tonight. Tonight, I want to be forgettable.

"No, ma'am," I say. "I've never been here before."

She tilts her head to the side, trying to get a better look at me. "Ya look familiar. Ya have family hereabouts?"

"No, ma'am."

"Then what're ya doing here?"

"Visiting a friend," I say, adjusting my cap, pulling the brim over my forehead.

"A boy?" she asks, her voice warming as she reaches into her purse and takes out her phone.

"Mm-hm," I say. I reach for her phone and dial Gus's number.

"Well, be quick. I got a man waiting at home for me too."

The phone on the other end rings, and I feel a jolt in my belly. Hope. So sharp, it almost makes me cry.

"Hello?"

"Um, hi. May I please speak to Gus?"

"Gus? He's sleeping. Can you ring back in the morning, please?"

"No!" I raise my voice, worried that he's going to hang up on me. "I *really* need to speak to him now, sir."

There's a pause, and the voice on the other end asks, "Who is this?"

I glance at the lady standing beside me. She's lit a cigarette, and the smoke exhaled from her lips catches a ride on the breeze. I turn away from her and cup the phone.

"Ash," I whisper, praying she doesn't hear me. Between my mother's face and my first name, the internet could deliver up my identity quickly.

The man on the other side of the phone gasps. Whoever he is, he knows who I am.

"Gus. Gus, wake up. Wake up, babe. It's Ashley. Ashley's on the phone!"

"Wh-what? Ash? Where?"

"Here. Here she is."

A moment later, my Gus is speaking to me. "Ash? Li'l Ash? You there, honey?"

"I'm at the Charlotte ferry stop," I say. "Come and get me?"

"You're . . .? Wait! You're here? Oh, my God! Yes! Stay there, honey! Stay there. I'm on my way!" Gus's voice is far away when he says, "Talk to her for a minute. I gotta get dressed."

"Ash? Ash, it's Jock, Gus's partner. He's on his way."

I'll be there. I'll be there for you.

For the third or fourth time tonight, tears prick my eyes. "I have to go."

"Stay put. We're coming. We'll be there in a few minutes. And Ashley? You're welcome here."

I clench my jaw to hold in a grateful sob, nodding my head even though he can't see it. I pull the phone from my cheek and press the End button. Before I can delete the phone call, the ticket seller plucks it from my fingers.

"All set? Boyfriend on his way?"

"Y-yeah," I manage with a small sniffle. "Thank you."

"Want me to wait with ya?"

I look around the empty parking lot, quiet except for the buzz of bugs dive-bombing the ticket booth's light and the footsteps approaching us as the captain and crew of the small ferry pass by.

"Night, Maude."

"Night, boys. See ya tomorrow."

"'Nother day in paradise," one of them jokes, his eyes lingering on me for an extra second as he walks by, heading for a group of four cars in the corner of the lot.

"N-no," I whisper, feeling uncertain about my surroundings, but also knowing instinctively that I need to be as inconspicuous as possible during my travels. At this point, I've drawn the attention of the woman next to me on the train, the conductor, the taxi driver, the ferry crew, and the ticket seller. I'm not doing a very good job of flying below the radar.

"No, thank you, ma'am," I say, pulling on the brim of my hat again. "He's on his way. I'll be okay."

She exhales a puff of smoke and clears her throat. "Sure. Take care of yourself, now."

"Thank you for letting me use your phone."

She turns and heads toward the last remaining car in the corner of the parking lot, then suddenly stops in her tracks and pivots around, the gravel squishing under her white canvas tennis shoes.

"Tígin! Tig!"

My heart drops, and my stomach flip-flops. For a second, I'm grateful I haven't eaten anything since lunch or it might have gurgled up and splashed onto her tennies.

Stay calm, Ashley. Stay calm.

I look up at the woman. "Huh?"

"That's who ya look like!" she exclaims, taking a step toward me as she scans my face. "Spitting image."

I furrow my brow like I have no idea what she's talking about. "I don't—"

"The *model*," she says, her tone straddling impatience and wonder. She takes an indignant step toward me. "She was the Christie Brinkley of the 2000s, don't ya know!"

As if. Christie was a glorified swimsuit model. Tig

modeled top-drawer Parisian and New York couture.

"Huh."

"Come on! Ya know who she is, don't ya? You've heard of her!"

I shrug my shoulders and shake my head. "Sorry. I'm not much for fashion magazines."

"Well, you're a dead ringer for her," says Maude, squinting at me as she takes another long drag on her cigarette. "Hey, what did ya say your name was?"

I didn't.

Think fast, Ashley.

"Christy," I answer in the same snotty tone that Tig used when she wasn't in the mood to deal with people.

"Ya don't have to make fun of me," pouts Maude.

I cross my arms over my chest and sigh like I'm bored even though my heart is racing inside.

"Bitch," says Maude, gesturing at me with the bright orange end of her cigarette. "I hope your ride doesn't show up."

I watch her head to her car, hating it that I had to resort to one of my mother's crappier behaviors to get rid of her after she'd been kind to me. I wish I could yell, "Sorry!" or "Yes, I'm Tig's kid!" or "You were right! Let's be friends, Miss Maude," but I can't. I've made way too much of an impression as it is.

Her car peels out of the parking lot a moment later with her middle finger jabbing through her window in my direction, and I am left alone, waiting for Gus's headlights to brighten the darkness around me.

Luckily I don't have to wait long.

A cream-colored Lexus screeches into the parking lot a moment later, the wheels kicking up gravel and dust as it stops beside me at the ticket booth.

I start laughing, my whole body shaking with ripples of giggles, tears streaming down my cheeks. I let my backpack slide off my shoulders, down my back, and onto the gravel. I run to the driver's side of the car, my arms outstretched, my body pulled, like a magnet, to his.

"Li'l Ash!" he exclaims, running to me from the passenger side, his voice a beloved mix of California sun, urban African American, and proud homosexual man. "Come here, girl!"

I am enveloped into Gus's arms, the smell of his cloves and cologne making me sob as he wraps one wiry arm around my waist and cups my skull with the other, pushing my head down on his shoulder.

"Baby doll," he murmurs near my ear, his voice gritty with emotion, "what on God's green earth are you *doing* here?"

***

Gus's car is big, but it feels small since he's climbed into the backseat beside me, keeping his arm around my shoulders and his hip pressed against mine as Jock, whom Gus called P.C. when he asked him to drive, sits alone in front.

"What's P.C.?" I ask, thinking that Gus has never given a flying fig for political correctness.

"What? You don't see his crown? His goddamned ti-ar-a? He's my Prince Charming, baby doll. After an endless parade of queer frogs, I finally kissed a prince."

Jock glances up from the wheel, catching Gus's eyes in the rearview mirror, and the look they share is so intimate, my stomach clenches with longing for a second. I don't have the slightest idea of how it would feel to be loved like that, but there isn't a cell in my body that doesn't yearn for it.

"He's being generous, Ashley," says Jock, and for the first time I realize he has an accent.

"You're English?"

"Yes. My mother was English. My father was American. From here, actually. Vermont. They divorced when I was small, and I grew up in London with my mum."

"You left London for . . . *here*?" I ask, looking out the window at . . . nothingness.

Jock nods. "I have dual citizenship. After 9/11, I moved to the States to serve. Marines."

"Oh," I murmur, quickly putting together that Jock, a half-American gay man, served in the military. "Wow. That couldn't have been easy."

"Don't ask, don't tell," says Gus, squeezing my shoulder. "Good luck getting anything out of him. I ask him for stories, and he tells me to mind my business."

Jock grunts softly. "They aren't the best memories."

"Poor P.C.," says Gus, clucking his tongue. "A fairy in fatigues." His voice is tender when he adds, "You're with me now, honey. I got your back. For life."

Jock catches Gus's eyes in the mirror again, and again I feel the intensely loving bond between these two men. "Thank God for that."

"Li'l Ash," says Gus, turning to me. "What happened to you? Why you here, baby?"

My stomach knots uncomfortably, and I burrow closer to Gus, biting hard on my lower lip. *Your body is mine! Your virginity is mine! Your pussy is mine! Your womb is mine, and I will pump it full of cum and fill it with son after son until you have built me a beautiful fucking empire, do you hear me?*

"Mosier," I murmur on a release of held breath. "He . . . he had plans for me."

"What kind of plans?" asks Jock.

"He . . ." I sob. The words are so filthy, so unthinkable, I can't bear to repeat them. "I can't, Gus."

"Don't grill her, P.C.," admonishes Gus. "She's not one of your grunts." He hugs me tight. "He wanted, uh, *things* from you, baby doll?"

"Mm-hm."

"He . . . made a move on you?"

"Mm-hm."

Jock growls softly from the front seat. "Did he force himself—"

"Sweet man, I'ma have to flog you later if you can't zip it now," warns Gus. He turns back to me. "You okay, Ash? Your body hurtin'?"

"N-no," I manage to whisper. "It didn't get that far. I . . . I puked on him."

"You . . . you . . . ha!" Gus chortles. "You puked on the man? Ha! Oh, li'l Ash, I wish I'd been there to see that!"

"No, you don't," I sob, my words suddenly rushing from my lips. "He was furious. He said terrible things. He . . . Gus, he said he only married Tig for me. He wanted to . . . to mold me into . . . I don't know . . . some perfect child wife. He . . . he . . . he said I was g-going to h-have his s-sons and . . . and . . . and . . ."

My sobs are choking me now, and I let them free, crying in terrible gulps and snorts as I think of my dead mother, my callous grandparents, and my terrifying stepfather. How could she have done this to me? How could Tig have married that man, knowing the life he planned for me? Did she hate me so much? Did she resent me that much? That she would consign me to a life of debauched slavery to a man thirty years my senior without a kind bone in his body? My God, what did I do to deserve that future?

"How *could* she?" I wail, my shoulders shaking, my body aching, my heart a pulverized thing, shredded and dying within my chest.

"How could . . .?" Gus pauses, turning to me, his eyes wide and horrified. "Oh, no. No. Are you . . . Ash, honey, you think *Tig* did this?"

I take a ragged breath. "He said that it was his p-plan all along. From the m-moment he first saw us. He m-married *her* for *me.*"

"And you think she *knew*?"

I don't know. I don't know, and that's what's killing me.

I shrug, feeling pitiful.

"Oh, li'l Ash . . . *No.*" Gus's voice is kind, but firm. "No. Absolutely not."

"She *hated* me, Gus," I manage to whimper.

"Oh, honey. No," says Gus, rubbing my back as I tuck my head under his chin. "No. Tig was a lot of things, but she was no pimp. And believe me, baby, she didn't hate a hair on your head. I promise you that. Your mama—oh, Tig. She was . . . lost. A lost soul. But this? No, baby. She wouldn't do this to you."

"Gigi," says Jock softly, "I'm going to bring Ashley's bags inside. She can stay here tonight."

Tonight? Only tonight? Panic grips me. "Do I . . . need to . . . *leave* tomorrow?"

"No, baby doll—"

"Tomorrow we'll go talk to Julian," says Jock, sliding out of the car and leaving me and Gus alone.

"We have to figure things out," continues Gus, his

low voice soothing. "*He* could find you here. Your pedophile step*monster.* If he tries to track you down, staying with me could be the worst possible thing for you. Jock and I already talked about it on the ride to the ferry. We need to hide you."

"But, Gus. I want to b-be with *you,*" I sob. "You're all I *h-have.*"

Gus leans away from me, cupping my cheeks, his dark eyes searching mine. "Then trust me. Trust Jock. We'll keep you safe, baby doll, I promise. But you have to trust us."

He's quiet, staring into my face, scanning my eyes, waiting for my reply.

And suddenly I am eight years old again, and Gus has pulled up in front of Tig's bungalow in his shiny, chrome-blue VW Bug. He is walking up the path from the sidewalk to the front door, and when he gets there, he squats down before me and says, *Your mama's in rehab, baby doll. Wanna roommate?*

We'll keep you safe, baby doll, I promise.

I have a terrible feeling that it's not a promise Gus will be able to keep, but in a world where I've loved few and trusted still fewer, one unassailable truth is law as I look into the eyes of a man who's been the truest family I've ever known.

"I trust you, Gus-Gus."

He blinks back tears as he pulls me into his arms.

"Let's get you inside," he says with an elegant sniff. "I just bet P.C.'s got cold milk and Oreos waiting for us."

CHAPTER SEVEN

Ashley

I wake up in Gus and Jock's guest room, bright sunlight flooding through the white, gauzy curtains, warming my body, which is utterly inert under an eiderdown quilt. My eyes open slowly, taking in the unfussy room: crisp white walls with several pop art reprints by Roy Lichtenstein hung at careful intervals. My eyes follow the story they tell, starting at my far left.

The first print is of a woman with a ribbon hairband in her bobbed blond hair and a vulnerable expression on her comic book face.

In the second print, the woman's finger is caught between her teeth in a gesture of angst, with tears about to fall from both eyes.

In the third print, her hair is royal blue and she's almost underwater. The bubble caption over her head reads, "I DON'T CARE! I'D RATHER SINK -- THAN CALL BRAD FOR HELP!"

On the wall across from my bed are two windows, but between them is a fourth framed picture of the same woman in a convertible. She's wearing a fur coat, facing forward, and a man—Brad?—looks at her with sinister eyes as he drives the car.

To my right are two more prints: the first is of a woman's hand and a man's hand, and the man is placing an engagement ring on the woman's finger. And in the sixth and final print, the woman and man are kissing passionately.

I circle my eyes around the room again: the young woman, the tears, the drowning, the car ride, the engagement, the kiss.

In broad strokes it tells a story: first love, conflict, a happy ending.

But why does the girl's face look so uncertain in the first print? And why is she crying in the second? She'd rather die than ask for his help in the third picture. But in the fourth, they're back together, though his expression is ominous, like he means her harm. Then there's a ring and a kiss. Somehow, they end up married.

What is the real *story?* I wonder. *Where is it? In the broad strokes or in the nuance? In the glossed-over happy ending? Or in her tears and his hostility? Where is the* truth?

A knock at the bedroom door ends my introspection, and I sit up in bed. "Come in."

Gus peeks in, his dark skin in stark contrast to the bright white of the room. "You decent?"

I giggle. That's the way he always woke me up when he stayed with us, and despite its inappropriateness, I love it just as much now as I did then. I pat the bed, and he sits down, crossing his legs, clad in crisp, cuffed khaki. He wears a Christian Lacroix tie as a belt and an ironed, long-sleeved Brooks Brothers button-down shirt in mint green, rolled at the cuffs. He looks like a movie director from the 1930s, cool and sophisticated, and I remember how much I've always admired his sense of style.

"Lacroix and Brooks Brothers?" I ask, raising an eyebrow.

"We *are* in the country," he notes with a sniff. " I could hardly break out my black leather chaps, baby doll."

I chuckle. "If anyone could pull them off, it's you."

"Speaking of *what we wear*," he says, his voice severe, "I sent that hat to the dry cleaner's after handling it with latex gloves."

My shoulders slump. "Gus! You didn't!"

"I did wrong?" he asks, placing long, tapered fingers on his chest in surprise.

"It's Father Joseph's," I mourn, "not mine."

"Well, Father Joe can thank you for cleaning it."

"You'll get it back for me?"

"Only if I must."

"You're impossible."

"You love me," says Gus.

"Yes, I do."

"You trust me?"

I nod.

"Then listen up, because my ex-military, all-manly man has a plan."

"Okay," I say, sitting up straighter, remembering what Gus said last night about my needing to hide somewhere.

"Jock inherited a house from his daddy. It's about fifteen miles from here, out in the sticks, and he has a tenant there, Julian. Julian is ex-police or military or ex-something, I don't know, but he's an artist now. There's a barn on the property, and Julian uses it for glassblowing."

"Glassblowing?"

"Mm-hm. Real high-end stuff. Remember the private dining room at Lala's? Over the table? It had that—"

"Oh, my God! Yes! That, like, um, Medusa chandelier?"

"—with the orange and red glass dangling down?"

"I would stare at it for hours while Tig talked to people."

"That's the sort of stuff Julian does, but on a smaller scale. Sculptures. Vases. He'll take commissions for glassware. Beautiful stuff."

"Hmm," I hum, feeling impressed. "That chandelier was amazing."

"So is his work."

"And he lives out there? At Jock's country house?"

"He does," says Gus. His eyes flick away from mine, and I wonder what he's not telling me.

"What else?"

Gus sighs. "Our Julian is talented and *hella* hot, sweet thing, but he is not the friendliest boy toy Jesus ever made."

"What are you saying?"

"We'll have to massage this situation a little bit."

"*Massage* it?"

Gus nods. "Make it . . . palatable."

I finally get his meaning, and my shoulders slump again, even though being unwanted is a familiar theme in my life. "He won't want me there."

"No, he won't."

"Then I'm not going," I say. "I'll . . . I'll figure out something else. I'm not going to—"

"Pipe down, li'l Ash," says Gus, putting just a bit

of umph into his tone to make me listen. "You'll stay out there because it's Jock's place, not Julian's. Julian can just pretend you aren't there, baby doll, but it's not his call who lives there and who don't. As long as Julian has his bedroom to himself and exclusive access to the barn, Jock can rent out the top floor of the farmhouse to anyone he wants." Gus taps the tip of my nose with his finger. "Boop. And we want *you.* We want you safe, sweet girl."

Safe. That word again. Oh, how I hate and love it at once.

"Staying with a man who doesn't want me there."

"Oh, he might stomp around and give you all sorts of frowny faces, but, like I said, he's some sorta ex-law enforcement. He won't touch a hair on your head . . ." Gus half grins, looking saucy. "Unless you ask him to."

I roll my eyes. "You know I'm not like that."

"*Everybody*'s like that," Gus says. "You just haven't had a chance, what with Sisters Mary and Margaret breathing down your sweet neck for the past five years."

"I'm not like *her*," I insist, lifting my chin a little. "I'll *never* be like her."

Gus's brows furrow momentarily, and it looks like he's about to say something, but then I watch him think better of it. He takes a deep breath and nods. "That's up to you."

I want to change the subject. I don't want to think about Tig, let alone chat about her. "So the plan is for me to go live out at this farmhouse in the middle of nowhere with a man who doesn't want me there? Fabulous. Then what?"

"You said that your Father Joe is going to talk to

the stepmonster, right?"

"He said he would. It's a sin for Mosier to even consider marrying me."

"His dead wife's sister?"

"I'm *not* her sister. I mean . . . I wasn't."

"Oh my." Gus looks grave. "He didn't know you were Tig's kid."

I shake my head. "Father Joseph's going to tell him."

Gus's eyes are deeply troubled. "How you think that's going to go down?"

I hold my breath and shrug. "I don't know."

"Me neither, baby. But if it doesn't go well, that demon beast will start looking for you."

"I know."

Gus sighs. "Jock still has some friends in the Marines. He thinks we should start looking into Mosier. Try to find something to give to the police."

Never, not once in all the time I lived with Mosier, was he approached by the local police, and there was plenty of cause. They steered clear of him. Whether out of fear or in response to bribery, they left him alone.

"He has the local police in his pocket," I say.

"Then the FBI," says Gus. "You know he's into all sorts of sordid shit, Ash. A guy like him has got to be on their radar."

I think about his men with guns, about the times my mother and I were banished to the basement apartment for unknown reasons, about the bloody noses and split lips, about the time he unleashed his dogs on one of his own guards.

Huh. I'd forgotten about that. Come to think of it, I never saw that man again.

"There was a guard," I say. "I think his name was .

. .” I rack my brain. The names of Mosier’s guards are all foreign, and though my brain is good at storage and recall, it’s hard for me to remember words that I only learn phonetically. “Dragon. I think his name was Dragon. He, um, he worked for Mosier. He was a perimeter guard. One day he was there, the next day . . . he was gone.”

“Dragon, huh?” Gus rubs his lower lip. “Nickname?”

“I don’t think so. I think that was his name.”

“What happened to him?”

I sigh. “You know? I think my brain filed this as a dream, but it wasn’t.”

“*What* wasn’t?”

“I was in bed, but the dogs woke me up. Barking. Loud, you know? Snarling. I looked down at the courtyard in front of the house, and two guys were holding Dragon. He was limp, and his face was bloody. Mosier punches him in the face while they hold him, and then they release him. He falls on the ground but tries to get up. Like, he was in so much pain, he almost couldn’t move, but he somehow manages to get up, holding his ribs, and Mosier yells something at him. He turns and tries to run toward the gates, but he’s slow and clumsy. Just as he gets to the edge of the light, close to the gates, the dogs . . . the dogs were on metal chains, but Mosier walked over to their handler and unclipped them. I watched them race into the darkness, following the man.” I gulp, hating that I have gruesome memories like this one stuck in my head. “I jumped back in bed. I don’t remember anything else. In fact, I think I tried to convince myself it was just a dream. But

. . . but, Gus . . . I never saw that guard again."

"When was this, Ash?"

I purse my lips, trying to remember. "Maybe, um, two or three years ago? There was still some snow on the ground. I remember because Dragon was barefoot. I thought his feet must have been freezing."

Gus nods. "Okay. I'll tell Jock. I don't know if it'll lead anywhere, but at least it's a start."

"You're going to try to get him arrested? Mosier?"

"If he's behind bars, he can't get to you, li'l Ash."

I stare at Gus, thinking that he has no idea how strong Mosier is, how far his reach extends, how brutally he will retaliate if he discovers that Gus and Jock are poking around in his affairs.

"Don't do anything dangerous, Gus. Please. Promise me."

Gus cups my face, a gentle smile on his lips. "*Life* is dangerous, baby doll. Don't let anyone tell you any different."

"I can't lose you too," I whisper.

Gus drops his hands and stands up. "Then get dressed. The sooner we get you over to Julian's place, the sooner I can breathe easy again."

***

The drive to Jock's farmhouse takes a little under half an hour over quiet roads dotted with farms both well-kept and dilapidated—quiet Americana in the middle of nowhere. Gus was right: it'll be the perfect place to hide for a while.

We turn down a nondescript road with farms on both sides, and then down another with woods on both sides. The woods thin to a clearing, and up ahead I see a house, barn, and meadow, with a circular gravel driveway in front. We pull in, and Jock cuts the engine as I look out the window.

The house and barn are pristine.

No flecks of peeling paint dot the shingles of the house, and the barn is a soothing maroon in the late-morning sun. The garden around the house blooms with sunflowers turning their cheerful faces to the sky, and a weather vane caps the roof's peak. It feels more like a top-rated bed-and-breakfast than a private home, and as I leave the car, I breathe deeply, feeling hopeful that this place will welcome me, even if its tenant does not.

"What do you think?" asks Gus.

"It's lovely."

"Yes, it is. P.C. renovated it when he came back from Afghanistan. It's how he dealt with everything."

"Hey," I ask Gus as Jock walks over to the barn and knocks on a maroon door with bright white trim, "how did you two meet anyway?"

"The Cape," says Gus. "He was browsing in an art gallery. I saw him through the window. I took one look and I died. I had to have him."

I nod, remembering that Gus had always loved his P-town getaways.

"Just like that?

"Oh, honey," says Gus. "When you know, you know. And with Jock? I knew. I knew the second I looked at him. He was mine, and that was that."

My eyes skitter to the barn, where I can hear voices raised in increasing anger. Suddenly a man comes stalking out of the door, wearing a T-shirt, jeans, and black leather gloves that cover his forearms. He takes them off and tucks them under his arm as he approaches me.

"Are you kidding me, Jock?" he asks over his

shoulder, practically spitting the words. "*Goddamnit.*"

Jock calls to the man from the barn door, and that's when I see a reddish-brown hound escape from behind Jock, rushing across the driveway toward me.

A dog!

I feel my face split into a grin. I *love* dogs. With the exception of Mosier's attack animals, I have *always* loved dogs, but Tig never let me have one. *There's a dog here? Oh, God, please let this work out.*

I squat down, holding out my hand to the animal as he approaches. He sniffs my hands before letting me pet him behind pendulous, curtainlike, velvet-soft ears. "Hello, baby. You're so beautiful, you sweet, sweet girl."

"He's *male*," spits a voice over my head.

I look up, rising slowly, unable to look away from the man yelling at me.

Eyes.

Bright green and heavily lashed, they widen in surprise, staring into mine for a long and life-changing moment before they narrow with anger, sliding away from me and back to Jock.

I don't hear anything as his voice lowers to a point of fury, likely telling Jock all the reasons I am unwanted here. Usually it would sting a little to watch someone reject me summarily on first meeting, but I am so mesmerized by his face, by his body, by his rugged and innate beauty, I can barely breathe, let alone force my ears to function in any sort of meaningful way.

He is tall. Taller than me, six two or six three, with a clearly defined, muscled body under a gray T-shirt and beat-up jeans slung low on his hips. He wears boots that, in the sunlight, appear to be flecked with a million pieces of diamond dust—they twinkle every time he moves them. With his hands on his hips, the cords of sinew in his forearms pop just enough to create a map of trails that lead to his wrists and hands. The backs of his hands, like his boots, are dusted with diamonds, and when he raises one to reinforce one of the many reasons I absolutely may not stay here, it catches the sunlight and sparkles.

As I stare at his hand, I realize it's quiet—*really quiet*—and the silence startles me back to reality.

I look at Gus, who darts a quick and disappointed glance at Julian.

"Happy now?"

I slide my eyes—slowly, bracing myself for impact all the while—to Julian, watching him flinch, his jaw tight and his pink lips pursed as he regards me.

"I'm not *trying* to offend you," he huffs.

"I'm . . . not offended," I answer, my voice lower than usual. I'm being honest. I haven't heard a single word he's said.

"Of course she's fucking offended," says Jock, the expletive almost comical when delivered in his British accent.

But Gus knows better, and the expression on his face proves it. He knows that I am accustomed to being rejected and it doesn't bother me in the way it would shock and distress another woman.

"She has nowhere else to go," he says quietly.

"And this is *my* land," Jock adds with quiet steel, his gentility back in check.

"So you're going to force me to have this . . . this . . . this *girl* stay here."

But *this* does offend me, in fact, because I've been waiting to be a woman for a long time, and at eighteen,

I'm allowed to wear the title.

"I'm an adult," I hear myself say.

"Barely," he shoots back, his eyes changing color to a dark and angry evergreen.

"I'll stay out of your way. I'm good at that."

He yanks his gaze away from me, gesturing to a dilapidated, outhouse-looking structure in a field, about a hundred yards away from where we're standing. "Fine. The cottage is all hers."

"The . . . *cottage*?" I grimace, wondering how many species of mouse I'll be sharing the "cottage" with.

"It's not habitable," argues Jock.

"I'll fix it up."

"No deal," says Jock. "She stays in the house."

"Absolutely not."

"The second floor," suggests Gus, looking up at the round window at the peak of the old house. "Give Ash the attic."

"There's no kitchen up there."

"She'll only use the kitchen when you're working."

"Fuck this," mutters Julian, running a hand through his hair and looking pissed. "Fine! But I stay rent free as long as she's here."

"Done," says Jock, holding out his hand to shake on it.

Julian raises his sparkling hand and shakes with his landlord before putting his gloves back on and leveling an angry gaze at me. "Stay the fuc—" He pauses, his jaw ticking as he struggles for self-control. Finally he manages to grind out: "Stay out of my way."

"No prob—" I start to say, but he turns on his heel and stalks back to the barn, disappearing into its inky depths. The dog stares up at me for a moment, his hound eyes mournful, as though wishing he could apologize for his owner's rough behavior. After a beat, he turns forlornly and lumbers after his master.

"That went well," says Gus.

"Moody bastard," mutters Jock.

Gus sighs as he flicks a lustful glance toward the barn. "But you must admit, he is sex on a stick, and then some."

"What?" exclaims Jock. "Keep your eyes in your head, Gigi. That ass is not yours to tap."

Gus shrugs. "But lovely to look at."

"He's straighter than Gisele's hair after a Brazilian blowout."

Chuckling as he crosses to Jock, Gus cups his partner's bristly cheeks and pecks him on the lips. "Ain't no harm in lookin', P.C. My heart *and* my ass belong to you."

Something inside me pinches hard as I watch this genuine display of affection between two humans who endured so much before finding each other . . . especially when they're about to leave me with someone who so obviously doesn't want me here.

As though he can hear my thoughts, Gus says, "You okay with this, li'l Ash?"

I force a smile and nod. "It'll be fine. I'm grateful."

"You're a good actress," says Jock under his breath.

I take a deep breath, glancing at the barn before turning back to the happy couple. "I can handle him. He doesn't want me here, fine. I have no problem staying out of his way. He'll barely know I'm around."

Gus's eyes are troubled as he stares at me for a second, then nods. "That's true. You're good at flying under the radar, Ash. Maybe a little too good."

"He won't bother you," says Jock, gesturing

toward the house. Gus links his elbow with mine, and we follow Jock across the gravel driveway and up the steps.

Jock opens a squeaky screen door, and we step inside the coolness of his family's old house.

Some places hold on to the evil or goodness of the people who have inhabited them, the planes of time helpless against the emotions that have ricocheted off walls and been quietly recorded and contained within a space.

I close my eyes and breathe deeply.

Chocolate chip cookies.

Laughter.

Christmas carols.

Tears.

Cinnamon.

Sweat.

Dried roses.

Good news.

Bad news.

Love.

Life.

This house—this instantly sacred place—reaches into my heart and squeezes, at once sharing its past and inviting me into its present.

Opening my eyes, I sigh with a longing so deep and painful, it makes my vision blurry with tears. *Here, I will be safe*, I think to myself, wondering how such words dare to bubble up to the top of my consciousness when I barely understand their meaning.

But lives have been loved here and shared here, broken and mended, lived and lost. And now my life, small though it is, will be a part of it too. There is quiet comfort in the idea. Fellowship. Solidarity.

The walls are butter yellow, and the trim is bright white in the late-morning sunlight. Dark wood floors gleam beneath red-patterned Persian throw rugs of various sizes, and attractive pieces of country furniture are artfully placed around the living room. In a large brass vase on the coffee table there is a red silk flower arrangement that is so lifelike, I am almost tricked into believing it's real.

"I love it," I say.

"Well, thanks, love. I renovated and decorated it myself." Jock chuckles. "It's old, but special, right?"

Yes. "How old is it?"

"My great-grandfather bought the land in 1919, when he returned from World War I. He was a banker in New York City, but he married his sweetheart when he returned home, and she wanted a summer place. Nothing grand. Just something out of the city where she could cool off in the summer. Everyone else headed for the Catskills across the river, but my old gramp wanted something different. He chose Vermont instead."

"And the house?" I ask, still frozen in the doorway.

"A Sears, Roebuck Vallonia bungalow that he bought from a catalog," said Jock. "It was a popular model in California back in the 1920s. Gramp saw one outside of Sacramento where he was stationed during the war."

"He bought the house . . . from a catalog?"

"Mm-hm. Filled out a mail-order form. Sent in a money order. Found some local men to take care of the construction. *Voilà.*"

"Amazing," I say, looking around the eclectic front

room that spans the width of the old house.

"It was a popular model for young couples because it was one-floor living until children came along. Living room, dining room, kitchen, bath, and bedroom all on the first floor. And upstairs the layout allowed for three bedrooms or a big, open space for storage."

I slide my eyes to Jock, eyebrows raised. "What did your great-grandparents opt for?"

"The three bedrooms," he confirms with a grin. "My great-aunt Charlotte, my other great-aunt, Mary, and my grandfather, George, all grew up here."

"Your father too?" I ask, gingerly touching a fur blanket folded carefully on the back of a cream couch decorated with bright red peonies.

"Mm-hm. He bought it from my grandfather for twenty dollars in 1968."

"Only twenty dollars?"

"Family deal."

"And you?"

"I inherited it when my dad passed. Did a lot of renovations. Gigi and I lived here for a while, but it's pretty isolated. Almost an hour to Burlington, where our second gallery is located, and a lot longer in the snow."

"Not to mention, there are no good martinis out here in the sticks," lamented Gus. "Not even a little ol' country bar. You have to drive to Shelburne to get a drinky-drink."

I shake my head at Gus before grinning at Jock. "So, including you, four generations of Sourises have lived here."

"Actually," says Jock, his cheeks coloring just a touch, "four generations of Mishkins. I was born

Jonathan Mishkin."

"Mishkin?"

"It means 'mouse' in Russian."

"And Souris?"

"'Mouse' in French," he says with a self-deprecating chuckle.

"P.C. wanted to be sophisticated in his wasted youth," says Gus, staring adoringly at his handsome boyfriend.

Jock clears his throat. "Come upstairs. I'll show you where you'll be staying."

We walk through the large front room to a doorway leading to a curved staircase up to the second floor. The upstairs landing is painted white and has been converted into a lovely sitting area. A plush aqua and white striped couch sits invitingly in front of a working fireplace, with a coffee table in the middle of the room, and pristine, sheepskin rug on the floor.

I can barely admire the charm of the small space before Jock ducks through a dark wood door and leads me into a robin's-egg-blue bedroom with white portrait molding on the walls, several windows framed with gauzy white curtains, and a big white bed, positioned like a cloud, in the center of the room.

"Heaven?" I whisper.

Jock shrugs, his expression pleased. "*I* think so."

"Me too," says Gus wistfully, and I'm wondering if he's rethinking their move to town.

"It's yours," Jock tells me. "Behind the sitting room is your own bathroom too."

Tears prick my eyes as my gaze lands on the matted prints of angels, framed in white, adorning the walls. "It's beautiful."

"You deserve it," whispers Gus, placing an arm

around my shoulders. "Rest here, li'l Ash. We'll help you figure out the rest."

I spin, burying my face in Gus's neck and bawling like a baby.

I know this is only temporary.

I know that this is not *my* house, *my* room, *my* sacred space.

I know that my housemate, short of hating my guts, does not want me there.

But after a lifetime of wandering, it finally feels as though I am home.

CHAPTER EIGHT

Julian

Beautiful.

Without a doubt, without any caveats or clauses or reservations, she's the most beautiful woman I've ever seen in my life.

Ever.

Which is a massive fucking problem.

Her bright blue eyes, all hurt and wide and vulnerable, and her pillowed lips, perfect for every debauched thing I want to do to them, promise nothing but trouble. And it pisses me off because I moved here to escape that particular brand of chaos.

I do not want her here.

But I am a tenant at Jock Souris's house, and I read my agreement five times before signing it. There was nothing in it prohibiting him renting vacant parts of his property to other tenants, and in fact, there was something about him and his partner having exclusive use of the second floor at any time without notice. So if he wants to let someone stay here, I really don't have the right to say anything.

Fuck.

I need to start thinking about getting my own fucking place so I don't have to worry about shit like this.

"*An adult*," I scoff, sitting on a paint-splattered stool at my workbench and staring at the little figurine I'd been firing before Jock knocked on the barn door. I look at it objectively for a second before releasing the clamp and letting the figurine fall from the tiny metal platform to the wooden table, where the cooled glass splinters.

I'm not good at the small stuff yet. Not nearly as good as my dad anyway.

My father, Luc Ducharmes, born in France and apprenticed to Baccarat straight out of secondary school, was a master glassblower. After ten years of working with the finest crystal in the world, his skills earned him a work visa to the United States, crafting a special collection for Simon Pearce over in Quechee, Vermont, where he met my mom.

And for a while? We were happy there—Dad, Mom, me, and my little sister, Noelle. Until we weren't. Until my mom wasn't. Until she left for greener pastures and destroyed our little family.

So, yeah. That was fun.

Bruno looks up at me and whines. How the hell he knows the difference between glass that breaks by accident and glass I break on purpose, I'll never know.

I slide off the stool and stare down at him.

"Sorry, boy."

His deep brown, sorrowful eyes look at up me for a thoughtful moment before he turns to the barn door and barks once before looking back at me.

You're so beautiful, you sweet, sweet girl. Her feminine voice echoes in my head like crystal wind chimes on a breezy day, and it makes me scowl.

"If anyone should have been offended," I tell my dog, "it was *you*. How could she mistake such a masculine specimen of hunting perfection for a *girl*?"

Bruno vocalizes softly, a cross between a complaint and a question, and I realize I said one of his favorite words: *hunt*.

"Nah, buddy. Not today," I say, gesturing to his bed in the corner of the barn. "Go lie down. I'll take you for a . . ." If I say *walk*, he'll go crazy, so I skip the word and finish with: ". . . in a little bit."

Bruno lumbers over to his bed and lies down with a soft huff, those all-seeing hound eyes watching me as he settles himself in a tight circle.

I've had Bruno for a year, since I left Washington, DC, on the worst day of my life and drove up here to Vermont to start over. I stopped in Middlebury to get some gas and a sandwich when I saw a notice on the service station bulletin board about a one-day pet adoption event two streets over.

His owner had been shot in a hunting accident, leaving three-year-old redbone coonhound Bruno without a home. I looked at him, he looked at me, and I guess you could say we chose each other right then and there. Two sorry bastards who'd been dealt unlucky hands. Not like our luck could get any worse together.

I adopted him on the spot, loaded him in the passenger seat of my overpacked car, and kept driving north on Route 7 until I reached Shelburne.

With my dad gone and my mom remarried to a guy in Florida, the only person I had to return to was my sister, Noelle, who is four years younger than me and a junior at Saint Michael's College up near Burlington. It's been good to live closer to her this past year—to see her on any random weekend she feels like driving down and visiting.

God knows I would do anything for that kid.

And woe to the prick who makes her cry because he will be dealt with swiftly and mercilessly.

I put on my left glove and sweep the broken pieces of glass on my workbench into a metal collection bin filled with other jagged pieces. Then I sit down on the stool again, staring out the dusty window at the green meadow behind the barn.

I like Jock Souris. I truly do.

I grew up in Vermont, where pretty much anything goes, so renting a house from a gay man and his partner is a nonissue for me. Besides, at one point in each of our lives, both Jock and I worked for Uncle Sam, so we have that in common. But he told me very little about the chick he dumped on my doorstep. Just that she's a "friend of the family" and "needs a place to stay" for a while.

Now, there is the fact that I'm living here rent free for as long as she stays. That should make me happy, right? Wrong. I am *not* happy about this new development. I have no interest in sharing the house I've grown to love with some girl I don't know.

I picture her face—her beautiful fucking face—and the way she stared at me with those wide eyes and her lips slightly parted. Those lips. Angelina Jolie lips. Scarlett Johansson lips. Liv fucking Tyler from the "Crazy" video lips. Except this chick doesn't look like Liv. She's got blonde hair and a perfect pout like Alicia Silverstone. I remember the beginning of that video when our girl, Alicia, climbs out a bathroom window in her Catholic school uniform, her skirt riding up to show her black lace panties . . . makes me feel dirty as fuck, but I feel my cock twitch when I imagine the waif upstairs in nothing but black lace panties.

Fuck my life.

Shit. Shit. Shit.

Because, yeah, I was yelling at Jock, but she was standing behind him, and I didn't miss the tight lines of her teenage body under a pair of new jeans and a long-sleeved T-shirt. Her rounded tits strained just a little against the fabric of her top. Not enough to be dirty. Just enough to hate her. Because no guy alive—least of all me—has a right to want someone like her. Or sure, we can *want* her, but we'll never have her. Not in a million years.

She looked to be about Noelle's age—somewhere between eighteen and twenty, and ridiculously young to suddenly arrive alone in the middle of nowhere, put up in an old farmhouse by a couple of aging queens.

How in the fuck is *this* her best option?

Who is she?

And what exactly is her deal?

I grimace because the headlines of her story—the easy parts—start materializing as I think about what little I know about her. I didn't do all that training for nothing. Plus, I have good instincts. I could practically smell it on her—the fear, the desperation, the way she wouldn't meet my eyes except to insist that she was an adult.

God, what a joke. If she's an adult, I'm a French poodle.

It was Jock's boyfriend, Gus, who gave away the

most important part of her story.

She has nowhere else to go.

And then something else occurs to me, and I wonder, *Is she in hiding?*

This girl—what's her name? Amber? Audrey?—is in trouble. *Big* trouble. The kind of trouble that gets other people in hot water when they were just trying to live their lives and mind their own business. And she's been dumped on my doorstep. Literally.

Not my business. Not my problem.

I take off my glove and hang it and its mate on a nail over my workbench. I never fired up the oven today, and after this morning's shit bomb of irritating developments, I don't have the patience to work on figurines anymore.

I put my hands on my hips and frown.

Nowhere else to go?

How is that even possible?

My mom left when I was twelve and Noelle was eight, and my dad died eight years later, when I was a junior at Granite State College and Noelle was a junior in high school. No way my mother was interested in disrupting her new life to take care of us, so I left my room at the dorm and came home to live in Quechee with my sister. I looked after Noelle, commuting to college for my final two years instead of living on campus. I got Noelle up for high school every day and made sure she had money for lunch before I got in my car and headed to class. I signed her permission slips and helped her buy a prom dress. I didn't start my FLETA training down in Georgia until Noelle had started her freshman year at Saint Michael's.

This girl over in the house doesn't have a mother? A father? A sibling? A grandparent? *Someone?* That doesn't seem possible to me. It doesn't make sense. It seems suspicious and puts me even more on edge.

While I've been sitting here thinking about my new and extremely unwanted housemate, I've been toying with a piece of blue glass—a solid tube about twenty centimeters long and half a centimeter in diameter. That it's approximately the same color as her eyes is a fact I try to ignore as I turn on the torch in front of me and pull a pair of safety glasses from a hook to my right.

Holding the tube in the fire, I twist the glass back and forth, watching it melt, creating a blob at the end. When I have a nice rounded marble, I press it against a cool metal slab, flattening it a little at the end of the tubing. Before it cools, I press the flattened blob against a few small white crystal pieces still lying on the metal from a previous project. They're picked up by the hot glass, and I heat them again. I do the same with a few granules of green, and now my flat blue blob is embedded with flecks of white and green. I hold it up to the flame again, twisting it into a blob again, watching as it transforms back into a smooth sphere, with white and green flecks of melted color trapped inside the light blue glass marble.

I turn off the torch, clip my marble with glass scissors before it cools, and then, as gently as possible, clasp it with tweezers and dunk it into a metal cup of water.

When I lift it out, I have a perfect marble, about the same diameter as a quarter; and when I hold it up to the light, it's like I'm looking at a tiny, distorted version of the world.

Huffing softly, I whistle at Bruno, putting the marble in my pocket and closing the barn door behind me as we head back to the pasture for a long walk in the woods.

***

Ashley

From the window of my new bedroom, I see Julian and his dog leave the barn, locking the door before slipping around the side, back toward the meadow.

I don't have much to unpack, but I hold a folded T-shirt tight to my chest as I watch them go.

The sunlight glints off his golden hair, which brushes his shoulders, and he reaches up and binds it into a short ponytail. His strides are long and even, and I can see a strip of tan skin between the waist of his jeans and the hem of his T-shirt with each sure step.

"Whew," I murmur, reaching up to fan my face as the duo disappear into the woods at the property line. Even though I can't see them anymore, I linger at the window, as if hoping for one last glimpse.

Finally turning back to the bureau between the two windows, I add the shirt I'm holding to the one in the drawer. Before we left New Paltz, Father Joseph handed me a plastic bag from Target that contained three pairs of size four jeans; a three-pack of T-shirts in white, black, and gray; a three-pack of white camisoles; a three-pack of white cotton underwear; a three-pack of white socks; and a pair of simple white tennis shoes. I found his Mets cap in the bottom of the bag when I used the train lavatory to change out of my school uniform, and his unexpected kindness made me cry. It was the hat he wore whenever the juniors played the seniors in softball. All the girls would tease him about being Coach Joseph instead of Father Joseph, which he accepted with good-natured chuckles. I will cherish it above all things. I need to remind Gus to get it back from the cleaner's for me ASAP.

I close the dresser drawer and sit down on the edge of the bed. With the window cracked open, fresh scents of the countryside breeze into my room: dark soil, fresh-cut grass, sweet flowers, and lighter, perhaps farther away, manure. I stop picking them apart and let them blend together seamlessly, inhaling until my lungs are full.

Rest here, li'l Ash. We'll help you figure out the rest.

I lie back on the bed, looking up at the white ceiling fan, and realize there are clouds painted on the ceiling. A tear rolls from the corner of my eye as I muster a smile. Heaven. I pull my legs onto the bed and let my tired eyes drift closed.

When I wake up, the sun is shining straight through my windows, lower in the sky, but twice as hot as before, and a new smell joins the others from before: fire. But not just fire. I blink, sitting up slowly on the bed. Charred wood. The tang of burning metal? Or, no. Probably glass. I stand up, walking across white-painted floorboards to the window and look out at the barn, where I expect to see smoke, but there isn't any. My lips twitch with curiosity, and I'm tempted to go downstairs and tiptoe across the gravel driveway to peek into the barn, but Julian's furious words echo in my head: *Stay out of my way.*

My stomach growls, and I realize that if I'm going to stay out of his way, I should probably use the kitchen to make myself some food now, while he's busy.

Leaving my shoes upstairs, I slip down the small curved staircase to the first level of the house. I turn through the living room and dining room and smile as I step into the bright, modern kitchen.

There are white tiles on the floor, and the walls are

painted a light yellow. In the center of the room is a slab of white and gray marble and a glass bowl holding oranges, lemons, and limes. I step forward and finger the bowl gingerly, staring at the swirling citrus colors melted into the glass, and instinctively I know that this is one of Julian's pieces. From the window over the sink, I glance out toward the barn, but I don't see my hot-tempered housemate, so I relax.

At my school, culinary arts and home economics are given the same weight as reading, writing, and arithmetic, and in fact, there are some sisters who insist that knowing how to keep a home and feed a family are skills more useful to a young woman than geometry or a comprehensive knowledge of Charles Dickens and the historical works of William Shakespeare.

I feel at home in a kitchen and am quite skilled, though I've never had my own in which to work. Mosier's was off-limits; the milieu created by his house staff was not a place for me or my mother. And the kitchen at school was always filled with dozens of girls, all charged with a task to bring breakfast, dinner and supper to the table.

The first thing I do here, besides celebrating the revelation that this kitchen is all mine for the next hour or so, is open every cabinet and drawer at the same time, then slowly spin around the room, memorizing the placement of every ingredient, utensil, pot, pan, sheet, colander, and storage supply. And I quickly realize that, while it's a beautiful kitchen, it's not exceptionally well outfitted. In fact, it's missing quite a bit. There's no slow cooker, a must-have for young mothers, or cake pans, with which to make hospitality sweets for new neighbors. Hmm.

There is, however, a good collection of basic items,

which are high-end and seem almost new. Plucking a baking sheet from the skinny cabinet beside the oven, I place it on the marble counter, then add a heavy iron skillet, a rolling pin, two wooden spoons, a lemon squeezer, and a garlic press.

As I close the cabinets and drawers one by one, I take out other items I might need, adding them to the growing pile on the marble island, then turn to the refrigerator. There is no garlic, but there is a sad, solitary onion in the crisper, a package of two chicken breasts in the back, and half a container of whole milk.

In a cabinet of baking supplies, I find flour, baking powder, salt, and Crisco, all of which Gus told me I could use

Working quickly, I grease the baking sheet, then mix the ingredients for simple biscuits, one of many recipes I know by heart.

Once I pop them in the oven, I remove the chicken from its package, pound out the cutlets until the membrane and muscle are broken, and rub them with lemon. Using the garlic press, I add minced onion, then set the breasts to the side. Just before the biscuits are ready, I'll fry the cutlets in olive oil, and *voilà!* chicken and biscuits. Not a perfect meal, but not bad for limited provisions. Sister Mary Claire would be proud, I think, grinning as I put away the ingredients I don't need anymore.

As I wait for the biscuits to finish, I snoop around the kitchen and find an old cookbook in the back of a lower cabinet. I place it on the marble slab, flipping through the pages as the smell of warm bread fills the kitchen.

Betty Crocker's Picture Cook Book.

Property of Annabelle Mishkin.

Hmm. Jock's mother? Grandmother? Great-grandmother?

I glance at the copyright date: 1956.

Probably his grandmother.

I flip through the pages, my mouth watering at the recipes, which are illustrated with black-and-white pictures and cartoon sketches. Nineteen fifties housewives with perfectly coiffed hair, wearing aprons over their crinoline-poufed skirts, smile adoringly at their business suit–clad husbands as they present a turkey tableside. It's a version of family I never remotely experienced, but as I lean over the book, my elbows propped on the cold marble, I feel a familiar longing for something I've never known.

Suddenly I picture Tig in an apron and crinolines, and for the first time since my mother passed away, I'm neither angry nor bitter. I chuckle softly at the picture in my head, thinking about how much she would have hated that life, and wondering if all daughters end up wanting exactly what their mothers didn't, wondering if women are like cuckoo clock pendulums, swinging back and forth with each successive generation.

The timer on the oven beeps, and I remove the sheet from the oven and place it on the counter, admiring the browned tops of my perfect biscuits. I light the fire under a burner and place the heavy skillet over the flame, adding a little olive oil. The flattened chicken cooks quickly, snapping in the grease, the lemon and onion adding another layer of delicious smells to the kitchen.

As I plate the food—two biscuits and a chicken

breast with pan drippings on each dinner plate—I suddenly realize that, unconsciously and *definitely* inadvertently, I've made two servings. Maybe it's because I've never made a meal for just myself, or because there were two chicken breasts, that it only made sense to plate two meals, but suddenly I picture Julian's angry face, shouting at Jock, yelling at me, the diamond flecks on his arms and the moody green of his eyes.

Maybe he's hungry, I think.

Putting away the mitt I've been using, and rinsing the skillet in the sink, I gather my courage. I'll run to the barn, place the plate on the stool just outside the door, knock, and run.

I cover the plate with plastic wrap and with shaking hands open the creaky screen door and make my way down the back-porch stairs. I grimace as my soft feet touch down on the gravel driveway between the house and barn, swallowing gasps as the tiny stones dig into my flesh.

Knock and run, Ashley. Knock and run!

My heart hammers as I reach the barn, and as quickly as possible, I place the plate on the beat-up stool, knocking twice on the door before turning and racing back to the house. I barely feel the gravel this time, but my lungs are burning as I scurry up the back steps. Bruno is barking by the time I reach the kitchen, but I don't look back.

Once safely inside the kitchen, I lean against the wall, catching my breath. When I finally peek out the window over the sink, I notice the plate is gone and feel a tiny rush of victory that makes me giggle softly.

Then I take my own plate from the marble slab, grab a fork from the correct drawer, and hurry back up to my attic sanctuary.

CHAPTER NINE

Julian

Knock knock knock!

My eyes jerk to the door, and I almost lose the spinning rhythm I'm using to etch a spiral design in the orange flecked vase I'm working on.

"What part of 'Stay the fuck out of my way' didn't she understand?" I mutter, using a torch to smooth the bottom before letting it cool on the rod. Gently I dip the unfinished vase into a metal bucket of water on the floor, then prop the rod, with the vase attached, on a holding rack.

By the time I open the barn door, she's gone, but on the stool beside the door is a plate of food covered in plastic wrap. I stare at the plate like it's a coiled snake instead of biscuits and chicken, then glance up at the house. No sign of her.

But I can smell the food, and it makes my mouth water instantly. It smells like butter, onions, and lemons, and stirs a long-forgotten memory.

"Joyeux anniversaire, Julian!"

My grandmother's green eyes, like my father's and mine,

shine in the late summer Provençal sunlight. She takes the top off a cooking pot with a flourish, grinning at me from across the table.

"Joyeux anniversaire, fiston!" says my father, squeezing my small shoulder with a burly arm. "C'est coq au vin. Your grandmother's special dish. She only makes it pour des occasions spéciales!"

"Merci, Mémère," I say, grinning up at her, wishing that our summer in Sault never had to come to an end.

"Treize ans." She reaches across the table and pinches my cheeks lovingly. "Beau garçon."

Thirteen years old. Beautiful boy.

Bruno's soft wailing lets me know that his hound nose has sniffed out the food, and I reach for the plate, closing the door with my back.

"You want some?" I ask him.

His insistent howl tells me he wants all of it.

"No chance, buddy. We're sharing."

She's forgotten to leave a fork, but it doesn't matter. I halve the first of two biscuits and rip off a piece of the still-hot chicken with my callused fingers. One half for me, one for Bruno. And I can practically hear my dog's sigh echo mine as he chomps down his share, then shifts his weight from front foot to front foot, hopeful for more. But it's too good to share.

"Sorry, boy," I say, halving the other biscuit and sandwiching the remaining chicken.

As Bruno licks the plate, I savor the rest. And it's good. It's *so* good. It's as good as my grandmother's coq au vin, and as much as I hate it, it makes me wonder about the girl inside.

Where did she learn to cook? Did she once have a grandmother like mine? Someone who made sure she felt loved the way I did when the sting of my mother's abandonment was at its sharpest?

My cell phone buzzes on the wooden workbench.

Noelle.

"Hey," I say, putting the phone to my ear as I wipe my hands on my jeans.

"Hi. What's up?"

"Nothing much. Working on a vase."

"Commission or gallery?"

"Gallery, I guess."

"You should open your own shop, so no one takes a cut," she suggests.

At twenty, she thinks she's the master of all things entrepreneurial just because she's majoring in business administration.

"Yeah, yeah. So you've told me."

"What're you up to next weekend?" she asks.

I shrug. "What am I *ever* up to?"

"Thought I might come down to see you and Bruno."

"Really?" I ask, wondering what's brought on this development. "You've only got a few weeks of school left. Don't you want to make the most of them? You'll be *here* all summer."

"Yeah. I know. I just . . ."

I lean back against my workbench. "What's going on?"

"Nothing."

"Spill it, *tamia.*"

Tamia means "chipmunk" in French, and it's what our father called her when she was little.

She sighs heavily. "We broke up. Me and Parker."

Fuck. She really liked that guy.

That said, I feel a small bit of satisfaction, because I *didn't.* Parker grew up in a wealthy family from

Connecticut, and I sensed he looked down his nose at me and Noelle the couple of times I met him, like maybe we weren't quite up to par. Now, I couldn't give two shits if Greenwich-born Parker Post thought I was inferior to him, but I fucking hated my gut feeling that he felt he was slumming by dating my sister.

"What happened?"

I can picture my sister shrugging when she says, "Nothing. I mean, he changed while he was studying in Barcelona. He's all about free love now."

"*Free love*?"

"Commitment free. He doesn't believe in relationships anymore. Or . . . for now . . . I guess."

"He cheated on you?"

"He didn't say that."

"Noelle . . ."

"Yeah, I'm pretty sure he cheated on me," she says, and her voice sounds thinner. I think she's about to cry, and my heart clenches.

"Fuck."

"Jules," she sniffles, her voice a mix of sad and peeved. "Don't go all ballistic big brother ex-Secret Service on his ass." She pauses. "He cares about me and said he still wants to see me. He just wants to see other people too. He feels it's important for our personal development that we be unencumbered with commitment."

More like for his personal *enjoyment*.

"You deserve better, *tamia*."

"I know. That's why I told him to take a hike."

"Good girl."

"Yeah, well . . ." She sighs. "There will be a lot of end-of-year parties next weekend, and I just don't feel like seeing him . . . hitting on other girls. Hooking up.

You know . . ."

Her voice is thin again.

"Yeah. Sure. Come home. Definitely. I'll be here."

"Cool. I miss my room."

My room.

Oh, shit.

Jock is cool with me letting my sister sleep in the upstairs room whenever she visits, but now that room's taken by the chicken 'n' biscuits foundling.

"Actually, um, you can have my room instead."

"What? I don't want *your* room, Jules. I want mine."

"Well, it's either mine or the couch. Jock and Gus have a friend staying."

"A friend?"

"Yeah. Some friend of Gus's. She's here for—"

"Wait! *She*?"

The question hangs between us, and I count 3 . . . 2 . . . 1 . . .

"Your roommate is a *girl*? Is she nice? Is she single? Is she pretty? Oh, my God. Do you *like* her? I can't wait to meet her! *Julian's got a girlfriend . . . Julian's got a girlfriend . . .*"

Aside from constantly riding my ass about opening a glass shop—even to the point of suggesting that I lean on our dad's old Simon Pearce contacts to get started—my sister has this notion that I'm lonely and need companionship. She's made it her mission in life to jump on any and all opportunities to pair me off with someone of the opposite sex.

Partially this is my fault. I never told her the whole truth about what happened in Cartagena. She doesn't know that I've sworn off women. Possibly, and probably, for life.

"*Merde, tamia!* You are the most ridiculous person on the planet. I don't even know her. I've barely exchanged two words with her."

"Oooo! Listen to you, cursing *en français!* You're . . . affected by her. Eeeep!"

"If, by *affected*, you mean that I'm annoyed to suddenly have to share my home with some stranger, you're exactly right."

"Now I'm *definitely* coming home next weekend!"

She sounds happy again, and I roll my eyes. Fine. If fantasizing about my nonexistent love life makes my sister's breakup easier, I'll take the bullet.

"Great."

"Blow up a mattress at the foot of your bed. We can be roomies. Like when we went to Sault."

A rare—*very* rare—grin tries to turn up the corners of my lips and almost succeeds. Almost. During those summer vacations to my father's native Provence, Noelle and I always griped about having to share a bedroom at our grandmother's house, but deep down, I think we both loved it. I know I did.

"Text me when you leave, and drive safely, yeah?"

"Yeah. Always," says Noelle. "See you Friday, Jules. Love you."

"You too."

She hangs up, and I lower the phone from my ear, wondering if my new housemate will mind my sister's visit, and then quickly deciding that I really don't give a flying fuck if she likes it or not.

***

Ashley

As I step into the kitchen the next morning, my eyes skitter instantly to the drying rack beside the sink.

There is a clean white dinner plate there, gleaming in the sunlight, and it makes me smile. I wonder if he enjoyed the chicken and biscuits. I hope he did because I really don't want to feel unwelcome here. I have no idea how long I'll need to stay, and it would be so much nicer if we didn't have to avoid each other the whole time.

Not that I don't love my attic retreat. I do. I am so grateful for it.

Last night, I had dinner in the upstairs sitting room, washing out my dish in the bathroom sink so that I'd stay out of Julian's way. Around eight o'clock, he turned on the TV in his bedroom, which, I now realize, is directly below mine.

I don't know what he was watching, but it was in French. Because I study French at school, I was able to understand some of the words that floated up through the floorboards between us: *bonjour* and *merci*, *je t'aime* and *au revoir*.

Hello, thank you, I love you, good-bye.

Mostly I wondered if he—*Julian*—was listening in French or reading subtitles in English.

His last name, pronounced "doo-shahm," doesn't tell me much about his background, but I saw it spelled on an envelope affixed to the fridge: *Ducharmes*, which looked French to me. There's something romantic about my grouchy housemate being French, so I decide that he is, and leave it at that.

The kitchen doesn't smell like coffee or breakfast, though I heard him rattling around down here an hour ago. Based on the small bowl, spoon, and glass also in the drying rack, I am guessing he had cereal and juice.

It's nice that he does his own dishes. The nuns led us to believe that most men were slobs but that an ideal wife would cheerfully look after her husband, cleaning up after him without derision or complaint. An ideal husband is, after all, the head of every family and must be afforded the respect due to a moral compass, protector, and breadwinner.

But for all that I've heard these learned words a thousand times, they ring hollow in my head now, just as they did at school. Neither my grandfather nor my stepfather were especially moral, protective, or generous. Not legally, anyway.

I don't even know for sure that such a man exists, though it is—in the words of Ernest Hemingway—pretty to think so.

I see a piece of paper on the marble counter, and my heart lifts. I wonder if it's a thank-you note.

Alas, it's not.

In straightforward print, it reads:

My sister is coming to stay next weekend.

I'm going to the store later today. If you need anything, write it down. Jock will pay me back.

-JD

As I take out two eggs and heat up a frying pan, I do a mental inventory of the fridge and cabinets, thinking about what ingredients I would need to cook for three.

Although he hasn't asked me to handle his meals, I am anxious to do anything I can to ingratiate myself to him, to make myself less of a nuisance and burden, and perhaps to lay the groundwork for us to become friends. Since I left all mine behind and he appears to be my only option, I'd very much like for Julian and me to be friends.

As my eggs fry, I write in careful cursive:

How kind. Thank you.

Please pick up a dozen eggs, some butter and flour, a package of sugar, pork chops, chicken breasts, sausage, ground beef, garlic, vegetables for salad, half a dozen baking potatoes, cheddar cheese, and whatever fruit is in season.

I will look forward to preparing dinner for you and your sister while she visits with us.

-Ashley

By the time I finish writing, my eggs are ready to be plated. I grab a paper napkin and an orange from the bowl on the counter, then push open the screen door with my elbow so I can eat my breakfast outside.

CHAPTER TEN

Julian

Knock knock knock!

And then . . . bare feet running over gravel.

I've grown accustomed to this routine after four days, and per usual, my watering mouth and Bruno's excited yelps overrule any objection I should make to her cooking for me.

We haven't talked since our quick conversation on Sunday morning—in fact, I've made a concerted effort to avoid her—but something about refusing her food would be, I don't know, mean. Or something.

I've thought about Noelle a lot over the past few days—about her living alongside some stranger like this girl sharing a house with me. Oh, sure, Jock and Gus showed up yesterday to check on her and bring necessities like shampoo and a new toothbrush, but they aren't here all the time with her like I am.

If something happened to me? And Noelle was suddenly living with some stranger? Well, I'd want him to treat her kindly. I wouldn't want him touching her or making moves on her, for Chrissake. But I'd appreciate it if he was kind.

She's long gone by the time I crack open the door and pull the white plate inside. I can already smell her latest creation and look down greedily at what appears to be simple macaroni and cheese. One bite, however, and I'm groaning because I don't know what the hell she does in that kitchen, but everything—every damn thing she makes—is delicious.

Tonight? Buttery noodles are bathed in a mix of molten cheeses. Flaky bread crumbs fried to perfection practically melt in my mouth.

As I take a second mouthwatering bite, I feel bad for every kid in the world who thinks bright orange goop over disgusting little rock-hard elbow pasta is food. It isn't. I know the truth now. And the truth is that when there's an angel in the kitchen, everything tastes like it's straight from heaven.

Sighing over a third bite, I retread that thought, annoyed with myself for referring to Ashley as an angel.

For all you know, she screwed over some guy royally, and now he's after her. For all you know, she's a little tease who could get you in hot water too.

It wouldn't be the first time, Julian.

"Angel," I scoff. "Right."

Bruno whines, tilting his head to ask if I'm almost done. He's waiting as patiently as he can to lick the plate, but I know the wait hurts, so I eat a little faster.

Well, she sure looked like an angel sitting on the porch Sunday morning and feeding my dog her eggs. Her blonde hair was loose, lit by the rising sun like a halo. And her blue eyes when she stared at me? Fuck, I could feel my whole body tightening and hardening when I caught her staring at my ass. She's sexy beyond words. Effortlessly gorgeous. Eminently fuckable.

That said, I *don't* sense that she's a tease. There's an artless innocence about her. An otherworldliness. An old-fashioned vibe that would be almost unbelievable if it wasn't so tangible.

Yesterday she fell asleep on the porch, in the sun, holding a book—not a Kindle, not a phone, but a real book with paper pages—on her lap, and while she was sleeping, I snuck upstairs to her room just to look around.

I didn't see a laptop charging on the coffee table or the bureau in her room. No phone plugged in beside her bed. No tablet propped up on her pillow. No electronics anywhere, in fact. Just a neatly folded quilt at the foot of a neatly made bed, and two books on the floor, like maybe they'd fallen from her fingers and slipped off the covers as she drifted to sleep.

And then there's her cooking.

She cooks things like pasta and cheese. She makes biscuits—the carbiest carb of all—with *butter*. Last night she made a little fruit tart that she delivered with a hefty slice of meat loaf. Dessert. No one eats dessert anymore! Who cooks like that? I mean . . . *butter?* The girls I dated in Florida and DC barely ate more than lettuce. *Maybe*, *once in a while*, they'd splurge big with a veggie burger. But under no circumstances would they eat the bun.

This girl? She's *all* about the carbs. I've seen her sitting on the porch, finishing off the same meals she makes for me. Seriously. What millennial chick eats like this?

Ashley. That's who.

Her cooking and eating, coupled with her blatant lack of technology, reads odd, but genuine, to me.

Genuinely odd. Genuinely lost. Genuinely down on her luck. Genuinely at the end of her rope. I watched her with Gus yesterday—the way she hugged him, the way she smiled at him.

So what's her story?

I know it's none of my business, and I hate it that I'm curious, but I am. I can't help it. Curiosity is hardwired into my DNA.

Is she a little lost waif? Or a damn good actress?

"Like you'd know th' difference," I growl through a shoveled-in mouthful of food. "Your 'stincts with women aren't th' best, dummy."

If her entire persona is an act, what's her angle? A free place to stay? Nah. What girl would go to such lengths just to skip rent? There must be more. Money? Maybe. Maybe this is all a long con. Jock and Gus do well for themselves. Maybe she wants to bleed them dry. Or maybe—as I suspected the first day I met her—she's hiding. But from who? Who did she piss off so badly that her best option is living in the middle of nowhere with a complete stranger?

I rub my eyes, feeling a headache coming on.

Whatever her story, I don't trust her. Not until I learn more about her situation. Because some women, like my grandmother and sister, are genuinely good-hearted and well-intentioned. For a good woman, I would give the world. I would help her, protect her, keep her safe.

But other women—like my mother, like Magdalena—are users. They prey on men, they destroy them. They would ruin a man—his reputation, his future, his very life—without a second thought.

My biggest problem? I have no gift for telling the

difference.

Estoy desesperada. Sin dinero, mi padre morirá. ¡Ayúdame, Julian! ¡Por favor, ayúdame!

I'm desperate. Without money, my father will die. Help me, Julian! Please, help me!

Magdalena's pleading voice, garbled with tears, enters my mind and circles, the words despairing, relentless, and, in *my* gullible ears, genuine. Even now. Even when I have twenty-twenty hindsight.

My stomach rebels, turning over. I clench my jaw to keep from throwing up all that good mac and cheese.

It's been a year.

A year, and the memory of that night can still double me over.

Magdalena Rojas was a user. A thief. In one night, she stole my dreams and my future. She destroyed my reputation and my credibility. She shattered any chance of my having the life I had worked so hard to build.

She broke me.

And I *cannot* let it happen again.

I stare down at what remains of my dinner, my heart thundering with something that feels like panic. There's still a chunk of pasta left for Bruno, but instead of putting the bowl on the floor for him, I cross quickly to the door.

No more dinners, damn it.

This has to stop.

I push through the barn door, stalking toward the house, only to find Chicken 'n' Biscuits sitting on the back porch in her favorite chair, a forkful of pasta in one hand and an open book in the other. She looks up at the sound of my approach, her face brightening with a smile before her brows furrow in confusion. She senses my anger and sits up straighter in her chair, her smile gone by the time I'm standing before her.

"No more dinners," I spit, practically throwing the bowl down on the porch floorboards, then putting my hands on my hips as I glare at her.

"I'm sorry?" she asks, her expression startled and confused.

Part of me—the part that would want Noelle treated with kindness were she in a similar situation—feels like a shit heel, but this conversation is a hundred and fifty percent necessary. In fact, it's overdue. I don't trust her. I *can't* trust her. If we're going to share this house, she needs to leave me alone and stay the hell out of my way.

"Don't. Cook. For. Me. Any. More." I enunciate each word just to be a dick. "Got it?"

"I . . . I don't know."

She blinks at me, and even though I steel myself, I'm not prepared for the hurt that seeps into her big blue eyes, making them glisten. I'm about to soften when an image of Magdalena's big brown eyes, glistening with similar tears, takes front and center in my mind.

"Are you hearing-impaired?" I ask. "I don't want any more fucking dinners."

She winces like I just smacked her, and I wince inside, hating myself.

"You didn't . . . like it?" she asks.

Her question takes me off guard. "It was fine."

"Then why . . .?"

"I . . . I asked you to stay out of my way, and . . . and you're not doing that." I take a breath, then release it in a huff. "You're just . . . bothering me." My eyes slide down to her breasts, which are small and round, like twin globes, pushing against the front of her T-shirt. "You're bothering the *fuck* out of me."

"Oh."

"Cut it out, okay?"

"Okay," she says, blinking as she lowers her gaze and stares down at the bowl of pasta in her lap like she's lost her appetite. I know she's going to cry, and I know I caused it, but man, I just don't fucking want to see it.

"Anything else?" she whispers.

"No. That's all."

I'm about to head back to the barn, but she surprises me by looking up, and although her eyes are shiny, she somehow keeps her tears from falling. Suddenly I have a terrible notion that she's had a lot of practice at that, and it makes me feel even worse.

"I'm sorry," she says softly, her voice gentle but strong. "I'm sorry I'm here. I'm sorry I fed your dog. I'm sorry I cooked for you. I'm sorry for all of it." She pauses for just a moment, her eyes searing as they stare unrelentingly into mine. "Will you forgive me?"

It takes me several seconds to realize she's waiting for an answer. She's waiting for me to actually *forgive* her, and the terrible irony of her request is not lost on me, since I'm the one yelling at her and she hasn't done anything wrong.

"Um." I gulp. "Yeah. Fine."

"You forgive me," she confirms.

"I forgive you," I say, feeling terrible.

"Thank you, Julian."

She stands up, leans down, and picks up my bowl. Then, without looking at me, she walks back into the kitchen.

And me?

I'm left staring at her perfect fucking ass before the

porch door slams shut, wondering why I feel like I just kicked the shit out of a chicken 'n' biscuits angel kitten when all I'm trying to do is protect myself.

***

Ashley

I place the bowls on the marble counter, head to the stairs, and make it up to my room before I allow a single tear to touch my cheek.

I didn't mean to upset or offend him, but I have a knack for alienating myself from other people, and it's happened yet again. I have no idea what I did, but he obviously hates me. Lucky me, now I get to live here for an undetermined amount of time enduring his daily scorn.

"What did I ever do to you anyway?" I mutter softly, sitting down on my bed as I swipe away a tear.

Through my window, I watch him walk back to the barn, standing at the door for a minute, then turning around, like he's about to walk back to the house, then pivoting back toward the barn, yanking open the door and letting it slam behind him.

"It was just a little pasta," I whisper.

Except it wasn't. If I'm honest with myself, I know it wasn't.

It was, though not ill-intentioned, a bribe.

Especially after our short conversation on Sunday, I was hoping that Julian could be my friend.

I was trying to buy a friend with food.

"You're pathetic, Ashley. Completely pathetic."

I see the barn door open again, and he steps outside with Bruno at his heels. Without even glancing at the house, they turn toward the meadow. Bruno races toward the woods with Julian following. They'll be gone for an hour or so.

Without making a conscious decision, I slip downstairs into the living room and through the small dining room, but instead of turning left into the kitchen, I turn right, down a short hallway that leads to Julian's bedroom and bathroom.

I know precious little about my housemate, but I'd like to know why he decided to dress me down today. Maybe his room will hold clues about who he is and why he's so desperate to have nothing to do with me.

Gus told me that he used to be in some sort of law enforcement before moving up here last summer. I know he has a sister. I can see he loves his dog. I suspect that he speaks French, though I'm not positive. Based on Gus's descriptions of the type of glass he blows, I feel like I can identify which pieces in the house are his. They're good—exceptional, even. He has an eye for color and a gift for unusual beauty.

"But he's moody as h—heck," I add, turning the bathroom knob and peeking inside.

I was about to say *hell*, which surprises me.

I'm no stranger to cursing, of course. Tig had a mouth like a trucker, and Mosier swore in several different languages, including English, but it's been years since I've muttered anything worse than "Fudge!"

"Fudge!" I say, reaching left and running my hand along the wall, feeling for the light switch.

I flick it on, look at my face in the mirror, and watch my lips form the word *fuck*.

Fuuuck.

I only think it, but Lord above, it is such a *foul* word. It makes me giggle.

I find a container of deodorant beside the sink and lift it to my nose. The container reads NATIVE in bold letters, and when I take off the cap, it smells like woods and spice. I close my eyes and take a deep breath, my bare toes curling on the tile floor because it smells so good.

I replace the cap and exchange the deodorant for a bar of soap. The word BEEKMAN is barely visible after multiple uses, but the bar itself smells like sweetgrass, and I sigh softly, murmuring, "*Fuuuck*," as I replace the soap in its little silver dish beside the sink.

There isn't much else in the pristine bathroom: a bottle of Pert shampoo/conditioner in the shower and a white towel hanging on the back of the door. It's clean and tidy, unremarkable even, except for the scents that have captivated me.

I close the door behind me and step down the hallway to his room. My heart quickens as I turn the knob—if he found me in his bathroom, the only lavatory on the first floor, I could make a plausible excuse. But there's no excuse for my poking around in his room, and I know it.

In for a penny, in for a pound, I think, stepping into the cool, dim room.

As my eyes adjust to the lack of light, I inhale the now familiar smells of Native and Beekman, which engulf me, making me whimper softly. The unique combination of woods, spice, and sweetgrass mark the room as his space, and it makes my stomach tighten like it wants something very badly. It almost feels like hunger, but I just ate half a bowl of macaroni.

My mind, looking for context and answers, offers up a memory from several months ago:

"What is the difference between hunger, desire, and lust, girls?"

Sister Agnes's Irish brogue sounds in my head, her lecture on the seven deadly sins in full swing now.

There is a dusting of giggles among the girls in my class, and Sister Agnes strikes her desk with the back of a wooden ruler. "Focus, girls. Hunger, desire, and lust. The difference, please?"

No one dares answer, and I look around, wondering if anyone will be bold enough to raise her hand.

"No one?" she asks, her eagle eyes sharp behind bifocals. "Then I shall explain: hunger is hunger. It is a physical need over which you have no control. Your stomach aches for food. If you eat—not to the point of gluttony, girls, but enough to satiate your hunger only—the ache will disappear." She pauses, watching us, and we nod at her in understanding. "Desire is a kind of hunger, but within the context of Christian marriage, a hallowed kind. Desire for one's husband may even be considered a Godly gift, for from that blessed hunger may come children born of wedlock, who are welcomed into Christ's kingdom."

She crosses her arms over her ample chest and lifts her chins. "Now, lust? A deadly sin. Satan's evil work. Beware lust, girls. Lust is also a kind of hunger. A very wrong and very bad sort of hunger. It is self-seeking. It is blinding. It is consuming, and you will never be full. And, make no mistake, girls: lust will separate you from the love of God."

Lust, I think, standing in the doorway of Julian Ducharmes' room, secret muscles deep within my body alive and quivering. *This must be lust.*

I gulp, hoping that my thoughts alone aren't enough to strike me down where I stand. When nothing happens, I exhale softly, stepping into his room.

If my room is heaven, then his room is Eden.

The floorboards, molding, and furniture are made from dark wood, sophisticated and deep, overwhelmingly masculine, but tempered by their placement within . . . a garden.

In the far corner, a tree is painted on the wall, the thick trunk rising up from the floor. Beautiful branches, covered with green leaves, pink buds, and delicate blossoms, billow out on both walls. Over my head, more painted boughs cover the ceiling, with blue sky and sunlight peeking out from under the branches. Hanging from the middle is a chandelier with arms of brown glass emulating branches, dotted with hundreds of tiny green glass leaves and pink petals.

I gasp softly at the beauty of this room, just as I did when I first saw my own, and think, *It's like standing in the middle of spring.*

In front of me is a bed, from which I avert my eyes quickly, finding a chair, a side table, and a lamp. On the table is a tablet plugged into an outlet. *For reading or watching TV*, I think, adding, *in French.*

Stepping over to the bureau, I find two framed pictures on the chest: one of a much younger Julian standing beside a young girl, who I assume is his sister, and another of a bearded man, with the same young versions of Julian and his sister. His father, perhaps. The man's eyes remind me of Father Joseph's, warm and wise, and I smile at the picture before setting it back down.

When I open the top drawer of the dresser, I find underwear and socks carefully folded. My cheeks flush, and I'm about to close the drawer when I see something in the back corner. I reach inside and pull out a black leather wallet. Only, when I open it, I discover it's not a wallet. It's a badge case. On the left side it reads *Department of Homeland Security* in gold embossed letters. On the right side is a place where a badge is supposed to go. But it's empty.

I run my finger over the letters before putting the leather case back where I found it and closing the drawer.

Turning around, I lean against the bureau, finally allowing myself to stare at his bed, which is huge and inviting. Covered with a soft, dark green velvet duvet—surely something that Gus chose—the bed is so tempting, I consider lying down for a moment to stare up at the painted sky through painted branches and inhale the scent of Julian Ducharmes all around me. I reach out, running my hand over the supple fabric, sighing softly with longing.

Since the moment I entered Julian's room, my stomach's been vacillating between tight and fluttery, but as I stare at the bed, my fingers rubbing the soft fabric, there is a delicious humming, almost a buzzing, between my legs that's making me vibrate with every shallow and increasingly choppy breath. In the recesses of my mind, I remember the sounds of Tig's moans and whimpers coming from under the door of her bedroom. I can't remember the faces of my many "uncles," but I remember them walking past me on their way to the front door, the musky smell of their skin lingering behind, familiar to me only because it matched that of my mother's sheets.

Lust will separate you from the love of God.

"I'm not her!" I yell, yanking my hand from Julian's bed and backing out of the room.

In my haste, I trip over the doorstep and into the hallway. Reaching out to break my fall, I knock a framed photo from the wall. It crashes to the floor and breaks, splinters of glass scattering everywhere.

"Oh, no!"

At the same time, I hear the high-pitched sound of Julian whistling for Bruno, and I freeze. It hasn't been an hour. It's barely been twenty minutes.

Here is your punishment, Ashley Ellis, says a voice in my head, *for your impure thoughts.*

Leaping over the worst of the glass, I step gingerly into the dining room, looking out of the window to see Julian and Bruno enter my line of sight, headed for the barn door. For just a moment, Julian looks at the house. His gaze lingers on the window in my room. He reaches for his jaw, rubbing it with his thumb and forefinger, then runs his hand through his golden hair.

I stare at his face, at the troubled expression in his evergreen eyes, and realize I'm looking at regret. It placates my hurt feelings to know that he's sorry for yelling at me.

You're bothering the fuck out of me.

I place my hand over my heart, wondering, for the first time since he said them, if he meant those words in a way that hadn't occurred to me earlier. Could it be that I'm bothering him in the same way *I* felt bothered standing in his room? Does he feel that same humming, that same buzzing, when he looks at me? Is *that* how I'm bothering him?

Lust.

As though answering my question, he shakes his head with a deeply irritated look, then disappears into the barn after one last, longing glance at my window.

When I remember how to breathe, I run to the

kitchen to find a dustpan and broom.

Day #15 of THE NEW YOU!

Dear Diary,

I've been staring at this page for half an hour and I still don't know how to start or what to say. All I can think is this:

I am fucked.

Fucked.

Frontways. Sideways. Backwards. Forwards. From every fucking side and every fucking angle.

I fucked up.

So bad.

SO SO SO SO SO SO SO SO SO SO SO SO SO BAD.

But this time I can't get away. I can't run away. I can't leave. I can't escape.

I am fucking trapped.

If I left, he'd find me, and I don't know if I'd survive it.

And then there's the kid. The goddamn fucking kid.

I can't even kill myself because of her. He'd eat her up and belch out her guts before I was cold.

I have always been a stupid bitch. A beautiful, stupid bitch. Mam and Tad knew it. Always knew it. Dw i'n pert, ond dw i'n twp. *And now I know it too. Pretty but stupid. Pretty stupid.*

What did I do?

Oh, my God, what did I fucking do to my life?

My husband.

My husband?

Jesus, Joseph, and Mother Mary, he is the villain cast in every gritty, under-the-table, porn-style piece of masochistic indie-shit movie I ever saw—the sort of sick stuff that makes normal people watch in morbid fascination for a split second before turning the fucking channel because they're about to throw up.

And who am I? What's my role in this piece of cinematic garbage?

Starring Tígin as . . .

The junkie who'll take it up the ass with a splintered broom handle for a fix!

The moronic fucking prostitute who's offered the kind of gig that'll get her killed!

The stupid, beautiful bitch who thinks she's got every man wrapped around her finger until she meets a monster!

That's me.

That's me on the fucking screen doing things normal people wouldn't make their fucking dogs do.

And I'm not even getting a fix when the horror is over. There are no drugs. There is no wine. I'm doing the show sober. I'm standing in the fucking shower until the water runs from red to pink, aching in places I didn't know existed while I pray I'm dead before tomorrow.

Except I can't make that prayer.

I can't fucking die.

If I die, what'll happen to the kid?

The fucking kid.

The fucking stone around my neck.

The fucking bane of my fucking existence.

I fucking hate her. I hate her.

I HATE HER. I HATE HER. I HATE HER. I HATE HER. I HATE HER. I HATE HER. I HATE HER. I HATE HER. I HATE HER. I HATE HER. I HATE HER. I HATE HER. I HATE HER. I HATE HER. I HATE HER. I HATE HER.

I FUCKING <u>HATE</u> HER.

CHAPTER ELEVEN

Julian

Noelle texts me at five o'clock on Friday evening to say she's on her way down, and I tell her to drive safe. It's only a forty-five-minute drive at most, so she'll be here soon.

I've finished the vase I was working on this week, plus a set of four stemmed glasses and a matching pitcher. I'm wrapping up these items in tissue paper, and when I'm done, I'll place them carefully into a wooden crate for transport. Tomorrow Noelle and I can take a ride into town and drop them off at Jock and Gus's gallery. I promised these pieces by Monday, and besides, I want to ask Gus a couple of questions about Ashley. Not that it's any of my business, but I think I have a right to know if there's trouble following h er or looking for her. If there is, it might be grounds for me asking her to leave.

And I *need* her to leave, I think, putting plastic wrap around each tissue-covered glass.

I haven't seen her since Wednesday afternoon when I yelled at her and told her that she was bugging the shit out of me, but I can't stop thinking about her and it's driving me nuts. I hear her moving around upstairs. I smell her shampoo after she takes a shower. I see her dishes in the drying rack. I think of her big blue eyes and pillowed lips, and I get hard as a rock. I've jacked off to the thought of her a dozen times since she arrived, and it's getting out of hand. Literally.

It doesn't help that I haven't had sex in weeks.

I miss it like crazy. I want it so fucking much, I can't stand it sometimes.

But aside from a drunken encounter with a couple of tourists over in Sugarbush, where I occasionally go for a night of beer and live music, it's been a quiet spring. The fact is, there aren't many opportunities for female companionship out in the sticks, which is exactly why I chose to live here.

My self-imposed punishment is that I can't have sex—and certainly not in any *meaningful* way—until I figure some things out for myself. I need to get my head on straight. I need to figure out a plan for the rest of my long fucking life. And I can't think straight or make plans for myself if I'm distracted by a woman.

And again I think: *Ashley needs to leave.*

She's not doing anything overtly provocative, per se, but she's messing with my head just by being here. I'm thinking about her all the time. I'm dreaming about her at night. I'm living in a state of constant fucking arousal, and it sucks.

I place the glasses and pitcher in the crate beside the vase and cover it all with packing shreds, then set the crate in the passenger seat of my truck. I look at my phone. I should have just enough time to take a shower before Noelle gets here.

I whistle for Bruno and head into the house. Bruno

pads across the living room to the stairs without my permission, and I listen to his feet click-clack up to her space. *Traitor.* Though I can't make out her words, there's the soft hum of her voice as she greets him, and although it's pure fantasy, I imagine her lying naked on her bed, smiling at him as he walks into her room. Her skin will be light and flawless, her nipples pert and pink. She has a flat stomach and slim waist, but a rounded ass teases me as she crooks a finger and invites me into her bedroom. I gulp, imagining myself stepping forward, my cock thickening and hardening until it's jutting out at her, and she grins at it, then at me.

"Fuck, Julian!" I mutter, stalking through the dining room and back to the hallway that leads to my bathroom. "Knock it off."

I throw my shirt on the floor. My chest muscles are bunched and firm. I slide my jeans over my hips, and they pool on the floor. I yank on my boxer briefs, but they snag on my erection, which points straight up at my chin. Lifting the cotton over the taut skin, I let the underwear skim down my legs. I stare down at my cock, half hating the way it has decided that it wants this foundling girl, no matter how strong the objections of my mind.

Opening the glass door to the shower, I turn on the water, waiting a moment for it to warm up before stepping inside. I stand in the hot spray, leaning my forehead against the tile wall, feeling the water pound on my back as I soap up my hands. I reach for my cock, stroking it while I think about Ashley, who is directly upstairs.

I imagine grasping her hips as I push into her from behind.

I think about how tight she'll be, how hot, how

wet, how welcome.

I imagine the soft voice that she uses with Bruno as she gasps and moans and tells me how huge I am and that she's never had it as good as she has it with me.

I fist her beautiful blonde hair in my hand, pulling back, watching the gorgeous lines of her neck as she extends it.

I watch the pulse in her throat as I feel the building of my own release, the tightening of my balls, the racing of my heart, the swirling inside that grows to a fevered pitch.

"Ah! Fuck! Ahhhh!" I groan, coming in hot spurts against the white tile walls. I pant through the waves of my orgasm, grateful for the relief, hating the inspiration.

When my knees no longer threaten to buckle, I lean my head back into the hot water and shampoo my hair, wondering what it is about this girl that has me so captivated. Is it as simple as her looks? Her beautiful face and gorgeous body? Or is it something more?

Let's face it: a man could get used to home-cooked meals and the sight of her wide blue eyes as she listens attentively to the details of his day. Not to mention, I'm pretty sure she's in trouble, and if—a big, unrealistic if, I know—but *if* she's a good person and not a user, *if* she's a victim and not a culprit, *if* she's someone worthy of protection instead of someone who would play on a man's protectiveness, then there is something in me that would answer her need. I would keep her safe. I would hurt anyone who'd try to hurt her. I would kill anyone who'd try to take her away from me.

My heart thunders as I rinse the soapy water from my hair, my hardwired instincts to protect and serve now as aroused as my cock was five minutes ago.

Ayúdame, Julian. Por favor, mi amor!

I bite my lip when I hear Magdalena's voice in my head, followed by a different voice from my past that makes me release my almost-bloody lip and clench my jaw instead.

Agent Ducharmes, at what point did you ascertain the true nature of Ms. Rojas's objectives?

I flinch at the memory, picking up a bar of soap and running it over my body as shame washes over me.

Agent Ducharmes, I repeat: at what point did you ascertain the true nature of Ms. Rojas's objectives? At what point did you understand what she intended?

I close my eyes, take a deep breath of steamy, scented air, and hold it in my lungs.

Never, I think, recalling my answer under direct testimony. *I never ascertained the true nature of Ms. Rojas's objectives. I didn't understand her intentions until it was way too late to stop them.*

The gavel bangs. A price must be paid.

Agent Ducharmes, you are hereby dismissed from the United States Secret Service. Your position with the Department of Homeland Security is terminated, effective immediately.

I turn off the water and grab a towel from the rack over the toilet.

Yes in-fucking-deed.

Ashley needs to go.

***

Ashley

Julian hates me, but he still allows Bruno to visit, which I regard as a kindness, even though I'm positive he doesn't intend for it to be.

I'm lying on my bed, my eyes burning with tears after reading Tig's diary, when my sweet friend walks into my room, his warm brown eyes meeting mine. He approaches the bed with soft, sure-footed steps, stopping directly in front of my face and sniffing tentatively. When he starts licking my tears, I'm so surprised that I hear myself giggling, despite the sharp pain in my heart.

"Aw, baby," I croon, "thank you for the kisses."

I scratch behind his ears as his soft pink tongue bathes my cheeks.

A noise outside the window distracts him, and he freezes before crossing my room and standing up with his front paws on the windowsill, his hound nose pressed against the screen. With a deep bark, he runs from my room, and I listen to his footfalls on the stairs.

I turn back to the diary, staring at Marilyn's smiling face on the cover. My mother's words are so terrified, so hopeless, so full of regret, so full of hate.

I remember her screams the night after Mosier found me in the pool with his sons, but when my mind shifts, trying to imagine what exactly was happening to her in his study, what degradations *her* body endured in *my* place, I can't bear it. I can't process this right now. I shut down my thoughts, push hard against the bed, and stand up, placing distance between her scrawled fury and my trembling heart, but it's not enough. I need to get out of this room.

Water rushing through old pipes tells me that Julian is in the shower and probably can't hear Bruno's baying and whining at the kitchen door. As long as my nemesis is showering, it won't "bother the fuck" out of him if I slip downstairs, let Bruno out, and make myself a cup of tea.

Bruno wags his tail gratefully as I open the back door, and he bounds down the porch steps in search of whatever he smelled from upstairs. I lift the kettle from the stove and fill it with water. I take a cup from the cabinet and plop in a tea bag, leaning against the marble counter as I think about Anders' words in the limo when he drove me back to school.

She loved you.

Did she?

Did she love me?

She writes over and over again that she hated me, and yet she could have run away, but she didn't. She could have killed herself, but she didn't. In fact, it appears that I might have been the reason she stayed with Mosier. Why? Because she knew what he intended? Did she know when she married him? Or only after? I have so many questions, and while I know that reading her diary might give me the answers I crave, every entry throws me into a chaotic emotional spiral that makes it hard to breathe. I have to pace my reading, or I feel like my head will explode.

There's a soft knock at the screen door.

"Um . . . hi?"

I start at the unexpected sound of a woman's voice, jerking my neck up to see a woman, more or less my age, standing on the porch.

"Hi," I say automatically.

She has light brown hair and a duffel bag hanging from her shoulder. "I'm Noelle."

Okay. I stare at her as the kettle starts to whistle.

She grins. "Noelle. Julian's sister? Noelle?"

"Oh!" I exclaim, crossing to the back door to open it. "Yes, of course. Sorry. I was—"

"I think your water's ready," she says, looking over my shoulder at the stove.

"Right. Yes," I say, stepping over to the stove and

lifting the kettle. I turn to her. "Can I make you a cup of tea?"

Her face blooms into a smile, and I can see so much of her brother in her pretty features, it makes my heart catch. I've seen Julian smile only once, but now I know what it would look like if he'd do it more freely.

"Tea? Oh. No. That's okay, but thanks."

She drops her bag on the floor and pulls a stool out from under the counter. I pour boiling water into my white mug, then pull out the stool across from hers.

"I'm so sorry," she says. "Jules didn't tell me your name."

Jules? Hmm.

"It's Ashley," I say, reaching my hand across the table to shake hers.

I know that "Jules" won't like it that I'm downstairs visiting with his sister, but it feels rude to leave her all alone, so I decide to stay just until he makes an appearance.

Noelle cocks her head to the side, her eyes narrowing. "You look *so* familiar to me."

"I get that a lot."

"Why?" She pauses, her brain trying to figure it out. "Who do you remind me of?"

Maybe it's because I've been reading my mother's diary today, or because I'm just so sick and tired of hiding who I am, but I sit up straighter and say, "Tígin."

"*Tígin*?" says Noelle. "The *model*?" I watch her face as she does a mental comparison, her eyes widening and lips parting as she makes the connection. "Oh, my God. I've seen pictures of you two in *People* magazine! *You're her sister.*"

I'm about to nod when a voice behind me makes

me freeze.

"Who's whose sister?"

I snap my neck to look over my shoulder.

Julian stands in the kitchen doorway in jeans and a T-shirt, his feet bare, his hair wet, and his face so spectacularly handsome as he grins at Noelle, that the humming and buzzing starts up between my legs again. I gulp softly, clenching my thighs together before turning back to Noelle.

"Ashley!" exclaims Noelle. "She's Tígin's sister!"

"Tígin . . . the model?"

"Yes!"

I don't face Julian, but I hear his feet step into the room, smell his freshly showered scent as he passes me. Now his eyes are staring back at mine from across the counter. Just like his sister, he scans my face, realization dawning on his features as he nods slowly.

"Oh, yeah. Huh. I missed that."

"I didn't mention it," I say.

"Why not?" he asks, his expression troubled.

"It's better if . . . I mean . . . she's . . . forget it." I purse my lips for a second before slipping off my stool and reaching for my cup. "It was nice to meet you, Noelle."

"Wait," she says, hopping off her own stool and rushing around the counter to stand before me. "Where are you going?"

I shoot a quick glance at Julian, who's still staring at me thoughtfully, before I look back at his sister. "I stay upstairs. In the attic."

"So?" she asks. "You eat dinner down here, right?"

"Yes . . . but . . . n-no. I can't. I . . . I mean . . ."

"Jules!" she says. "Ashley has to join us for dinner

tonight. Tell her."

"I'm sure she has other—"

"You'll join us, won't you? We always order from Pizza Hearth in Charlotte. It's decent for Vermont. I promise!"

Julian crosses his arms over his chest and shrugs. It's clear he wants me to decline, but the thought of going back upstairs to my attic room and Tig's vitriol makes me feel so desperate, I find myself nodding at Noelle.

"I'd love to. Thank you for inviting me."

"Great. That's settled." She steps back around the counter and grabs her bag. "I'll put my stuff in your room, Jules. Open a few beers for us?"

She breezes from the kitchen, leaving me and her brother alone. He gives me an appraising look from across the counter.

"Really?"

"Really what?"

"You're Tígin's sister?"

I nod.

"Kind of a big detail to omit about your life, don't you think?"

I know he doesn't really want an answer, so I shrug, taking a sip of my tea and ignoring the opportunity to point out that he's never really asked.

"So why are you here?" he asks. "In a fight with your big sister? You must know a million people, have a million places where you could go."

"Gus is here," I say simply.

"Who is he to you?"

"My godfather. He was her best friend."

"Wait . . . *was*?" His brows furrow.

"She died two weeks ago."

"Oh, man." He flinches. "Fuck. I didn't know. I'm sorry."

I reach for my mug and take a sip of my tea, quietly accepting his sympathy.

"Were you . . . being hounded? By the press?"

It would be a lie to nod because, for most of my life, the press has left me alone, especially since Tig got married and retired. But I am not prepared to tell Julian the specific reason I'm hiding here. Besides, Gus hasn't given me permission to talk about it, and I wouldn't want to put him and Jock in danger by saying too much.

I take a deep breath and lower my cup. "I just needed to get away."

"Yeah." He nods slowly, though he's still scanning my face like he has about a hundred more questions for me. "I get that. It's tough to lose someone."

"It was sudden." The words spill out of my mouth, though I didn't feel them coming.

"What do you mean? Like a sudden illness?"

"The coroner said she overdosed on heroin, but she was clean. She got married a few years ago, and she hasn't . . . I mean, she wasn't doing drugs anymore. I don't . . . I don't know why she'd backslide."

His face changes a little as he absorbs this news. "She was an addict?"

"Years ago," I say. "But she was clean. I'd know if

she was using."

He leans forward, bracing his elbows on the counter as he looks into my eyes, and I don't know why, but I keep talking.

"I saw her at Easter," I say, the words falling from my lips in a nervous rush. "She seemed fine. A month later, she overdosed? It doesn't make sense to me."

"I'm sure it's a painful time for you, but . . ." He sighs softly. "It's hard for addicts to stay clean. It doesn't take much for them to—"

"No," I say firmly. "She took her sobriety seriously."

Julian's eyes widen. "Okay. Then what do you think happened?"

"I don't know," I answer honestly. "I was at school. I . . ." My voice trails off. When I find it again, it's thick with emotion. "I don't know."

"How 'bout those cold beers?"

Noelle bounds back into the kitchen, headed for the refrigerator. She takes out three amber bottles and places them on the counter, looking back and forth between me and her brother.

"Whoa. Who died?" Suddenly she flinches, which means that, unlike her brother, she read somewhere about my sister's death. "Fuck! I'm an idiot, Ashley. I saw the news on Twitter. Sorry." She blows out a breath, wincing at me. "God, I'm such an asshole. Sorry, again."

"It's okay," I say, watching her pop the caps off three bottles.

"Do you drink?" asks Julian, glancing at my untouched beer while he and his sister clink bottles in cheers.

"No, thanks," I say. "I'll stick to tea."

For most of my childhood, I had a front-row seat to the ravages of addiction. I have no interest in setting off down a similar path. Because I like the way some wines pair with specific foods, I will occasionally drink it with a meal. But only then in moderation.

Julian draws a bottle to his lips, sipping as he stares at me. When he sets the bottle back down on the counter, he asks, "So . . . what do you like on your pizza?"

His voice is warm—*almost* kind—and something inside me sighs, feeling lighter, better, easier, than it did when I came downstairs half an hour ago. I'm not entirely certain what's prompted the change in his demeanor—learning that my "sister" was a supermodel? finding out that she recently died?—but right this second, I don't really care. Right this second, he doesn't hate me anymore, and I'm surprised to discover that's all that matters.

CHAPTER TWELVE

Julian

As I sit across a picnic table from Ashley, staring at her sister-of-a-supermodel face in the glow of a flickering citronella candle, I admit to myself that I've enjoyed tonight. Perhaps more importantly I've *allowed* myself to enjoy it.

Learning a little more about who Ashley is, and that she's here to mourn her sister, has been a game changer for me in my feelings about her living here. It's not that I suddenly trust her, per se, but I finally have some answers about who she is and why she's hiding out in the middle of nowhere. I'm no stranger to loss, and the truth is—as I look across the table at *my* little sister—losing Noelle would break me. I can't imagine what Ashley is suffering, and that I have added to her pain by snapping and barking at her fills me with shame. Gus brought her here for sanctuary, and I have compromised her peace by rejecting her modest efforts to live companionably.

You can do better, Julian, I tell myself, and as I watch Ashley in the flickering candlelight, an intense longing takes root within me.

Noelle nudges me under the table, and I curse internally. Like every little sister in the world, she has effortlessly picked up on something I just as soon would have kept to myself: my newly sanctioned crush. Fuck. When we get back to my room, she's going to be relentless. *Hell, she's probably already planning our wedding.*

Thankfully Ashley's stories are so compelling, I find myself alternately grimacing and chuckling at another misadventure of Tígin's instead of brooding. The tales she's told us about growing up with her famous sister are riveting. At turns hilarious, unbelievable, and awful, she paints a vivid picture of Tig as a hedonistic, headstrong woman who said "Fuck the world" a lot more than she probably should have.

"Then what?" asks Noelle, sipping her third beer.

Whether she likes it or not, it's also her *last* beer. I've been counting, she's underage, and a fourth beer will make her bold enough to say things that will embarrass me and Ashley. I'm cutting her off when this one is cashed.

"Well, the ratings on *Lure Me* were still really good. I mean, *The Devil Wears Prada* had started this fascination with fashion magazines, and *Ugly Betty* was still their only major competition."

"So they didn't fire her?" asks Noelle. "I mean, I know they didn't, because she was still on the show, but what happened behind the scenes?"

"The network said she had to apologize to Vanessa Williams and give ten thousand dollars to the NAACP." Ashley's smile is small as she shakes her head. "I mean, the weirdest thing of all is that Tig wasn't racist at all.

Not even a little bit. She just *really* hated Vanessa."

"Like, personally?"

Ashley nods. "Which is so strange because she's seriously the nicest woman in the world." She picks up her glass and takes a drink of water. "Maybe Tig was jealous of her. I don't know what the problem was between them."

Noelle has stars in her eyes. "I bet you know *a ton* of celebrities."

"I met a lot when I was little," says Ashley. "But I'm not really from that world. Not anymore, anyway. We moved away from Hollywood when I was thirteen and my mo—*sister* enrolled me in Catholic boarding school."

"Boarding school?" I ask.

"Mm-hm."

"Where?"

She stares at me for a second, and I can read her face like a book: she doesn't want to tell me. Why not? I wonder. Why is the location of her boarding school a secret? I suddenly realize that, while she *seems* forthcoming, sharing stories with me and Noelle over pizza, she's been telling us a lot about her famous sister and precious little about herself. She mentioned, at some point, that her sister was born in Wales, where her parents still live, but *she* was born in Ohio. And I know that Gus is her godfather. But it startles me a little to realize I haven't learned much else about her tonight.

She smiles politely, her expression closing before my eyes, and says, "It's late, isn't it? Thank you so much for dinner. I haven't had pizza in a long time. It was really good."

"Thanks for joining us," says Noelle, smiling at

Ashley like she's her newly minted BFF.

"I invited Gus and Jock for dinner tomorrow," Ashley says, holding Noelle's eyes and pointedly ignoring mine. "I hope you'll both join us at six."

"We'd love to!"

I kick my sister under the table. In retaliation, she reaches over and pinches the top of my thigh. Hard.

"Can we pick up dessert?" she cheerfully asks.

Ashley shakes her head. "Nope. I'll take care of everything."

She pushes away from the table, reaching for our plates and stacking them on top of her own. Gathering the empty cups and used cutlery, she cradles the pile of dirty dishes in her arms as she stands. It occurs to me now, after learning that her sister was runway royalty, that she's actually pretty humble. She cooks and washes dishes. She grew up in Hollywood, flush with cash, witnessing God only knows what, but was moved, at a young age, to a Catholic boarding school.

Without realizing it, I'm piecing together the two strange halves of who she is.

Part temptress, part angel.

Part shrewd, part foolish.

Part wisdom, part innocence.

Our past determines our future, I think to myself as Noelle stands up and moves around the table to say good night to her. *If she is part Hollywood chaos and part Catholic school virtue,* I wonder, *who am I? What makes up the parts of me?* Without warning, three faces pass through my head: Noelle's. My mother's. Magdalena's. Three different women who have influenced my life, my journey, my future.

I look up as Noelle opens her arms, and Ashley seems lost for a moment before realizing that Noelle wants to hug her. She puts the stack of plates on the table, steps forward into my sister's arms, and hugs her back.

"I'll see you tomorrow," says Ashley.

Noelle nods, pulling away. "For sure. Night, Ashley. Thanks for the awesome stories!"

"Anytime," she says, picking up the plates. Her eyes land on mine.

"Good night," I say, holding her gaze in the candlelight before she turns away, walks back up to the house, and disappears into the kitchen.

As soon as she's out of sight, Noelle looks at me with huge eyes. I can feel my sister's energy building, like a mega-wave coming at me from a distance, getting closer and closer, bigger and bigger, the funnel widening to the height of a fully-grown man until she blurts out:

"OH. MY. GOD!"

She whispers so loud, my head whips toward the house to see if Ashley is listening.

"Noelle—"

"She was *so* nice! And she's *so* pretty! Don't you think she's pretty? Oh, my God, and she's *Tig's sister*! Tig! The *supermodel*! Holy cow! Her life was so glamorous, wasn't it? JULES! She's making dinner for us tomorrow night! Oh, my God! SAY SOMETHING!"

The answers to her questions are: no and no.

No, she's not pretty. She's *gorgeous*.

And no, her life wasn't glamorous. Growing up with a junkie sister before being shipped off to Catholic boarding school? Doesn't sound so great to me, honestly. Sounds like a little bit of a mind fuck.

But I will say this: her life has aged her, maturity-wise. She's only eighteen, and yet she speaks, thinks, and carries herself like someone years older. My sister is twenty and she's much younger in many ways. As evidenced by her next question . . .

"Are you *totally* going to ask her out?"

"No."

"What?" Noelle climbs up on the bench next to me and sits on the table, frowning down at me. "What do you mean, *no*?"

"No, I'm not asking her out."

"You don't like her?"

She says this like it is absolutely unthinkable.

"She's fine," I answer.

"Fine? She's *beautiful* and like, *so nice*!"

True. Noelle's right on both counts . . . so far.

But my mind flashes back to the way she hedged my final question about where she attended school. Hmm. There's something going on with Ashley. I don't know if I believe that she's only up here grieving out of the public eye. I think there could be more to the story, and until I find out what it is, it would be smart to keep my distance, no matter what my cock wants.

I cross my arms over my chest and give my sister a look. "Did you know Parker was cheating on you in Barcelona?"

Hurt dusts over her features, and I'm sorry, but only a little bit. I need to make a point that my sweet little sister will understand.

"No."

"When he left, did you expect him to be faithful?"

"Yes," she says, lifting her chin.

"So would it be safe to say he deceived you?"

She sighs. "Yes."

"That sucks, right? Believing one thing and finding

out later that you were wrong."

"Obviously," she huffs.

"Well, Ashley's not telling us everything, *tamia*. I can promise you that."

My sister stares at me for a second, her green eyes hard. Finally she practically hisses, "What the hell *happened* to you, Jules?"

"What do you mean?"

She shakes her head, her expression a mix of sympathy, exasperation, and disgust. "I mean, you changed. *What happened?* Why did you lose your job?"

"I've told you before: I made a protocol mistake that—"

"What mistake?"

"Doesn't matter."

"Why'd you move up here? Why'd you become such an *asshole*? You don't trust anyone anymore. You won't even give someone a chance! When she's perfectly fucking nice!"

"Noelle, calm down."

"No!" she cries. "Tell me what happened!"

"I can't," I say, and technically, at least, this is true. I'm not supposed to talk about what happened in Cartagena. It's embarrassing for the Secret Service that one of their own screwed up so completely.

"That's bullshit. I'm your sister. You could tell me, and you know I'd take it to the grave."

"Let it go, Noelle," I say, a sharp edge in my voice warning her that I'm not kidding around. "This conversation is closed."

My sister returns to her original tack, mellowing her voice. "She's pretty. And nice. And the way you two look at each other? Like you want to eat each other sideways with a spoon? God, Jules—"

"We do *not*—"

"Parker *never* looked at me like that," she continues. "I don't understand why you won't, I don't know, let yourself like her, Jules."

I place my palms on the table and push away. Standing up, I'm looking down at her instead of the other way around.

"I just can't."

"Then you're stupid."

"And you're a brat."

She hops down from the table, looking up at me with narrowed eyes. "You know what? You don't have a right to call out anyone else on keeping secrets. You're hiding out here. Your *whole life* is one big secret."

Then she huffs softly and heads into the house, leaving me alone.

It's on the tip of my tongue to yell "Fuck you!" at my sister's back, but while I've used that sort of coarse language *around* her, I've never said it *to* her. Hell, my father would have smacked my mouth off my face if I ever had.

But damn it, I'm frustrated by our conversation.

She's right. I'm attracted to Ashley like I've never been attracted to anyone in my entire life. She's been here for a week, and it's turned my whole life upside down. I'm aware of her in a way I've never experienced before. I want to know more about her. I want to know everything about her, in fact. And until I do, there can be nothing more between us than sharing this house and occasionally offering one another pleasantries when we happen to cross paths.

That I want our paths to cross as often as possible

is my problem, not hers.

But I will fight whatever force draws me to her until she's gone.

***

Ashley

Morning sun streams into my windows, and I wake up slowly, breathing deeply and smiling as I recall dinner with the Ducharmes siblings last night. Since losing Tig, I haven't spoken of her like that—with both affection and exasperation, but it felt good to remember her with laughter instead of pain. It felt . . . new.

To be frank, I don't know the last time I thought about Tig without a deep and terrible ache, which is weird because her diary entries are so furious, so desperate, they should make me sad. And on one level, they do. They make me angry too. But at least twice, she says that she stayed alive for me. That counts for something, doesn't it? It makes me wonder if maybe—just maybe, despite her efforts to reject and conceal it—she loved me just a little.

Anders and Gus, in their own ways, have both insisted that she did.

My mind slips from Anders to Mosier, who still believes I am at school.

When Gus visited on Wednesday, he told me that he called Father Joseph from a pay phone, introduced himself, and asked the priest if he had reached out to Mosier yet. Yes, he had. But Mosier and his sons were on a business trip in Las Vegas when he called, so Father Joseph had asked that I remain up here a little longer, until he could get in touch with them. Gus said I was welcome for as long as I wanted to stay.

"You don't think Mosier would *do* anything to

Father Joseph, do you?" I asked Gus.

Something dark flickered behind Gus's eyes, but his smile was brave. "Ain't no man alive wants to tangle with a priest, precious."

I, however, don't share Gus's certainty, and still fear for Father Joseph when I imagine him sitting down with Mosier to discuss my future. Mosier doesn't have the type of temper that can be easily controlled. Not as far as I've seen, anyway.

And if anything happens to Father Joseph, Gus, or Jock—or Julian, for that matter—I would never forgive myself. These people, in various degrees of welcome, have embraced me in my time of terrible need, and I will always be grateful to them.

Julian.

Julian.

I close my eyes and sigh, remembering his chiseled face in the candlelight last night. Watching him with his sister—so effortlessly affectionate and loving—was a revelation to me. Now that I know how Julian's face looks when he loves someone, I won't ever be able to unknow it.

And how does it look?

Still rugged. Still masculine. Still beautiful. But softer, in a way that is tender, not doughy. Maybe even a little vulnerable—something I haven't seen on Julian's hard face at all until last night. I didn't even know he was capable of it.

"Lord," I pray, "help my terrible lust."

But my heart is already racing, and that deep and throbbing ache is growing between my legs. Reaching for the hem of my modest nightgown, I pull it up, over my hips, to my waist, baring my sex under the covers.

Tentatively I trail my trembling fingers over the

skin of my belly, landing on the triangle of curls at the apex of my thighs. I flatten my palm over the soft hair, as my breath grows choppy and shallow.

My fingers are the first to reach between my legs and slide into the hot valley of slickened skin, gasping when the pad of my finger inadvertently brushes over a nub of firmer flesh. I arch my back against the mattress, running my finger back and forth, a mewling sound rising from my throat as I pass over the little button.

I rub faster now, pushing my head back into my pillow and raising my knees to open my thighs wider. I moan loudly, then bite my lip to stifle the sound, my eyes rolling back in my head as my body explodes in wave after wave of almost painful pleasure, of intense contractions, like fireworks bursting inside my body. I pant and giggle at the same time, riding out this newfound bliss until I open my eyes and release my lip, which tastes slightly metallic. I think I've split it with my teeth, but I don't care. I've never experienced anything remotely as earth-shattering on a physical level, and it's left me feeling sated and spent.

I open my eyes and sigh softly. At some point during my orgasm, a warm heat rushed from between my legs, and the area I was rubbing is now soaked and slick from it. I fondle myself lazily for an extra minute before skimming my hand back to the hem of my nightgown to pull it down.

I've never touched myself like this before. Never dared, either at school or at Mosier's house. I know the mechanics of sex, of course, and that having desire for one's husband will lead to the kind of sex that will be pleasurable for both married partners, and, hopefully, fruitful.

But hearing a sanitary version of "how sex works"

from Sister Agnes, who had no firsthand knowledge of the act, and experiencing my first orgasm, are two different things entirely.

Remembering Julian's face across the table last night—his green eyes softer because of his sister's presence—makes me feel confused and tired. Now that I know how he looks when he loves someone, I can't help the impossible, ridiculous yearning that suddenly skyrockets to the very pinnacle of my longing:

For Julian Ducharmes to love *me* someday too.

***

Julian

I was wrong about last night.

Noelle didn't grill me when I went back to my room to go to sleep.

She didn't grill me, because she refused to speak to me at all.

Even when I put on *Princes et Princesses*, her favorite movie of all time, she wouldn't speak to me.

Since waking up this morning, she's been reading on the front porch swing, ignoring me completely and looking disdainfully at the sandwich I placed on the table beside her at lunchtime.

When I returned an hour later, she hadn't touched it.

My little sister is freezing me out.

After making my delivery in town—Noelle refused to come along for the ride—I return home and stand at the foot of the porch steps.

"Enough is enough, Noelle."

"You're right," she answers, turning the page of

her book, but not looking up.

Phew. "So come for a walk with me and Bruno."

"No, thanks."

"But I thought you just agreed that enough is—"

"Enough of *you* shutting *me* out," she snaps, closing her book and marching into the house.

And *of course*, who is standing there in the doorway watching the drama unfold? Ashley.

Great.

She stares at me through the screen, her expression unreadable.

"She's a fucki—she's a *brat*!" I yell, loud enough for Noelle to hear. A door slams shut in the back of the house in response.

"She loves you," says Ashley softly, pushing open the door and stepping onto the porch with me. "And you love her."

"I guess you know something about difficult siblings, huh?"

She offers me a small smile, but I feel it everywhere. "Tig? Oh, she was . . . *terrible*. Yes."

"But you loved her?" I ask, feeling strangely invested in her answer.

She averts her eyes as her smile fades. "I did. I think I did. It was . . . hard to know Tig."

"My sister won't come for a walk with me and Bruno," I say, ignoring the warning bells going helter-skelter in my head as my lips form the following words: "How about you?"

Her eyes widen, and her lips part in surprise. "Me?" I'm about to yell, *No! I take it back!* when she nods emphatically. "Sure. I'd love to."

I whistle for Bruno, who's sniffing for something

at the white lattice under the porch. "Come on, boy."

I don't know why I asked her. And I don't know why I didn't take back my invitation when I had the split-second chance. But I blame it all on Noelle. If she hadn't harassed me about dating someone and opening up and being a big, fat liar last night, I never would've suggested this.

Well, suck it up. You asked and she accepted. Besides, it's just a walk.

As we round the barn, Ashley moves into step beside me, and I take note of her little white tennis sneakers. No good for traipsing through the woods. We'll have to stay on the path.

"Have you seen the pond?"

"No," she says, her voice breathless as she tries to keep up with me. "I haven't seen anything."

I slow my pace a little. "It's not much, but if we follow the path, we'll come to it."

"Sounds good," she says.

We walk in silence for a few minutes, Bruno's happy baying breaking the quiet every few minutes.

"Is he chasing raccoons?"

"You have a good memory."

"Photographic," she says.

I glance at her. "Really?"

"Mm-hm. With a few exceptions, I only have to hear or see something once." She taps on the side of her head. "It's in here forever."

"Huh. Interesting."

"Not always," she says softly.

I assume this is because there are some things she'd rather forget, and I am struck with a sudden sympathy.

"Are there a lot of things you'd like to forget?"

"Yes," she answers without embellishment, explanation, or excuse. Her one-word answers are maddening when, more and more, I want to know everything about her.

"Why didn't you grow up with your parents?" I ask.

"I did," she says, "for a while."

"Then you moved to Hollywood. To be with your sister."

She stops abruptly, and I turn around to face her, shrugging sheepishly at the expression on her face. Just short of pissed, she appears unnerved. "How . . . ?"

"The internet," I say simply.

After Noelle fell asleep last night, I spent a good hour surfing Tígin, born Teagan Ellis, in Anglesey, Wales. There was a lot of information about her career, her addiction, the many wild things she'd said and done, her whirlwind marriage, and her death. But aside from the fact that Ashley was born in Ohio, sixteen years after her sister, there wasn't much else about my elusive housemate.

When she says nothing, I add, "Tig has a Wikipedia page."

"I know."

Her blue eyes look so hurt, so betrayed, I almost want to comfort her. I remember Noelle enfolding Ashley in her arms last night and my own ache to do the same.

"There's not a whole lot about *you*, though."

"I'm not a celebrity," she says, her tone accusatory.

"I just don't know a whole lot about you," I say, being honest with her. "We live here together. I see you every day. I mean, we share a house, for Chrissakes, but I don't know you at all. It's weird. It's disconcerting. It makes me edgy."

"Please don't blaspheme."

"Sorry," I say, exhaling softly, feeling frustrated with the situation.

"You know . . . it's hard to get to know someone when you ask them to stay away from you," she says in a cool tone, but I'm relieved to note that she's started walking again.

"Yeah, well, I'm cagey," I admit. "My sister gave me an earful about it last night."

She doesn't say anything, but I see her lips twitch, and I know she's holding back a grin.

"It's okay. You can smile about it."

"Noelle yelled at you?"

"Mm-hm. And she won't talk to me today."

"The silent treatment."

"She's good at it," I say, thinking that she learned from the master: our mother. "Are you surprised?"

"A little. She's younger."

"Doesn't matter. She's in charge."

"But she's so small, and you're so . . ." Her words have tumbled out, but now she lets them trail off.

"I'm so . . . what?"

". . . much bigger," she murmurs, a pink bloom coloring her cheek. "Why, um, why are you, uh, *cagey*?"

I shrug. I know why, of course, but I'm not anxious to tell her the sad story of my destroyed career. I fall back on an easier story instead. "Our mom left us when we were young. It affected me, I guess."

"I'm sorry. She passed away?"

"No. She physically *left*. Took off. She moved from Vermont to Florida, divorced my dad, married Greg fucking Kellerman, and started a new life."

"How old were you?"

"Twelve."

"Noelle was eight," she figures out quickly. "That's young."

"I think it fucks you up," I say, articulating something I haven't said aloud in a long time.

She nods. "It's hard to trust other people when the one who was supposed to love you most lets you down. It's a betrayal. I don't know if you ever get over it."

"Sounds like you have experience with this."

"My mother . . ." She pauses. "My mother let me down too."

"She pawned you off on your older sister," I say.

"It's more complicated than that," she answers, and I feel her closing up again. But then she surprises me. "Make up with Noelle. She's your sister. She's all you have. You never know when . . ."

You might lose her.

The unspoken words are heavy between us as the pond comes into view. Ashley moves toward it without me as I stand at the end of the path, watching her. For whatever reason, her own mother abandoned her too—left her with her junkie sister in LA and returned to Wales after that sister died. Why didn't they take Ashley with them? Because she was enrolled in school here? Why didn't her parents offer her a decent life with them instead of mayhem with her sister? And where are they now when she, arguably, needs them more than ever?

I catch up with her at the pond.

"I don't know what happened to estrange you from your parents, but maybe you should take your own advice and reach out to them. Now that your sister's gone, they're all you have too, aren't they?"

When she looks up at me, her eyes are so heavy, so sad, I instantly regret my words and the heavy-handed way I've given her unsolicited advice on something I know nothing about.

"I have no one," she says softly, turning back to the pond and ending our conversation.

Day #17 of THE NEW YOU!

It's been a year.

A year since I married Mosier, since I wrote in this diary, since I chose this ~~fucking~~ life.

(Since I chose this slow and painful death.)

I have learned the rules to this life.

I have learned how to shut up.

I have learned how to keep my head down.

I have learned how far a human can bend without breaking.

I have learned that bending can be another kind of breaking.

I lost another baby today.

Taking a ~~shit~~load of vitamin C a day every day basically ensures that I'll stay sterile, but this time I was scared. It took a couple of weeks, but finally, today, my period came. Big clots of red and black tissue falling to the toilet in loud plops while I cried tears of ~~fucki~~ thanks.

Good-bye, baby.

Thank ~~fuck~~ God.

If I brought a child into this life, I would be damning my eternal soul to hell.

It's bad enough I brought Ashley here.

When Mam and Tad visited in March, I begged them to

move back to Anglesey with Ashley. She can be your daughter, I said. She can be beautiful and dutiful and good. She can be the me you never had.

But Mam doesn't want to raise my ~~bastard~~ kid. And Tad looked at me with disgust.

"What do you think of us taking Ashley back to Wales with us, Mosier?" my mother asked my sadistic husband over dinner. "Teagan feels the change would be good for her . . . younger sister."

I froze in my seat, cold, hard dread seeping into my bones like a never-ending disease.

My fingers curled into my napkin, and I bit the side of my cheek until I tasted blood.

I don't know if she knew the price I would pay for her words. Maybe she did. Maybe that's why she said them.

His eyes, so dark and furious when he looked at me, promised unimaginable pain in retaliation for my suggestion.

"Ashley stays here," he said lightly, "at school, near her family."

My mother shrugged when she looked back at me. "That's that. Ashley stays here."

I died sitting in that chair that night. Everything about me is ~~fucki~~ dead now except my body, which can still feel pain. My body that was subjected to extreme horror when my parents left after dinner that night.

If he finds out that I lost a second baby today, there will be more pain tonight.

But I will close my eyes and think of Ashley and of the baby I lost today. The baby I SAVED today.

And I will take it.

CHAPTER THIRTEEN

Ashley

"Did you know that Tig got pregnant again?" I ask Gus as he helps me set the picnic table outside. "After me, I mean?"

Jock, Julian, and Noelle are playing something with beanbags called cornhole on the front lawn while Gus and I lay plates and silverware on a crisp, white, just-ironed tablecloth.

He doesn't look up at me. "Yes."

"How many times did she miscarry?" I ask.

"Too many to count."

I wince at this information. While at school, part of our service requirement was to participate in the annual March for Life rally in Washington with other Catholic girls' schools. It was our biggest annual field trip and mandatory for every girl in upper school.

I have been taught that willful miscarriage is a terrible sin, but all I can think is that for Tig to resort to such measures, her life must have been utterly unbearable, and I feel more sympathy than judgment.

"How did you know?"

"She wrote to me," says Gus, sitting down to roll and fold pink napkins into rosebuds.

"E-mail?"

"No, sugar. Pen to paper."

"She did?"

"Started the third year she was married. Out of the blue. Then, once a month, like clockwork."

"How?"

He shrugs. "I don't know. Said she had someone on the inside who'd mail the letters for her."

"You don't know who?"

"Never asked."

"Did you write back?"

Gus shakes his head. "Couldn't."

I have many unresolved feelings about my mother, but to think of Tig sharing her terrible life with an old friend who wasn't permitted to write back—who wasn't allowed to comfort her through all those secret losses—makes me so sad, I stop what I'm doing for a moment, hugging a plate to my chest. I close my eyes and breathe deeply to stanch the tears that want to fall.

"I would've *liked* to write back," says Gus, "but it would have made things harder for her."

This is indisputable, and we both know it.

"I found her diary," I say. "I took it. I have it. Now. Here."

Now Gus looks up at me, his forehead creasing as he searches my face. "Tig had a diary?"

I nod. "She found it in her bedside table two years after she left rehab and started writing in it."

"Where the hell did you find it?"

"She hid it under a mattress at her house. I . . . I

found it in her room. At Mosier's."

"What does it say? Oh, my God, Ash, what does she say?"

"I can't read too fast, Gus. It's . . ." I wince. ". . . hard."

He's holding my eyes, but now he rounds the table and pulls me into his arms. "Aw, li'l Ash."

"She was so unh-happy," I say, tears burning my eyes.

"Yes, she was."

"I thought she hated me."

"No, honey. She only stayed alive for *you*," says Gus.

"B-but, all those b-babies."

"She couldn't keep them, honey. Couldn't bring them into that life."

I rest my forehead on Gus's wiry shoulder and close my eyes.

"I saw her over h-holidays," I say. "It wasn't m-much time, but I c-could've c-comforted her."

"Wasn't your job, Ash. She screwed up a lot, our Tig, but she knew it wasn't your job to comfort her."

"She was so alone. I c-could have . . . I c-could—"

"No, honey. You couldn't have done a thing. She made her choices," says Gus. "Some good, some bad. But you don't owe the universe any debt because of them."

For a while, he just rubs my back, and I feel my tears recede in the safe haven of his arms.

"Ash, baby," he says, his voice gentle, but firm, "I know you feel far away from all that right now, but you're still in danger."

I clench my eyes shut because I don't want to think

about it.

"Jock reached out to an old friend," he says, his voice low, his lips close to my ear. "Someone he knew at the Department of Defense. He put Jock in touch with someone at the FBI. We're working with a special agent named Jack Simmons."

"Working with?" I lean back, looking up into my godfather's eyes.

Gus nods at me, but his expression is bleak. "Ash, that guard you told me and Jock about? Dragon? Could his name have been Dragomir? Dragomir Lungu?"

And even though I told Julian earlier today that an eidetic memory can be a burden, in instances such as this one, it can also be a blessing.

"Yes. That was his name. Definitely."

"Okay, so Dragomir Lungu emigrated from Moldova seven years ago, sponsored for a work visa by Mosier Răumann. But his trail ends *three* years ago. No more passport entries or exits, no tax returns, no credit cards, not even a speeding ticket. Nothing. It's like he disappeared. Or . . . was murdered. Just like you said. Do you know of any other guards who went missing?"

Murdered. Even though I knew that was probably what happened, it's chilling to have it confirmed.

"Ash? Honey?"

"I was barely ever at Mosier's house, and even when I was, I wasn't allowed near his guards. It was a coincidence that I happened to wake up and see anything that night. I thought I dreamed it."

"Well, keep thinking," says Gus. "Your priest is supposed to talk to Mosier later this week, when he returns from Vegas, but Jock's going to keep digging, just in case Father Joseph can't change Mosier's mind about his plans for you. Agent Simmons said that

Răumann and his sons are bad men. The FBI's been trying to build a racketeering case against the family for years."

While this news doesn't surprise me, it's still *news*, in that I've never had it confirmed before now.

"If you were up for it, baby doll, you could even be a star witness in putting him away," Gus adds softly, gauging my reaction. "For murdering Dragomir Lungu."

Sudden and unexpected chills turn my arms into gooseflesh. "Gus! He'd hunt me down! He'd—"

Gus drops his hands to my shoulders. "Never. Never, sugar. No one will touch a hair on your head. That's rule one."

"How?"

"Witness Security Program."

"You mean . . . changing my name? Moving somewhere far away? Hiding? Forever? What about my *face*, Gus? People recognize my face wherever I go!"

"Easy, Ash. Easy." Gus pulls me close and rubs my back. "Listen, honey, let's shelve this for now. I'm going to ask you to trust me again. Can you do that? For Gus-Gus? Jock has it all under control, I promise. I don't want you to worry. You just . . . rest a while here. Maybe your Father Joseph can get things ironed out, but if he can't, Jock's on the case, okay? That's all I wanted you to know."

Gus kisses my forehead, then sits down to make three more napkin roses while I put water and wine glasses at each place.

My nerves are still jumping. I want to change the subject. I want to think about anything else but Mosier.

"Did Julian make these?" I ask, holding up a

wineglass with a bright blue stem.

"He did." Gus looks up at the glass I'm holding and sighs dramatically. "Oh, but the talent, honey. The *tal-ent*."

I feel a grin quirk the corners of my mouth, but I don't turn away in time. Gus sees.

"Oh, look here, now. Wait wait wait wait, baby doll. Is that a blush I see? Oh, my gracious Lord above, does my li'l Ash have a crush?"

"Stop," I hiss, looking across the yard at Julian, who throws a beanbag into a hole, then taunts his sister with his victory.

"He is a *manly* piece of man," Gus swoons, covering his chest with a manicured hand, his lacquered nails shiny in the dying sun. "You could choose worse."

"Stop staring," I plead. Julian's going to know we're talking about him.

"You're no fun."

"We went for a walk today," I say, studying the place settings like my life depends on it.

"Oh, *reeeeeally*? Tell me more."

"We talked a little. Walked a little."

"Did you let him touch your—"

"Gus!"

"—*hand* a little?"

"You weren't going to say *hand*," I say, raising an eyebrow at him. "Cut it out. I'm a good girl."

"Maybe *too* good," Gus mutters under his breath, standing up to place napkins on plates.

"What does *that* mean?"

Gus puts his hands on his hips, giving me major attitude. "Your mama was the fiercest bitch I ever met. And Lord knows she was trouble, but she had some *spirit*!" He tilts his head to the side. "I get you, honey. I get that you don't want to turn into your mama. But damn, girl, you ain't the Virgin Mary either. Live a little. Have some fun. That boy gives you tingles in the tinderbox? Well, hell. Let him strike a match already."

"You *can't* be serious."

"Why not?" He widens his dark eyes with exasperation. "Is you eighteen? Is you hot? Is you ready?"

"Gus . . ."

"Don't you *Gus* me. When's the last time you kissed a man?"

I stare at him.

"Tell me you have kissed a man, Ashley Carys Ellis."

I sigh softly, blinking at him. "When I was thirteen."

His index finger flicks back and forth. "Thirteen is not a man, peaches. Thirteen is a boy."

"Well, there it is."

"Now, honey, *you* can't be serious."

"Who *exactly* was I going to kiss?" I ask, putting my hands on my own hips to mirror him. "Father Joseph? Mosier? My stepbrothers? Where, exactly, O wise one, was I supposed to find a man to kiss?"

"Lord, child," he says, shaking his head at me like my entire existence is impossible now that he's discovered I've been kiss free since thirteen. "You must be backed-up to China. You are *way* overdue to let loose."

Jock bellows a triumphant whoop from the grass, and Gus's eyes slide to his partner, who's jumping up and down like he just won the lottery. Jock high-fives Noelle, then shakes hands with Julian, who offers Jock a rare grin, and a *feeling* sweeps over me. A feeling so sharp, it hurts. The kind of hurt that knocks the wind from your lungs and leaves you gasping.

Gus and Jock. Julian and Noelle. Me. A sunny evening. Lawn games now and dinner coming. Five misfits who don't have a lot of somebodies, who suddenly have each other.

I don't have much experience with family, but I long for it so terribly right this minute—with the four unlikely people around me—that it makes me dizzy, and my eyes sting while I try to catch my breath.

"You okay, baby doll?" asks Gus.

I nod, setting the last glass in place, then I turn and run back up to the house.

***

Julian

There is no comparison between last night's dinner and tonight's.

Last night, we sat at a bare picnic table with paper plates, a roll of paper towels, and a citronella candle, eating pizza slices directly out of the box. Tonight? As part of a security detail, I've attended dinners with the most powerful movers and shakers on the planet, and I can say without reservation that tonight is elegant. Tonight is decadent. Tonight is not just a meal, it's an experience.

On one side of the table, Jock and I share a bench. On the other side, Gus is flanked by Noelle and Ashley. The table has been carefully set with white and pink linens, plates, and my own glasses—clear bowls with royal blue stems that I made for the house. At some point, Ashley must have picked flowers and has arranged them in bud vases. She found floating candles hidden somewhere and put them in two hurricane vases filled with water so that the candlelight pings off the glass and the water.

Couldn't she find any candlesticks? I wonder, making a mental note to craft some for her—er, the house.

To start, she spoils us with a cold soup; vichyssoise, I think, as Jock pours each of us a glass of wine that pairs with it.

Across the table, I watch Ashley bring the glass of wine to her lips, and I stare until she catches me, then I smile at her over the rim of my own glass.

"Do you like it?" I ask, thinking that the cold, dry Chardonnay is a perfect match for the creamy soup.

"Yes, I do."

"I thought you didn't drink?"

"I only drink a little," she says, replacing her wineglass, "when a meal commands it."

"Does this meal command it?" I ask.

She nods, her head moving just a little, like a queen acknowledging a loyal subject. "I hope so."

"Li'l Ash has always been a good cook," offers Gus, grinning at his goddaughter beside him. "Used to spoil me rotten when I looked after her, putting bacon in the mac and cheese and potato chips on the PB&J."

"Was that often?" I ask. "That you looked after Ashley?"

"Often enough," answers Gus, shooting a look at Jock.

"Julian," says Jock, as he clears his throat, "we've already gotten inquiries for Christmas ornaments. How many are you planning this year?"

I see what they're doing. In their own gentle way, they're protecting Ashley, and while I respect that, something in me longs to be on Team Ashley too. I want them to trust me. Even more importantly, I want *her* to trust me. It's not a good idea. It could get me in trouble. But I can't help the feeling that zings through me—of wanting to be useful, of wanting to keep her safe too.

"We had one lady come in and buy half a dozen," says Gus. "She had a bunch of ornament swap parties coming up and said your pretties would make a splash."

Last year, I made almost fifty blown-glass ornaments, some round, some teardrop shaped, some onion shaped like the domes on a Russian cathedral, but each original and unique. They sold like hotcakes, especially, I think, because of the skiers at Sugarbush who often swing over to quaint Shelburne for the restaurants and shopping.

"How many do you want?" I ask.

"At least a hundred," says Gus. "Right, P.C.?"

"At least."

"What will you sell them for?" I ask.

"Fifty each?" asks Jock. "Twenty-eighty split?"

Not bad. I'll make $4,000 for the batch, and who knows how long I'll be living rent free with Ashley? I'll be able to bank most of my commission.

I nod at Jock. "Done. And if you need more, let me know. I can make four or five a day."

Noelle looks up at me from where she's sitting, her smile grudging as she speaks to me voluntarily for the first time since last night. "Dad would be proud, Jules."

I shrug, but her words mean something to me, and my voice is warm when I thank her. "*Merci, tamia.*"

"French," says Ashley. "You speak it. I knew it!"

My eyes shift from my sister, across Gus, to rest on the sparkling blue eyes of my housemate. *Damn, but she's pretty*. "You did?"

Her cheeks color pink. "Well, you . . . sometimes

you watch movies in French, and I wondered if—"

"How do you know what I watch?"

"I can hear it," she says, her cheeks coloring dramatically as she confesses, "through the floor."

I take another sip of my wine. Fuck. What else has she heard? I've beaten-off thinking about her about a dozen times since she arrived. My cheeks are as hot when I set down my glass.

"The plot thickens," hums Gus. He looks at me and winks. "How 'bout you help Ash take these bowls into the kitchen, tiger? I want to catch up with your *adorable* little sister."

Gus proceeds to ask Noelle questions about her classes, while Ashley and I collect the bowls from each side of the table. My sister, Gus, and Jock are laughing companionably as I follow Ashley to the house, up the porch steps, and into the kitchen.

She places her three bowls in the sink, then turns and takes mine, her fingers sliding against mine as the bowls change hands. I'm not going to lie—I feel it everywhere, and it makes me lean a little closer to her.

"Where did you learn to cook like this?" I ask, my eyes focused on the intricate braids in her hair that start at her crown and trail to her back. Her hair is white in some places, silver in others, and gold in still others. It's like something out of a fairytale—I'd almost believe that Rumpelstiltskin spun Ashley's hair on his wheel if she told me it was so.

There is a lavender sunset outside the window, where people we love sit at a candlelit picnic table, and for the first time in a long time, a rare peace descends over me. People. Food. A beautiful girl. An amethyst sunset. It feels good. It feels so good, I want to sink into it and find a way to hold on to it forever.

"Um, at school," she says, her voice just a little nervous. "Service and teamwork are important parts of the, um, curriculum."

"Service and teamwork?"

She turns on the water to rinse the bowls, and I pivot slightly so that my back is against the counter and I'm looking at her askance instead of facing her.

"Mm-hm. Preparing meals for the homeless and elderly and taking turns in the kitchen, assisting the numeraries—"

"What-a-raries?"

"They're helpers. Like nuns."

"Your school's pretty conservative, huh?"

"I don't know," she says. "I guess so, but I have nothing to compare it to."

"It's Catholic."

"Yes."

"Is it Opus Dei?"

"Yes, it is."

Huh. Well, that explains a little more.

For the short amount of time I worked in DC, I rented an apartment in a suburb called Vienna where Hartridge, an Opus Dei all-girls prep school, was being built.

Out of curiosity, I googled "Opus Dei" and discovered that it's a branch of Catholicism that practices strict adherence to rules and whose schools offer a traditional and conservative education. Its detractors might throw around words like *misogynistic* and *oppressive*, while its supporters would tout its commitment to values and faith.

Personally, I was raised as a Christmas Eve and Easter morning sort of Catholic. Yeah, I made my First

Communion. No, I wasn't confirmed. And honestly, I don't have much of an opinion on the church in which Ashley was raised but knowing that it was influenced by Opus Dei certainly answers some questions about why she seems so sheltered.

"That must have been quite a change from Hollywood."

"Yes, it was," she says, "but I'm grateful for it. I was, I mean, it's good I went away to school."

I realize that she's opening up to me little by little, and I feel much the same way I do when I'm crafting something particularly delicate out of glass. One false move and I could destroy its shape, or shatter it completely.

"Was it?"

She rinses the last bowl, then stacks all five neatly in the corner of the sink, turning slightly to look up at me. I've never been quite this close to her, and it's impossible to look away from her upturned face, so innocent, so lovely. I fist my hands at my sides to keep from reaching out to her, but the temptation is strong.

I want to kiss her.

I want to feel the softness of her lips beneath mine.

I want to pull her into my arms while my tongue explores the hot, wet recesses of her mouth.

I want to crush her breasts against my chest and feel the points of her nipples against my pecs.

I want to devour her.

I want to mark her.

I want—

"What?" she asks, her eyes searching mine, her voice a breathy whisper.

"What?" I whisper back, feeling myself lean closer to her, my own breath short and choppy as I lose myself in her eyes.

"The way you're looking at me . . ."

Does she realize that she's stepped closer to me? That, if we synchronized our breaths, our chests would touch each time we inhaled?

"It's because . . . I want . . . Ashley, I want . . ."

I dip my head, my lips closer and closer to hers.

"Yes," she murmurs, and I don't know if it's a question or permission, but I choose to believe it's the latter as I drop my lips to hers.

A week of potent attraction and months of abstinence make it difficult for me not to grab her hips, lift her to the counter, and grind my hard parts against her soft. But what I've just learned about her tells me that she probably has very little experience with men, and moving too fast will get me pushed away, maybe forever, which is precisely what I *don't* want.

Her breath is sweet, and her lips taste like cream and wine. I raise my hands to her face and cup her cheeks gently as I deepen the kiss, running my tongue along the seam of our lips. She gasps softly, and given the chance, my tongue slides effortlessly between her lips. Her palms have been flattened on my chest since we started kissing, but now her fingers curl into the fabric of my T-shirt, and I increase the pressure of my hands against her cheeks, pulling her closer to me as my tongue glides along hers.

She gasps again, this time with a little whimper, and I can feel my heartbeat in my cock, which is hardening and throbbing between us. I am careful not to push it against her, though I long to draw her into my arms and ferry her to my bed.

Slow down, I think. *You've* got *to slow down.*

Breaking off a perfect first kiss with a beautiful,

pliant woman isn't something I ever imagined myself doing, but my desire to have more than one kiss with her overrules my immediate hunger. Tomorrow, when Noelle leaves, Ashley and I will be all alone again, and unlike last week, when I pushed her away, all I want this week is time with her.

Drawing my lips away from hers, I kiss her right cheek, then left, the tip of her nose, and her forehead. I move my hands to her shoulders, keeping my pelvis a respectable distance from hers, and rest my forehead against hers until I feel her fisted fingers on my chest slowly loosen.

When I look down at Ashley, her cheeks are flushed. Her eyes slowly open. Well, slowly at *first*. Then they fly open wide in horror. Her hands push me away.

"No!" she cries. "Oh, my God! I'm so . . . *That* shouldn't have happened."

I take a step away from her, but cover her hand, which has landed on the rim of the farm sink. "Hey. It's okay. It was just a kiss."

"Just a kiss," she mutters, yanking her hand away, her eyes stricken when they look up into mine. "I barely know you. We shouldn't have . . . Julian, I'm not . . . I'm not *dirty*. I'm not a bad girl. I'm not fast."

"Of course you're not. I know that."

"What you must think of me," she whispers, placing her hands on her bright red cheeks and staring down at the floor in misery.

"I think you're beautiful," I say softly. "I think you're kind. I think you're a little sad."

She raises her head, and I realize she has tears in her eyes, which I hate. I am desperate to reach for her, to hold her just for a minute, but I know it would comfort me more than her.

"But I don't think you're dirty," I say, somehow knowing that she needs to hear this more than anything else. "I don't think you're bad, and I don't think you're fast. Ashley, I . . . I *like* you, just the way you are."

Over the course of the past week, my jury has been out on Ashley, but as I say these words, I realize they're true. I still think she has secrets, and I don't trust her completely, but I have yet to see a way that she can hurt me. She hasn't brought anything to my doorstep except sweetness. Whatever else may happen between us, she doesn't deserve my disdain anymore. She deserves to feel welcome at this house. She deserves a chance.

"Are you just saying that?"

I shake my head. "I wouldn't lie to you. I don't lie. Ever."

"How do *I* know that?"

"You don't," I say. "But I hope you'll take my word for it."

"Are you going to take advantage of me?"

"I'd like to," I say, risking a grin because she's so damn young and sweet. I reach up and whisk a tendril of blonde hair behind her ear. "But I won't."

"I don't know how to trust you," she says, her eyes so serious as they search mine.

"Hmm. How about this?" I hope I won't regret the next words that come out of my mouth. "If you're worried about me taking advantage of you, then I promise I won't make another move on you. I won't kiss you again. I won't even reach for your hand. Nothing. I promise. Not unless you want me to. Not unless you *ask* me to."

Her entire body relaxes, a smile tilting up her lips, tentatively at first, and then she's smiling at me, the tears in her blue eyes receding, and damn if I'm not smiling right back at her, because Ashley Ellis is not a woman easily resisted.

"Okay?" I ask her, holding out my hand as though making a deal we should shake on.

She nods, taking my hand in hers. "Okay."

CHAPTER FOURTEEN

Ashley

It's almost midnight by the time Gus and Jock hug me good night.

"Can't remember when I've been so spoiled. Thanks, little Ash," says Jock in his half-British, half-American accent, which I've grown to love. He turns to Gus, his eyes full of tenderness. "I'll go get the car started, Gigi."

Noelle insisted on clearing the table and washing the dessert dishes, and she has pressed her brother into service, so we are alone on the front porch when Gus embraces me. "*You* are quite a lady, Ash. I'm so proud of you, I could burst."

His words make me flush with pleasure. "The wines were perfect. Thank you for bringing them."

"That dinner was sheer perfection. Thank *you* for inviting us."

The sounds of Julian and Noelle washing dishes come through the screen door. Over Gus's shoulder, I catch a glimpse of Julian replacing a vase I used. His gaze meets mine, a small smile warming his eyes, and I swear I can feel a shot of heat all the way to my toes.

Gus lurches back, placing a hand over his heart. “Oh, Lord! You’re smitten, peaches.”

“Stop,” I chide him, but the truth is, I don’t know *what* I am.

Ever since he kissed me, all I can think about is kissing Julian again. Sitting across the table from him at dinner, I felt myself withdrawing from the conversation around me, from Jock and Gus’s banter and Noelle’s encouragement for Gus to tell more stories about models and actresses behaving badly. I stared into Julian Ducharmes’s eyes, and I was lost in them.

“Jock likes him,” says Gus. “My P.C. said that even if Julian seems prickly, he’ll look after you while we figure things out. Apparently our boy has a protective streak as long as his, ahem, well, you know.”

I roll my eyes at Gus.

I love it that Julian is protective. I’ve seen it in the way he speaks to his sister, the love he has for her, the way he looks after her.

As Noelle helped me prep for dinner today, cutting up vegetables for the soup and making a half decent piecrust under my tutelage, she talked about her brother, about how he more or less adopted her at the age of sixteen, becoming her guardian. He left behind the fun of college to live with her, to parent her, to make sure that she could finish high school in Vermont after they lost their father.

“He was in the Secret Service,” she added. “He even met the vice president.”

“Wow! Really?”

“Mm-hm. It was his lifelong dream. His bedroom was covered with pictures and decals he got in Washington whenever we went there on vacation. We must have watched *In the Line of Fire* five thousand times. I know that movie by heart."

I haven't watched many movies in the past few years, except a few times when I was home on break and watched one with Tig, but I think I'll try to get a copy of this movie from Gus. I'd like to know what Julian loves so much about it.

"What happened?" I asked, wondering why he'd leave his dream job and return to Vermont. "Did he quit, or . . .?"

She shrugged, her lips pursing like she was unhappy about something.

"I don't mean to pry," I said, sorry that my curiosity about her brother was making her uncomfortable.

"You're not," she said, rolling the dough out on the floured surface. "The answer is that I don't know. I don't know why he left . . . or how. I just know that one day he worked in Washington, and the next, he was moving up here. All he's ever told me is that he broke protocol, but I'm not even sure what that means."

Hmm. A mystery.

But I'm glad that Jock likes Julian. I wonder if Jock knows why Julian left the Secret Service, but I don't feel it's my business to ask about Julian behind his back. If I want to know what happened, the right person to ask would be Julian.

"Gus," I ask, reaching for his hand and holding it in mine. "Would it be wrong? For me to . . . like him?"

"No, baby. It wouldn't be wrong. You can't help who you like." Gus releases my hand, then reaches up to run his knuckles gently over my cheek.

"It *feels* a little wrong," I murmur.

"To like him?"

I shake my head no as my cheeks flush.

"Ah. To *want* him?" I nod and Gus sighs. "Listen up, li'l Ash. I loved your mama. But I don't agree with how she raised you. The life we lived, me and Tig, was no place for a kid. I know the visitors Miss Tig had comin' and goin' every night. I know what you heard. I know what you saw. And then suddenly, out of the goddamned, ever-lovin' blue, she marries a dirty old man and throws you into a church school that tries to make a nun out of you."

"Oh, they didn't—"

Gus holds up a hand. "It's chilly out here, and P.C.'s car is warm, so you let me finish, now." He is wearing a pale pink pashmina over a white tennis shirt, and he swings the fringed end over his shoulder before continuing. "It was wrong the way your mama done it, with all those men parading in and out the door. But Ashley, listen to me now: if you were told by those nuns that *wanting* someone, that *liking* someone, is wrong, well, baby, that's crazy too. It's not wrong to want someone. It's not wrong to like them. And it's not wrong to give yourself over to loving if the chance arises." He glances at the car, where Jock patiently waits before searching my eyes. "Do you understand me? It's not wrong. None of it. It's just . . . *human*."

I take a deep breath and exhale, letting many of my misgivings and fears hitch a ride on the cool air and float, like cinders at a campfire, like fragments of ash, into the night sky.

"Thanks, Gus," I somehow manage to whisper.

"Just . . . take precautions," he says, leveling a no-

nonsense look at me.

"What do you mean?"

"No glove, no love."

"What in the—"

"Sock that wang before you bang."

"Gus, I don't—"

"For God's sake!" Gus shakes his head with a thoroughly exasperated expression. "Use a condom if you decide to have sex!"

I gasp in surprise, covering my mouth as my cheeks flame with heat. "Gus-Gus!"

"I'm just sayin'," he says. "Be smart."

"That isn't even a . . . I mean, there's no need . . . Gus! Really!"

He gives me a knowing look. "Oh, honey, just *have some fun*. Damn, girl, if anyone deserves some fun, it's you. And that boy is the very one to give it to you." He grins. "If you know what I mean."

I smack him on the arm, blinking at him with disapproval. "Oh, look! Jock's waiting. Time for you to go!"

"I love you, baby doll," he says, chuckling softly as he gives me a Gus-scented hug.

"I love you back," I say, then wave good-bye from the porch steps as he and Jock drive away.

Instead of going in, I walk around the house, to the backyard, to see if I can help bring in any dirty dishes, but the picnic table is empty. All traces of our dinner party have already been cleaned up by the Ducharmes siblings.

I look up at the midnight sky, at the thousands of stars, and I wonder if Gus is right. What he says *feels* right, but I feel very young and very small as I stare up at the universe. *It's not wrong to give yourself over to loving if the chance arises.*

"We get beautiful night skies up here."

I look over my shoulder and find Julian, tall, barefoot, and beautiful, walking toward me.

"Yes, you do," I answer, giving him a shy and tentative smile before I turn my attention back upward.

My skin prickles with awareness. My lips tingle, remembering the insistent pressure of his. And elsewhere in my body, I clench hard, willing those deep-set tremors not to start up again right now. I want to believe what Gus has told me—that liking and wanting a man isn't wrong—but it's new to me, and I need a little time to marry my desire and conscience together.

"When I lived in DC, it was what I missed the most, besides Noelle. More than the cheese. More than the beer. More than the skiing." He stops, standing beside me, staring up at the firmament. "I missed Vermont's night skies. And the millions of stars."

"I can see why," I say. "When I lived in LA, I never saw stars." I giggle. "I mean, I saw the *people* kind, not the sky kind."

"Who's the most famous person you ever met?"

"Hmm. Maybe . . . Gigi Hadid . . . or Bella? Hmm . . . Or Cara Delevingne? Kate Moss mentored my mo—Tig for a while, um, and she knew Gisele, of course. Also—"

"Wait a second! Gisele? Did you ever meet Tom Brady?" he asks, his voice eager.

"Let me guess." I glance at his face. "Patriots fan?"

"The biggest."

"Tig went to their wedding, but I never met him. Sorry," I say, giggling as he lays a hand over his heart and pretends to cry. "Speaking of the rich and famous, Noelle tells me you met the vice president while you worked in Washington."

"She did?" His teasing expression disappears quickly as he straightens, dropping his hand. "Uh, yeah. Long time ago."

"Not *so* long," I say.

"Yeah, well . . . I guess it just *feels* like a while ago." I wait for him to say more, hoping to learn why he left Washington so abruptly, but he stretches his arms over his head and yawns. "I'm tired. You must be exhausted."

"At school I was on the dining hall rotation, which meant cooking for one hundred souls regularly. Tonight was a breeze."

"Your soup was amazing."

"Thank you."

"The lamb too."

"Thank you again."

"And the tart."

"That was your sister. Let her know you thought so."

"And the kiss."

"Thank—" I'm grinning at him, but my eyes widen at his unexpected compliment, and I immediately look back up at the sky. It's dark out so he can't see my blush.

His chuckle is soft and low beside me, and maybe I'm wicked for not feeling more guilty, but I feel my smile grow as I trace Orion's belt. I don't dare look at him, but I feel Julian step closer to me, the warmth of his chest radiating against my back. If I moved slightly, one step even, his body would be flush against mine, and the shiver down my arms has nothing to do with the night chill.

As though he can read my mind, he whispers, close

to my ear, "Not unless you ask."

I close my eyes and say a prayer for strength and virtue, which, sadly, works, because the next thing I hear is his footsteps receding.

"Good night, sweet Ashley," he says to my back, his voice a low rumble.

My eyes open slowly to the glittering heavens.

"Good night, sweet prince," I whisper to Julian's stars.

***

Julian

She's tempting.

She's so very fucking tempting.

But I gave her my word, and no matter how much I fucking want her, I can't have her until she says so. My come-on was gentle and playful enough, but pushing her any further would have been obnoxious and off-putting. Nothing about her posture invited a repeat performance tonight. It seems I might have a wait on my hand before I get kiss number two.

I stop by the kitchen to discover the dishwasher running and the serving bowls drying beside the sink. Noelle's finished the cleanup without me, and Ashley's advice from earlier today circles in my head:

Make up with Noelle. She's your sister.

The thing is, Noelle's not just my sister. Our brother–sister dynamic was irrevocably impacted by my father's death. Sure, I'm her brother, but I was also her guardian. I was her de facto parent for two years. I don't want to tell her about the most embarrassing, most regrettable chapter in my life. I don't want to fall from grace in her eyes. I don't want her to be ashamed of me. My silence is as much for her protection as my own.

That said, she's leaving for school tomorrow, and I don't want to leave things like they are between us, with Noelle freezing me out because she wants the truth about what happened in Washington, and me refusing to give it. I'd never forgive myself if something happened to one of us while she was away, if we were at odds when parted.

I hear the front door open and close. Ashley's footfalls are light on the stairs, and I can hear her singing as she heads upstairs to her attic quarters. As I walk to my bedroom, words to match the melody pop into my head, like they'd been sitting somewhere in my psyche all along.

Stars fading but I linger on, dear,
still craving your kiss.
I'm longing to linger till dawn, dear,
just saying this . . .

I lean against the wall of the dark corridor that leads to my bedroom and close my eyes because my memories of this song go further back than tonight. Suddenly, like time has no meaning whatsoever, I hear the soft, low tone of my father's voice singing the same song in his workshop:

"Des souvenirs comme ça, j'en veux tout l'temps. Si par erreur la vie nous sépare, je l'sortirai d'mon tiroir." My father sings off-key, but with gusto, spinning the rod deftly while I etch a spiral into the vase we're making together. "Zis song, Julian. Oh, mon coeur, zis song."

At fourteen, I am not interested in his dopey music, and even less so when it's in French.

"You understand it, son? Ze words?"

"Something about memories?" I ask, concentrating on my

work, not on translating.

Since my mom left, Noelle spends a little time with Mrs. Willis up the street every weekend, watching movies or baking cookies or other girl stuff. I think it's because she misses our mother. As for me? I don't miss her. She left us. Not the other way around. And anyway, sometimes while Noelle's hanging with Mrs. Willis, my dad invites me into his workshop and teaches me how to make something cool out of glass.

"Listen, son. She sings, 'If we should ever be separated by mistake, you and I, I'll take my memories from ze drawer and remember you,'" he says, a very French sigh heavy in his voice.

My dad is the greatest man I've ever known, but he's also so completely cheesy, it's crazy.

"Okay, Dad." Whatever.

"Julian," he says, drawing out the "j," which he pronounces with a mash-up of the "j" and "sh" sounds, "you know zat your mama, she left me, not you. You know, right?"

Behind my safety goggles, I blink my eyes in surprise. My fingers slip a little, and I mess up the perfect spiral I was making. "Oh! Oh, no! Sorry, Dad!"

"Ce n'est pas grave. Keep going," he says, spinning the rod without a break in rhythm. "Some mistakes are good. Zis one? It will be a memory for you. It was me, Julian. It will remind you, fiston. She didn't leave you. Only me. Not Noelle, not you. She left me."

Opening the door to my room, my eyes fly to the vase on my dresser, which sits beside a picture of me, Noelle, and my father. The top half of the glass has a beautiful spiral design, while the bottom half has a single jagged slash, like a rogue lightning bolt crashing through a once-peaceful sky.

Missing my father is, without warning, a hit to the chest, and my breath catches from the intensity of it.

"What?" asks Noelle from her air mattress on the

floor. "What happened? Jules?"

It's only the second time she's spoken to me directly all day.

"Huh?"

"Your face. What happened?"

I take a deep breath. "Nothing."

"Nothing? You look like you've seen a ghost."

I reach down for the remote on her lap and turn off the TV.

"What the—?"

"Listen."

Though my sister looks away from me, I assume she is listening because she doesn't say anything else. As we share the dark silence, I can hear Ashley's voice, far, far away. I can't hear the words, but I can hear the same melody that my father loved so long ago.

"Do you hear it?"

"Mm," she hums. "Yeah."

"Do you know it?"

"*But in your dreams, whatever they be . . .*," Noelle sings softly. "Yeah. I know this one."

"Dad loved it," I whisper.

"*. . . dream a little dream of me*," she finishes, her voice following Ashley's soft notes as the shower upstairs is turned on, muting the song.

"I'm sorry," I say.

She snatches the remote out of my hand and turns the TV back on. "For what, exactly?"

Ambient light brightens the room, and I sit down on the side of my bed, feeling like an old man. "For not telling you what happened in Washington."

Turning to face me, her eyes widen. "You . . . you

are?"

I nod. "If it hurts you, I am."

She takes a deep breath and sighs, tilting her head. "I just . . . I don't know. Dad's gone. Mom's . . . I mean, we haven't seen her in years, right? It's you and me against the world, right, Jules? I just . . . I don't like secrets, I guess. Not between *us*."

"You really want to know what happened?" I ask, wincing at the thought of telling her the whole sordid, shameful story.

She twitches her lips, looking so much like our dad for a second, I grin at her.

"What?"

"Dad used to do that with his mustache."

She smiles back at me, doing it again.

"I miss him," I hear myself say.

If we should ever be separated by mistake, you and I . . .

"Me too," she whispers.

"*Il nous aimait.*"

"Yes," she agrees. "He loved us a lot."

"Don't be mad at me, *tamia*."

She rolls her eyes at me. "You know what? I'd settle for the CliffsNotes version, Jules. You don't have to tell me every detail of your secret past. I just want to understand."

And so, while my foundling siren, with lips like honey, showers by herself upstairs, I tell my sister the shorthand version of what happened. She is held rapt by the story of a young Secret Service agent called up from a routine detail in Annapolis to cover for a sick agent in Cartagena, Colombia. Unfortunately, however, I also have to hear her gasp with shock and sympathy as I continue the story, as I tell her the dirty details of a job gone wrong and a lapse in judgment that will haunt me for the rest of my life.

"Oh, Jules," she sighs, and for the first time since I started talking, thirty minutes ago, I realize that it's quiet upstairs. No more shower. No more singing.

I lie back on my bed, looking up at the ceiling, at the tree of knowledge taunting me with its perky blossoms and shiny red apples. "Yeah."

"How could you—" She breaks off whatever she was about to say and sighs again. "It is what it is."

"Mm-hm."

"No one died," she says, then amends her statement. "As far as you know."

Except my career. Except my life.

"Thank you for telling me," she says. "I won't . . . I won't tell anyone."

"Great," I say, feeling like there's a fifty-pound block of concrete on my chest. I can't bear it. "*Tamia*? Are you . . . I mean, are you, you know, disappointed in me?"

I hold my breath, waiting for her answer. Thankfully she doesn't take long to say, "I'm disappointed *for* you. It was your dream."

That's true. It was.

Protecting the president? The vice president? What higher honor could there be in the world than giving my life for that of a great man? Even now, even here, I can think of no greater calling.

"But," says Noelle, and as she shares her next thought, I need to remind myself that she's a college student in liberal Vermont, "considering the current administration, maybe it's for the best. Would you really want to take a bullet for one of *them*?"

"Hey, now," I warn her. "Love or hate the person,

you need to respect the office."

She snorts.

After a while, she says, "Actually, yeah, you're right."

"What do you mean?"

"It's not really about a specific person, is it? It's about protection. It's about protecting someone who needs you. Hmm." She hums softly at the foot of my bed, like she's having a revelation. "You know what? It's not too late for that. There are lots of ways to protect someone weaker than you, Jules. Heck, everyone's pretty much weaker than you. It's easy pickings."

Her words, so unexpected, surprise me. "What do you mean?"

"The Secret Service is glamorous, right? Sure. Protecting a president is cool. But if your heart wants to protect someone, well, you could join the local police force, you could teach a self-defense class, you could get a job in private security. I mean, there are a million ways for you to still do good, you know?" She clucks her tongue. "Anyway, thanks for telling me."

I think over what my smart little sister has said and murmur, "Mm-hm."

"I'm all sweaty. I'm taking a shower before bed."

I hear her open and close the bedroom door, and a moment later, the water rushes next door.

It's not really about a specific person, is it? It's about protection. It's about protecting someone who needs you.

Staring at the ceiling, I wonder about the girl upstairs, returning to the original questions that plagued me when she arrived: Why is she here? Why does she have no one else? And why do I have the persistent feeling that she's in hiding?

Except, instead of like they did before, when these questions made me want to put distance between us, now I feel just the opposite. I lean into them.

She's young and all alone in the world.

Who the hell could mean her harm?

I ask myself this question again and again, until it's deeply embedded, until it's an unexpected mission, and I promise myself:

I will find out who or what is hunting her.

And whoever or whatever it is, I will protect her.

I swear on my life—on the wasted chances I have squandered before today—this time I will do it right.

I will keep her safe.

Day #22 of THE NEW YOU!

I don't know where else to write this.

Where else I can share it.

And I HAVE to share it.

Where to begin . . . Oh, God, I don't even know. I can tell you that my cheeks are hot and my legs are weak and my stomach . . . God, I want to throw up. But I also want to—I don't ~~fucking~~ know . . . laugh or something.

Laugh.

Oh, my God, for the first time in two years, maybe I don't want to die.

How is that possible? How is it remotely possible that I can live in a nightmare and—right here RIGHT NOW*—feel . . . good? Is that what this is? I mean, I don't trust it. ~~I almost hate it~~. No. I don't. I take that back. I don't hate it. I don't—My God, I just don't know what to do with it.*

I thought I was dead.

But I'm not. I'm not dead. How can that be? Who the hell am I now?

I was Teagan, the daughter. Then Mam, the teen mother. Then Tig, the model. Then Tig, the bad bitch. Then Tig, the junkie. And then back to Teagan, the sad sack wife of ~~a fucking~~

~~monster.~~

So who am I now?

~~(Fuck knows.)~~

(Mae'r diafol yn gwybod.)

I didn't mean for it to happen.

I didn't see it coming.

It was an accident.

I know that for sure.

Over soup, Mosier reached to his right, grabbing the back of Damon's neck and slamming his face into the full tureen of borscht. He was pissed about something. I don't know what.

It doesn't matter.

~~Fuck.~~ I don't know what came over me.

Usually, when he gets into it with one of his boys, I stop eating. I fold my hands in my lap. I look down, wait until it's over and he gives us permission to eat again. But last night—for no reason I can think of—I didn't look down.

I looked up.

For once, I looked up.

And Anders—18-year-old Anders, with the blackest eyes I've ever seen—looked back at me. At me. Into me. Through me.

Oh, God, why did I look up?

Something happened. Mary, Joseph, and baby Jesus, something happened. Between me and Anders. Something ~~fucking~~ happened.

Time froze.

It ~~fuck~~—I mean, it stopped.

Everything stopped.

Life stopped.

Breathing stopped.

My heart stopped.

Somewhere outside of me, Mosier was yelling, and Damon was drowning and grunting and I felt soup splash onto my chin, but I couldn't look away from Anders. I couldn't. I . . .

HE looked away. He looked away, and I still couldn't. I kept watching him. It was like I'd never seen him before. And maybe I hadn't. I don't know. I stared at his face. I watched his jaw—it clenched so hard, then relaxed, and then he looked up at me again and mouthed, "LOOK AWAY" just in time.

I looked down as fast as I could.

A second later, and Mosier would have caught me. Caught us.

Us.

No, no, no. No. NO. There is no "us."

It <u>can't</u> happen. He's my stepson. I am 13 years older than he is.

Wait. Wait. Wait. I'm going too fast. Slow down, Teagan.

After dinner, Mosier took them to his room. Damon with his head red from blood and purple from the soup, gets up and follows his father. But Anders.

He stopped at the doorway, turned, and looked at me. Again.

AND. TIME. STOPPED.

AGAIN.

And maybe it was THAT look. That second look.

Because this is worse than coke. I feel like my heart's going to explode because it's beating so fucking fast.

I don't know.

Yes, I fucking do. I know. I know. I know. I remember. I remember that look.

I remember it and I can barely fucking breathe right now because I know what it means.

Because I felt it.

I FELT it.

Everywhere.

CHAPTER FIFTEEN

Ashley

Whenever our circumstances changed, Tig was fond of saying, "This is the new normal, kid. Get used to it."

After that, she'd snort a line of coke, light a joint, and watch the BBC News.

The new normal could mean her throwing a bag of kale chips at me and expecting me to eat them for dinner.

The new normal could mean standing in our front doorway, watching our new Jaguar being repossessed.

The new normal could be Tig showing up at my classroom one afternoon, taking me via limo to a posh private school two towns away, and enrolling me there without warning or explanation. It could also be that same school kicking me out because my tuition hadn't been paid and Tig reenrolling me in the school I'd just left.

It could, literally, be anything. There was no rhyme or reason to the old normal, so the new normal meant nothing. Very little about my life ever seemed normal at all.

But it made me flexible. It made me more adaptable to the changes around me. It kept my expectations low. Nothing was permanent. Nothing was forever. And when circumstances changed, I learned how to roll with the punches.

But that entire philosophy was flipped on its head when I turned thirteen and we moved to New York. Suddenly, normal *was* a static thing.

For five years, from eighth grade through twelfth, I attended the Blessed Virgin Academy, coming home at Thanksgiving for five days, Christmas for seven, Easter for three, and for two months in the summertime, which I mostly spent alone in my room, reading, except for the rare times when my mother wanted to watch TV with me. It was a regimented and predictable life, and had it not included an intimate association with the Răumann family, would have been welcome. I quickly learned that, although I had developed coping skills for chaos, I much preferred order.

But here and now, waking up on Monday morning, I am grateful for my early education. Something shifted between me and Julian over the weekend, and I have yet to figure out the new normal. As I open my eyes, breathing in the welcome smells of freshly brewed coffee, eggs, and bacon, however, I'm suddenly eager to figure out what it is.

"Ashley? Hey, Ashley, are you up?" I hear Julian's voice from the foot of the stairs. "I made breakfast. Um, if you're awake, come down." As I sit up in bed, I hear him once more. "Ashley?"

"I'm up," I call, my toes curling under the covers.

His voice surges. "Oh! You are? Great. I made

breakfast."

"It smells good," I say, swinging my legs over the side of the bed.

"Are you hungry?" he asks. "I made enough for two."

My stomach is so full of butterflies, I don't know if there's room for food. "Thank you. I'll, um . . . I'll be down in a few minutes, okay?"

"Yeah," he says, and after a second I hear his footsteps moving away from the stairs, back to the kitchen.

Is this *the new normal?* I wonder, standing up and stretching my arms over my head. *Because I'd love to get used to it.*

I pull my nightgown over my head, and as it falls to the floor in a soft heap, I suddenly remember Tig's diary and the entry I read before falling asleep last night. Sitting naked on the side of my bed, I pull the diary onto my lap and flip to the last entry. I skim the words quickly, refreshing them in my mind and wondering if they mean what I *think* they mean.

Deep down—deep in my heart, where I am becoming a woman—I understand them I know *exactly* what they mean.

I know because Julian looked at me that way before *and* after our kiss. He looked—how did Tig put it?—*at me, into me, and through me.* And like Tig, I felt it everywhere.

So . . . Anders had feelings for my mother? Romantic feelings? Did she return them?

I remember back to finding Anders in my mother's bedroom the day after her funeral. I can picture him clearly, sitting on the edge of her bed, his head in his hands, his shoulders shaking with soft sobs.

She loved you.

His words, muttered so angrily, so fiercely, in the car ride back to school, resonate in my head, and . . . oh, my God . . .

Tig and Anders?

My mother and her eighteen-year-old stepson?

I gasp softly and place the diary back on my bedside table, then I cross my arms over my chest and hold on tightly, letting this new information—and all the questions it raises—sink in.

Tig and Anders. Anders and Tig.

I never saw it. I never even suspected.

I stand up and take a clean bra and underwear from the top drawer.

My God, she was old enough to be his . . . his . . . well, no, actually, she wasn't, I think.

Neither Tig nor I got our first period until we were fourteen, so technically I guess she *wasn't* old enough to be his mother. But she was still thirteen years older and married to his father.

My mother and my stepbrother.

Were they just friends? Lovers?

Mosier would have *killed* them if he'd ever found out. He beat the boys for swimming with me. He barely let them look at us. If he'd known about this, he would have—

"Ashley? Did you fall back to sleep?"

"N-no!" I yell. "I'm . . . I'm coming!"

I pull my hair back in a ponytail and head downstairs barefoot, trying to calm the chaos in my head before breakfast.

***

Julian

I think Ashley was hiding from me yesterday.

She came downstairs only once, to give Noelle a hug good-bye in the late afternoon. Well, and at some point, she popped into the kitchen to make a plate of leftovers, but her clean plate was in the drying rack when I came back from my walk with Bruno. Which means, yep, she was hiding from me.

I must have stared at that plate for ten minutes, feeling disappointed and wondering why she was purposely avoiding me. Because we're developing feelings for each other? Because we kissed? Because we're alone now?

By late afternoon, it was bothering me so much, I thought about calling upstairs to ask if she wanted to walk over to the pond again, or watch a movie, or go into town for ice cream, but I also wanted to respect her privacy, so I left her alone, falling asleep to thoughts of kissing her and waking up hard.

But this morning, my patience is gone. I want to see her.

Making breakfast and laying it out as pretty as possible is a bribe to get her to come downstairs. Aside from the fact that I am mistrustful of women in general and really need a temperature check, I also want to know what she's hiding from and if I can help her. Today, more than anything else, my mission is Ashley.

"Good morning," she says, stepping into the kitchen wearing her usual uniform: gray T-shirt, jeans, and bare feet. Her blonde hair is up in a ponytail, her blue eyes are shining, and fuck my life, she is the prettiest fucking thing I have ever seen.

"Hey," I say, gesturing to the breakfast I've laid out on the island. "Hungry?"

I feel her pleasure in my gut when her eyes widen and her lips part. She looks up at me and offers a small, surprised smile. "Oh, wow! Yes. Thank you."

"Tea?"

"Yes, please," she says, her feet soundless as she walks over to the island and pulls out a stool.

I keep my back to her from where I'm standing in front of the Keurig. "Hey . . . were you avoiding me yesterday?"

"Maybe just feeling a little shy after . . . "

I wait until the tea is made, then turn back to find her sitting at one of the two set places, blue eyes wide.

"Kissing?" I ask.

A blush blooms in her cheeks as she nods, a sweet little smile pulling at her lips.

And maybe it makes me stupid, but this is all the temperature check I need to move forward with her. While I stand there, smiling back at her like a dummy, I almost feel like I've known her forever, like the connection we have is more real and more intense than anything else I've ever known. There is even a part of me—the most cautious part, which feels less and less cynical as the seconds tick by—that desperately hopes she won't let me down.

I place the mug in front of her, pointing to the various offerings between our plates. "Cream and sugar there. Scrambled eggs with cheddar cheese here. Bacon. Home fries."

She doesn't say anything. She just smiles. But it's . . . dazzling.

I know she's eighteen and I'm twenty-four, so by

default I should be more confident than she, but suddenly I'm nervous as hell, and I don't know how dudes like Tom Brady and Tony Romo marry models and keep it together on a daily basis. How do they get used to waking up to a girl who looks like this every day? Or do they *not* get used to it? Maybe they're blown away every time they look at their wives. Maybe they wake up tongue-tied every morning for the rest of their lives. That sort of makes sense to me right now.

One of my college fraternity brothers had a thing for Tig—she was on his screen saver, and he had a big poster of her over his bed wearing a white string bikini. And I can see Tig in her little sister, physically speaking. Blonde hair, check. Blue eyes, check. But Tig looked hard to me. Pissed. Fierce. Angry as all hell, like fucking her would be a combat sport at best, and she'd deck you hard if you called it "making love."

But Ashley?

She's soft. And sweet. Surprised by everything. Taking nothing for granted. Jesus, I wish I could just sink into her and stay there for days. For months. For-fucking-ever.

"What?" she asks.

"Huh?"

"You're staring at me."

"You're nice to stare at," I answer, feeling smooth.

Unsmiling, she shakes her head and looks away, reaching for the serving spoon sitting on top of the eggs.

Hmm. Her expression makes me feel a little *less* smooth. "Should I not say that?"

She shrugs as she places some eggs on her plate. When she replaces the spoon, she snags a piece of bacon and bites it, looking up at me.

"Don't take this the wrong way," she says, crunching on the fried deliciousness, "but I've heard that a lot."

"That you're nice to stare at?"

She nods. "Mm-hm. *Beautiful. Pretty. Gorgeous. Stunning. Hot.* I've heard it all."

What's amazing about what she's saying is *how* she's saying it: without a hint of conceit. She's calling out the world on its banality without pressuring herself to agree or disagree. She genuinely doesn't like being boiled down to "pretty," and I realize that I like and admire this about her.

What I don't like is the way she's looking at me, like she's disappointed.

"Are you calling me unoriginal?"

She pops the rest of the bacon into her mouth, raising an eyebrow.

If the shoe fits . . .

"Okay. How about this?" I say. "You look unexpectedly good for a woman who woke up five minutes ago. You're unshowered. You probably smell pretty ripe. But you still look . . ." I shrug for effect. ". . . okay."

She giggles softly, digging into her eggs. "Better."

"Ashley doesn't like being called pretty. Check."

"Triple check," she says. "You actually got points for *not* recognizing me last week."

This surprises the hell out of me. "I did?"

She nods, chewing thoughtfully. "Mmm! These are good. What's in them again?"

"Eggs, cheddar, salt, pepper. How come I got points?"

"You're leaving something out," she says, licking

her lips. "Lavender? Thyme?"

She's scrambling my head with her little pink tongue. "Uh. Yeah. Maybe. The cheddar. It comes from a dairy where they free-feed the cows. It's called Lovely Lavender Farm."

"That's it!" she says. "The cows are fed on lavender, and it's in the cheese. Oh, my God, it's so good!"

"Ashley! Why did I get points?"

"Hmm? Oh." She reaches for her tea and takes a sip. "I don't like being recognized."

"Why not? Your sister was one of the most beautiful women in the world."

"Yeah," she deadpans. "And *that* role came with zero pressure and produced a super-well-adjusted human."

Good point. "You don't want people to know you're related to Tig?"

"I don't want them to judge me based on the fact that I am. People expect something of me once they find out. They even expect something from me because I'm pretty. It's a lot to live up to." She places her mug on the counter and snags another slice of bacon. "I just . . . I just want to be *me*."

I get this. I truly do. I get it because my sister wants me to lean on my father's old Simon Pearce contacts to open my own glass shop, and I refuse to. Either I can make it on my own or I can't, but I don't want to make bank on my father's legacy. I just want to be me, which makes me wonder: what else does Ashley want?

"I'm guessing you don't want to be a model?"

"I have zero interest in that life."

"So what *does* interest you?" I ask, finally scooping

some eggs and potatoes onto my own plate.

She grins at me over the rim of her cup. "Cooking, I guess. Baking. I used to like fashion when we lived in LA, but the glamorous uniforms at school didn't give much inspiration, and I'm out of touch with the latest trends. Honestly? I don't know what comes next. Technically, I haven't even graduated from high school yet."

"But you're eighteen."

She nods. "And all of my requirements are done, but graduation isn't for two more weeks."

"Why'd you leave school early? Because of Tig? Because she passed away? Or something else?"

She opens her mouth to speak, then drops my eyes and sips her tea instead. When she puts her mug back on the counter, she looks up at me, her expression unreadable.

"Thank you for breakfast."

Oh, shit. I know this routine. I asked too many questions, and she's about to run for the hills. As she braces her hands on the counter to stand up, I reach out and grab her wrist, holding it gently until she looks up at me.

"Ashley. Don't go."

She stares back at me, but I note that she doesn't try to pull away, which I take as unspoken permission to hang on to her.

"Can I be frank?" I ask, my voice low and urgent.

She nods once, but her smile is long gone, and her eyes are wary.

"I think you're in trouble," I say softly. "I think you're in trouble, and I want to help you. I mean that. I'm sorry I was such an ass last week."

She doesn't say anything, just watches me, her

wrist resting loosely in my grasp.

"You can trust me," I add. "I promise, I just want to help." She still doesn't answer, so I press on. "I don't know what's going on with you, but you seem really alone to me. Your sister is gone, your par—"

"My mother," she blurts out, the words audible, but just barely.

"What?"

"Tig wasn't . . . my sister."

"What?"

"She was my mother," she says.

She barks out a garish, high-pitched laugh, and a weird chortle follows, her eyes widening as she pulls her wrist away from me and slides off the stool slowly, as though dumbstruck.

I keep my voice as soft and gentle as possible. "Okay. Um, I didn't realize—"

"Fuck," she whispers, staring at the counter like she can't believe what she just said. She crosses her arms over her breasts, hugging herself, her eyes blinking wildly, her breath coming out in little pants, like she's about to have a panic attack. "Forget I said that. Please just . . ."

She shakes her head and starts for the door, but I rush around the counter, fighting against my instinct to reach for her shoulders and pull her back to me. "Wait! Ashley! It's okay. It's fine! Don't run."

She stops just inside the living room but doesn't turn around.

"It's okay," I say to her back. "Seriously. It's okay. I want to help. You can tell me anything. You can trust me. I don't . . . I don't want to hurt you or make things worse for you." Her shoulders are bunched up so tightly, they graze her ears. "So . . . Tig was . . . your mother?"

She turns around slowly, her face white when she faces me. "Yes."

Whoa. Okay. But her body language tells me that she is completely uncomfortable, which I need to fix or she's not going to want to keep talking. Because I can't help her unless she invites me in.

I have an idea and hold out my hand to her. "Hey. Come with me."

This was an important tactic I learned during my months of training: people with big secrets are often more inclined to share them if it doesn't feel interrogative when they're speaking. Sitting across from her at a table or facing each other in a classic standoff position, like we are right now, aren't scenarios likely to lessen the tension. Side by side is sometimes best, so that you don't have to meet someone's eyes as you converse.

She flicks a glance at my hand. "Where are we going?"

"The pond?" I suggest.

"The . . . pond?"

"Yeah. Remember from Saturday? Where we took Bruno for a walk? We could, you know, walk there. Talk. Chill. Whatever."

"Oh," she says, her face relaxing just a touch. "Okay."

Without taking my hand, she walks around me and heads to the back door, sliding into her little white tennis shoes and stepping onto the porch.

I think about whistling for Bruno, who's asleep in the barn, but decide against it. I want to focus all of my attention on her. I follow her, copying her rhythm, falling into step beside her. But I don't say anything until we round the barn.

"Tig was your mother," I say softly. "You just lost your mother."

Glancing to my left, I watch her nod, the single movement jerky. "Y-yes."

"That's tough. God, that's . . . terrible."

She nods again, this time more easily, and I can feel her body loosening up beside me as we walk through the tall grass.

"Thank you for sharing, you know, the truth . . . with me," I say.

"Nobody really knows," she says. "My grandparents, of course, but they've just returned to Wales. Gus and Jock. Father Joseph. That's it." She pauses. "Well, now . . . you, too."

"Father Joseph?"

"The priest at my school." Without looking at me, she adds, "The Blessed Virgin Academy in New Paltz, New York."

"Why was it a secret?"

"My school or my mother?"

"Both," I say, "but I was asking about your mother. Why did your family keep it a secret? That you were her daughter?"

She stops at a cluster of Queen Anne's lace, fingering the delicate white flowers. "I never knew my father. I don't even know if Tig knew who my father was. And my grandparents are . . . Catholic. *Very* Catholic."

"Is that why they left you here? After Tig died?"

"I am," she pauses, and when I glance at her, I see her jaw tighten like she's clenching it hard, "their great shame." She gathers a bunch of the flowers together before leaning down to smell them. "They wanted Tig to give me up for adoption."

I wince at this news, at the way she states it so matter-of-factly, so offhandedly.

"I'm sorry."

"Sometimes I wish she had. Maybe I could have had a normal life."

"And sometimes you're glad she didn't?"

"What kid *wants* to be abandoned by their mother?" she asks me, and I know the answer only too well.

I try to look on the bright side because it feels like the right thing to do in conversations like these. "She kept you, despite their disapproval. She must have loved you."

She caresses the blooms before releasing them. "People keep saying that."

She's right. They do. After my mother left, many people in my own life, including my father, made the same claim. *She loved you. She loved you and your sister. It wasn't your fault she left.*

Except, she did, in fact, *leave* us. No pretty words offered out of kindness could change that damning fact.

We walk in silence for several more minutes, until we're standing side by side at the pond, which is dotted with bright green lily pads. Our quiet presence disturbs a frog, who croaks indignantly at us, making a small splash as it jumps into the water.

I feel the back of her hand brush against mine. Without saying anything, I turn my hand so that our palms touch. When she doesn't pull away, I lace my fingers through hers, feeling like she's given me a gift when she bends her fingers and clasps my hand against hers.

"I'm so sorry," I say softly, "that you lost your

mother."

***

Ashley

I don't know why I suddenly blurted out that Tig was my mother.

I don't know why I told him that my grandparents pressured her to put me up for adoption.

I don't know why I'm holding his hand.

But I guess I'm sick of carrying other people's secrets, and the truth is that I am so *fucking* tired in general—of being alone, of being unwanted, of being frightened—I feel like I can't lose much more by letting Julian in.

And holding his hand is even less complicated.

I *want* to hold his hand.

In every way imaginable, it feels nice. It feels right.

After this weekend—seeing him with his sister and, perhaps more importantly, knowing of Jock's confidence in Julian—I am willing to trust him. He's right. I'm in trouble. I need all the help I can get.

"My stepfather," I say, "is a very, *very* bad man."

Beside me, Julian's posture shifts, but I keep my gaze trained on the tip of a rock protruding from the water about fifty feet away. He doesn't say anything, but he squeezes my hand, which I take as encouragement to continue.

"He . . ." There is no good or easy way to share Mosier's plans for me. They're dark. They're sordid. They're twisted. All around, they're pretty terrible. "After my mother's funeral, he came to my bedroom to speak to me . . . to, um, to explain his plans for me now that she's gone."

Julian takes a breath through his teeth and holds it.

"He, um . . . he made it clear that he married my

mother for me. I mean . . . he wants me to, well, take her place."

"What does *that* mean?" Julian asks, his voice tight and biting.

I swallow again, my cheeks burning with shame and embarrassment and fear. "He intends to marry me. To have . . . children by me. He wants a lot of children . . . I mean . . ."

"He wants to . . . to *breed* you?"

My breath catches at the disgusted tone in his voice, and I wonder if I should pull my hand away, but before I can, he demands,

"Is that what *you* want?"

"No!" I cry. "Never! Not at all! That's why I ran away! Why I came here!"

His fingers squeeze mine and I squeeze his back, feeling unaccountably relieved.

"Did he . . . try to force you?" he asks me, his voice so sharp and menacing, it's walking the edge of deadly.

"No," I say. "I think he was going to, but I vomited on him."

"Ha!" He laughs, but it's not an amused sound, more just surprised.

"I couldn't help it. He was making me so nervous, t-touching my thigh, . . . and I was so, um, upset, I don't know. I couldn't help it. I threw up on him. The next day, he sent me back to school. He said I could graduate, and we'd get married right after."

"Does he think you're there now? At school?"

"Yes." I tell him the plan. "Father Joseph is going to call him and talk to him this week. Mosier doesn't know that Tig was my mother. Father Joseph believes that once Mosier knows, he won't want me like that.

It's a mortal sin to marry your wife's daughter. It's incest."

Julian scoffs. "Somehow your stepfather doesn't sound like the type of guy who cares about his mortal soul."

"He values religion. He cares about piety."

"For himself? Or everyone else."

Good point. "Everyone else."

"And let me guess," says Julian. "Especially you."

"Yes."

"He married your mother for you. For her little sister."

"Yes."

"And how old were you? When they got married?"

"Thirteen."

"*Sick fuck*," he mutters. His breathing is choppy and agitated. Then he growls, "I'll kill him."

I turn my back to the pond, facing my would-be protector.

"No, Julian."

His eyes are wild when he looks down into mine. "Yes."

Slowly I shake my head. "No. That's not the way."

"Then what?" he whispers. As he scans my face, he draws our bound hands to his mouth, pressing his lips to the back of mine.

I step closer to him, grinning at his lips against my skin. "You said you'd wait for my permission."

"Then give it to me," he murmurs, his breath hot on my hand.

"Kiss me," I say, stepping closer and leaning my head back to offer my lips to him.

He reaches for my cheeks, cupping my face, his mouth falling hot and hungry onto mine. As I flatten my hands on his chest, his tongue traces my lips, first the top, then the bottom. I part them with a soft sigh, wanting to feel his tongue slide against mine again. He obliges me, pulling me closer, his hands sliding down my arms to my hips. As he pulls me against him, I arch my back, and the tips of my breasts rub against his muscles. My nipples are so sensitive, the touch makes me whimper, makes the pulsing between my legs faster and more urgent. He tilts his head the other way, slanting his lips over mine, sealing his mouth over mine, stealing my breath, stealing my heart. My legs are jelly by the time his lips skim gently along my cheek. His teeth nip at the lobe of my ear, sending shivers down my spine, and I wrap my arms around his neck, holding on.

"Ashley." His voice is breathy, almost drunk, as he speaks close to my ear. "Tell me what you want me to do."

"Wait," I whisper, not positive if I want him to wait a little longer for the rest of my body, or if I want him to wait for Father Joseph to talk to Mosier. Maybe both.

"I hate waiting," he says gruffly.

This makes me smile. "Please, Julian. I'll tell you everything. But for now, just wait with me. Okay?"

He tightens his arms around me, and I close my eyes, burying my face in the crook of his neck, and hoping that this new feeling bursting inside me—of finally feeling like I'm not so very alone—will be the new normal for a little while.

CHAPTER SIXTEEN

Julian

Ashley likes kissing me, so we kiss a lot over the next couple of days.

I like kissing Ashley too, but I want so much more from her, it hurts to stop. It hurts when she pulls away from me. It hurts all over to make myself wait.

I remind myself not to push her—that we just met and we're still getting to know each other. Sometimes that helps. Mostly it doesn't. My body pretty much aches for her all the fucking time.

She still considers the barn my private space, but when I'm alone in there, I stare out the window, thinking about her. I work with more blue glass than usual because it reminds me of her eyes. I count down the minutes it takes to make whatever I'm working on, so I can walk back over to the house and find her.

And when I do? She smells like vanilla and cinnamon when she throws her arms around my neck without asking. I kiss her like the world is ending tomorrow because our time feels fragile and finite . . . but also because she is so sweet and so beautiful and—

right now—so very mine.

Over the past couple of nights, after I kiss her good night and send her upstairs, I head to my room, take out my laptop, and work.

What do I work on?

In the Secret Service, we called it tactical planning.

Sun Tzu would have called it knowledge and strategy: *If you know the enemy and know yourself, you need not fear the result of a hundred battles.*

The enemy is Mosier Răumann, and what I have learned so far chills me to the bone.

Following the death of his first wife, seventeen years ago, Răumann immigrated to the United States from Bucharest with his young sons and settled in Brooklyn for a short time. I couldn't find much about his first wife. Only that she died in a "tragic accident" at the Răumann vacation home on the island of Crete. She was found facedown in the family's swimming pool, a red rose floating beside her.

Not long after his arrival in the States, Răumann bought a mansion in Westchester County, New York, and, seemingly overnight, outfitted the estate with a high, black, wrought-iron wall around the perimeter, much to the consternation of local planning and zoning, from which he did not obtain the proper permit. After a small dustup and a heavy fine, the matter was settled with Răumann's promise to plant shrubbery around the exterior of the wall, which effectively hid the ugliness of the eight-foot-high monstrosity.

Not the intent of it, however: it keeps gawkers out and the Răumanns in.

And from what I can gather online, the Răumanns are *in*to a little of everything. Most notably, drug, weapon, and sex trafficking from various corners of Eastern Europe into the United States. There's ample chatter on the dark web about the FBI looking into their dealings, but the Răumanns have been clever—they run dozens of legitimate offtrack betting operations across the state of New York that are kept in good standing, though I suspect these are laundering businesses for their more nefarious dealings.

I'm also trying to figure out Răumann's relationship with his second wife, but while there are thousands of pictures of Tig online, very few of them are of Teagan Ellis Răumann. I am able to find only a couple of paparazzi snapshots of Mosier and Tig together: one of them sitting at a table—at a wedding reception, maybe—with his arm slung possessively over her shoulder, and another of them leaving a funeral in Brooklyn, with Mosier looking over his shoulder while Tig, in a conservative black dress and veil, makes her way down the church stairs behind him.

In both photos, their age difference is obvious, and in neither does Tig look like the feisty model who took the world by storm. She is still beautiful, of course, but in both shots, her shoulders are hunched and her eyes are haunted. God only knows the messed-up shit she saw behind that high black fence.

Here's what I know for sure: both of Răumann's wives died young and under mysterious circumstances. And I can't help wondering if it's a coincidence, though a sickening chill down my spine says it isn't. And the thought of Ashley being wife number three makes me want to smash my fist through a wall . . . or kill someone.

This guy? Mosier Răumann? He's a criminal. A wealthy, powerful, established, international criminal. If he originally set his sights on Ashley, waiting for her to mature to eighteen over the past five years, he's not going to let her go just because a kindly old priest asks him to. No way. This guy's a thug and a powermonger. From what Ashley's told me, her attendance at Catholic school was *his* idea—he was *grooming* her to be the perfect wife. Frankly I think he's the kind of man that would prefer to see her dead than with someone else. In fact, I am positive of that.

I slam my laptop closed and wonder how long her whereabouts can remain a secret from Răumann. According to Ashley, the only people who know she's here are the priest, Gus, Jock, me, and Noelle. Noelle and I are nonissues because there's nothing to tie us to Ashley. Same with Jock. That leaves: 1. The priest, and 2. Gus.

Ashley assures me that the priest would never betray her. Nor would Gus, but Gus is *known* to Răumann, and unfortunately, if he tracks down Gus, it could easily lead him to Ashley.

Ashley told me that her stepfather disapproved of Gus and forbade Tig to continue their friendship. It was risky for Gus to attend Tig's funeral, but Ashley insists that her stepfather never saw them together.

But if he wants to find her, he's going to start with her mother's dearest friend. He's going to start with the friend who made an impression, the friend he hated. Mosier Răumann didn't get where he is by being stupid. No doubt Tig's preference for Gus was noted at some point in time. Sooner or later, Răumann will be coming for Gus.

I think about calling Jock to discuss all of this with him, especially because Ashley has already told me that Jock's been in touch with the FBI, but then I remember that Gus and Jock are coming over for dinner on Friday night. It'll keep until then.

I swing my legs over the side of the bed and undress. Wearing only my boxer shorts, I slip under the covers, lacing my fingers under my head.

I stare at the ceiling and think about Ashley.

After I made her breakfast again this morning, we took a walk to the pond with Bruno, then drove to a berry farm over in Charlotte. I watched her as we walked up and down the rows, eating as many as we picked and kissing under the blue sky whenever we felt like it. At one point, as she knelt in the dirt and filled a little basket with berries, I marveled at the fact that this girl, practically drowning in secrets, is someone that I'm growing to trust. For just a moment, my breath caught, heavy and painful in my lungs before I set it free. I hope I'm not throwing caution to the wind. I hope that inviting another woman into my trust isn't a choice I'll come to regret.

Above me, I hear her footsteps across a hardwood floor. A toilet flushes. A faucet is turned on, then off. I imagine her walking back through the little sitting room to her bed, and my cock stiffens beneath the sheets. I lick my palm and reach for the thickening flesh, stretching it until it's sticking way out of the elastic waistband, then flick my thumb over the tip. As I stroke up and down, I force my eyes to stay open, staring up at the ceiling she's lying right above.

When I come—in hot, white ribbons across my chest—I finally let my eyes close, burrowing the back of my head into the pillow as I picture her face and softly growl my pleasure.

***

Ashley

"Julian is not your boyfriend," I whisper to my reflection in the bathroom mirror on Thursday afternoon. "You're sharing a house, and yes, I think he's *becoming* your friend. Also, you kiss him, and he kisses you back, but that *doesn't* make him your boyfriend."

I stare at myself, willing my brain to accept this as fact, but it's getting harder with every passing day, with every passing *hour.*

It's been five days since he first kissed me, and from that time I've learned the hidden places inside his mouth, the hot, wet recesses that I leisurely explore, that belong to me. My fingers know the peaks and valleys of his chest, the soft skin on the back of his neck, the way he tastes and smells. My body knows what it is to be held by him and against him. I am excited by the hard length of him pushing against my secret places, wanting more.

I want more too, but I've only known him for less than two weeks. My feelings for him are so intense, they frighten me. They *feel* real, but how can I know for sure? I don't know how to do this. He is the first man I have ever fallen for.

"But that doesn't make him your boyfriend," I snap. My lips turn down, and I look so sad that I add in a whisper, "Not *yet* anyway."

Maybe, someday, he *will* be.

Maybe, someday, in the not-so-distant future, when Mosier has given me up and I have graduated from high school, I will come back here. Jock and Gus will let me live in the attic I love so much, and Julian will still be my housemate. And then? We can *really* get to know each other. We can spend every waking moment together. We can fall in love and get married and have a bunch of blond, blue- and green-eyed babies. And I will never, ever be lonely again.

I sigh at my reflection. "You're insane. You know that, right?"

My hopes and wishes are like a runaway train. My body is hurtling down a track at the speed of light, with Julian waiting for me at the end of the line. It makes me feel so young. Like, *tragically* young. When I think about Tig and Mosier and Anders and Gus—the mess I am in, the living nightmare that my life could easily become, the danger my very presence poses to those I care for—I feel so scared, it makes my breath catch. It makes me freeze. It makes me so frightened that no place on earth will ever be safe.

It's no wonder I have a massive crush on Julian.

I feel Mosier's breath on the back of my neck, getting closer and hotter every day. But Julian gives me hope that maybe, somehow, someday, I *will* be safe, and that hope is more precious to me than anything else.

I splash my face with cold water and pull my hair into a ponytail. The forecast calls for thunderstorms this afternoon and evening, but we're hoping to beat the clouds with a quick walk to the pond first, and I can hear Bruno in the kitchen, baying at me to hurry up.

I smell the impending rain as I scramble down the stairs and into the kitchen, where Julian and his canine companion are standing by the back door.

"*Woof!*" exclaims Bruno, wagging his rusty-red tail.

"Yeah," says Julian, grinning at me. "Woof."

This is happiness, a voice whispers in my heart, and I pause for a second by the marble counter, touching it lightly as I smile back at the pair of them.

A man and his dog, waiting for me, in a farmhouse kitchen.

This is all I need, I think. *This man. This dog. This place. I could be happy here forever.*

I feel my smile slipping and blink my eyes at the intensity of my feelings. I remind myself that these are fleeting moments—that the likelihood that this story somehow ends in my favor isn't strong. But no matter what, this time—right here, right now—is mine. One day, I will remember that once upon a time, I knew happiness, and it will help me bear my sorrow when it's gone.

"Look at you two," I say, trying for a bright tone.

Julian gestures outside with his chin. "It's going to downpour any minute. Sure you're up for it?"

"I'm not sugar."

"I don't know about that," he says, winking at me. He offers me his hand, his arm long and strong as he extends it in my direction. "Let's go, *doudou*."

"*Doo-doo?*" I ask, pulling back the hand that was about to take his.

"Oh! It doesn't mean—" He puts his hands on his hips, his shoulders shaking with laughter. "*Doudou* in French means . . ." He shrugs, swallowing his giggles. ". . . like, 'sweetie' or 'honey.'"

"Really?"

"Cross my heart."

"Just so you know," I say, taking his hand and pulling the door shut behind us, "I'm checking that with Noelle the next time she comes to visit."

"Don't trust me?" he asks.

"I'm getting there," I answer honestly, "but calling

me poop won't help your cause."

"I promise it means 'honey.' You made me think of it when you said you're not sugar. Sugar, sweet, honey, *doudou.* It's nice. Really."

I can tell from the tone of his voice—from the humor and warmth in it—that he's telling me the truth, but I sort of love teasing him too.

We lace our fingers together as Bruno runs ahead and thunder crashes in the distance. Julian looks up, pointing at a group of dark gray clouds up ahead and to the east. "It's coming."

"We'll make it," I say, speeding up and pulling him with me.

"We won't," he says.

"Want to make a bet?" I ask, laughing at his dubious expression.

"Absolutely. What do I get when I win?"

I stop running to turn and look up at him. "You can kiss me anytime you want."

He raises an eyebrow. "You'll reverse our arrangement?"

"Just for kissing," I say.

"Deal," he says. "And what do you get if *you* win?"

"Same thing," I say solemnly.

He chortles with laughter just as a fat raindrop plops onto my head.

"You lose," he says, pulling me into his arms and dropping his lips to mine without permission.

Raindrops dot my arms as I reach up and lock my hands around his neck. More rain pelts my hair. Drops fall on my upturned face as his lips move hungrily over mine. And then suddenly, unexpectedly, his hands land on my bottom, cupping it, and he lifts me. His legs, rooted firmly to the ground, split mine, and I straddle his hips, instinctively locking my ankles around his back as he holds me.

I slide my hands to his jaw and cup his face as his tongue sweeps into my mouth to tangle with mine. He skims his lips along my jaw, licking the rainwater from my skin. I open my eyes and find that his long eyelashes have caught tiny droplets of water that glisten and shine like the glass dust that sometimes sparkles on the backs of his hands.

I'm crazy about you.

The words bolt through my head like that runaway train I was thinking about before.

He is so beautiful, I feel it everywhere—in every frantic beat of my heart—and I stare at him until he realizes I've frozen in his arms. When he looks at me, when his eyes meet mine, I'm so overwhelmed with emotion, I can't speak. I loop my arms around his neck and rest my forehead against his. Then I close my eyes and breathe deeply, memorizing this perfect moment.

***

Julian

I like her—*so damn much*—it scares me.

The way she looked at me in the kitchen . . . the way she's looking at me now . . . I can sense the depth and intensity of her feelings, and my heart answers them. If I wasn't enjoying every second with her, I'd realize how enormously fucked I was. This girl is *way* under my skin, and I'm starting to wonder if this will be a passing fling, or if she's there to stay. Some people breeze in and out of your life without leaving a mark. With Ashley? I'm pretty sure there's going to be a mark. Nah. There's going to be a big fucking gash.

I'm not an idiot.

I fucking realize that I haven't known her that

long.

But it just doesn't matter. The heart wants what the heart wants. Mine wants her.

I loosen my hands on her ass, sliding them to her hips and holding her steady until her feet hit the ground.

My voice is hoarse with emotion. "We should go back, baby."

She tilts her head and grins. "First, *doudou*. Now, *baby*. Which one is it?"

"Whichever one you want."

"Both, please," she says, just a tiny bit sassy, and I can see her mother so clearly in her for a split second, it almost knocks me on my ass.

"Both it is, baby *doudou*."

"If that means 'baby crap,'" she says, "you're in hot water."

She makes me laugh again, which is the wonder of Ashley. She's in a world of shit up to her eyeballs and she's still making me laugh. What a woman.

I whistle for Bruno and take her hand, turning us around and leading us back to the house. When the barn is in sight, I realize that there's an unfamiliar car in the driveway, and every muscle in my body tenses. I'm immediately on high alert.

I yank Ashley against me, pivoting to hide us behind a tree trunk and look down into her eyes. "Are you expecting anyone?"

"No," she says.

"There's a car in the driveway."

"Is it Gus?"

I shake my head. "No. The car's black, not white."

"Is it an SUV?" she asks.

I take a peek and shake my head. "No. A sedan."

I can see her thinking before she whispers, "A Cadillac?"

"A Honda."

Her shoulders relax. "It's not Mosier."

I nod, squeezing her hand and wishing I had my gun. I'll clean it tonight and start carrying it with me at all times. "Stay behind me, okay?"

"Don't take any risks."

"I won't. Come on."

There's no way he could know where she is already, I think to myself, unless the priest gave her up. Would the priest give her up? Shit. Ashley was positive he wouldn't, but my initial feeling was that Răumann would stop at nothing to get her back. I should have followed my instincts. What if the priest fucking buckled and Răumann's sent one of his men to grab her?

As I get closer, I realize there's someone in the driver's seat, and someone else, in a trench coat with the collar up, is knocking on the front door. Fuck. What the fuck is going on?

"Stay here behind the barn," I whisper to Ashley. "I'll go see who it is and let you know if it's safe."

"Okay," she says. "Be careful."

I drop her hand, walk around the barn, and call through the ebbing rain, "What do you want?"

To my surprise, *Gus* turns around and looks at me.

"Julian!"

"Gus?" I look pointedly at the car and then back at Gus, a clear question in my eyes. *Who the fuck is that?*

"Him? Ohhh! No, no, no!" he says, reading my expression. "It's just an Uber! Julian took the car."

Shit. Okay.

As Gus thanks the driver for waiting and waves him away, I go back for Ashley.

"Gus is here?" she asks. "Hmm. I wonder what's up."

We meet Gus at the front door, then step into the living room. Gus takes off his khaki trench coat as I run to my bathroom for towels since Ashley and I are soaked. When I return, Ashley's still standing just inside the front door, staring at Gus.

"You're scaring me," I hear her say. "Just tell me what happened."

For the first time, I notice that Gus's expression is deeply troubled, bordering on grave.

"Sit down, li'l Ash," he says.

Gus sits in a wingback chair by the fire, and I sit across from him, beside Ashley, on the edge of the sofa. I place a towel in her lap, which she ignores. She is totally focused on her godfather.

"Please," she whispers.

"Oh, honey. There's no easy way to share this . . ." He winces, staring at the folded hands in his lap before looking up at Ashley. "I called your school today. Your, uh, Father Joseph . . . last week when I talked to him, he told me that he had a meeting set up with Mosier on Wednesday night. Uh, that was yesterday, um, night. So I called this afternoon . . . just to see how the talk went."

Ashley's entire body has tensed up beside me. Her

arms are crossed over her chest and her shoulders brush the lobes of her ears. She nods at him to continue.

Gus licks his lips nervously. "Father Joseph . . . aw, baby doll, he had a heart attack last night." Ashley gasps, covering her mouth with her hands, and I can't stop myself—I put my arm around her rigid shoulders. "I'm so sorry, Ash, but he's gone."

"No!" she cries, her voice keening. "No. No, no, no. No. Please, no."

"Aw, honey," says Gus, leaning forward in his chair, his brown eyes brimming with tears. "I'm so *damned* sorry."

She is shaking her head, sobs racking her small body as she repeats the word *no* over and over and over again. The depth of her sorrow is shocking and terrible, and I wish I could halve it for her, share it with her, make it go away.

But I can't.

I look up at Gus, and to my great dismay, I realize that he isn't finished. He has more to say.

"What else?" I ask, sliding closer to Ashley and rubbing her back.

"I asked . . ." Gus pauses before starting again. "I spoke to Sister James. She said that he was fine yesterday. She saw him at dinner, and he asked her to pray for him. He said he was meeting with the stepfather of a student at eight thirty that evening and called it a 'complicated matter.' When he wasn't at Mass the next morning, she sent a student to the rectory. They found him at his desk. He was gone." Gus sighs. "According to the coroner, the time of death was approximately nine o'clock the night before."

Ashley has been cradling her head in her hands,

but now her neck snaps up and she looks at Gus. "What?"

Gus looks sorry as hell to have to share this information, but he nods as Ashley adds up the facts in her head. "He either died while Mosier was still there, or directly after he left."

"What do you mean?" Ashley demands, springing to her feet. "Did Mosier hurt him?" she screams. "Did Mosier *kill* him?"

Now Gus is on his feet. "Baby doll, your Father Joe wasn't a young man."

"Sister James said he was fine the night before!"

I stand up too, looking at Gus. "Did you get a sense of foul play? From the nun you talked to?"

Gus looks thoughtful for a second, then shakes his head. "No. She didn't tell me that anything was off, aside from the fact that he seemed concerned earlier in the evening." He takes a deep breath and releases it slowly, crossing his arms over his chest, his expression bleak. "But are you asking if *I* suspect foul play? I don't know how you'd go about giving someone a heart attack, but the answer is yes. The timing stinks."

I nod because I feel the same way.

"There are untraceable drugs that will induce a heart attack," I say. "They aren't easy to find, but someone like Răumann, who deals in the importation of illegal drugs, wouldn't have trouble getting his hands on something. With a tiny needle, it would be virtually impossible to detect a puncture wound." I take a deep breath, imagining an alternative. "Or he could have been threatened and frightened to such an extent that his heart sped up to dangerous levels and gave out. Either way . . ."

"You think Mosier killed him," Ashley murmurs,

her body falling limply back to the sofa. Her head falls forward, her shoulders shaking with sobs. "Oh, my God. Mosier killed him. Mosier killed him . . ."

Gus says, "We've been working with someone at the FBI who's taken a great interest in the case. Special Agent Simmons. Jock called him today, and he's flying up here tonight from Langley. Jock already went to go pick him up at the airport. That's why I Uber'd here. We'll put him up at our place for tonight and bring him here tomorrow. We need to figure out what comes next."

"Good," I say, grateful there's a plan in the works. "Whatever you need, I'm in."

Gus looks at Ashley, moving around the coffee table to sit beside her, to gather her into his arms as she cries. And although a part of me wants to be the person comforting her, I know that I have a much more important job ahead: to protect her from whatever is coming.

So while Gus rubs her back and lets her cry, I head out to the barn to clean and load my gun.

I'm not letting anyone hurt her.

Even if I have to protect her with my life.

Day #32 of THE NEW YOU!

Crazy.

I am crazy.

It all started that night at the table: Damon's head in the beet soup and a look from Anders that I could have missed if I hadn't raised my eyes to his.

But I did raise my eyes.

And he did capture my heart with that look.

And it became almost a game.

At first, it was all so overwhelming—to feel connected to someone again. My heart would thunder every time we were in the same room together. I would hold my breath. My whole body would BUZZ, *like I was ALIVE.*

I remember this old game, Operation, that Mam and Tad bought me at a tag sale when I was a kid. You'd put a metal pincher around a body organ and try to extract it without making a buzzer go off.

Our game is kind of like that, but this game is called Attraction. Him to me. Me to him. Like magnets. And if we're caught—if we make the buzzer go off—we're both cooked and we lose the game. So we're quiet. We've learned to be quiet, to be careful, to be . . . flawless in our silent extraction of feelings.

We can't talk.

We can't touch.

We can only look.

And I have become very good at looking.

In fact, Tig—who was once such a loud, brash bitch—has become an EXPERT *at looking.*

He has 100 looks when something is funny. Another 100 for frustration. 1,000 for sadness. 10,000 for anger. Glances. Smiles. The many moods of his mouth and seasons of his eyes. I have learned them all this year. I know every nuance of his face, every twitch, every crease, the manifestation of every possible emotion you can imagine painted on the canvas of his face.

I have unlocked them, studied them, and memorized them.

I live for them.

I live for him.

The days he is away are my purgatory. The days he is here are my heaven and my hell. Because I want so much more. But I can't live without what I have.

Today was a regular day.

Anders left early for Albany. M and Damon went to Newark.

No one was supposed to be back for three days. Thank God. A little peace.

M left a small crew behind—only four guys, with one inside and one outside at all times.

Boian had perimeter duty in the morning. Costin was beside the front door. After dinner, Sandu and Marku took over for the next twelve hours. Like fucking dogs. M's kennel of thugs.

Grosavu, that evil fucking witch, had her eyes on me all day. Like I would do what? Start an illicit affair with potbellied, foul-smelling Costin? Get hammered on the cooking sherry on the fucking sly? She knows M locks up the alcohol whenever I am alone. That's the joke of it all. I can't get into trouble and she still fucking watchdogs me, typing texts to M, her lord and master, every time I walk from my room to the kitchen, following me around like she's my fucking shadow.

Anyway, at midnight, I'm in my room watching some stupid horror movie where the girls run into the basement instead of out to the car, and there's a knock on the door, and I just fucking know it's Grosavu coming to check on me, and I've had it with her bullshit.

I yell, "If you come in here, you fucking troll, I will throw this crystal vase at your fucking head." I know she'll tell M that I was yelling and swearing, and he'll call me and tell me to expect a special punishment. He'll say a good wife doesn't swear and doesn't yell. And I'll get beat for it when he gets home.

But it might be worth a beating just to clock Grosavu in the fucking face.

I hear the door open and close, and I think to myself, Is this bitch actually walking into my fucking room?

I pick up the vase on my bedside table and it's like a cement block it's so heavy. I grab the white roses and throw them on the carpet, ignoring the thorns that dig into my palm, and launch the water on the wall across from me. And I swear to CHRIST I'm about to hurl that $4,000 20-pound monstrosity at her, when I hear a voice say,

"I surrender."

Fuck.

It's not Grosavu, it's a man.

And at first? It didn't click. I didn't know who it was.

I didn't. I swear.

Because I barely ever hear his voice, and when I do, it's directed at his father or brother, not at me.

So I'm wondering which of the four brainiac mongrels from downstairs has lost his goddamned mind, coming into my room at night, when he rounds the corner.

And . . .

The world . . . stops.

It isn't one of M's moron guards.

It's Anders. Standing in my room. Smiling at me. And I know this smile. I know it like I know my own soul and it says, "Hello. How are you? Stay strong. I love you. I'm here."

And that's what I hear myself whisper aloud, the words dusting over my lips, feather soft:

"Hello. How are you? Stay strong. I love you. I'm here."

He puts his hands on his hips, darting a quick glance at the vase I'm holding over my head.

"You wanna put that down, killer?"

I place it beside me on the comforter and ask, "How are you here?"

He takes the remote control from my bedside table and turns off the TV, then presses the button that closes the shades over my windows.

"Albany is two hours away," he says, watching as the shades lower, the gears a soft hum as darkness slowly envelops us. "I'm not actually here. I'm there. In my hotel room. Asleep."

"You're not here?"

He shakes his head. "Nope. I can't be here."

"Okay, you were never here," I say. "How did you get in?"

"The tunnel to the wine cellar," he says, replacing the remote. "My brother and I discovered it years ago."

"How long do we have?" I ask him, rising to my knees and reaching out my arms. They're shaking because they want to hold him so badly.

He steps over to me, cupping my cheeks like he loves me. "Two hours."

"You're driving four hours for two alone with me?"

"Teagan," he says tenderly, leaning down to kiss my forehead, "I'd drive a thousand hours for two minutes alone with

you."

Oh, my heart.

Every wall within me fell. Every barrier slipped away. Every terrible, forbidden longing that we'd silenced for a year was given a voice.

He had me.

And I had him.

Again and again and again. In every way. In all the ways that singers write about in love songs and actors try to capture on the screen.

He treated me like I was loved. Like I was a person. A real person. Not a model, not an actress, not his father's purchased whore. Not a pretty bitch to try on like jewelry. He touched me like he loved me. All of me. The bad parts and the shattered parts and the scared parts and the beautiful parts.

I have never been touched like that. Not ever before. And maybe never again.

It was like a rebirth. Or a baptism. Like his tenderness had the power to soothe or . . . or even erase all the horrors of my life—parents who didn't love me, a daughter I never wanted, a career that tried to eat me alive, a husband who wants to beat all of the spirit out of me.

Anders just . . . loved me. And, my God, if I have to, I will live on those two hours for the rest of my miserable fucking life.

At two o'clock, his watch alarm went off. He rolled off me without a word and put his clothes back on in the dark.

"This can't happen often," he says.

"I don't care. I'll take whatever I can get."

He checks his phone and nods at me, one of his thousand sad looks stealing over his face, soft in the ambient light from his phone. His eyes seize mine.

"Stay strong," he says. "I love you. I'm here."

I blink at him because my eyes are burning. No one. No one except Gus has ever told me that they loved me, and I don't know what to say back. But it scares me because it's the most precious gift I've ever been given, which means that someone's going to take it away.

"What if he finds ou—?"

He lurches forward, covers my mouth, and shakes his head. "Don't say it. He can't. Not ever, Teagan. He'd kill us."

I nod because he's right.

"I'll come back when I can."

"Stay strong," I whisper. "I love you too. I'm here."

He kisses me, examining my face carefully, fiercely. "We will find a way out."

And then he was gone.

And I am alone again, but my body is aching from missing his touch, and I wonder if I'm a good enough actress to act like nothing happened when he sits down across from me at dinner on Wednesday night.

Oh, God. Oh, God. Oh, God.

Don't let me be a stupid bitch who gets herself killed.

Who gets Anders killed.

Please let me have this one, tiny piece of happiness.

Teagan

CHAPTER SEVENTEEN

Ashley

I am lying on my bed, my eyes so swollen from crying, I can barely see the words.

Father Joseph is dead, and my mother was not only in love with my stepbrother, but it appears that she engaged in a full-blown affair with him that started years ago.

. . . and this gives me a possible motive for her sudden and suspicious death.

My chest tightens, and I lay my hand over my heart.

I knew that Mosier was a bad man. But to kill my mother? To kill Father Joseph? A woman—his *wife*—and a priest? He is worse than I ever imagined, and it makes my blood run cold. I draw my knees to my chest and hold them, crunching my body into a fetal position and trying to get warm even though it's a mild evening.

Why my response to Gus's tragic news was to come up here and read my mother's journal is a question I can't answer. Maybe to find comfort. Maybe to wallow in more misery.

It's been an hour since the Uber came to the house to take Gus home, and since then, Julian's been out in the barn. I've been curled up in bed, reading Tig's diary and wondering how my life ended up here.

"Father Joseph," I say, more tears sliding down my cheeks to dampen my pillow. "I'm so sorry. I'm so, s-so s-sorry if I b-brought d-death to your d-door."

"You didn't," says Julian's voice from the doorway of my room.

I gasp in surprise, so relieved to see him, and reach out my arms to him without thinking. He crosses the room and sits down on my bed, across from me, concern and sorrow etched into his handsome features.

"You didn't do anything wrong," he says, holding my eyes with his as he gently cradles my face in his hands.

My shoulders shake with sobs, and I lower my head. He releases my face, and I hear him lie down, depressing the mattress with his weight. A second later, he pulls me to his chest as he sits with his back against the headboard. I cry against his chest, wrapping my arms around him as he hugs me close to him.

"You didn't do anything wrong, baby."

He says it over and over again as he holds me, rubbing my back and occasionally dropping kisses to the top of my head.

"This all started long before you, sweet girl," he whispers. "Listen to me: it's not your fault."

"B-but if I had j-just . . . j-j-just . . ."

"Just what? Allowed yourself to be married off to a monster?" An edge has crept into the soothing timbre of his voice. "Let him buy you? Own you? Breed you?" I hear his disgust, and it resonates with me because I feel it too. "No, baby. That's not your life. That's someone else's version of your life. You *never* agreed to that."

"D-do you think he k-killed F-Father J-J—"

"I don't know," he says, taking a deep breath that I can feel under my cheek. "The timing doesn't look good, though."

"He was only t-talking t-to Mosier for m-me, Julian!" I lean up, looking into his eyes. "It was m-my fault!"

"NO!" he bellows. "It wasn't!" He cups my face, his eyes fierce as they stare deeply into mine. "It *wasn't* your fault. Not even a little bit. Tell me you get that. Tell me you understand that."

I scan his eyes, back and forth, seeing the truth in them, and desperately wanting to trust it.

"Tell me, Ashley, because guilt over something like this is too heavy to bear. It's too heavy to carry."

"B-but if it's m-mine . . .," I sob, reaching up to cover his hands with mine.

"It's *not*," he says, his own eyes filling with tears. "It's not, baby. It's not your fault."

"It's . . . n-not my f-fault," I murmur.

"It's not your fault," he repeats. "Tell me again."

I nod at him, sniffling. "It's not my f-fault."

"That's right."

Julian puts his hands under my arms and drags me back to him. I lie half on his chest with my hip pressed against his side, where something hard bulges into my pelvic bone. I lean away and see the outline of a gun tucked into his waistband.

He lifts his shirt and takes it out, showing it to me. "I'm not letting anything happen to you."

I stare at the black weapon, which almost looks

like a child's toy. I am not a stranger to guns—Mosier's men carried them. But I've never seen one this close-up.

"What kind is it?"

"A Beretta," he says, tucking it under the unused pillow next to his other hip. "Just to be safe."

"I don't like guns," I say. I lay my cheek on his chest again, yawning as my heavy eyes close. "But I'm glad you have it."

"Sleep, *doudou*," he says softly, threading his fingers in my hair and sliding them down my back in long, slow strokes. "Just sleep. We'll talk more later."

"Thank you," I sigh, trying for deep breaths, but still finding it hard to get a good one. "Thank you, Julian."

"I'm here," he says, his strong heart beating under my ear like a lullaby. "I'm here."

And the last thing I think before I drift off to sleep is:

Stay strong. I love you. I'm here.

***

Julian

She's asleep in a few minutes, her breathing even and deep, and I'm glad because I can't really get my head around what she's gone through in the past hour. She's lost someone she really loved and who, I believe, loved her. And from what I can gather, the list of people who have Ashley's best interests at heart is getting pretty fucking short.

Gus. Jock. Me.

That's it.

Well, I think, stilling my hand on her hair, maybe this guy Simmons will be part of Team Ashley too. God, I hope so. She needs all the help she can get at this point.

And we need a plan. A good plan. A plan that will keep her safe, not just for now, but forever. Which means I need to bring my A game tomorrow.

Do I think Răumann killed the priest? I whitewashed my answer for her because she's frightened enough. But yes, I do. A hundred and fifty percent, I do.

I don't know if he went there with a syringe and the intent to kill, or if he ended up scaring the shit out of the old guy, but I'm fairly certain that Father Joseph was a goner the moment Răumann stepped into his office. Răumann's plan doesn't work if someone objects to the marriage. If the priest couldn't be useful—by telling Răumann where she was hiding—and was categorically opposed to the match, he was better off dead.

How Răumann did it? I don't know. And frankly I don't care.

All I know is that this bastard will do whatever it takes to get Ashley back, which means I need to be prepared to do whatever it takes to keep her safe.

She stirs in her sleep, snuggling closer to me, and my heart swells with something I've felt before, but only in small doses. It's like comparing the first time you jerk yourself off with how it feels to sink into a willing woman for the first time. One packs a punch, sure, but the other leaves you breathless and changed forever.

I've felt protective before—over Noelle, over girlfriends in high school, even over Magdalena—but this is different. It's deeper, and it's growing in ways I can't explain. When I think of keeping Ashley's life safe, there's a part of me that wants to be included in that life, in that forever. There is a part of me that doesn't want to envision a future that can't or doesn't include her. Not just because protecting a young woman like her is the right and noble thing to do, but because I'm getting attached to her. And not knowing her—not being allowed or able to see what might happen between us, given time and space and freedom—makes me unspeakably sad.

And that's when I realize it:

I'm falling for her. Hard.

Which is *not* convenient.

She's several years younger than I am, almost completely alone in the world, and being hunted by a madman. She doesn't need the added emotional complication of me pining after her, does she? Not to mention, I've only known her for a handful of days.

But despite these logical reasons for keeping my distance, I can't help how I feel. I care about her. And even though I've heard that feelings can deepen quickly under stressful conditions, that doesn't make mine any less real.

I hold her closer and rest my lips on her head, wondering how much time we have and how all of this will end, and hoping that falling for someone all over again won't cost me as much as it did last time.

***

Ashley

When I wake up, my room is dark, and I can tell, from the deep and even way his chest rises and falls under my cheek, that Julian is asleep.

I've never slept beside a man, and I allow myself to marvel in the wonderfulness of it for a moment, keeping my dark thoughts at bay until they won't be held back any longer and they crash around me.

My mother died suspiciously, and I'm starting to wonder if Mosier killed her.

Father Joseph is also dead, and it seems likely that Mosier killed him too.

He's scorching a path to my door, burning down anyone who would stand in his way of having me. I should feel terrified, but profound sorrow overtakes my fear. My breath catches as my mind plays a montage of memories about my beloved Father Joseph.

I remember the first day I arrived at the Blessed Virgin Academy—how warmly he welcomed me and how, over time, he became a cherished friend and stand-in grandfather. I remember him blessing meals and wearing his Mets cap at softball games. I can hear his voice of absolution in my head, forgiving my transgressions. I think about his face when he drove me to the train station in Poughkeepsie and said good-bye to me. He died keeping me safe, and I will be forever grateful.

"Thank you, Father," I whisper, "for everything."

Julian sighs in his sleep and mumbles, "You okay?"

"Mm-hm." I nod against his chest, feeling a little shy. I lean up to go to the bathroom, but he reaches for my wrist, grasping it hard.

"Where are you going?" he demands, his eyes wide open in the darkness, shiny in the moonlight filtering through my window.

"Just to . . . pee."

He relaxes his grip. "Of course. Sorry."

I blink at him, a little surprised that he grabbed me. "Are *you* okay?"

"Yeah. I just . . . sorry," he says, letting go of me to

reach up and rub his eyes. "Vivid dreams."

"Bad?"

He nods. "Not great."

I pee and wash my hands, then splash some cold water on my face because my eyes and cheeks are swollen from so many tears.

When I return, Julian is lying on his back, holding his phone over his head, the glow lighting up his face.

"What are you doing?" I ask.

"Checking the news," he says. "I found Father Joseph's obituary on the school website. Sounds like he was a great man."

"I can't go to his funeral," I say, a sad realization. I would have liked to honor his memory by attending the service.

"When all of this is over," says Julian, "I'll drive you to the cemetery so you can pay your respects."

"Thank you," I murmur, sitting with my back to him.

Julian clears his throat, sitting up behind me. "Do you want me to go? Give you some space, maybe?"

"No!"

"No?"

"Please don't go. I don't want to be alone."

"I'll be just downstairs," he says.

"Can you stay, Julian?" I whisper. "Just for tonight?"

He gives me a half smile and nods, placing his phone facedown on the bedside table. His fingers slide to Tig's journal and rest on Marilyn's smile for a moment. "Your diary?"

"No," I say, picking it up. "My mother's. I'm getting to know her."

Julian adjusts the pillow behind him, then sits back,

beckoning me to join him. I plump another pillow and put it beside his, leaning back beside him.

"You didn't know her?" he asks.

It's nice, sitting side by side like this, though part of me misses the intimacy of half lying on him, with my cheek resting on his chest, over his heart.

I shrug. "She was a lot of different people. I don't think I knew her very well at all."

"I didn't know my mother very well," Julian says with a sigh. "But my dad was amazing."

I'm warmed by the tone of his voice, full of love and admiration. "Was he?"

"Yeah. He was a good man, you know? He'd listen to these old French records—this music from the sixties called yé-yé."

"Yé-yé?"

"Mm-hm. It was sort of this mix between English rock and, I don't know, maybe . . . bossa nova? Soft, but still with a light rock beat. Mostly women singers. Started in France and swept through Europe. There was this one singer, Françoise Hardy. She had this voice like butter." He chuckles softly. "My father used to say, '*Elle est si belle qu'elle me brise le coeur.*'"

"What does that mean?"

He looks down at me. "She is so beautiful, she breaks my heart."

I know he's translating his father's words, but I also sense that he's speaking to me. The expression in his eyes is so tender, so intense, I can't bear it, and I look away. I put Tig's diary back on the bedside table and lean my head on Julian's shoulder. I like listening to him. And it feels safer than looking directly into his eyes.

"Tell me m-more," I say through a yawn.

"Hmm. She sang this song called 'Dans Le Monde Entier'—'All Over the World.' And this song . . . it was beautiful. Sad and beautiful. My dad played it all the time after my mom took off."

"Do you have it?" I ask. "On your phone?"

He reaches over me for his phone, swiping at the screen a couple of times, and suddenly the darkness of the room is filled with the low, soft, mellow voice of a woman singing in French. And Julian's right. It's so beautiful, I just want to stay here forever, leaning my head on his shoulder, hidden from the world, in a beautiful farmhouse, in the middle of the nowhere, with a sixty-year-old love song playing just for us.

"What's she saying?" I murmur.

"She's apart from someone she loves, and she wonders if he's forgetting about her. It's breaking her heart."

"Did your mother break your father's heart?"

"I don't know," he says, pressing his lips to my head and kissing my hair. "Maybe." He sighs. "It's sad."

I'm not sure if he's talking about the song or his parents. Or maybe, it occurs to me, he's talking about himself too.

"Have you ever loved someone like that?" I ask.

It's an incredibly personal question, but there's something about being here with Julian that makes me feel like there aren't any rules. We say what we need to. We ask what we want to. I know he will answer me honestly.

"No," he says. "I haven't. You?"

"No," I whisper, feeling unexpectedly pleased by

his answer. "Not yet."

The song ends, and Julian swipes the screen before reaching over me again to place it on top of Tig's journal.

"How about we get some sleep?" he says.

My breath catches because I've never spent the night alone with a man. "Uh . . . okay."

"Or I can go now?" he asks, his voice tentative.

I am shy about spending the night with him, but I know—with everything I am—that I don't want him to leave. I want him to stay with me, and a peace overtakes me as I realize that nothing will happen between us if I don't want it to.

Therein lies the problem.

I want things from him that I shouldn't want, that I could regret, that might hurt me later, years from now, when he is part of my past and I wish we'd met under circumstances that could have allowed him to be a part of my future. But I'm not a fool. There is no man on earth who'd want the baggage I carry. I get that. I know it's true.

He starts to get up, but I place my hand on his chest and push him back.

"No."

Even though I am younger and far less experienced than he, his eyes look helpless in the moonlight as he gazes at me. "What do you want, Ashley?"

"I don't know."

"Tell me."

"Take this off," I whisper.

My hands bunch the fabric of his T-shirt, and I slide the cotton up his chest, over the ripples of his muscles, the heel of my hand brushing against the warm skin and wiry hairs that trail up the middle of his chest.

He stares hard at me before reaching behind his neck and taking the shirt off.

My eyes slide down. To his lips. To his throat. To his chest. I lean forward and press my lips against his skin, humming softly with pleasure at the contact. His hands land on my hips, and he lifts me onto his lap so that I'm straddling his waist. As I dust his chest with kisses, he threads his hands through my hair. Under my lips, his heart races, his pulse beating against a million sense receptors and sending the message to my brain that this man, this beating heart, are under *my* control. At least for now.

It's a heady sensation, to know the full force of my womanhood for the first time, the power I can wield over the human being lying beneath me. For just a second, Tig's face flashes through my mind, and I wonder if this is why she entertained so many men? Because her life felt so chaotic, but for the few minutes a man was lying beneath her, she was omnipotent?

My thoughts scatter as another part of him throbs against another part of me. A different muscle against different lips. And suddenly I remember that no matter how powerful I feel, I am probably half Julian's size. Whatever control I have, he is giving me. And by taking it, I'm trusting him not to turn the tables on me. That's where decency and emotion enter this equation, I think. He is decent. And we are falling for each other.

I raise my face and drop my lips to his, kissing him madly as he reaches for the hem of my shirt. He fists it in his hands, his question clear, despite the blinding distraction of our passionate kiss. I drop my hands to his and help him slide my shirt up. It swoops over my head and lands on the floor with a soft plop, leaving me clad only in my bra. His hands land on the clasp, and I tear my lips away from his to whisper, "Take it off."

It follows the same fate of my shirt—over my head, onto the floor—and Julian sits up, holding me tightly against him. I'm still astride his lap, my naked chest against his as his tongue slides against mine. I moan softly, arching my back, the hairs of his chest tickling my throbbing nipples. I reach for his face, my fingers digging into his cheeks as we kiss fiercely.

Suddenly he flips us, and I'm on my back, his hips still nestled between my legs, and his breath catches as he thrusts gently against me, the hard zipper of his jeans clashing against mine. The pressure against the secret places between my thighs is glorious, and I cry out, biting his bottom lip as he pushes against me again.

"Ashley," he growls, jerking his head back, his tongue darting out to lick his bleeding lip.

"Sorry," I pant, my chest heaving into his. "I'm . . . so sorry."

His lips tilt up in a bemused smile, his eyes gentle as he reaches up to cradle my face. "You've never done this before."

This isn't a remark about my skill. It's said with wonder, with awe, even. It's a realization that experience is unnecessary when chemistry is perfect. And ours is off the charts.

"Neither have you," I say, taking a chance that the way we feel about each other is as unique for him as it is for me.

"No, I haven't. Not like this. Not with someone like you." He chuckles softly, leaning down to kiss me softly before rolling onto his side. "But I think we should pause here."

Like a petulant child, I want to demand, *Why?* But

I already know the answer. Because too much, too fast, leads to regret.

He gathers me against him—my back against his chest and his arm slung protectively around me, resting under my breasts. His breath is warm near my ear when he whispers, "Try to get some sleep."

His erection presses against my bottom, which I like. It makes me feel uncharacteristically sassy. "*You* try."

He laughs again—just a soft rumble of amusement—and the sound makes me smile. "*Doudou* baby, don't tempt me."

Unbelievably, after the horrific day I've had, this makes me smile, and I fall asleep feeling something I have always longed to feel . . . safe.

For the first time in my life, and against all odds,

I feel safe.

CHAPTER EIGHTEEN

<u>Ashley</u>

We sit in the living room, where I have laid out a simple breakfast of fresh-baked strawberry scones, hot coffee, cream, and sugar. It's not fancy, but I want to be useful while these men—Julian, Gus, Jock, and Special Agent Simmons—discuss my fate and the best way to save me from Mosier's clutches. And frankly I don't know how to be helpful to them. I feel young and vulnerable and, therefore, endlessly grateful that they are interested in protecting me at all.

I sit on the couch between Julian and Gus, while Jock and Simmons sit in the wingback chairs across from us.

"Shall we get down to it?" says Agent Simmons, wiping his mouth before placing his empty cake plate on the coffee table. "Great scone, by the way."

He has reddish-blond hair with gray streaks at his temples and a smattering of freckles across his nose, and he wears a wedding ring on his left hand. I'm not good at guessing ages, but I'd place his somewhere between thirty and forty.

Jock nods. "Let's get Julian and Ashley up to date."

Agent Simmons clears his throat before speaking. "The bureau's been tracking Răumann for years. We know that he's into nefarious dealings—trafficking and smuggling mostly. He brings weapons in from Russia and the Middle East via his contacts in Moldova, Romania, and Bulgaria. With over ninety percent of the world's opiates now originating in Afghanistan, Răumann's overseas operations in Eastern Europe are strategically placed. We suspect that a fair amount of the heroin in New York is being imported and distributed via the Răumann family and its associates." He grimaces. "This is in addition to human trafficking—stealing children from smaller ethnic groups in Albania and Romania and bringing them to the States to work in the sex trade. Of the estimated 4,000 children being exploited in New York, we suspect a significant percentage were smuggled in by someone in Răumann's network."

My stomach churns as I listen to Agent Simmons speak, remembering the princess room prepared for me at Mosier's compound and the luxurious suite of rooms where my mother lived. Beautiful things purchased from the terrible suffering of others. I knew he was a bad person, but I had no idea *how* bad. Suddenly I hate it that I ate his food, washed my body in his shower, and slept in his house. I was a child, of course, not complicit in Mosier's business dealings, but right this second, it makes me feel sick that I ever accepted anything from him.

"Stop," I say. "Please."

Simmons sighs, looking slightly annoyed. "Miss Ellis, I'm sorry if this information is troubling, I truly am. But you need to know who he is."

"I *do* know," I say. I know better than anyone here what he is capable of.

"Let's move on," suggests Jock. "Tell them what you told me this morning."

"Right," says Simmons, looking at me. "I troll the dark web for chatter. Do you understand what that means?"

"Dark web? No."

His lips twitch. "Think of it as a layer beneath the internet."

To be frank, I have very limited knowledge of the regular internet, but I nod for him to continue.

"People can use it anonymously. Post messages. Send out feelers for information. Buy weapons. Sell drugs. Think of it as this huge bazaar where there are endless stalls, and in each one, you can buy or sell anything: people, children, weapons, drugs. No laws, no rules."

"She gets it," says Julian sharply from beside me, taking my hand in his. I'm grateful for the comfort of his warm, strong hand enveloping mine. "What did you find?"

"He's looking for her. Răumann has been sending out feelers since last night. Her picture, her description, and a bounty of $100,000 dollars for information that leads to her whereabouts."

"He's hunting her," says Julian, squeezing my fingers.

"Yes," says Simmons. "Actively. Aggressively."

Jock clears his throat. "Ashley, tell us about leaving school. Tell us every detail until Gigi and I picked you up in Charlotte."

I tell them about the woman who woke me up

when the train stopped in Westport, about the conductor who called me a bitch, about the taxi driver who noted my good manners, and about the ticket seller at the Charlotte ferry who recognized me.

Simmons shakes his head with a grim expression. "I remember your sister. Her face is memorable, and you look just like her. That's at least four people who could remember you. And frankly, Miss Ellis, there are probably countless others who didn't make an impression on you, but on whom *you* made an impression."

"What does that mean?" I ask.

"It means he'll find you," says Simmons, not mincing words. "I don't know when, but I'd estimate you've got less than two weeks before he shows up in Charlotte looking for you." He glances at Jock, then at Gus. "Your name is Gus Egér? That's your official name? Your legal name?"

"No. It's, uh, Augustus Edgerton," he says.

I look askance at Gus, my eyes wide, because I really thought I knew everything about him. "Edgerton?"

He shrugs. "*Egér* sounds better, baby doll."

Simmons asks, "Is your home owned by Egér or Edgerton?"

"It was mine before we met," says Jock. "It's still under my name only."

"That's good. What about the gallery?" asks Simmons. "Is it registered under Egér or Edgerton?"

"Edgerton," says Gus.

"That could buy a bit of time," says Simmons, "but not much. Once Răumann figures out that Gus Egér and Augustus Edgerton are the same person, Ashley's one step away." Simmons glances at Jock. "You two should leave town. Go on vacation. Stay away until this is sorted out."

"No!" says Gus, putting his arm around me.

Jock clears his throat. "Gus, honey—"

"Don't you *honey* me, Mr. Mishkin. I'm not leaving Ash! How can you even suggest that?"

"Because I love you," Jock says simply. "Because if a priest is expendable, you're *less* than expendable. And I can't lose you, baby. I won't."

My heart thunders as I look at Gus. *Be brave, Ashley. Be brave.* "Gus-Gus. You need to do what Jock says. If he says you need to go, you need to go."

"I'm not leaving you," Gus says.

Simmons interjects. "You should. It's stupid to stay."

"Excuse me," says Jock, flicking a furious glance at the agent, "but that's not necess—"

"You know," says Gus, interrupting Jock as *he* turns to Simmons, his brown eyes flashing with irritation, "you show up here last night, ordering us around, telling us we need to shut down the galleries. Now you're telling me that I need to leave my goddaughter—"

"Do you want a way out of this or not?" Simmons demands. "Do you want to help her or not? Because I feel like I'm just spinning my wheels here."

"Do you have a plan?" I ask, turning away from Gus and staring at the FBI agent.

"I do."

"And do you think it will work?"

He tilts his head for a second, then straightens it

and grimaces. "I think it's your best chance."

"Then tell us what it is."

"Ash, honey—"

"Gus!" I cry. "We need help! We need to listen to him!"

His face is stoic and hurt as he stares back at me. "Fine."

"Tell us the plan, Simmons," says Julian, sitting forward on the couch, still holding my hand in his.

"Jock and Gus close their galleries and leave town. Get away from here. Somewhere obscure. Somewhere inconvenient." He looks at Jock, who nods, avoiding his partner's exasperated gasp from across the room. "I'll move into the barn. Ducharmes," he says, looking up at Julian, "I understand you were Secret Service?"

"I was."

"I read your file."

Julian grunts softly.

"I wasn't impressed."

"It's in the past," says Julian, his body tense beside mine.

"Is it? Can you stick with the plan this time?" asks Simmons, his tone intentional and tinged with doubt. "Or will you get distracted?"

I slide my eyes to Julian, wondering yet again why this man, whose dream was to be a Secret Service agent, ended up losing his job.

"Yes, I can stick with the plan," growls Julian. "I learned my lesson. You can count on me."

"I hope so," says Simmons, "because we're using Ashley as bait. I'll be staying in the barn, watching surveillance of the galleries and the house. I'll know when he makes his move and when he's getting closer.

You stick to her like glue. Together we'll trap him."

"Done," says Julian, his tone grave.

"It's a matter of days, a week or two, tops, before Răumann tracks Ashley to Shelburne and Shelburne to Gus. When he does, he'll send men to the galleries looking for Gus, to press him for information about Ashley's whereabouts. We'll plant the location of this house in Gus's desk, and then we'll wait. If I know Răumann, and I do, he'll come for Ashley himself. This is personal to him so he won't pawn off the job on some lackey. *He'll* come. And when he tries to take her, we'll arrest him for attempted kidnapping. With Ashley's additional testimony about Dragomir Lungu, we should be able to file a murder charge too. We'll subpoena his employee and financial records. Once we have them in hand, we'll get a search warrant for his Westchester property. We'll nail him and his entire operation. He'll go away for life. His sons too. And since Răumann never trusted anyone besides his sons with the entire operation—unlike other organized crime bosses, Răumann has no lieutenants-in-waiting—the business will collapse." He's excited, his eyes shining, when he finishes laying out his plan. Looking around the room at the four of us makes him calm down a little, and his shoulders relax. "But Ashley's the key. Ashley makes it personal. He'll come for her."

"I don't like it," says Gus, but Julian's voice is stronger: "If it works, it's worth it."

Jock leans forward, staring at Julian, searching his face. "Can you protect her? Are you sure?"

"Yes," says Julian. "With my life, if it comes to that."

"Okay, then." Cocking his head, Jock gives Gus a

loving look. "It's the only way, Gigi."

"What happens to Ash after that?" asks Gus. "As long as her stepmonster's alive, he'll still come after her!"

"From jail?" I ask.

"It's possible." Simmons grimaces. "She can go into the program."

"Witness Security?" asks Julian.

"Yeah," says Simmons. "It's the only way to *guarantee* her safety."

I gulp. "So I'll have to leave? Leave here?"

Leave Julian and Gus and Jock? Leave this wonderful place? Start over somewhere totally unknown and utterly alone? "I'm afraid so," says the agent. "Or you can take your chances here, of course. We can't *force* you to go anywhere. But if he puts out a hit on you, you'll be a sitting duck here. Good luck."

I inhale shakily, all my dreams about staying here and making a life here disappearing with a pitiless poof.

"There's no other way?" I ask. "No way I can stay here? Afterward?"

"Remember when I said that you make this personal for Răumann? It's possible, even from prison, that he won't be able to let you go, to imagine you with someone else," says Simmons. "He may prefer you dead."

Jock huffs softly. "Come on, Simmons."

"You want me to sugarcoat it for her?" asks the agent, nailing Jock with an impatient look. He turns back to me. "Like it or not, Witness Security will be the best way to keep you safe for the long term. But it's up to you."

"She'll go into the program," says Gus softly.

"Won't you, baby?"

I lift my eyes to Gus, but I can't see him because my eyes are swimming with tears. I just got him back, and I'm about to lose him again? And what about Julian? Will I ever see him again after all of this is over?

But here is the thing about being out of options: you do what you have to do. And I have no choices left. My grandparents are gone. My mother is dead. My confessor is dead. My dearest friend is in danger. A madman will stop at nothing to get to me. Here and now is the end of the line, and just as I suspected, it doesn't include a happy ending.

But at least I'll be free.

"I'll go," I whisper, slipping my hand from Julian's so that I can swipe at my eyes.

"Then that's settled," says Agent Simmons, leaning forward to grab another scone like the entire course of my life wasn't just altered forever.

Gus stands up. "Well, I'm *hella* upset. I'ma need a stiff drink."

Jock stands too, looking down at the agent. "This better work, Simmons."

"I'm confident it will," he says between bites of scone. "Hey! Are you two fly fishermen by any chance?"

"Do we *look* like fly fishermen?" asks Jock, who is wearing a silk cravat with a tailored button-down shirt and charcoal-gray trousers.

"No. No, not really," says Simmons with a shrug. "But Montana is the shit this time of year, you know. Salmon up the ying yang."

"Great tip," mutters Jock, shaking his head as he heads into the kitchen.

Simmons finishes his scone with a satisfied groan,

then turns to me and Julian, and grins like we're old friends. "So. Who wants to give me the nickel tour?"

***

Julian

Though I'm glad he's here and I appreciate his quirky confidence, I'm not a big fan of Special Agent Simmons.

Besides having zero bedside manner and scaring the shit out of both Ashley and Gus this morning, he spent the afternoon rearranging *my* barn as *his* new office. He's had technicians install cameras at both gallery locations, and a live feed is being sent to a computer monitor he set up in the barn. Four more cameras are being installed here at Jock's house, and he'll be monitoring those too.

And yes, I get that having eyes on these places—the Shelburne and Burlington galleries, in addition to the driveway, the front and side of the house, and the back of the barn—are important, I feel like Ashley's and my privacy has been completely invaded, and I'm not crazy about that.

Plus, he asked if I'd pick up some groceries for him, like some damn errand boy, and the amount of Mtn Dew, Cheetos, and Hostess CupCakes (orange, not chocolate) on the list has me raising my eyebrows.

At the store, I purchase a few extra things for Ashley—a candle that smells like Christmas cookies and a romance book by Kristan Higgins. I pause in front of a shelf of condoms, staring at them for a second before grabbing a box and tossing it into the cart.

As I wait in line, my eyes slip over to the aqua box several times, and I chide myself for being presumptuous and then for being hopeful. Yes, last night we slept together naked from the waist up, but that's still a long way from having sex, isn't it? Not to mention, Ashley folded pretty easily when Simmons suggested that she enter the Witness Security Program, dropping my hand at exactly the same time.

I'm not going to lie. It stung a little.

Because if Ashley needs to leave and hide somewhere, she'll be lost to me forever, a fact she appeared to process and accept at the speed of light.

I can't leave with her—I have a twenty-year-old sister who has no one else, and besides, I've only known Ashley for a few weeks. Our relationship isn't far enough along for me to consider following her, and yet my heart aches when I think about losing her. I lean down and pluck the little box out of the cart, about to jam it into the gum and candy rack beside me when I realize the cashier is speaking to me and probably has been for some time:

"Sir? Sir! Are you ready?"

"Uh, yeah," I say, throwing the condoms on the conveyer belt and adding the other items from my cart.

As the cashier rings me up, I recall Simmons asking me about my ability to protect Ashley and stay on task. How fucking embarrassing. Yes, he had a right to wonder, but outing me as inept in front of the woman I'm seeing? That didn't feel so great. In fact, maybe that's why she was in such a fucking rush to drop my hand. Maybe she didn't want to be tangled up with a loser who can't hold down a real job because he got "distracted."

I pay for my purchases and wheel the cartful of groceries to the truck, wondering how long we have until Răumann shows up at the farmhouse, and then I hate myself a little for hoping we get a few more days together. But the truth is, I've fallen hard for Ashley over the past couple of weeks, and I don't want our time together to end.

When I get home, I deliver Simmons's bags to him in the barn, for which I'm rewarded with a curt "Thanks"—he's still setting up monitors and getting himself situated in the space that used to be mine—and then I head over to the house with the rest.

Ashley's nowhere to be seen so I put the groceries away, then take out her little gifts—the candle and the book—and stand at the bottom of the stairs. Am I still welcome upstairs? Last night was incredibly intimate, of course, and I'd like to think that we can move freely around each other now. Besides, Simmons said that I was to stick to her "like glue." But does she still want me after Simmons's insinuations about why I lost my job?

There's only one way to find out.

I start up the stairs.

***

Ashley

I hear footsteps on the stairs and sit up in bed, swiping at my eyes.

While Julian's been at the store, I've been having a pity party for myself. Gus and Jock stopped by on their way to the airport. They're flying to somewhere in Canada called Lake Louise for the next two weeks, and as I held Gus's wiry body to mine, I had the most terrible feeling that I'd never see him again. My heart thundered with fear and sadness, a thousand memories bombarding my mind as I clung to him.

"It'll be okay, li'l Ash," he said, blinking back tears.

"You don't know that," I sobbed.

"Aw, I see. You want solid facts, huh?"

I felt his jaw clench against my cheek as I nodded.

"Okay," said Gus, "then this is the solidest fact I know, doll baby: I love you. You and your crazy mother brought more love into my life than I ever could've found on my own. She was my family. You are too. I loved her and I love you." He leaned back, looking fiercely into my eyes. "We *will* see each other again."

I watched from the upstairs window as he waved good-bye, and stood there, with tears streaming down my face, until the car was out of sight. Then I lay down on my bed and wept.

"Ash?" comes Julian's voice from the sitting room. "You up here?"

I sniffle. "Y-yeah."

"Can I come in?"

"Of course," I say, wondering why he's asking. After last night, he should know that he's welcome wherever I am . . . unless last night was a onetime thing. Oh, no. Wait. Is that what's happening here? Now that I'm Mosier's bait, about to be shuttled into witness protection, has he decided he's not interested in me anymore? It hurts my heart to even consider this thought, and I wince, pressing my hand against my chest.

"Ashley, you okay?" he asks from the doorway.

I look over my shoulder, lifting my eyes to his. "Was last night a onetime thing?"

His face, which was soft a moment ago, changes completely. First, he flinches. Then his eyes narrow at me. "Was it for you?"

"N-no. I mean, I didn't want it to be."

"Neither did I," he says, his face relaxing a little.

"But I would understand," I say, trying to be brave for his sake, "if you felt it was better not to . . . to . . ."

"To hook up anymore?"

Hook up.

Oh. Oh, my God. Okay. I breathe through the pain of those two tawdry, dismissive words. *Here I was, with dreams of forever, when we were only . . . hooking up.*

I turn away from him, looking out the window at the barn, where Special Agent Simmons is setting up cameras—traps for Mosier to fall into.

"Yeah," I whisper, the single syllable bitter on my tongue.

I close my eyes because I feel more tears coming, but fuck, I am so goddamn fucking sick to fucking cuntish bastard death of them. I search my mind for more swear words—*asshole, dick, cock, fucking, fucking, fucking*—

"Ash."

He's moved so quietly into my room and around my bed, I don't even realize that he's squatted down in front of me. But when I open my eyes, there he is, on the floor, looking up at me.

His eyes—his beautiful, long-lashed eyes—are so green, I think that I will never see their equal again, and it makes me hold my breath, staring into them, focusing all my attention on them, so that my photographic memory will never be without them.

"It *meant* something to me," he says.

"What?"

"Last night. Being with you. It wasn't *just* a hookup," he says. "Last night *meant* something to me.

You mean something to me. I . . . I have feelings for you, Ashley."

I blink at him. "But there's no future for us, is there?"

He winces, then shakes his head, his words soft and sad. "Probably not."

I gulp because I know he's telling the truth, but I hate it. I close my eyes again, breathing through my sorrow.

"All we have is now," he says.

"Now," I murmur.

". . . if we want it," he adds. "If *you* want it. It you want . . . me."

"I do," I say, leaning forward until my forehead touches his. "I want whatever time we have left." I pause, holding my breath, measuring the words I'm about to say and letting myself exhale before I say them: "I want *you*, Julian."

His forehead leaves mine, and a moment later his body depresses the mattress beside me. I open my eyes and look up at him.

"I *want* you," I say.

I search his eyes and find such tenderness there, such hopefulness, it makes my tired heart sing with a sudden shot of renewed energy.

"How do you mean?" he asks, his voice low and fierce. "In what way?"

Again, I think about what I'm about to say before I say it, just to make sure, but it doesn't take long for me to know my mind, for me to own my truth. My heart and my mind have already been in communication about what they want, it seems, and they are in perfect communion.

"In *all* ways," I say, reaching for his face with my

hands. The scruff of his unshaven jaw tickles my palms and makes me smile. "In *every* way."

"You mean it, Ash?" he whispers, his breath rushing at me like he's been holding it.

I nod, slowly at first, then with more and more confidence. "I want you to be my first, Julian. I have no idea what will happen tomorrow, but I know what I want today: I want you to be my first."

He starts to smile, then rolls his lips between his teeth for a second before asking, "Are you *sure*, baby?"

I think about Tig having sex with all those men who meant nothing to her. And then I look into the eyes of the man before me. I haven't known him that long, it's true. But in a handful of days, he has become my friend, my protector, and my first love. And in another handful of days, I will likely lose him—either to a life with a man I hate, or a life of unknowns that cannot include him. We are *in between* right now, on an island between the past and the future. It's finite and it's fragile, and no matter what happens next, I want to make the very most of this moment with him.

"I'm positive," I say, leaning forward to press my lips to his.

We fall back on the bed together, kissing each other, grappling with our clothing. His hands fall to the hem of my shirt while mine land on his belt buckle. But after a moment of struggling, he breaks away from me and stands up.

Grinning down at me, he reaches for the button on my waistband and unsnaps it, unzips the zipper, and pulls the jeans down my legs. Then he reaches behind his neck and yanks his T-shirt over his head. His chest is solid and beautiful, and I sigh.

"Do you work out?"

His grin widens.

"Yeah." He flexes his pecs on purpose, and they pop. "I have weights in the barn."

I sit up and run my fingers from his shoulders to his waist. He's not overly ripped like a football player or bodybuilder. He's still human, but with some very nice definition, including a V of muscle that disappears into the waistband of his jeans. I love that V. I want to know everything about where it leads.

I undo his belt buckle and unsnap his jeans, which he shoves down his legs. Underneath, he wears tight cotton shorts in navy blue, and his sex, his—my cheeks flush as I think this word—*dick* is a rigid column underneath the thin fabric, bulging up and slightly to the right. My eyes fix on it, wondering how *that* is going to fit inside me.

As though he can read my mind, Julian whispers, "It's okay. We'll go slow."

I look up at him, holding his eyes as I slip my fingers into the elastic waistband of his underwear and pull down. My heart is thundering as he reaches down to help me lift the fabric over his erection and down his legs.

I am tempted to look down, to look at him—*all* of him—but a feeling of shame, or maybe of shyness, overwhelms me, and suddenly I can't look anywhere. I close my eyes, clenching them shut. Intense heat suffuses my cheeks, and I imagine how ridiculous I must look, perched on the edge of the bed in white panties and a T-shirt, with a naked man standing in front of me.

"Ash," he says softly, and his voice is so close to

my ears, I know he's not standing over me anymore.

When I open my eyes, he's squatting before me, just as he was before.

"We can stop here."

"No!" I say, reaching for the hem of my T-shirt and whipping it over my head. What was it Gus said? *It's not wrong to want someone. It's not wrong to like them. And it's not wrong to give yourself over to loving if the chance arises.* "I want this. Please." I reach behind my back and unclasp my bra. "Help me, Julian."

His fingers skim up my arms to the straps of my bra, and gently, slowly, he pulls them down my arms, uncovering my breasts and leaving me almost naked. His eyes look into mine for a moment before he drops them to my chest. He flinches, biting his lower lip.

"You're beautiful." He glances up at my eyes. "I know you hate hearing that, but it's true."

"I don't hate it," I say. "Not from you."

"Lie down, baby."

I lie back on the bed, sliding my head up to the pillow and watching as Julian joins me, kneeling on either side of my hips. He leans down and kisses me, his lips gentle and tender on mine. He sucks my bottom lip between his and then the upper. He licks the loose seam between my lips, and they open for him, my tongue seeking his as I reach up, threading my fingers through his hair and pulling him closer. Between us, rubbing the valley of my sex through my panties, I can feel his dick, hard and hungry, and I am scared, but I also want this.

His lips skim down my throat to my collarbone, then lower still, to my breasts. I feel his tongue, hot and wet, lick a circle around my left nipple, and I gasp in surprise, though my fingers, still in his hair, press his head to my chest. He kisses the bud of sensitive flesh, laving it with his tongue, sucking it between his lips, and my hips buck off the bed. He moves to my right breast, reaching up with his hand to massage the left, and sucks my right nipple between his lips, licking and sucking until I am whimpering from the sharpness of the sensation.

"Too much?" he mutters, his breath hot on my skin.

"N-no. Just . . . new," I sigh, my voice low and breathy,

He suckles at me again, his fingers toying with the nipple that isn't being loved with his mouth, while his other hand slips over my belly and into the waistband of my panties.

One of his fingers, warm and wet from my nipple, slides between the soft folds of flesh between my legs, finding its mark, and I cry out softly, a sound halfway between a whimper and moan. As he tongues my breast, his finger moves in slow circles, sliding over my aroused, slick skin. My knees rise and my toes curl. My eyes are closed, and I push the back of my head into the pillow. My body is his playground, and he is doing things to it that I never imagined. Even more, my body is responding like it's been waiting for him to touch me like this. Like maybe it's been waiting forever. It knows what it wants, and as my hips start to thrust softly against his hand, I feel a gathering within me. I am holding my breath, the same way I would if I was in the shallows with a massive wave coming straight for me. I hold . . . hold . . . hold . . . and then it breaks, and I gasp, fireworks bursting behind my eyes as my body relaxes into trembles and I fill my lungs. I am shattering under him, off the bed, floating in the stars, only the sound of his low, satisfied rumble of laughter returning me to earth.

"You're . . . laughing at me," I murmur.

"I'm enjoying you," he answers, his voice low and hot, but still tinged with amusement.

"What?" I whisper, realizing that he's sliding my panties down my legs, and further realizing that I am not embarrassed to be lying prone and naked before him. "Why?"

"Because you're so sensitive. Because this is all new for you, which makes it new for me." He spreads my legs, kneeling between them. "Because I bet you taste as sweet as you look."

He dips his head, spreads me with his fingers and tastes me with one slow, long lick.

"Mm-hm. I was right."

My fingers curl into the sheets on either side of my hips as he does to my sex what he did to my nipples. Licking, kissing, and sucking on my tender flesh, he brings me to orgasm number two, but his voice is more taut and less playful than before when he asks me:

"Are you sure you want to have sex, baby?"

I open my eyes to see him reaching over the bed. I hear the jingle of his belt buckle and then the crinkle of plastic. He holds up a condom.

"Do you know what this is?"

Remembering Gus's warning, I giggle. "No glove, no love?"

Julian's eyes widen. "Where did you hear that?"

"Sock that wang before you bang?"

He blinks at me, still holding up the condom. "Where does a nice Catholic schoolgirl learn an expression like that?"

"From a sassy gay man."

"Ah. Gus."

"Gus," I confirm. I lean up on one elbow, feeling bold. I point to the packet in his fingers. "That's a condom."

"I'm clean," he says quickly, out of the blue.

I stare at him. I'm not sure why he feels the need to tell me this, but maybe I should reassure him too.

"I showered earlier."

He looks confused for a second, and then his lips twitch. "No. I mean . . . I don't have any diseases. I don't sleep around."

"Oh." Now my cheeks flush with embarrassment, and I look down at the white sheets, feeling young. "That's good. Me neither."

He lies down beside me and slides his fingers under my chin, forcing me to look at him. "I'm using a condom because I don't want to get you pregnant."

I've been taught that trying to prevent pregnancy when you're married is a sin, but then again, everything I'm doing today is a sin, and besides, Julian and I aren't married. The strangest thing of all, however, is that I don't feel guilty about what we're doing. I don't feel dirty, and I don't feel bad. It feels right, and a rush of peace, of goodness, washes over me like a blessing.

"I'm not ready to be a mom," I say, thinking about Tig. She was only sixteen when she had me, unmarried, unsupported, alone. I want to do things differently. When I have my first child, I want to be ready.

"I'm not ready to be a dad," says Julian, though he's looking at me peculiarly, like maybe he's looking at his future and liking how it looks. "Someday."

"Me too," I say. "Someday."

"I care about you, Ashley" he says, looking into my eyes. "So much."

"I know you do. I feel the same." I lie on my back. "And yes, I'm sure I want to have sex."

He rips open the package with his teeth, then, presumably, puts it on his penis. I don't look. Part of me wants to, but suddenly, even after two orgasms that made me feel like jelly, I'm tense and a little shy. I *want* to do this, but part of me is a little scared too.

He's still kneeling between my legs, but now his head is over mine, and he leans down, kissing my lips. "I'll go as slow as I can."

"Okay."

Bracing one elbow by my ear, he reaches down with his other hand, guiding his erection to the opening of my sex. I feel it there, brushing against me, seeking entrance, but not yet pushing inside.

"It might . . .," Julian pants, "hurt a little."

"I know," I say, gulping nervously as I look up at him. "It's okay."

He starts sliding into me, slowly, gently, and I try to stay relaxed, but the sensation is so new, so different. I feel vulnerable, but not in a bad way. Exposed, but not on display. I am sharing something with him that is only mine to share, and he is taking it as tenderly as he can. I take a deep breath and let it out slowly, willing myself to relax.

Something eases where he is pushing inside me, but something else is blocking his way. I look up and see a bead of sweat break out on his brow. He winces, then drops his lips to mine in a passionate kiss while surging forward into my body, burying himself inside me to the hilt, until his pelvic bone is flush against mine.

I whimper, but his tongue is massaging mine, his hands cradling my face as he kisses me hungrily, desperately, and I realize that his kiss is distracting me from the waves of pain that I felt when he thrust through my virgin barrier.

The pain comes and goes. Comes and goes. Goes.

It's over now. I'm a woman. I'm *his* woman.

"Are you okay?" he asks me, his eyes concerned and soft, dilated to huge black orbs that look heavy, but stay focused on mine.

"I'm okay."

"If anything hurts, tell me to stop," he says, moving his hips away from me and then plunging slowly back inside.

And then I feel something else entirely. That buzzing between my legs is back. But it's so much louder than before. This is different from the way he pleasured me with his fingers and tongue. It's so intimate, it makes me even more emotional, and tears spring to my eyes. I pull him down to me, lacing my fingers behind his neck and kissing him as he thrusts into my body again and again.

When he cries out my name, shuddering and gasping on top of me, I don't orgasm with him. Not physically. But my heart, which he doesn't know I've given to him, hammers to the beat of utter and complete devotion. He looks down at me like I breathe fire into the sun, like the stars are my children and every single one is a miracle.

"*Elle est si belle qu'elle me brise le coeur*," he whispers reverently, rolling to my side and pulling me into the sanctuary of his arms.

As I am falling asleep, my mind repeats these words over and over, and at some point, I remember what he told me about his father's favorite song—the song he listened to after Julian's mother went away.

I remember what the words mean:

She is so beautiful, she breaks my heart.

Day #45 of THE NEW YOU!

Tonight is the two-year anniversary of the first time Anders came to me.

Two years of stolen moments, stolen glances, stolen love.

True love.

It's a miracle that M has never found out.

But then again . . . there's been a shift with him over the past year or so—like he's growing tired of me. He doesn't fuck me anymore. He never complimented me, but he doesn't criticize anymore either. He barely speaks to me and looks at me even less. I can't remember the last time I left this house with him. I'm positive he has a girlfriend in Newark because his appetites are strong and someone's meeting them, but it's not me.

If we weren't married, I'd say we were in the wind-down phase of our relationship, and that any day now, he'd call me to his study, hand me a check for $100,000, tell me that all the clothes and jewelry are mine to keep, and tell me to get lost.

But we are married.

So I don't really know what happens next. For M, that is.

But fuck him.

I know exactly what happens next for me . . .

Anders has purchased a remote island in the Hudson Bay, a thousand miles north of here. He bought it in cash, under a fake name, from the Cree Nation so there's no paper trail. There is a small house on the island. A generator. A boat. And it's ours.

He argued that we should leave as soon as possible, in April, after the thaw, but I won't we leave without my daughter, and Ashley deserves to finish school first. I never got my high school diploma. She has a right to get hers. And my love, my reason for living, he agreed.

He'll be here soon . . . and I can't wait to see him, to touch him, to hold him, to hear more about this beautiful plan he's been putting together for us.

I can't wait to be free to love him, without fear, without looking over my shoulder.

And the kid—Ashley—I'd like to get to know her. I'd like for her to know me now—the person I've become since Anders has been a part of my life. I'm the most stable I've ever been. I'm not on drugs. I'm not all over the place. Now that I am loved—truly loved, for the first time in my life—maybe I'm strong enough to be someone to her. Someone good. Someone who's not a fucking mess.

I'd like for us to be friends. Maybe that's possible now that she's all grown up. Maybe she could find something about me that she could like. I hope so. I really do.

Anders is here.

Teagan

CHAPTER NINETEEN

Ashley

I am lying naked against Julian in the white claw-foot tub in my bathroom, my bare back against his bare front, his arms on the sides of the tub and bubbles covering us like a blanket of clouds. While I slept, he ran the hot water and lit about a hundred votive candles, so the room is warm and soft, bathed in a magical glow that perfectly matches my mood.

The many times I heard Tig in her room having sex, with groans and grunts filtering through the walls, I never imagined that she was experiencing something as beautiful as Julian and I just shared. But then, I doubt she felt about many of those men, if any, the way I feel about Julian. And maybe, I think, that's the difference between the emptiness I always sensed in our LA bungalow and the feeling of wholeness I'm experiencing now.

In one of her recent diary entries, Tig wrote that Anders touched her like she was loved. She said that his tenderness had the power to soothe the horrors of her life, and now—*right now*—I understand what she meant by that, because, hunted as I am by Mosier, I should be terrified, yet I'm not. I feel safe. And soothed. And loved.

It would be absurd for Julian to tell me that he loves me, or for me to answer, *"I love you, too . . . so much that it's bursting inside me every moment I'm with you!"* but it's possible to *feel* loved, even if you're not certain you're actually *in* love. And for me, for now, it's enough.

I also feel a rare sense of fellowship with my mother, over the ages, through time, despite her passing. I imagine her lying against Anders in her bathtub, as I am lying against Julian now, and I am strangely happy that she knew what it was to be loved by someone. At her funeral, I wondered if anyone had truly loved her. Now I have my answer. Anders did. And I am grateful to him for giving her that gift before she died.

"My mother planned to take me away," I say, resting my hands under the water on Julian's thighs as he wraps his arms around me.

"How do you know? She told you?"

I shake my head. "I read it in her diary."

"Where was she going to take you?"

"To a cabin in Canada," I say. "With Mosier's son Anders."

"What?"

His voice is incredulous, and I twist my neck to catch his eyes. "My mother was in love with him. I think he loved her too."

"They had an affair?"

"Yes . . . No . . . It was more than that."

Affair sounds as tawdry and cheap as *hookup* and has no place between my mother and Anders, or me and Julian, for that matter.

"But she was his—"

"Stepmother," I say. "Yes. But she was closer in age to Anders than she was to his father."

"How in the world did they keep it a secret?"

I lean the back of my head against his shoulder and sigh. "I don't know if they did."

"Do you think Răumann found out?" asks Julian.

"I don't know," I say. "It would be a motive for him killing her, and I'm more and more certain he did. Kill her. The same way he induced a heart attack in Father Joseph, I'm positive he injected my mother with enough heroin to kill a horse. Because she was clean, Julian. I swear."

"It *would* be a motive," said Julian.

I think of Anders at the funeral. He didn't have a mark on him.

"No," I murmur, deep in thought.

"No?"

"No. I don't think Mosier found out," I say. "He would've beaten Anders to within an inch of his life if he'd known. Once, a long time ago, he found me swimming with his sons and broke Damon's nose and gave Anders a black eye. If he found out one of them was sleeping with my mother—his *wife*?—Anders would have spent weeks in the intensive care unit. But he was fine. At the funeral, physically he was fine."

"Then why did Răumann kill her?"

At some point the terrible truth must have occurred to me, and I chose not to look at it, not to examine it, not to accept it. But now? Safe as I feel in Julian's arms? I have the strength to admit its truth.

"For me," I whisper, the awfulness of the words making my eyes brim with tears. I am the reason for my mother's death. "He killed her a few weeks after my birthday. Mosier killed Tig to pave the way to me."

"Oh, baby," he whispers, horror thick in his voice. "You don't know that."

"I do," I say, thinking back to the reading of my mother's will. My grandparents weren't surprised about the arrangements and conditions for a life of comfort. Mosier had already spoken to them. He'd planned it all, right down to his visit to my bedroom. In fact, I'd probably already be married to him now if Tig hadn't insisted that my education be completed. "I know. And I also know that I'd be in his clutches now if it wasn't for Tig . . . for my mom."

"How so?"

"She only had one chance to speak publicly from the grave—via her lawyer at the reading of her will. He insisted that it was her final wish for me to finish school. That's the only reason I was allowed to go back to Blessed Virgin. Don't you see? If I hadn't gone back, Father Joseph wouldn't have been able to help me."

Tears slide down my cheeks, and I let them because I am learning that sometimes love isn't in the words we say, but in how we give and what we sacrifice, and in the hundreds of quiet, unsung actions we make on behalf of someone else, someone we care about *more* than ourselves.

"He was right," I say, closing my eyes. "Anders said that she loved me, and I didn't believe him at the time. But now I'm starting to think, well . . . that she did."

"Of course she did," says Julian, dropping his lips to my shoulder. He rests there for a moment, and I close my eyes, taking the comfort he offers me so selflessly, letting it wash over me like a warm breeze.

There is no part of me that expects to hear what he says next.

"It was a woman," he whispers, the words so soft, I almost miss them.

"What?" I murmur, opening my eyes.

"I lost my job over a woman."

The water swishes around us as I face him. "What do you mean?"

His eyes are haunted, and he stares *through* me, but then he blinks, shaking his head like he needs to clear it.

His voice is normal when he says, "I'm sorry. I don't know where that came from. You were talking about your mom."

"I was finished." I'm anxious that he not shy away from this topic now that he's actually broached it. "You said it was a woman—that you lost your job over a woman?"

He sighs. "I didn't mean to say that."

"But you did," I press. I turn my body around so I'm facing him, kneeling in front of him, so I can look squarely into his eyes. "You can trust me, Julian. Tell me what happened. What woman? When?"

He takes a deep breath and holds it, reaching for my shoulders as he exhales. For a moment I think he's going to pull me forward for a kiss, but then I realize that he's moving me back to where I was. He turns me around so that I'm sitting in the V of his spread legs with my back against his front.

"I'll tell you," he says, resting his arms on the sides of the tub. "But it'll be easier like this."

I lean back against him, my head on his shoulder. He turns his head just slightly so that his lips are near my ear.

"I wanted to be in the Secret Service all my life," he begins. "At Halloween the other boys would dress up like zombies and superheroes. I'd put on a black suit, black tie, white shirt, and sunglasses, and place a fake com in my ear." He chuckles softly. "My dad used to have this picture on his desk. It was Noelle on a tricycle and me running behind her in full gear, pretending she was the president and I was part of the motorcade security. I even taped an American flag to her handlebars. She was called Madam President quite a lot in those days."

I smile at his memory, reaching for his hands and putting them on my stomach under my breasts. I keep mine on top of his so we're holding each other.

"I studied criminal justice at Granite State College. I was accepted into the Secret Service program and went down to Georgia for training the August after I graduated. Ten weeks of basic criminal investigation down there and eighteen weeks of special agent training outside DC. By March, I was sworn in as an active agent and assigned to the L Street office in DC. All my instructors called me promising. I was on my way."

"Go on," I say, caressing his hands under the water.

"You have to understand. For most agents, working in the field for a few years is standard. It's investigative work, working with more seasoned agents. Actually it's pretty humdrum stuff, but it's almost like on-the-job training. You learn the culture of the agency, the way things work. You might not get your first protective assignment for years. You *shouldn't* get your first protective assignment for years. I learned that the hard way." He takes a deep breath and pulls his hands away. "Are you getting cold? The water's cooling off."

"I can add some hot," I say.

"Nah," he answers. "Let's go back to bed, huh?" As he pushes me away gently, I feel him stand up behind me and hear him step out of the tub. His hand appears before my face, and I take it, letting him help me out of the deep tub. He smiles down at me in the candlelight, his eyes tender but sad. "You're so beautiful, Ash."

I let my eyes trail down his glistening body—the muscles of his chest, the deep V of muscle that leads to his penis, and his long, strong legs. When I look back up at him, I smile back. "You are too."

"Make love to me," he says, his hands landing on my hips. He pulls me closer so that my breasts press against his chest and his growing erection pulses against the triangle of soft, blonde curly hair between my legs.

I lean back. "Tell me the rest first."

He groans, letting me go. Reaching over my head for two fluffy white towels, he hands me one, then wraps the other around his waist, tucking the loose end in.

"Come on, then," he says, taking my hand as I secure my own towel under my arms. "You sit. I'll light the fire, okay?"

I sit down on the couch, curling up in a corner and watching the muscles in his back ripple as he leans down, removes the screen, and strikes a match to the newspaper under the grate. It catches quickly as he starts talking again.

"Typhoid is spread through contaminated food so agents on assignment in South America are not supposed to eat the same things at the same place, but in May, two months after I finished training, typhoid ran through a detail of agents in Cartagena, just before the VP was supposed to arrive on a diplomatic visit. Eight agents down at once. They called the DC field office in a panic, and eight guys were sent down. Among them? Me. How? Because the guy I was assigned to work with—Javier Fuentes—was fluent in Spanish. He was chosen to go down there right away and decided I should go too. He said it would be a great experience for me. He essentially got me on the transport at the last minute.

"I had stars in my eyes. I mean, I was probably two years out from an international posting and four more from a protective detail. And there I was, going down to Colombia with guys way more experienced than me. I was hot shit that day. I was on top of the world."

He stops poking at the fire and turns to look at me. "Move over."

I do, and he takes my place in the corner of the couch, resting his legs on the coffee table and pulling me back against his chest. He kisses the top of my head. "I had no business being down there."

"For the record?" I say, snuggling against him as he takes a blanket off the back of the couch and pulls it over us. "I think you're still pretty hot shit."

"Is that right?"

"Absolutely."

"I want to fuck you, Ash," he murmurs, biting on my earlobe.

"Then finish your story," I say, a thrill shooting through me from the combination of his dirty mouth and sharp teeth.

"Okay. So there I am in Cartagena, the youngest agent by far. I've never been out of the country. Hell, I've only been an agent for two months. Honestly I didn't know what the fuck I was doing." He huffs out a breath. "There's no field office in Cartagena—the only one in Colombia is in Bogotá—so we check into the hotel and meet the security detail, mostly made up of Marines assigned to the veep's visit. We go over the agenda in the hotel conference room, but the meeting breaks up by eight. I assume we're all going to get a good night's sleep, but one of the Marines is old friends with Javi, and they start talking about this club we need to go to.

"And I realize that we're *all* going. And hell, I'm twenty-one, and the women there were crazy beautiful, and sure, yeah, I was up for some liquor and dancing. Why not?

"We get to the club, and it's dark and loud, and the whiskey starts flowing. I'm hammered two hours later, and I see Javi and this other agent, Mark, talking to these two girls at a table. Then I notice there's one more woman at the table, but her eyes are down. She's dressed like the other two, but she's not talking, not touching her drink. And you know—God, I was so stupid—I thought she looked young. I thought she looked . . . lost.

"Javi waves me over, so I sidle up next to this girl, using my high school Spanish . . ."

I clear my throat, surprised by the sharp surge of jealousy I experience. "Feel free to skim over the details of this part . . ."

He chuckles softly. "I didn't sleep with her."

"Oh," I sigh, feeling relieved.

"But I wanted to."

"*Exactly* the sort of detail you're welcome to skim over," I say.

"I hang out with the guys for a while, but I'm

looking at her, and she's stealing glances at me, and fuck, but here I am: I'm a goddamned Secret Service agent, and I'll be guarding the VP tomorrow while he tours Cartagena. I'm on top of the world. I've made it. I'm thinking, if this goes well, it could fast-track my whole career. I'd be a legend. And this girl was so pretty, I just . . . I just . . ."

"What?" I whisper.

"I never even saw it coming," he says. "Talk about stupid."

"Not stupid," I insist, grabbing his forearm and pulling it across my chest. I rest my fingers on the wiry hairs that dot his skin. "Inexperienced. Maybe cocky. But not stupid."

"You haven't heard the rest."

"Doesn't matter," I say. "Whatever it is, it won't change the fact that you shouldn't have been in that situation. You weren't ready. Whatever happened wasn't your fault alone."

"Hmm," he hums. "You might think differently when I finish. My superiors sure did."

I know I won't, but I don't say so.

"So the six of us are walking back to the hotel, with Magdalena and I bringing up the rear, and I realize that the other two girls are prostitutes negotiating their price for the night. I look down at Magdalena and notice her wiping at her eyes, and I tell her that I don't expect anything of her. I tell Javi and Mark to go ahead, that we'll see them at the hotel in a little bit, and Magdalena and I sit down on a bench. She's still crying, talking to me in Spanish, and I make out that her father is sick. She doesn't want to be a *puta*, a whore. She tells me that this is her first night out, and she's terrified. I tell her she's not a *puta*. She hasn't done anything yet.

She's crying about medicine and her father, and I ask her how much money she needs. She tells me that a hundred dollars will buy the medicine her father needs, and I have that in U.S. dollars, but I have it back in my hotel room safe. I tell her that I'll give her the money; she doesn't have to do anything to earn it. I just want to help her. And so we start walking back to the hotel."

"You were just going to give her the money?"

"For one hundred dollars, I thought I could save his life," Julian explains. "My dad . . . I mean, my dad had died the year before, and I would've done anything to save him. I couldn't say no to her."

"Julian," I murmur, holding his arm tightly, knowing that this is the sort of man I am falling in love with: one who gives selflessly, who's blinded by the need to protect others, even at the expense of his own safety, and the tenderness I feel for him is . . . overwhelming.

"Pretty stupid, huh?"

"Not stupid," I insist, turning in his arms to look at him. "Not at all." I lean up and press my lips to his. "You're the best man I've ever known."

He kisses me back, his tongue swiping against mine, his lips hot and hungry. My towel slips a little, and my breasts, now warm and dry, press against his bare chest, and I sigh from the contact. I want him to finish talking. I want to go back to bed. I want him to fuck me like he suggested a few minutes ago.

"Finish up," I say, though I think I know where this story is going. It explains why he didn't want me here, why he fought against his initial feelings for me. Once upon a time, a woman who appeared vulnerable and in trouble was his Achilles' heel.

"We got back to my room, and I opened the safe

while she poured us two drinks. That should have been my clue. That should have told me that something was off. A girl like her? Who claimed she *wasn't* a prostitute? Why was she suddenly making drinks? Making herself comfortable in my room? The girl I *thought* she was wouldn't have made me a drink. She would have waited for me in the hallway, thanked me for the money, and left as soon as she had it. But I was still a little drunk . . . and maybe part of me even hoped that by helping her so gallantly, there'd be something in it for me."

"Was there?" I ask.

"No." He looks down at me, shaking his head. "I remember giving her the money and throwing back the drink. She suggested we sit on the bed and talk. All I heard was the word *bed.* After that . . . I can't remember anything. Still. To this day."

"She drugged you."

He nods. "And cleaned out my safe. My money. My passport. My weapon. My badge. My phone. My laptop. And most importantly, a printout of the VP's itinerary. Where he was staying, where he was going, who he was meeting with. Everything."

"Oh, God."

"Yeah. When I woke up a few hours later and realized what had happened, I ran down the hall and banged on Javi's door. Magdalena's friend had cleaned out his wallet, but not his safe, which he'd kept locked while she was in his room. I had to . . . I had to tell him what happened. Oh, my God, that was bad. He was pissed. Like, he couldn't believe it, and . . ."

"And what?"

"They had to cancel the vice president's visit to Colombia." He pauses, then adds, "I was sent home on a commercial flight. When I got to DC, I was fired."

"I'm sorry," I say, my heart breaking for him. "I'm so, so sorry."

"I was stupid. I was so stupid to think that she was some foundling waif who needed my help. I mean, how could I be so goddamned stupid? And of course it got out that Secret Service agents were sleeping with prostitutes at a hotel paid for by the American taxpayers. Guys like Javi and Mark—I mean, they had big careers, you know?—were put on probation. The head of the agency was replaced. A lot of shit went down. But it all started with me."

"You're *not* stupid," I say, reaching up to cup his cheeks. He doesn't look at me, his long eyelashes shielding his eyes from my view. "Julian, look at me. Please."

When he looks up, his expression is grim. Sad. Hurt. Ashamed.

"I killed my dream, Ash. In one night, I killed it."

My eyes water as I shake my head. "No, you didn't. *She* killed it. You were just trying to be kind."

He blinks, his Adam's apple bobbing as he drops my eyes. "Doesn't matter. I lost my job. I embarrassed the agency. I can never show my face in Washington again."

"It wasn't on my list of places to visit anyway," I say, leaning forward and pressing my lips to his. I kiss his lips, then the tip of his nose, the lids of his eyes, and his forehead. "And besides, if you hadn't been here, who would keep me safe? Who would protect me? Who would save my life?"

He lifts his head, and his eyes meet mine. His expression is inscrutable, and I think about what I've just said, how selfish it was.

"Not that . . . not that protecting me is worth losing your job. I didn't mean that. I didn't mean to say that . . ."

He reaches for me, lifting me onto his lap. His towel has come loose, and as he moves me, mine slips away as well. I lean forward, then settle back onto him, sliding my body onto his waiting erection and whimpering softly as I am impaled to the hilt.

"It's okay," he murmurs, his breath shallow and quick. "For the first time . . . since it happened . . . I'm glad."

I place my hands on his shoulders and arch my back, sliding against him as he clutches my hips.

"Thank you . . . for telling me," I say as he thrusts up, his throbbing sex filling me to bursting.

"Thank you . . . for giving me a chance . . . to keep you safe," he says, panting between his words, his eyes holding mine with blistering intensity.

"Thank you . . . thank you . . . thank you . . .," I murmur in a whispered litany. I close my eyes and hang on as he hammers into my body, his hot, silken skin mating with mine.

I feel the building passion between us, the gathering, the hot, sweet culmination of our union quickening until I am barely hanging on, and when he leans forward, razing my throat with his teeth, I realize that he's been saying a litany of his own:

"Ashley . . . Ashley . . . Ashley . . ." He whispers my name with reverence, like it is a holy word, like it is sacred, like it is his only prayer.

We orgasm together this time, and after the wave of pleasure crashes over us, leaving us clinging to each other in the soft glow of firelight, replete and exhausted, Julian rests his head on my shoulder.

Holding me tightly against him, he whispers, "Ashley . . . you're safe."

And deep in my heart, where I am falling in love with him, I know that it's true.

Yes, I am.

I am safe with you.

***

Julian

Last weekend, when Ashley and I were in the tub and making love before the fire, when I shared my greatest shame with her, and she offered me absolution, I found new meaning in the path my life has taken.

And since then, I look at what happened in Cartagena not as a disgrace, but as a means to an end I would have chosen, given the chance. It got me here, to her. And for the first time since it happened, I am grateful for an episode of my life that I expected would always be painful.

Without my work space available to me, this week has been one long vacation, and we have treated it as such.

We take long walks, hand in hand, to the pond.

We watch movies in French, curled up together on my bed, with Bruno at our feet.

We eat delicious dinners that Ashley makes for us, flirting with each other over candlelight and swapping stories about our lives.

We make love everywhere: in my bed, in hers, in my shower, in her tub, in front of the fireplace, and under the stars.

We ignore the fact that our time is finite . . . that Răumann's arrival to take his bait means that these precious days will soon be over. Probably forever.

I try to enjoy every moment with her—to memorize her smiles and the way she says my name. I stare deeply into her eyes when she comes. I hold her close to me as we sleep.

If I think about her leaving, I will go crazy.

So I don't.

And she doesn't bring it up.

We are living in a fairytale world, my love and me.

But the day will come when, like a fragile piece of glass dropped to the ground, our world will shatter around us. Until then, we steal our piece of heaven, quietly hoping that the strength of our growing love can trounce the hounds of hell, knowing all the while that it can't.

Nothing can hold back what is coming.

The knock on the front door is urgent, and Ashley, who is lying beside me in bed, sits up and looks at me.

"Who's there?"

"Probably Simmons," I say, reaching forward to pause our movie and tuck my gun in the back of my jeans. "I'll go see."

"I'm coming too," she says, straightening her shirt. When she lies beside me, I like to push her shirt up and rest my palm on the warm, soft skin of her belly. I think she likes it too.

I kiss her quickly before slipping out of my room, just in time to hear another bang at the door.

"Coming!"

Sure enough, Simmons is standing on the front porch, and man, I hate the look on his face. I hate it so much, I can barely force myself to unlock and open the front door and screen. When I do, he rushes inside.

"It happened," he says, looking back and forth

between me and Ashley. "The gallery in Shelburne was broken into tonight."

"When?" asks Ashley.

"Half an hour ago. Three men in ski masks. They ransacked the place."

"You saw it?" I ask. "On the monitor?"

Simmons nods. "Yeah. Wasn't pretty either. They trashed the place. And one of them spent a long time at Gus's desk. He found the address. I watched him write it down, then make a call on his cell."

Ashley gasps and takes a step back. "They're coming."

I put my arm around her. "It's okay, baby."

"No, *baby*," says Simmons, giving me a look, "it's *not* okay."

"Don't be a dick," I mutter.

"Then try being realistic," he suggests.

"Did you call the police?" I ask.

Simmons nodded. "Yeah, but they used the siren, of course. It's the Keystone Kops in these little towns. Răumann's guys peeled away from the curb before the police arrived. But more's the better. I didn't actually want them caught. I just wanted Jock and Gus to have a police report for the insurance claim."

"So?" I say. "What's your best guess on Răumann showing up here?"

"Could be later tonight. Could be tomorrow. Could be a week from now. I have no clue."

"What's your instinct?"

"By tomorrow," says Simmons with a heavy sigh. "I called the field office in Albany. They're sending backup."

"When'll they get here?"

"They've got to assign someone. Plus, it's a three-hour ride from there to here."

"But you said it was urgent, right?"

"I asked for backup," says Simmons, looking annoyed. "I can't control when it gets here."

"What about local police?" I ask. "You want to alert them?"

"They know I'm here," says Simmons, "but this is a sensitive operation. The less they know, the better." He lifts a finger and pantomimes a siren, crooning, "*Whoo whoo whoo.*"

This fucking guy.

"What's next?" I ask.

"Don't go to sleep tonight." He takes a walkie-talkie from his belt loop and hands it to me. "Keep this with you. I'll radio if someone's coming up the driveway."

"What about me?" asks Ashley.

"You're the bait," says Simmons. "Do what you always do. When the doorbell rings, *you* answer it. Ducharmes, you cover her from the living room. I've got the barn. We'll flank them."

"And it'll be okay?" asks Ashley.

"Hope so," says Simmons at the same time I cry, "Yes!"

Simmons rolls his eyes, and I'm starting to wonder if that ring on his finger is just a fucking prop. What if it was *his* wife in danger? Would he be this much of a fucking asshole?

"Yes," I say again, squeezing her gently, "it'll all be okay."

I'll keep you safe, baby. I promise. I promise on my life.

"I'll be in touch," says Simmons, stepping back out onto the porch just as a pair of headlights brightens the driveway.

CHAPTER TWENTY

Ashley

Agent Simmons steps back into the house and switches off the lights in the living room.

"Car coming. Shit. Sooner than I thought." He pats his chest, but his holster's empty. We can hear Bruno barking from the barn. "Dog's locked up and I left my gun in the barn. I'll go out the kitchen door and sneak back over there. Ashley, you open the door. We won't let him take you. We'll intervene before it gets to that. Julian, you good?"

"I'm fine," he says, but his eyes are wide and worried when he shifts them to me. "You're going to do great, baby. I'll be just inside the door. I won't let anything happen to you."

My racing heart makes me feel light-headed. I'm not ready to come face-to-face with Mosier.

"Okay," I say. "I'll just . . ."

The car pulls into the driveway and parks in front of the house.

Julian pulls me into his arms and kisses me hard.

"Be strong. It'll be okay. I'm right behind you."

Then he steps to the side of the door so he'll be hidden when I open it.

I hear footsteps on the stairs. Three more to the door.

Knock, knock.

I close my eyes and take a deep breath, counting from five. Five . . . four . . . three . . . two . . .

Knock, knock.

"Coming!" I call.

I dart a glance a Julian, who has his gun drawn, standing against the wall behind the door. He nods at me.

Be with me, Tig. Please be with me, Mam.

I reach for the lock and turn it, then twist the doorknob, opening the door. There is a screen between us, but it's unlocked from Agent Simmons's visit.

And there he is. My stepfather.

Dressed in a dark suit and a white dress shirt, open at the neck, he reeks of aftershave and cigar smoke, his jet-black hair slicked back from his ugly face. A shudder slides through my body and across my arms over my chest.

"*Cenușă*," says Mosier, his eyes dark and angry, his lips tilting up into a humorless smile. "Surprise."

"*Frate*," I say, gulping softly. "How . . . how did you find me?"

"*Frate*?" He chuckles like something is funny. "No, no, no. Don't you mean . . . *Daddy*?"

I stare at him, realizing that this is information he could only have gotten from Father Joseph, and it squeezes my heart.

"You saw Father Joseph," I whisper.

"Poor man. I heard he passed away. Heart attack,

yes?"
"Yes."

"Old men die. It happens."

"Especially when they come into contact with you," I say, willing myself not to cry.

"*Cenușă*, my darling . . . he told me lies about your dear sister." He grins. "Such lies about my beloved wife."

"What lies?"

"He told me that she had a baby eighteen years ago. A little girl she passed off as her sister."

I lift my chin. "It's true. She was my mother."

"Her name is not on your birth certificate."

"My grandmother wouldn't let her claim me."

"Ah, yes. Your . . . grandmother, who is now happily living far away across the sea. There's no one to corroborate your story, *cenușă*."

"It's the truth!" I cry. "You . . . you *can't* marry me, Mosier. I'm your stepdaughter."

His faces changes from amusement to anger in an instant.

"I don't care if you're my daughter by blood, you pious little bitch," he spits. "You're *still* going to be my wife."

He reaches for the screen door handle, but before he can come inside, I push it open and sidestep out onto the porch. I look over his shoulder and see Anders standing in the driveway, at the foot of the steps. My eyes meet his, and he flinches.

All my life I've been told I look like her, but I've never felt it more strongly than now, face-to-face with my dead mother's lover.

Finally—maybe when he can't stand it anymore—

Anders looks away.

"Where's Damon?" I ask.

Mosier doesn't leave his house without Damon, his second-in-command.

"He's dealing with your fucking fed," says Mosier, flicking his eyes down my T-shirt and jeans and then back up to my face. He looks over my shoulder at the dark living room. "Once he's dead, I think I'll fuck you here. Tonight. Bareback. See if we can't get our family started sooner than later, eh, *cenușă*?"

My skin crawls, and I inch closer to the steps, to Anders. Leaning against the railing, I remind myself that just inside the front door, Julian has a gun. He won't let me be taken.

"I don't *have* a fed," I say, but a second later, I'm startled by gunfire coming from the barn. Two shots are fired, and I gasp, waiting to see who walks out of the barn: Damon or Simmons.

The barn door swings open, and at first I'm relieved, because I see Agent Simmons . . . but then I realize that his hands are laced behind his head and he's followed by Damon, who holds a gun to his back. There's a dark spot on Simmons's shoulder and it's widening and dripping. He's been shot.

"Good work, son!" yells Mosier.

"I knocked out the dog. What do you want me to do with *him*?"

"Bring him here," says Mosier, staring at me. "Maybe *cenușă* needs a reminder of how we handle men who dare to look at our women."

Simmons crosses the driveway, his eyes on mine telegraphing nothing. He must be in pain, but his face is expressionless. Maybe he's frightened. I certainly am. Nothing is going according to plan. How is Julian supposed to take on three men?

"He didn't look at me," I say, thinking fast. "He stayed in the barn. He was only there to protect me."

Simmons stops in front of the car, head down.

"*Protect* you? Then he's worthless," says Mosier, darting a glance at Damon. "Fuck him up."

I watch as Damon takes the butt of his gun and slams it into Simmons's temple. He gasps in pain, falling to his knees. Damon takes that opportunity to kick Simmons in the stomach, over and over. He takes the blows without a sound, lying on the ground, protecting himself by curling into a fetal position.

Damon pauses, running a hand through his dark hair, which is mussed from his exertions. "More?"

"Eh," says Mosier, flicking his fingers. "He's not screaming. It's better when they scream." He sighs, then turns to me. "You know who was a hell of a screamer? Your sister. Ah, forgive me. Your fucking tramp mother. She screamed like a fucking champion."

My stomach flips over as I remember the sound of her screams coming from his study.

I sneer at him. "You are a monster."

He reaches out and grabs me by the back of the neck. "I will be your fucking husband, and you will be respectful."

"No!" I cry. "Fuck you!"

"Ahhh, listen to that dirty mouth! The apple don't fall so far from the tree, eh? *Cum e mamă, e și fiică.*" He pulls my face to his and licks my cheek slowly, starting at my jawline and stopping at my forehead. He whispers close to my ear. "I'm going to make you scream too."

I struggle, but his grip is strong, and he keeps my face close to his.

"Your mama was one stupid bitch." He laughs, his

fingers pulling my hair, hurting. "She came out to New York, thinking I was going to make her life easy. She could take her drugs and do her stupid shit and, well, well, well, it didn't work out like that, did it? The dumb cunt. I only wanted her for you."

Out of the corner of my eye, I can see Anders. He's staring at the porch steps, his jaw twitching in anger as his father talks about Tig.

"I used to dream of you while I was fucking her," continues Mosier. "Ashley. Ashley, I'd think. One day, I'm gonna pump you with my cum and watch your belly grow huge. I'm gonna fuck you while your tits are full of milk. I'm gonna use you like a fucking cow."

His words are so repulsive, I swallow back a mouthful of vomit.

I flick a glance at Anders, then back at Mosier. "She fucking hated you."

"Oh, yeah? Well, guess what. I don't give a shit," he says. "Good screamer, though. Real good screamer."

"Did she scream when you killed her?" I demand as tears stream down my face.

"Ha! You got some spirit now, eh?" he says, his voice both admiring and disgusted. "Tsk, tsk, little beauty. That won't work for me. I'll have to beat that out of you, *cenușă*. I raised you the way I want you. Pure. Dutiful. Ready to fuck whenever I want you."

"Admit it," I sob. I fist my fingers at my sides and scream at him. "Admit you fucking killed her!"

He leans close to me. So close, I can smell the cigar he smoked in the car on the way up here. "She didn't scream when I put the needle in her arm. She was fucking quiet. For once."

My head falls forward, my shoulders shaking with

the force of my sobs. "I'm sorry, Tig. I'm so sorry."

"What are *you* sorry for? I was done with that dumb fucking cunt. I was ready for—"

A gunshot rings out, and Mosier lurches back. I stumble as he falls to the porch floor. His hand on my neck loosens, and I scramble to my feet again just as Julian bursts out of the house and grabs my arm, pulling me behind him.

"Ash! What happened?"

I stare at Anders, who stands at the bottom of the steps, the gun in his hand lightly smoking.

"Anders!" I gasp.

Julian points his gun at my stepbrother, who drops his piece to the ground.

"He fucking killed her," says Anders softly, as though in a trance. "He killed her."

"What the *fuck*, Anders?" screams Damon, forgetting about Simmons, who is still lying in a heap on the gravel. "You shot him! You shot our *father*, you crazy bastard!"

"But . . ." A dazed Anders turns to his brother. "He killed her, Damon. He killed Tig."

"Who gives a shit? I don't fucking care!"

"You *should* care!" screams Anders. "You should fucking—"

Another gunshot interrupts the brothers, and I watch in horror as Anders stumbles backward, a large bloody spot marring the crisp light blue of his dress shirt. He reaches up to his heart, then pulls his hand away, staring at the blood as he collapses to the ground.

"Anders! *No!*" Damon falls to the ground beside his twin. "Fuck. Oh, Jesus. Fuck! No!"

At my feet, Mosier is holding a gun. In a low, breathy voice, he says, "She was mine. Mine to fuck.

Mine to . . ."

Whether he passes out or dies, I'm not sure, but Julian pushes me to the side, kicking Mosier's gun out of reach and training his own on my stepfather. Mosier's chest doesn't rise or fall. I think he's dead. I think he used his last second alive to kill his child, and I'm filled with such bleakness for this twisted family, I'm weak.

Agent Simmons staggers to his feet and takes off in the direction of the barn while Damon cradles his brother's head in his lap, crying.

I rush down the stairs, toward my stepbrothers, and Damon looks up at me, his cheeks wet and glistening in the moonlight. "Do s-something, Ashley. H-Help me. Help *him*!"

I kneel down on Anders's other side, looking into his face, into his eyes, which he's fighting to keep open. He looks at me, his face softening, relaxing.

"Teagan," he says softly and slowly, his lips tilting up into a smile.

"It's . . . Ashley," I sob.

"Ashley . . .," he sighs, his smile fading. "You're safe now . . . kid."

"Anders," I say through tears. "She loved you. She loved you so much."

"I . . . loved her," he says, his voice threadier by the second.

"You can't leave me!" says Damon, his tears falling onto his brother's dying face. "Please, Anders! Stay with me! *Stay with me!*"

"Help's coming," says Simmons, running from the barn. "An ambulance is on the way."

I hear Julian ask about Bruno and feel a small, short-lived burst of relief when Simmons says he'll be okay. The agent reaches down and grabs Damon's gun. "I'm taking your weapon, son."

"I don't want it," murmurs Damon, his attention focused on his twin.

"You'll . . . be . . . okay," says Anders to his brother, his voice a whisper now. "Go home. Leave . . . America and go . . . home." His eyes, barely able to focus, look up at the starry Vermont sky. "She's safe . . . Tea . . . gan. She's . . . free." He wheezes softly, a dying gasp. "I love you . . . I'm coming . . ."

Damon reaches under Anders's shoulders, pulling his brother onto his lap and rocking him. Through tears of disbelief and agony, he sings a haunting lullaby: *"Hai Luluțu, dormi un picu' . . . Dragul mamii, puiuț micu' . . ."*

On the porch, Julian keeps his gun trained on Mosier's lifeless body.

In the driveway, Damon sings softly as his twin brother passes from this life to the next.

And in the distance, I can hear sirens, coming closer and closer.

She's safe, Teagan. She's free.

"Thank you, Mam," I breathe, looking up at the heavens, where Tig and Anders are finally together. "Thank you."

Day #50 of THE NEW YOU!

We are leaving tomorrow.

It's a month earlier than I wanted.

I wanted Ashley to finish high school. But Anders insists that tomorrow—when M and Damon leave for their weekly trip to Newark—must be the day. And after learning what he knows, I agree. We need to get the fuck out of here because if Anders's suspicions are correct, M has been making plans. Plans I knew nothing about. Plans that I must stop.

Anders told me that just after Easter his father started acting strange—saying things about me, about Ashley, about how one sister is just as good as another. For a while now, I've felt the distance between me and M. I've felt him pulling away from me. I've wondered what happens in a marriage likes ours, when a husband like M decides he's done with a wife like me.

Is it possible that he means to replace me with Ash?

Divorce me and marry her?

HELL NO.

FUCK NO.

NEVER.

I'd die first.

He can't have her. No. Never. Fuck. Fuck. Fuck. I didn't see this coming. I didn't know that this was his plan. Maybe it was even his plan all along. It makes me sick to think about my baby ending up with him. It makes me want to kill him.

Thank God for Anders. He has a plan.

He's given me ex-lax to put in Grosavu's morning tea. The amount I'm going to give her will keep her shitting for hours.

An hour after M and D leave the house, Anders and I will leave too.

Forever.

The plan is for me to dress warmly and take nothing. I will sneak into the garage and get into Anders's car, behind the passenger seat, under a black tarp he'll leave on the floor.

When he leaves for Albany as usual, it won't appear that anyone or anything is in the back of the car. Nothing will appear amiss as he drives out the front gate, waving good-bye—FOR-fucking-EVER—to M's dogs.

I'm staying under the tarp the whole way to Ashley's school. Anders will sign her out for a dentist appointment and she'll get into the car.

Anders has three fake passports for the Cerne family. I am Marie Cerne. Ashley is Pauline. Anders is Jacques. We are three siblings from Vermont, visiting family in Montreal.

And then? And then? (Oh, my God . . . I can barely write because my hand is shaking. We are so close. We are so fucking close to happiness, to freedom.)

We'll drive north. To the ends of the earth. So far north that no one will ever find us again.

On an island of our own, in the coldest place in the world, we will keep each other warm.

Far, far away from this terrible place, we will keep each other safe.

Me and my love and my kid.

A woman who loves a man.

A man who loves a woman.

A mother who loves—who, in her own fucked-up way, has

always loved—her daughter.

And for the rest of this sweet life, I'll be free.
I'll finally be free.

Someone is coming . . . .Shit . . .

EPILOGUE

Ashley

I close my mother's diary, but hold it in my lap, shutting my eyes and turning my face to the late-afternoon sun, which warms my cheeks. This spot on the back porch is still my favorite place to relax, and Tig's journal, especially the last few chapters, is my favorite thing to read.

A mother who has always *loved her daughter.*

Until I read those words, I didn't realize how badly I needed them. And now that I have them, I grieve her loss in a different way. But I also celebrate the mother I never knew I had. She loved me. She didn't know Mosier's plans for me, and she would have given her life to stop them. There is such peace in knowing that—in knowing that my mother loved me.

A cold breeze picks up from the north, and I open my eyes, wondering what life would have been like for her on the little island Anders had purchased for their new life together.

Julian drove me up there a few weeks ago, just to see it. We took a boat from Waskaganish to the small island, and as the cold wind whipped my hair, I spoke to Tig, telling her she would have been happy there, wishing she'd made it.

I still don't know *exactly* how she died, if she knew what was happening, and what she was thinking as she slipped away. The specific details of her death died with Mosier, but that night—the night of her last diary entry when she wrote that someone was coming—was him getting rid of her. I imagine her shoving the diary under the mattress and pretending to be asleep. My hope is that he used a small needle that didn't hurt and that she died quickly and without pain. I think of her journal—under the mattress where she breathed her last—filled with hope, filled with second chances, filled with love, filled with sweet dreams for a life she'd never get to live.

My heart bleeds when I think of how close she came to escaping him.

I take a deep breath of the crisp fall air and sigh.

Thinking about it will only make me sad. And I don't want to be sad. By finding her diary, she was returned to me. Finding out that she loved and protected me in her own way has given me more quiet contentment than I've ever known.

I can smell a fire in the distance—burning leaves, like a campfire—and it makes me smile.

It's pumpkin season.

Apple season.

Thanksgiving is coming, and Noelle, Gus, and Jock will be spending it here with us. Sometimes I remember that spring evening when Gus and I set the table for dinner while Jock, Noelle, and Julian played cornhole on the lawn nearby. I remember wishing that we five could be a family. I can still feel that longing in my heart some days . . . and then I remind myself that dreams can come true. Gus isn't the only man with a Prince Charming. I have one too.

When Julian drove me to New Paltz to visit the grave of Father Joseph two weeks after the shoot-out at the farmhouse, he said he wanted to talk to me on the ride home. I stressed out about that, wondering what was on his mind, wondering if our relationship was coming to an end. Realistically speaking, we'd only been together for a few weeks, and under duress. Now that Mosier and Anders were dead, and Damon had been extradited to Bucharest to answer for the Răumann family's crimes in Eastern Europe, I didn't need Julian's protection anymore. My mother's jewelry fetched a decent price at auction, leaving me solvent. Maybe he wanted to tell me that it was time for us to go our separate ways.

But that wasn't what happened.

As we drove up the New York State Thruway toward home, he took a deep breath, and said, "You have your whole life ahead of you now, Ashley."

I gulped and nodded, bracing myself for his rejection—for him to set me free, even though the only freedom I craved included the space and permission to love him.

"I just . . . I just wanted to say that if you choose to go . . . if you're ready to move on, I won't stop you."

"You won't?"

"No. I don't have the right to keep you with me if you want to be free."

I turned to him, staring at his handsome profile. "You don't love me?"

He took a deep breath, his voice lowering with emotion. "I love you with everything I am. That's why

I'd never stand in your way. You don't owe me anything, baby. It's *your* life. Whatever comes next, it's *your* choice."

"What if I want to stay with you? What if I want to live my life with you?"

His Adam's apple bobbed, a giveaway that he was nervous. When he spoke, his voice was raspy, like he was desperately trying to stay calm and reserved. "That would be your choice too."

It was glorious on one hand, to make a major life decision for myself . . . but maddening on the other, because I didn't want to stay unless he wanted me with him. I didn't want to impose myself on him. For the first time in my life, I was free. I needed to be somewhere that I was *wanted.*

"Julian," I said. "What do *you* want?"

He jerked the steering wheel, the tires shrieking as he skidded onto the side of the highway. After putting the car in park, he turned to look at me.

"What do you *think* I want?" he demanded, his voice thick with emotion. "But I was fired from my job. I failed at it. I rent a house in the middle of nowhere. I blow glass for a pretty pitiful living. I'm not good enough for you, Ashley. I'm not—"

"Stop. Please stop telling me why I shouldn't want you. It hurts."

"I'm just trying to say that . . . you can do better than me."

"No," I said softly, "I can't."

And finally—*finally*—I saw it in his face, at the way he was looking at me like something so beloved, he'd give it up rather than trap it. *He loves me, and I am wanted.*

"I love it that you make beautiful things," I told him, turning his words around. "I love the house that we share. I don't need you to support me—I just need you to love me. I need you to let me love you."

"Are you sure?" he asked me, his hands clenching and unclenching the wheel.

"All I want," I said, reaching over to take his hands in mine, "is the life we have together. I don't know how it'll look a month from now, or a year from now, or five years from now. I don't even know who I'll *be* five years from now. But right here, right now, all I want . . . is you."

He unbuckled his seat belt and mine and pulled me into his arms. "Thank God, thank God, thank God," he whispered over and over again until his lips found mine, and we made out on the side of the highway. Finally Bruno started barking, telling us he was impatient to go home.

Home.

Gus and Jock have rented this house to us on a five-year lease with an annual fee that covers the taxes and nothing else. It's ours, Jock told us, for as long as we want to live here together. *It's our home, mine and Julian's,* I think as the timer on the kitchen buzzes.

I place Tig's journal on the table beside my chair and head inside to take my pies out of the oven.

Blessed Virgin sent me my diploma in June. Two months ago, in September, I enrolled at the New England Culinary Institute in Montpelier, where I attend college-level classes three days a week.

One of my favorite things to do is experiment at home. Today's bounty includes a pumpkin spice pie with a lattice top and an apple–raisin pie with an oatmeal crust. Sometimes I even make baked goods for Jock and Gus to sell at the gallery. Between Julian's ornaments and my muffins, we're going to take over the place. Noelle, with her sharp business acumen, approves.

"Is that pumpkin pie I smell?"

I turn around and feel it—as I always do—in me, around me, and through me . . . how much I love this man standing behind me.

"For later," I say, turning to face him.

His arms are covered with diamonds, and his eyes are soft with love for me.

As his hands land on my waist, he drops his lips to mine, but our kiss is short-lived as Bruno sandwiches himself between us.

"I think someone wants a walk," says Julian with a chuckle. "Come with us?"

"Of course."

As the porch door swings shut behind us and we leave the spicy smell of waiting pies behind, I lace my fingers through Julian's and think of how sweet life can be when you are loved, when you are wanted, when you are safe.

I squeeze his hand and hold on tight.

My sweet life is just beginning.

THE END

A LETTER FROM KATY

Dear Reader,

Since my first modern fairytale, I have always donated part of my royalties to a nonprofit organization that could benefit from a little extra money.

YEAR	TITLE	BENEFICIARY
2014	*The Vixen and the Vet*	UCLA Operation Mend
2015	*Never Let You Go*	Operation Underground Railroad
2016	*Ginger's Heart*	The Ridgefield, Connecticut, Fire Department
2016	*Dark Sexy Knight*	The Prospector Theater
2017	*Don't Speak*	P.E.O. International
2017	*Shear Heaven*	Locks of Love

I am proud to announce that 5% of the gross profits of e-book and paperback sales of *Fragments of Ash*, for purchases made before and throughout October 2018, will be donated to the Women's Center of Greater Danbury.

From their website:

Each year, the Center serves over 20,000 individuals from our area communities. Our free and confidential services are available 24 hours a day, 7 days a week, 365 days a year. The Center's key areas of focus include emergency shelter and support services, counseling and advocacy, crisis intervention, and community education, primary prevention and training.

That there are over 20,000 women and children in the town neighboring my own who require assistance breaks my heart. That the Women's Center is there to provide it, humbles me.

Please know, dear readers, that some portion of the money you spent on purchasing this book will go toward saving another woman from an abusive household. I hope you will hold your head high with pride.

Thank you so much for reading my books!

Love,
Katy
Xoxo

***For more information about The Women's Center of Greater Danbury, please click** HERE.*

FRAGMENTS OF ASH
Playlist

Cinderella (original motion picture soundtrack) Patrick Doyle
Keep in Touch (music from the motion picture) Gabbi McPhee
I'll Be There Jess Glynne
We Are Stars The Pierces
Must Be Something The Pierces
Crazy Aerosmith
Dream a Little Dream of Me The Mamas & the Papas
Ashokan Farewell Jay Ungar
Dans Le Monde Entier Françoise Hardy

The Vixen and the Vet
2015 RITA® Finalist
2015 Winner, The Kindle Book Awards
(inspired by Beauty & the Beast)

Never Let You Go
(inspired by Hansel & Gretel)

Ginger's Heart
(inspired by Little Red Riding Hood)

Dark Sexy Knight
2017 Finalist, The Kindle Book Awards
(inspired by Camelot)

Don't Speak
2017 Silver Medalist, International Book Awards
(inspired by The Little Mermaid)

Shear Heaven
(inspired by Rapunzel)

Fragments of Ash
(inspired by Cinderella)

Swan Song
(inspired by The Ugly Duckling)
Coming in March 2019
PRE-ORDER NOW!

For announcements about upcoming
a modern fairytale
releases, be sure to sign up for Katy's newsletter at
http://www.katyregnery.com!

PRE-ORDER MY NEXT FAIRYTALE NOW!

SWAN SONG
(inspired by The Ugly Duckling)

COMING MARCH 4th 2019

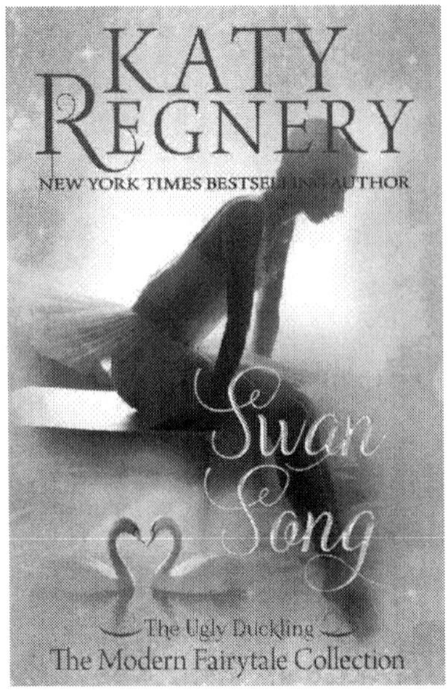

ALSO AVAILABLE
from Katy Regnery

a modern fairytale
(A collection)

The Vixen and the Vet
Never Let You Go
Ginger's Heart
Dark Sexy Knight
Don't Speak
Shear Heaven
Fragments of Ash

Swan Song
Coming Soon!

THE BLUEBERRY LANE SERIES

THE ENGLISH BROTHERS
(Blueberry Lane Books #1–7)

Breaking Up with Barrett
Falling for Fitz
Anyone but Alex
Seduced by Stratton
Wild about Weston
Kiss Me Kate
Marrying Mr. English

THE WINSLOW BROTHERS
(Blueberry Lane Books #8–11)

Bidding on Brooks
Proposing to Preston
Crazy about Cameron
Campaigning for Christopher

THE ROUSSEAUS
(Blueberry Lane Books #12–14)

Jonquils for Jax
Marry Me Mad
J.C. and the Bijoux Jolis

THE STORY SISTERS
(Blueberry Lane Books #15–17)

The Bohemian and the Businessman
The Director and Don Juan
Countdown to Midnight

THE SUMMERHAVEN TRIO

Fighting Irish
Smiling Irish
Loving Irish
Catching Irish

STAND-ALONE BOOKS:

After We Break
(a stand-alone second-chance romance)

Frosted
(a stand-alone romance novella for mature readers)

Unloved, a love story
(a stand-alone suspenseful romance)

Under the paranormal pen name
K. P. Kelley

It's You, Book 1
It's You, Book 2

Under the YA pen name
Callie Henry

LOVE IS FOR EVERYONE

A Date for Hannah

ABOUT THE AUTHOR

***New York Times* and *USA Today* bestselling author Katy Regnery** started her writing career by enrolling in a short story class in January 2012. One year later, she signed her first contract, and Katy's first novel was published in September 2013.

Forty books later, Katy claims authorship of the multititled *New York Times* and *USA Today* bestselling Blueberry Lane Series, which follows the English, Winslow, Rousseau, Story, and Ambler families of Philadelphia; the six-book, bestselling ~a modern fairytale~ series; and several other stand-alone novels and novellas, including the critically acclaimed, 2018 RITA© nominated, *USA Today* bestselling contemporary romance, *Unloved, a love story.*

Katy's first modern fairytale romance, *The Vixen and the Vet*, was nominated for a RITA® in 2015 and won the 2015 Kindle Book Award for romance. Katy's boxed set, *The English Brothers Boxed Set*, Books #1–4, hit the *USA Today* bestseller list in 2015, and her Christmas story, *Marrying Mr. English*, appeared on the list a week later. In May 2016, Katy's Blueberry Lane collection, *The Winslow Brothers Boxed Set*, Books #1–4, became a *New York Times* e-book bestseller.

Katy's books are available in English, French, Italian, Polish, Portuguese, and Turkish. Her books soon will be available in German and Hebrew.

Katy lives in the relative wilds of northern Fairfield

County, Connecticut, where her writing room looks out at the woods, and her husband, two children, two dogs, and one Blue Tonkinese cat create just enough cheerful chaos to remind her that the very best love stories begin at home.

Sign up for Katy's newsletter today:
www.katyregnery.com!

Connect with Katy

Katy LOVES connecting with her readers and answers every e-mail, message, tweet, and post personally! Connect with Katy!